# CIRCUS OF SINS

Forget everything you've ever been told about angels. Those fluffy-winged do-gooders you see on Christmas cards are about as similar to a real angel as newborn kittens are to a man-eating tiger.

Real angels have wings made of fire and carry swords made of solid light. They can level an office block with the flap of one wing, or summon a plague of locusts with the wave of their hand.

And trust me when I say that you never, ever want to get on the wrong side of them....

NATASHA RHODES

# CIRCUS OF SINS

## A KAYLA STEELE NOVEL

SOLARIS

*To Chris Rohner, with love.*

First published 2010 by Solaris
an imprint of Rebellion Publishing Ltd,
Riverside House, Osney Mead,
Oxford, OX1 0ES, UK

*www.solarisbooks.com*

ISBN: 978-1-906735-72-2

A CIP catalogue record for this book is available from the
British Library.

Designed & typeset by Rebellion Publishing

Printed in the UK

*'Well-behaved women rarely make history.'*
– Laurel Thatcher Ulrich

# CHAPTER ONE

FUNNY THING ABOUT Apocalypses. They always strike out of the blue, when you're least expecting them. Just when you think you're starting to get a handle on the world, getting a few of life's notches on your belt, then - *boom*. Apocalypse.

Life can be like that sometimes.

I stood on a high ledge on the roof of the church, gazing out at the bright lights of Los Angeles as I waited for the world to end. My chestnut hair streamed out in the hot blast of the Santa Ana winds, wrapping around me like a living cloak as the clock ticked ever closer to that final hour.

I wiped the sweat off my face as I looked around me, grumbling softly under my breath. It was almost November, but the night air was hot and oppressive. It tasted of the grit and ash which rained on the city from the annual LA wildfires, drifting gently down from on high like papery black snow.

I turned to the East, studied the burning skyline. Every hilltop and canyon surrounding the city was ablaze, from the lofty peaks of Malibu to the scrub-covered hills of the Valley, fanned by the hot winds which rolled down from the desert and torched the hillside McMansion homes of the rich and famous with alarming regularity.

They would rebuild. They always did.

But the fires always came back.

I spat flakes of ash from my tongue and glanced down at my military-style watch for what felt like the hundredth time that hour, gently stroking its glossy face. It was a gift from the man I loved, a man whose life had ended less than four weeks earlier.

But more about him later.

*It was ten past nine.*

My lips moved swiftly as I did the calculations. If it was ten past nine, then that meant I had exactly two days, two hours and fifty minutes until the official End of the World.

Great.

I paused in my obsessive pacing and took a deep, calming breath. Panicking wouldn't help at this point, although it would probably make me feel a hell of a lot better.

Almost unconsciously, my hand dropped down to touch the warm steel hilt of the Smith and Wesson handgun hidden in my belt, then slid along to stroke the bandolier of silver stakes strapped on either side of it. The weapons should have reassured me, but knowing what I was up against, they didn't.

I stepped forward and looked downwards, scanning the crowd that thronged in the night-time streets below.

Beneath me lay the seedy sprawl of West Hollywood—entertainment capital of the world, my home for the last year and a half. A place where it was famously said they'd pay you a thousand dollars for a kiss and fifty cents for your soul. A place where half the town was dying to be discovered, and the other half was afraid they would be.

I peered downwards, blinking against the wind. On the streets surrounding the church, the annual Halloween parade was well under way. Five entire blocks of Santa Monica Boulevard had been cordoned off, and the night-time streets were alive with thousands of costumed revelers: vampires, werewolves, aliens, movie villains and presidential candidates. Ferris wheels danced and spun, children screamed, multicolored lights bathed the streets in a hallucinogenic blaze of color, the neon candy-bulbs burning bright enough to rival the spinning lights in the heads of the drug-addled street peddlers that roamed the backstreets nearby. From the safety of a tenement building an evangelical preacher screamed eternal damnation at the happy revelers through a bullhorn, while a woman in the opposite block shouted sleep-deprived obscenities back at him.

The year's biggest party was well underway.

I checked my watch again and scanned the skies above me.

Everything looked normal.

Cheerful, even.

Not even so much as a whiff of brimstone or a rain of flaming toads to disturb a perfectly ordinary Thursday night in Hollywood.

I snorted. The way my life was going right now, the world ending might actually come as a relief. At least then I'd have some reprieve from the fear and the guilt, from the endless, terrible worry that had consumed me ever since the terrible events of one month ago, when...

I mentally slapped myself, slamming the brakes on that particular line of thought. *Focus, Kayla*. There would be time enough for regret later. And besides, it was bad enough feeling like this without remembering that the coming Apocalypse was probably all my fault...

I slid a hand under my hair and pressed a finger to my ear, more out of habit than hope. White static hissed up from the tiny modified Bluetooth earpiece I wore clipped to my right ear. I strained my hearing to no avail. The channel which only days before had been awash with shouting voices, barked commands and coded bleeps was utterly and chillingly silent. Not wanting to think about what this meant, I turned off the earpiece, raised my infra-red binoculars and started scanning the crowd again, biding my time.

Then—

*There!*

Every muscle in my body tensed as I stared down at the dark figure far below me.

*A vampire*. It had to be. The man stood out in cool shades of blue and black in my heat-sensitive binoculars, a dark outline amid the yellow-red masses of warm-blooded people that surrounded him. Vamps have an internal body temperature of around fifty degrees, slightly higher if they've just fed.

The man was moving purposefully through the milling crowds, in stark contrast to the aimlessly drunken revelers all around him. He was dragging a young teenage boy with him. I snapped off the infra red on my binoculars, hit the zoom. The boy was dressed as a zombie, with painted bloody bite-marks on his face and neck. He was drunk, stumbling every couple of feet, forcing the man to practically carry him as he fought and shoved his way through the crowd.

In West Hollywood it was a common enough sight in the after-hours club scene, but something in the boy's demeanor made me take a second look. I zoomed in with my binoculars, and my free hand tightened on the ledge as I saw his panicked expression.

*Ten bucks said those bite marks weren't fake.*

Adrenaline flushed through me as I readied myself for action. My heart sped up as I ghosted along the roofline, tracking the path of the pair as they cut across behind the main band stage.

As I reached the corner of the roof, the vampire's head snapped suddenly up and he looked directly up at me. He immediately spun away and sped up, doubling back and vanishing into the dark mouth of the street beside the church as though spooked, dragging the young boy with him. *Shit.*

I memorized the name of the street - San Vincente street - then with a burst of mad energy I turned and sprinted across the church rooftop, darted through the fire door and pelted down the fire escape, my metal-capped biker boots clanging on the metal staircase. I'd been up on the roof for well over five hours now, and this was the only vamp I'd managed to ID. I couldn't let him get away. The lights in the disused stairwell were out, smashed and flickering, so I found my way downwards by touch, moving as fast as I dared in the darkness. I had only minutes to get to the boy in time, to save him, or it would all be over.

No time for screw-ups…

I yelped as someone leaped off the staircase above and slammed into me with bruising force. I dropped instantly, letting the weight of my attacker roll us both down the stairs until I was clear of him. It hurt but it was worth it. I hit the bottom with a jarring bump, grabbed the cold steel railing and heaved myself up with all my strength. My hand flew to my belt and I ripped my hammerless pistol from my hip-holster, spinning to aim it double-handed down at—

I sagged, letting out my breath in a rush of relief and anger. The broken light cast flickering shadows over my face as I jammed my gun back into my belt, spun on my heel and headed for the next set of steps.

I jerked to a halt, and sighed.

'Mutt,' I said, with strained patience. 'You have a choice. Either you let go of my arm, or—'

'We all have a choice, kitten. That's what makes us human.'

'You're a fine one to talk.'

Mutt tugged gently on my arm, turning me back around to face him. I felt the awesome power in the young man's grip and flashed him a warning look, squaring off against him in the semi-darkness. Mutt grinned and backed up a pace or two, looking me over with cautious amusement. He didn't relax his grip.

'So… what? We're not even friends now?' he asked lightly.

'I didn't think you knew that word.'

Mutt's smile faltered a little. He scratched at his three-day stubble, eyeing me warily, then let go of my arm, his expression becoming strangely intent. The svelte muscles beneath his T-shirt rippled and bunched as he backed off a pace or two and circled me like a jungle cat, as though searching for an angle to attack. In the unearthly green light of the stairwell EXIT sign his amber eyes looked bright yellow, burning with a fierce flame. For a moment Mutt looked very alien to me.

I felt my heart thump with sudden fear in the enclosed space. I abruptly shoved my way past him, heading on down the stairwell without a word.

Words were wasted on Mutt. I knew that much by now.

'You know you can't do this by yourself,' he called after me.

I stopped halfway down the steps and paused, staring into the pitch blackness.

'Who else is going to stop them?' I asked.

Mutt shrugged, running a hand through his mop of thick dark hair. He pushed himself off the wall and started moving towards me with a slink of jean-clad hips. My hand slid silently down as I checked my handgun, making sure the safety catch was off.

*Just one shot, and all of this would be over.*

I felt the surprising heat of Mutt's body as he stepped up behind me, felt the gentle touch of his hand on my shoulder as he lightly stroked my bare skin, caressing the muscle beneath. It was all an act, I knew, these 'accidental' meetings. A calculated ploy to undo me, to start me thinking about things I didn't want to think about.

*Not now. Not then.*

*Not ever.*

I closed my eyes as he moved in close—*too close*— and started gently kneading the tense muscles on either side of my neck.

'Let me help you,' Mutt said softly, pushing my hair away from my face. 'I promised Karrel I'd protect you, if anything ever… you know.'

His fingers slid down my arm, traveled lightly up my forearm. Paused at the now-tarnished engagement ring on my left hand. Tactfully drew back. I followed his gaze as I stared down at that ring, feeling a knot rise in my throat at the sight of it.

*The man who gave me that ring was dead, killed by werewolves less than a month ago.*

I sharply pulled away, disarming my pistol with a stab of my thumb.

'How can you help me when you're one of them?' I asked quietly.

Mutt's smile faded as he stared down at me, stunned.

I dropped my pistol back into its holster, then turned my back on him and quickly headed for the stairwell, leaving Mutt staring after me in the darkness.


IT WAS HOT down in the crowd. The air tasted of soot and ash from the wildfires, clinging to the back of my throat and leaving a gritty taste in my mouth with each breath.

I swore as I shoved a creature from one of the less popular Star Wars movies out of my way, my gaze fixed on the dark mouth of the alleyway. There was hardly room to stand on the packed streets, let alone to try to get somewhere in a hurry.

I tightened my grip on my hidden pistol and made my way with frustrating slowness through the heart of the crowd. I passed the big band stage, shoved a path through the horde of sweaty, dancing humanity who had formed a seething mosh pit in front of the stage. Beer splashed on my costume and drunken hands grabbed at me, but I was oblivious to everything but the rapidly approaching alleyway, and the job I knew I must do.

*For I was a Hunter, the newest recruit of a secret underground fighting force who devoted their lives to ridding the streets of LA of the supernatural menace. Our destiny: to fight the forces of darkness, to do the unthinkable, to say the unsayable, to wear the frequently unwearable. To stand boldly alone against the creatures of the night, and make the world a safer place for the unwashed and traditionally ungrateful masses.*

I just wished that I'd had more than thirty days of training, and longer than forty minutes of sleep the previous night.

*It was also a shame that all the other Hunters were dead, their base blown up by a mass-murdering master vampire just a week earlier.*

No matter.

I scratched at the black bandana that was tied tightly around my left wrist as I forced my way through the crowd. It had been itching like crazy all day. Just the thought of what lay underneath caused a black knife of dread to push its way a little deeper into my heart. Even if by some miracle I managed to sort out the impending Apocalypse, I still had *that* little problem to sort out…

I picked up my pace, trying to push thoughts of my rather unique injury out of my head. I'd been bitten by a werewolf just over a week ago when our base was attacked, and had since been holding the change at bay with a complex cocktail of drugs developed by the Hunters. ADHT was the Hunters' new 'wonder drug.'

When injected, the compound temporarily halted the change, keeping a Hunter human long enough after being bitten to go get help. The effects lasted a bare twelve hours before it wore off again, but the upshot of all this was that as long as I had a canister of the stuff on me when the moon was full, I could buy myself some precious time.

But my supply had almost run out. I'd been lucky to find this canister, after returning to the Hunters' base to scavenge what we could from the charred rubble. When the canister ran dry, I wouldn't be able to put off the change any longer…

*Don't think. Just move.*

As I neared the alley I'd seen the vampire run down, a pale boy dressed as a zombie spun out of the crowd and grabbed at me with clammy hands. He stared into my eyes with drugged-out pin-prick pupils.

'*It's you,*' he said, his voice filled with wonder.

I gave him a strange look before shoving him aside. Day or night, Hollywood was rife with whack-jobs, and I didn't have time or patience to deal with this one. I hadn't gone far before a second hand fell on my shoulder. I growled and spun around to see a tall, thin man dressed as Jack Skellington staring down at me. His mouth fell open as he drew me close, his expression a mixture of fear and awe.

'*It's you!*' he breathed. '*You killed them, Kayla!*'

'Huh?'

The man silently stepped aside with a sweep of his arm, and my heart almost stopped. Scrawled on the wall behind him, in amateurish, blood-red graffiti, were three numbers.

*Three-Five-Nine.*

Fear crawled in the pit of my stomach like a march of acid spiders. *How could he know?* Nobody knew my horrible secret. Hell, if I drank enough, some days even *I* didn't remember what I had done. And how the hell had he known my name?

I pushed 'Jack' away without a word. Someone was trying to freak me out, throw me off the scent. Probably the vamp I was tracking. Mind control was a common vampire trick, and these drunken folk must be easy prey. I hadn't gone more than ten feet before the phrase was picked up by the young kids nearby, traveling back through the crowd in a creepy hushed chant.

*'It's you... it's you... it's you...'*

The revelers' faces were expressionless, their eyes unfocused as they turned to watch me pass like zombies. I felt the tiny hairs on my arms rise as a legion of plastic demons and witches stared at me, through me, their lips moving in spooky synchrony.

'Hell yeah, it's me,' I said, trying not to show my fear. 'I can't be anybody else.'

I turned a corner and gave a grunt of triumph as I finally spied the mouth of the alleyway. Breaking free of the stifling crowd, I darted down the alleyway in pursuit of the vampire. Just a couple more blocks and I'd catch up with him, and then I'd show them. I'd show them all.

*For I was unstoppable. I was an animal, a living, breathing tracking machine, and nobody and nothing was going to stand in my way...*

'Ow!'

I clutched at my forehead, which had just struck something hard and immovable. My vision swam for a moment before refocusing on the face of the winged man I'd just walked into. Alarm bells clanged in my mind and I leaped back, automatically reaching for my pistol.

*The man was an angel!*

My gaze fell on the cryptic tattoo on the man's pale white shoulder and I relaxed, although not much. As far as I knew, real angels couldn't get tattoos.

'*Organized Religion*,' I read. '*Same Guilt, Different Holidays.*'

The Angel Guy turned around and beamed at me, revealing a set of stained, oddly pointed teeth. I recoiled at the stench of alcohol on his breath. He held a steaming hot-dog in one huge hand, and wore a thick pair of silvered sunshades, even though it was night-time. *Poser.*

'You like mah tattoo?' he asked, in a thick, strange-sounding accent. 'Mah mother did it for me.'

'Oh really? That's nice.'

I flashed the guy a quick, tight smile as I tried to step around him. Angel Guy moved with surprising speed, blocking my path.

'What about mah wings? You like mah wings? My mother made them for me, too.' He gave me a slow, shy smile. 'She makes me everything, you know.'

Behind the angel, a younger guy dressed like a demon glanced around, regarding me with a look of sudden interest. I met his gaze and blinked, momentarily dragged out of my world of vampire tracking by the guy's intense eyes. They were pure black, some kind of crazy Halloween contacts. His hair was black too, spiked up like a reject from an 80's-style hair-metal band. He was shirtless, his powerful naked body smeared with red ochre. A legion of tattoos crawled up over his strong upper arms, just visible under the paint. A half-finished bottle of scotch dangled from one hand, in blatant defiance of California's strict No-Drinking-In-Public laws.

He grinned at me, rolling his eyes at the angel. *Nut-job.*

I pulled a pained face at the Demon Guy, who responded by hanging his tongue out and winding an imaginary noose around his neck. I smiled back, although my smile was slightly strained.

'My mother is a *wonderful* woman, ah'll have yew know,' continued Angel Guy. 'She helped me find God.'

'You found God?' I clapped him on the back. 'Hey, if nobody claims him in ninety days he's yours. Listen, I really gotta go—'

'Say. You sure do look a lot like my mother. I like your eyes. You have *real* kind eyes.' The angel moved to block my way, staring at me with an open fascination that was as unnerving as it was creepy. 'Last time ah seen eyes like that, I was looking into the eyes of my lord Jesus Christ. It was a dream ah had, you see? A *pro-phet-ic* dream. You wanna hear about ma dream? Oh…'

I was already gone, pushing my way through the last few partygoers as I made a beeline for the mouth of the alleyway.

'Always when you're in a rush, huh?' the Demon Guy called after me, grinning.

'You have no idea,' I threw back.

*The hunt was on.*

# CHAPTER TWO

I PULLED UP short at the mouth of the darkened side street, sandwiched in between the church and a bar packed full of boisterous revelers. I stood stock-still, listening. Was it my imagination, or could I hear the sounds of a scuffle coming from the other end of the street? I only hoped I wasn't too late.

I touched a finger to my Hunter Bluetooth earpiece and hit Transmit, my voice vibrating with tension.

'Heading north off Santa Monica Boulevard,' I barked, trying to sound all official. 'Intercepting possible vamp attack down San Vicente. Target: white male, late teens. Pickup on Sunset in ten.'

'Kayla,' a male voice sounded in my earpiece. 'You're not dead yet. I'm shocked.'

'Working on that,' I snapped.

'Get here fast,' the voice crackled. 'You're being followed. There's six of them, non-human I'm told. I have a very bad—'

The radio signal screeched, then cut to static.

I swore and smacked the earpiece a couple of times.

*Damn piece of knockoff eBay crap.*

I glanced over my shoulder to check that Angel Guy wasn't following me, then clicked on my flashlight and strolled casually down the alleyway.

My casual pace turned to a headlong run as I darted past a small offshoot side-street partially blocked by heaped garbage, then slowed to a trot as I rounded the corner, staring around me with trepidation. The side-street was wide and dirty, in typical LA-style, easily big enough for two cars to pass each other. Half a dozen businesses backed onto it, with a number of large wheeled blue dumpsters parked on the sidewalk outside the delivery entrance of each one. Disused packing crates and flattened cardboard boxes partially blocked the sidewalk in big piles every ten feet.

But something was wrong here. This side-street ended in a dead end, a solid-looking chicken-wire fence twenty feet high that screened off the industrial parking lot behind it. A big yellow sign hung on the wire pronounced ominously 'END.'

I gawked up at the nearest street-sign, half-hidden behind a curl of rusting razor-wire, and swore. Instead of 'San Vicente,' the sign read 'Hilldale Ave.'

I'd gone down the wrong street!

Footsteps pounded behind me.

I whirled, darted forwards, paused, dodged back like a cornered animal.

No way out. I was trapped.

Six winged shadows loomed on the far wall.

I snapped off my flashlight and backed up quickly, squeezing myself into a narrow gap between a dumpster and the back of a pawn shop, my heart thundering in my chest. The broken brickwork scraped gouges in my bare arms and shoulders but I didn't feel a thing. All my attention was locked on the dark shapes of my pursuers. They slowed to a leisurely walk upon seeing the dead end, then began looking around for me.

I seemed to blink and suddenly their leader was standing in front of my hidey-hole. Of course, it was Angel Guy, still clad in his costume with the big fake wings. But he seemed different now. The vacant, dull-eyed look had gone from his face and he moved with a new, sinuous grace, like a cat stalking its prey.

I pressed myself as far back into the crevice as I could go, holding my breath. As I did so, Angel Guy turned his back on me and removed his mirrored sunshades with an impossibly fast snap of his wrist, not showing any of the slowness or goofiness I'd seen in him just a moment ago. He glared into the shadows and cocked his head. He could obviously sense my presence, but he couldn't seem to see me in the darkness. *Thank Christ.*

He turned in a slow circle, fists clenched, nose raised as though scenting the air.

I held my breath. Maybe I would be lucky.

*Maybe...*

A sudden squeal of interference came from my Bluetooth headset. I slapped at it, in my panic somehow managing to turn it up louder. The effect on my pursuers was electric. All six bowed at the knees and banged their hands over their ears, all moving in creepy unison.

'Kayla, you still there?' A tinny voice blasted out of my earpiece, nearly deafening me. As I reached frantically for the 'off' switch, Angel Guy's arm shot into the crevice like a striking snake. He dragged me out into the light and threw me to the ground. I hit the asphalt hard and my earpiece went flying. It skittered across the ground beside me, where it continued to blare from several feet away.

'Listen to me,' my backup's voice was saying from the earpiece, heavy static shrouding his voice. 'Kayla. Wherever you are, *get out now.* These things... don't let them touch your skin. They're—'

I made a mad grab for the earpiece, accidentally hitting the *off* switch as Angel Guy stamped towards me. I snatched it up quickly. Seconds later a steel-heeled boot slammed down in front of my face, right where the earpiece had been. I threw up my hands to protect my head. When it became clear that his next kick wasn't going to shatter my skull, I uncurled, cautiously.

Six impassive, alabaster faces stared down at me in a silent ring of contempt. I looked from one to the next of them, ending my fearful inspection with Angel Guy.

'Hey, pretty lady,' he grinned. His goofy, idiotic expression had gone, as had his phony accent. His voice was flat and cold and his black eyes held no expression as he looked down at me, through me. *The gaze of a killer.*

'Thought I'd better introduce myself. The name's Caleb.' I noticed a cockroach run out of Angel Guy's shirt, disappearing under his hairline. *That was never a good sign.* 'I've been watching you all night. You're perfect for the program. You will come with us now.'

He smiled widely, revealing rotted yellow fangs.

'I'll pass, thanks.' I scrambled to my feet and backed off fast. I noticed that one of Caleb's followers was the vampire I'd seen just minutes ago, back in the crowd. My heart gave a quick thump. I flung a quick look over my shoulder, scanning the dark alleyway for the boy. There was no sign of him.

'That boy you took,' I called out to him. 'Where is he? I'll trade you for him. His life for mine.'

The six men sniggered, throwing a look at Caleb.

'Whoever said we wanted your life, lady?' said one of them.

Ah. So it was going to be one of *those* nights, was it?

Caleb smiled at me strangely, and the look on his face made my skin crawl. I stood my ground, staring back at him. Six guys against one girl. It didn't seem fair, but that's life for you.

I pulled myself up to my full height, resting my hand lightly on my belt above my hidden pistol as I stared Caleb down. I didn't scare easily but this guy was freaking me out. In the bleached lamplight his features were shadowed, shiny with sweat, hollow-looking as an addict. His skin was so translucent that, for one unnerving moment, I fancied I could see his skull through it.

I silently kicked myself for ever taking him for human.

The wind blew again, harder. I backed up a step and glanced at Caleb's bright reflection in the bar window as pulley-chains rattled in the wind against the nearby garages. Something felt very wrong here. There was something strange about these vampires that I just couldn't put my finger on...

'The boy is dead,' said Caleb, in a slow, drawling voice. He stepped forwards and looked me slowly up and down. 'Still want to trade?'

I shook my head, distracted, looking around for the boy. *Never believe it till you see the body.* I looked up at the bar window opposite to see myself reflected, surrounded by a circle of dark figures. I was trapped, cut off. My gaze flew back to the window and it suddenly hit me.

*Vampires with reflections?*

Caleb smiled slowly and I swallowed, cursing my own stupidity. The silver stakes in my garter and the gun in my belt suddenly felt as useless as toy weapons.

*I'd messed up. I was screwed.*

'Whoever said we were vampires?' said Caleb, with a smile.

He pulled a strangely shaped white blade out of his pocket and started moving towards me, grinning like a corpse...

A STRANGE SENSE of calm overcame me as I backed away from Caleb, goosebumps flashing over me despite the heat. Above him, a tiny spear of silent summer lightning flicked down from the heavens. A heavy roil of heat pulsed down the alleyway, as though energy was building up in the sky, and suddenly everything clicked into place.

These guys weren't vampires, and they weren't hairy enough to be werewolves.

There was only one other thing left that they could be.

'Oh, I get it,' I croaked, as Caleb's five followers started closing in on me, moving as one. 'You're Them, aren't you? The Seekers.'

'*Seekers?*' Caleb said, as though tasting the word.

'You know,' I replied, with what I thought was an admirable amount of sanity. 'The Avenging Angels. The Bringers of the Apocalypse.'

I felt dumb saying it, but I knew it was real.

In case you don't know, Seekers are an ancient species

of Warrior angel. I didn't know this until about three weeks ago. They live in the place that modern humans call Heaven. Other species have another name for it, which for the sake of my own sanity I was choosing not to think about at this minute.

Forget everything you've ever been told about angels. Those fluffy-winged do-gooders you see on Christmas cards are about as similar to a real angel as newborn kittens are to a man-eating tiger. Real angels have wings made of fire and carry swords made of solid light. They can level an office block with the flap of one wing, or summon a plague of locusts with the wave of their hand.

Trust me when I say that you never, ever want to get on the wrong side of them.

Another name for a Seeker is an Avenging Angel. In case you don't know what they do, imagine humanity as a screaming two-year-old having a tantrum and God as The Father. Avenging Angels are God's belt, a tool he uses to dispense justice to the world, on a grand scale.

The only problem was that this time, it was the whole of Humanity that had messed up and was overdue for a spanking... and I had a very good feeling that I knew why.

I backed up further, my gaze flicking between the six tall, winged figures. I suddenly felt very small.

'I've never met real-life angels before,' I said, trying to keep my voice from cracking. 'They warned me I might bump into you guys around about this time.'

'Angels?'

I pointed a tremulous finger at Caleb's wings.

He began to laugh, a bitter, incredulous note in his voice. I stepped back, my eyes flicking down to the silver gleam of my Bluetooth earpiece, clutched out of sight in one hand. *Perhaps it was still transmitting. Perhaps my backup could get a fix on my location, come save me...*

As if on cue, a loud engine roared nearby. I let out my breath in relief. About time! Thank God for technology. I backed off as a pair of too-bright blue-tinted headlights lit up the end wall, throwing the winged men into sharp silhouette.

I was saved!

The six men leaped back in alarm as a heavy armored ground car rocketed around the corner, doing close to fifty as it bounced and jolted crazily up the wide rutted alleyway. Its lights washed across us and it braked so violently that its front bumper kissed asphalt. Road debris flew as its back end slewed around a full ninety degrees, jumbo-sized back tires bouncing off the brick wall of the alley.

It rocked to a smoking standstill. Smoke drifted up from its tires to frame a brand new silver SUV, outfitted with so many lights and racks and add-ons that it looked like the carapace of some outer-space giant bug.

As the dust-cloud cleared, a horrible sinking feeling went through me. This wasn't a Hunter vehicle. In fact, I'd never seen this car before in my life.

Before I could make a break for it, a second identical SUV rounded the corner to join the first car, this one driving more sedately. It maneuvered around nose-to-nose with the first car with a smug metallic whine, until the two cars formed a 'V' shaped metal barrier across the alleyway, hiding all view of us from the main street.

I was penned in the dead-end alley, blocked off by the two cars.

That couldn't be good.

My gaze flew back to Caleb as he strode towards the vehicles, moving impatiently as if he'd been kept waiting. As he walked he grabbed hold of the brown leather straps that held his white angel-wings on. He pulled the straps away from his chest, snapping the thick leather one-handed.

Behind him his 'fake' wings sprang open, doubling in size as though they'd been bound up. They trembled as he stretched them upwards in evident relief. I stared in surprise as the entire surface of his wings sloughed off in a rain of white feathers, which slid to the ground with a muted *flump* to reveal a black, shiny, scaly surface underneath. The other five men followed suit, freeing their own wings, again acting in creepy unison.

I stared at them as feathers flew. Their wings weren't fake.

But these were no angels.

Caleb sighed in relief, folding his black horned wings sedately behind him, his white-blond hair streaming out in the soft blast of the scorching midnight winds. He touched his ear and muttered a rolling command in a language that sounded a little like Russian. Behind him, the top-door to the first car popped open with a hydraulic hiss.

My heart stopped dead in my chest as a giant, leather-clad figure stepped out, swiveling his massive leonine head to take in the scene. Bright amber eyes narrowed at the sight of me, and the figure's mouth stretched in a sudden, violent grin.

I swore, feeling suddenly dizzy. It was Harlem.

Harlem was a werewolf, one I had never wished to see again in my life.

The winged men stepped back respectfully, moving out of the way. It was a trap. I'd been set up.

I slowly backed away in horror as three more dark figures emerged from the cars and joined Harlem, each equally familiar, equally terrifying. They were all werewolves, and their names were burned into my soul.

*Flame. Jackdoor. Mitzi.*

The hitmen who had killed my true love, Karrel.

And now, they had come for me.

# CHAPTER THREE

IT'S STRANGE, THE tricks the mind plays on the body when confronted with certain, inescapable, horrifying death. I felt my heartbeat slow to a crawl as I backed away from the monsters who had butchered the only man I had ever loved, and stared with a certain grim finality at what I felt for sure would be the last thing I ever saw.

Werewolves are not human. Sounds self-evident, really, but at this point I feel it bears repeating. They look cool in the movies in wolf form, but when you see then in real life, in human form, they just look... *wrong*. Their bodies are too tall and gangly, they have muscles in all the wrong places. Their hairlines and bone structures are more canine than ape-like. I watched in a trance as the four wolves stretched and turned to face me, casually spacing themselves apart and easing into pre-attack positions that would ensure my swift and efficient death.

They had a job to do, and I was it.

'Hi, baby,' grinned Harlem. 'Miss me?'

'More than you know,' I called out, backing up a pace.

Harlem's broad-shouldered, wild-haired, barrel-chested figure had already earned itself a permanent place in my nightmares after his previous abortive attempt to kill me. Last I'd heard of him, he was doing five consecutive life-sentences for the first-degree murder of not less than seven Scientology recruitment trainees in LA County's State Pen. How he'd escaped and why he wasn't currently splashed all over CNN's *'Most Wanted'* was a matter that didn't bear thinking about.

Standing next to him was his second in command, a big red-haired werewolf known as Flame. Word had it that he used to be a pastor who lived and worked in one of the worst parts of downtown Southside LA. That was before the accident that had burned down his church—with him inside it—and scorched the entire left side of his face into a twisted mask. Some said it was arson, others whispered that it was some kind of misguided revenge attack by one of the young boys he 'saved' from the streets—rumor had it that it hadn't only been confessions that had gone on in his confessions booths.

Flame freaked me out almost as much as Harlem. Almost.

Behind him stood Mitzi, a shorter, sinuous man with waist-length hair and an elegant, regal bearing. He was albino and the white roots of his dyed black hair were showing, a social *faux-pas* I found unsurprising given the fact that he was completely blind. His spooky black contacts seemed to follow my every move as I slowly backed away from him, trying to put as much distance as possible between myself and his wickedly curved *tachi* katana sword as I could. I'd felt the end of that blade once, and was in no rush to encounter it again.

Mitzi was tailed by his faithful shadow Jackdoor, a greasy jackal of a man in a voluminous leather duster. I'd seen him remove that duster only once, and what lay underneath still haunted my dreams. I wasn't quite sure of the technicalities of werewolf breeding or of what supernatural races could interbreed with others, but the fact Jackdoor had tatty, stumpy wings made him a very good banner-boy for werewolf birth control.

I sucked in a breath and looked at each of them with increasing panic, searching for some softness or warmth in their eyes that I could use to my advantage. I found none. The werewolves' faces were alight with the feral, stone-cold stare of born predators.

I was nothing to them. Barely even lunch. My twenty-four years of life wouldn't even pass muster as after-dinner conversation to them once I was no more than a bloody smear on the street.

So much for my great career as the savior of the world.

I saw Harlem's smile broaden and cleared my throat, my hand creeping down again towards my gun. I had six silver bullets in there. If I could pull it out in time, I could take at least one of them down with me before they tore me to pieces...

I hesitated as the door to the second ground-car hissed open. A pair of steel-buckled, white calfskin boots stepped down to the sidewalk. A tall, elegant woman swathed in a snow-leopard skin wrap emerged from the car. All eyes turned to her as she strode past the four big werewolves and paused in front of me, freezing me to the spot with a stab of her intense violet eyes.

Her name was Cyan X, and she was a vampire.

But not just any vampire. If Michelangelo had painted

his famous work *The Temptation of Adam and Eve* a hundred years later, he would have used Cyan X as a model. Men and woman alike feared her as much as they wanted her. Even master vampire Harlequin had once dumped her complaining that she was 'too much for one man to handle.'

Looking at her now, I could well believe it.

The four big werewolves eased away from me, straightening their backs and sucking in their stomachs. I almost laughed out loud. It was unusual for werewolves to follow a vampire, overcoming their traditional species enmity, but this was something of a special case. Cyan had recently captured their Alpha Wolf, Magnus, and sold him into slavery to the vampires. Since then she had commanded the pack. It was more than a little surreal to see these four murderous scumbags running around after Cyan like frightened little boys, but these wolves weren't dumb. They knew when to cut their losses and follow the stronger leader.

And that wasn't all.

I glanced sideways at Harlem as Cyan stared at me. The six-foot-five behemoth was standing with his shoulders hunched, hands pressed together, bushy eyebrows pinched together in worry as though he was afraid she'd somehow strike him down for just existing. I'd seen the way his fire-colored eyes had dropped almost religiously down her body as she'd walked past him, seen his shoulders rise and fall in a sigh.

Harlem was smitten with her, head over heels in love with this deadly siren.

I didn't blame him.

Cyan looked me up and down as I stood there in the alleyway, a look of undisguised contempt on her perfect face. I stood up straighter and raised my chin, trying to look as unimpressed as possible, to match her six foot height with my less-impressive five-foot-six. If I was a cat I would've turned sideways and gone all spiky. The mortal fear the wolves inspired in me was nothing compared to what I felt in Cyan's presence.

For she'd been the one who'd given the order to the wolves to kill Karrel, under direct order from the master vampire, Harlequin. To say I wanted her dead was the understatement of the century.

'All this fuss just for me?' I managed, reaching for my stakes. 'I'm flattered.'

'Don't be.'

Cyan's voice was like jeweled silver bells tied to the end of a rattlesnake's tail. She regarded me for a too-long moment, laughing at me with her eyes.

I glared back at her, my hand closing on the reassuring shape of a silver stake. I desperately searched my mind for a Dark Arts spell. My brain drew a blank.

Before I could move any further Cyan blurred out of existence, moving with the preternatural speed that only older vampires have. She was suddenly standing beside me, one fist clamped tightly around my wrist. She squeezed and I felt the bones in my arm creak and bend alarmingly. I grabbed my forearm and yelled as the vampire jerked her arm up, hoisting me high into the air, dangling me painfully by one wrist. My fingers opened of their own accord and my stake dropped to the ground with a sad little *clink*.

Two seconds flat and she'd got me. *Shit.*

'What were you going to do with that, girlfriend?' said Cyan, her gaze as cool as ice. 'Pick my teeth for me…? *Hey!*'

She cried out as her hand suddenly burst into flame.

She threw me away from her with a shriek as the smell of burning flesh filled the air. I hit the side-wall of the alleyway and fell to the ground, clutching my head in pain. I watched as the vampiress ripped her steel-strung pearl bracelet off and flung it into the dirt beside me. The red-hot pearls landed on the sidewalk, which immediately began to bubble.

Cyan started to laugh, shaking her head in derision as the angry red burns on her hand flash-faded to white and instantly began to heal. Behind her, the little spike of lightning did its thing again, impaling a black thunder cloud like a child stabbing a pillow.

I shivered, unnerved.

'So you can do the *Dark Arts*,' she mocked, making the phrase sound like the dirtiest, lowest thing imaginable. 'Please. A *child* can do fire tricks.'

'Can a child do *this*?'

I scrambled to my feet and threw up my hands dramatically, concentrating with all my might. A tiny, spinning golden fireball formed between my hands. I uttered a brief prayer, shivering as I felt the magic suck all of the heat out of the air around me, while the dragon-charm that hung around my neck—the source of my magical powers—heated up. As the fireball blossomed to full size I gave a shout of triumph and flung it towards Cyan as hard as I could.

Nothing happened.

A moment later, the fireball spluttered and went out. I staggered as a black wash of tiredness swept over me, almost falling before I caught myself against a wall. I was still a novice at the Dark Arts, and the fireball spell represented the grand pinnacle of my learning so far.

'Very impressive,' Cyan's lip curled in derision.

'Could you do it again? I think I blinked and missed it.'

I gave her a look of barely-disguised loathing before turning my back on her. As soon as I turned away my haughty expression crumpled. Performing magic was exhausting, and even that small fireball spell had taken almost everything I had out of me. My heart was racing as though I had just run a mile in ten seconds, and my head was filled with a black dizzy fog that was characteristic of magical fatigue.

I couldn't give Cyan the satisfaction of seeing that, or I was dead.

The wolves snickered as they glanced at each other and closed in on me, ready to kill me. Thoughts of my gun were tempting me, but there were too many of them and I didn't have enough bullets. If I left even one of them alive they'd take that gun from me in a second, and then it would be all over.

I spun around as Cyan made a grab for me, groggily snapping up my hands to fend her off. The vampiress swayed aside, easily avoiding my wild blow, then dove towards me and slipped under my reach before I could draw in a breath. Her arm blurred as she brought her elbow around in a quick, clean strike to my solar plexus with the force of a kicking mule. I collapsed on the ground, gasping, all the strength knocked out of me. I rolled over and clutched at my side, glaring up at the vampiress.

That was when I noticed that she was now holding my gun.

*Shit.*

'Nice workmanship,' she said with a grin, checking the clip. She tapped the silencer screwed onto the barrel with approval. 'Know any spells to repel bullets?'

She aimed the gun at my head, and started to pull the trigger.

*CRASH!!*

The one remaining unbroken window of the bar behind us exploded. Cyan whipped around in surprise and the bullet went wide, embedding itself in the back of the dumpster with a *chink*. The vampiress's eyes widened as a madly flailing dark form sailed through the window above her head, blotting out the light…

*CRUMP.*

I blinked. An oddly-familiar male figure was sprawled on top of Cyan, who lay cursing and groaning in a puddle of broken glass. She'd dropped the handgun, which lay a few feet away from her in the gutter. A moment later a whisky bottle flew through the broken window and shattered on the ground beside her.

'How dare you!' shouted an irate female voice through the broken bar window. 'I'm calling the cops!'

'*Mmphr*,' muttered the fallen man, flopping over on the ground. He was dressed as a demon. I blinked as I recognized the newcomer as the young guy I'd seen just minutes ago, in the crowd. He raised himself up on one elbow and scanned the ground around him with forlorn hope. One of his horns had broken off. His eyes fell on the smashed whisky bottle beside him and he sagged in disappointment.

'They cut me off,' he muttered. 'Bastards.'

Beneath him, the vampiress's eyes snapped open. She snarled.

I was already on my feet, diving for the dropped handgun when Cyan flung the Demon Guy off her, hissing in outrage. She snatched the gun up before I could get to it and backed off quickly, aiming the barrel at the newcomer's head one-handed.

'Who's your friend?' she snarled at me, finger on the trigger.

'No idea,' I said truthfully.

I watched in alarm as Demon Guy climbed unsteadily to his feet and stood there swaying. He flashed me a drunken, cocky grin, all bravado and swagger, then turned to square off against Cyan. He was reeling slightly, his long, backcombed black hair sticking up in all directions like a disheveled hedgehog. I could smell the booze on his breath from five feet away.

'Damn vampires,' he slurred, pulling a crumpled roll of twenties from his pocket. He peeled off one bill from the mess and waved it at me in a half-hearted fashion. 'Hey Lady,' he hissed to me in a loud, slurred stage-whisper. 'Could you pick me up a can of Cockroach Killer from the store, sweetheart? It seems we have,' he dropped his voice, 'a *little problem*.'

He waggled the bill at me sheepishly, then blew Cyan a kiss.

'You're drunk,' snapped Cyan, her nostrils flaring with anger. 'Caleb over here tells me that the Lord does not look kindly on alcoholics.'

'He taught His son to turn water into wine,' replied Demon Guy, shaking glass from his hair like a dog. 'I'd call that a big heavenly thumbs-up.'

Two seconds later he was sitting in a very surprised heap on the ground, clutching his chest as smoke spooled upwards from the barrel of Cyan's gun. A slow trickle of blood welled up from between his fingers. He looked up at the vampiress in genuine surprise.

'You shot me,' he said, disbelieving.

'I'll shoot you again if you don't leave.' Cyan bared

pearly white fangs between her blood-red lips. 'Quickly, please. We have business to take care of.'

'Quite the little bossy-boots, aren't we?' grinned Demon Guy, apparently unaffected by the gaping bullet wound just two inches to the right of his heart. I recognized the warning note in his voice and quickly backed off. Whoever this guy was, he wasn't human.

He got to his feet in a slow, slinky kind of way that made all the hairs on my arm stand on end. He spat on the ground and backed off, circling Cyan, sizing her up.

'Last warning, freak,' said Cyan, raising her gun.

'The name's Niki,' he said, winking at me. 'And you wanna fight, you got one. Any last words, sweetheart?'

Harlem growled.

My subconscious registered the flicker of movement before it happened. Harlem charged forward like a bull to protect Cyan, moving so fast his huge bulk became a blur. I yelled as his gloved fist smashed out with crippling force towards Niki's face, but to my surprise the newcomer swayed aside without so much as blinking, easily avoiding the wild blow. He stepped back from the advancing werewolves, putting his arm around me and pulling me back with him. At first I thought he'd come to rescue me. Then I realized that he was just using me to hold himself up.

'S'okay, kiddies,' he told the advancing wolves earnestly as he stumbled away from them, dragging me in tow. 'Don' you worry now. S'okay to be a li'l intimidated the first time you meet me. I know it's not easy to be this good looking and this modest all at once, but lemmie tell you, I got years of 'xperience.'

He struck a heroic pose, grinning.

I didn't even see Mitzi draw his katana sword, but

suddenly it was in his hand and arcing down towards Niki's head. I tried to make a break for it but my new friend didn't even move. He simply brought one powerful arm up and over his head, shielding us both from the killing blow. I shrieked and ducked down as the blade bit deeply into his forearm, glancing off the bone with a sickening little sound.

The next thing I knew I was on the ground, tucked quickly but firmly against the wall as Niki exploded into a one-man whirlwind of action.

I sat up and watched in amazement as Mitzi went flying backwards as though fired from a cannon, his sword blade scraping a shower of blue sparks up from the sidewalk as he jammed it down to halt his mad slide. Jackdoor and Flame reached up and clutched their faces almost simultaneously as large, dark bruises blossomed where Niki's fists had just landed in quick succession. Harlem—always the brightest of the bunch—swayed back as Niki's gloved hands jabbed for his eyes, then brought up a booted foot in a punishing backwards kick that should've by all rights broken the new guy's spine... except it didn't.

The impact drove Niki flat on the concrete, face down in a pile of scattered broken glass, but an instant later he was somehow back on his feet like a spiky-haired jack-in-the-box, reaching out for Cyan as she shoved Harlem away in a fury and circled around him, hissing like a bobcat...

Which was everybody's cue to stand back.

I heard the familiar *sssshhhhiiinnnggg* sound as Cyan deployed her bio-blades—four organic bone blades, each a foot long. They had been embedded in both her wrists and elbows by Harlequin, an experimental biotech weapon gone very wrong. She flicked her arms straight and rotated her wrists ninety degrees, locking the four spurred bone blades together into two bone-white organic swords. She bared her impressive fangs and stepped back into a samurai's crouch, the look on her face promising instant messy death to anyone who dared stand between her and Niki.

Silence fell like a club.

I saw Cyan's eyes travel with disdain over Niki's demon costume as she circled him, sizing him up. I followed her gaze, taking in the guy's tight, ripped leather pants which clung to his muscled thighs in a way that did strange things to my breathing. I watched as the newcomer stepped back into an easy fighting position, brushing the dirt off his flat stomach, and cinched his silver devil's-horn belt buckle tighter with a defiant jerk where the end had come loose, causing a shower of glass to fall to the ground with a tinkle.

The sudden movement proved to be a little too much for him and he stumbled again, almost losing his footing.

He wasn't bullshitting. He really was drunk.

*Crap*.

With a yowl Cyan sprang at him like a bobcat, moving faster than I could follow. Niki yelped in pain as her half-inch fangs sank deeply into his neck, tearing at his flesh. Blood spurted and I cried out in frustration, starting to get up, to help him. Jackdoor turned to me and bared his teeth in warning. I held up my hands and swiftly backed off.

Cyan suddenly broke away, gasping. I couldn't see what had happened. I only saw the look of profound distaste in her eyes as she violently shoved Niki away.

She wiped at her mouth, then turned and spat into the nearest gutter.

'How dare you?' she snarled.

Niki gave a nonchalant shrug, a grin still on his face despite the ugly bite wound on his throat. He opened his mouth to reply, then whirled in alarm as a sudden thumping sound came from the end of the street.

I turned to look too. The strange thumping sound got closer. My view of the street was blocked by the two silver Hummers which closed off the end of the alley. But what I *could* see was the seven-foot-six humanoid shadow which fell on the far wall, backlit by the glare of carnival lights. Even Cyan paused, staring up at it.

Nothing human was that tall.

My breathing stopped.

There was a moment of deep silence, and then metal groaned as the fronts of the two armored cars were lifted off the ground and slowly raised up to form a ten foot tall archway of shining metal.

The big cars' frames instantly started to buckle and crack under the crazy pressure of their own weight. Their windows shattered and popped out in festive fountains of glass as they were lifted higher still, propped up on their rear wheels, before crashing over backwards onto their roofs, sending a huge cloud of white dust billowing down the alleyway towards us.

A tall, hulking, insanely muscular figure was revealed, framed by the twin dust-clouds and backlit by the whirling neon lights of the carnival. His head swiveled to scan the scene, using one giant hand to fan away the great cloud of road dust that plumed up around him, lit yellow by the sodium lights.

His eyes lit on me and he winked.

I grinned back, reaching for my dropped stake.
Finally, my backup had arrived.

# CHAPTER FOUR

I STOOD STARING at the giant figure blocking the alleyway in relief. I was saved!

I moved eagerly forwards as the behemoth turned to face me, ignoring the others. His eyes lit up with a gleam of unholy mirth and he tutted in a patronizing fashion, as though amused to find me bleeding from the head and neck-deep in werewolves.

The winged men started to fall back as the giant man shoved his way through the ruins of the two armored cars and started striding towards me with a long, easy gait.

'Monster!' I yelled, waving my friend over.

'You don't say,' murmured Niki from beside me, *sotto voce*. His eyes were very wide.

'No. His name. It's Monster.'

'One of yours?'

I nodded, not taking my gaze from the hulking figure.

'Thank Christ. Thought we were royally fucked for a moment there.' Niki paused, then held out his hand. The gunshot wound to his chest seemed to have sobered him up a bit, although not much. 'Didn't catch your name.'

'I'm Kayla.'

'Niki.'

I shook his hand without looking down. I was too busy watching the action. At the end of the alleyway, Monster briefly disappeared under a barrage of flapping wings and flailing fists as Caleb's minions charged him, trying to pull him to the ground. There was a brief, tense moment, then the winged men were flung outwards as though a bomb had detonated beneath them.

'Kayla! Duck and cover!' Monster yelled, his rich, cultured British baritone music to my ears. I instantly complied, dragging Niki down with me and covering my ears. I knew what was going to happen next.

I peeked out through my hands as the winged men regrouped in mid-air, wings blurring, conferring among themselves in a strange, chittering language. They turned as one and bore down on Monster en masse in a swirl of leathery wings.

Before they could reach him, Monster flung out his arms and opened his enormous fists to reveal a jagged pair of large blue crystals. Judging by the sudden look of horror on the winged men's faces, he'd just done the equivalent of pulling out Kryptonite in front of Superman. They squealed and writhed and formed a kind of mid-air pile-up in their efforts to get the hell away from him.

They weren't fast enough.

Monster muttered the first few words of an advanced Dark Arts spell under his breath. The blue crystals heated up and liquefied, swirling around his hands in twin balls of raw energy.

'Show off,' I muttered, putting my hands over my ears. I knew what was coming.

The winged men screamed as the two giant fireballs levitated up from Monster's hands, spun around like miniature tornados then turned into fierce spears of white light which silently streaked towards them, lighting the darkened alleyway up as bright as day.

Now *that* was how you did the Dark Arts.

The deadly light struck the creatures full force, freezing them into black winged sculptures in mid air. They crashed to the ground, shattering into thousands of tiny evil pieces that immediately began to *move*, wriggling and squealing and trying desperately to roll together and become whole again. *Gross.*

An instant later, the sound hit me. I should say it was more like anti-sound. Even through my ears were covered I still heard it, or rather, I didn't hear it. A great *WHUMPH* of dark energy poured over me, around me, dropping me and everyone else to the ground with my hands clamped tight over my ears. The anti-noise forced itself into my skull, as though trying to suck out every sound I had ever heard in order to fill the gaping vacuum in reality Monster had just created by performing the Dark Arts without a shield spell.

The pain went on for a long time.

When it was over, I was amazed to find I was still conscious. I coughed and risked a glance sideways, spitting out blood from where I'd bitten through my lip.

Cyan was gone, vanished without a trace. I wasn't surprised. She usually split at the first sign of trouble, and I had no doubts that she would be back. If she'd been ordered to kill me, she wouldn't stop until one of us was dead. The four werewolves were lying in the gutter, curled up into individual balls of pain. If the spell's concussion had hurt me, I shuddered to think of what it must have felt like to the werewolves, with their supernaturally enhanced senses.

I staggered my feet and stood there a little shakily, looking around at the mess that Monster had just made—the two wrecked Hummers, the cowering werewolves, the goopy wriggling remains of what just ten seconds ago had been six living, breathing winged beings. One of the bloody pieces crawled towards me. I glanced down at it and it reached tiny deformed hands out towards me, crying like a baby. I kicked it away from me with a shudder.

As if on cue, a distant siren started to wail.

I brushed my hands off on my dress and risked a glance sideways at Niki. He was staring at me with a kind of horrified fascination, his eyes almost comically wide.

'Does this always happen to you when you get drunk?' he asked.

'Sometimes,' I admitted. 'And I'm not drunk. You are.'

'Then why is the world spinning?'

I gave Niki a Look as he rubbed at his neck, regarding me ruefully. The flow of blood from his vamp bite had almost stopped, and his bullet wound had almost completely healed. He had to be a vampire to be able to heal that fast. At least he wasn't about to bleed to death before I thanked him for saving my life.

'I need to sit down,' I said, to no-one in particular.

'I have a better suggestion,' said Niki, taking my arm and pulling me to the side. 'How about we go find a bar, where it's safe and warm and *normal*, and then you can buy me a drink and explain to me what the hell just happened. Then I might just think about asking you out on a date.'

'Sounds good, I replied, gingerly exploring one of the long scrapes on my stinging wrist. 'Just one small flaw in your plan.'

'Which is?'

'I have to go with him now.' I pointed to Monster.

Niki's face fell. 'Of course. Your boyfriend.' His shoulders rose and fell as he heaved a huge, over-dramatic sigh. 'That's okay. I'll be okay. Don't you worry about me, I'll just go back to the car and...' His face crumpled into a frown as he patted his pockets. 'Did I give you my keys?'

I smiled, unable to help myself.

'Monster's not my boyfriend,' I assured Niki, touching his arm. It was a very nice arm, I had to admit. It was well toned and firmly muscled beneath the red body paint. I wondered what he looked like without his devil costume on.

A voice called my name and I glanced over my shoulder. 'In a minute!' I yelled back to Monster, who was cheerfully driving off the werewolves with a little weapon of his own devising, a miniature disposable flamethrower. I leaped back as Jackdoor fled past me with a yelp, trailing smoke like a werewolf comet, throwing an evil, vengeful glare back at me.

I could see that he was going to make me pay for this.

Job done, Monster torched the fleeing pieces of dead winged man with a flamboyant sweep of his hose. He switched the flamethrower off then walked over to me, baring his gold front teeth in a warm grin.

I couldn't help but smile back. My oversized friend's origins had always been something of a mystery to me. He was human, at least partially, and from what I could gather he'd always been something of a gun for hire, working with the Hunters for considerable sums of money whenever they needed a little extra muscle.

Rumor had it that he also had a nicely-paying side-job working security down at some of the more risqué new Hustler casinos in Vegas and LA. He made still more money trading on the company's lucrative stock options, usually buying on the months that he went to visit his latest love interest at the Playboy mansion, who just happened to be a registered psychic.

Monster was not, as he always told me, just a pretty face.

As to the million-dollar question about what species his parents had been, I'd heard several competing teams of Hunters place large bets on whether he was part Troll, semi-Ogre or just plain full-blooded Giant.

One upside to being a Hunter. You sure wound up with some interesting friends, in some cases whether you wanted them or not.

Monster's eyes flicked briefly over Niki without interest before coming to rest fully on me, a look of concern settling into his face when he saw my injuries.

'Having fun, little 'un?' he asked, his soft English accent as always making me smile. He looked me up and down, touching my bleeding forehead with a sausage-sized thumb. 'Stone the bleedin' crows, you look like a dog's dinner. What the 'ell happened to you?'

'She got in a fight with a wall,' said Niki, with a disarming grin. 'But I think the wall came off worse.'

Monster turned and gave Niki a look of cool assessment. 'Beat it, creep,' he said, without changing his easy, friendly tone or altering expression.

'Monster!' I scolded him. 'He just saved my life!'

'Not my problem.' Monster reached into his bulky tool belt and withdrew a wicked-looking German micropistol.

'Now wait a minute!' I protested.

*Click.* The silencer was on. The barrel swung around and settled between Niki's eyes, pressing lightly into his skin.

'We don't need the likes of you 'round here,' said Monster calmly, as sirens turned into the end of the devastated alleyway. 'Nothin' personal, you understand.'

Whirling blue and red lights washed over us as we stood in a frozen little trio, the two men staring each other down.

Monster's forefinger tightened on the trigger. 'Last chance, scumbag.'

Niki sighed. He gave a bored one-shoulder shrug, then pulled his hand from the twin puncture wounds in his neck as though making a point and wiped the blood on his ruined jeans.

'Suit yourself,' he said quietly. 'I've done my good deed for the day. Be seeing ya, Kayla.'

With the briefest of nods in my direction he turned and strode away into the shadows, weaving very slightly. I stared after him in dismay, then whirled and glared at Monster.

'What the hell was that all about?' I almost yelled. 'He saved my life!'

'No, dearie. *I* saved your life. *He* almost got you killed.'

Monster was already walking back towards the side alley, his flamethrower slung over his shoulder like a knight with a sword. 'You coming, princess, or you just gonna stand there prancing around like a nincompoop till the cops get here?'

I took a couple of deep breaths, still keyed up and vibrating with delayed-action shock. I didn't even know what a nincompoop was or why one would prance, but he was right about the cops. It was time for all of us to scram.

I saw the welcome shape of the Hunters' black SUV parked down the turnoff street and picked up my pace, suddenly desperate to get back to safety, back to normalcy.

'What were those things, anyway?' I called out grumpily, tailing after Monster as we got close to the car. 'The guys with the wings?'

'They were Nephilim, that's what they were, my dear.'

I looked at Monster blankly.

'The offspring of a fallen angel and a human.' Monster rubbed his immense jaw as he walked, making a sound like sandpaper on brick. 'Cocky little bastards, let me tell you. They can give you a headache and a half if you don't know how to deal with them. They can see into the future, and they feed on human souls.'

'Oh.' I thought about this. 'What were they doing hanging around the werewolves?'

'They're like vultures, Kayla. They smell a kill about to happen, they'll be all over it like stink on shit. They probably attacked that boy just to draw you out, then *pow!*' Monster stopped dead as we reached the car and gave me a piercing look. 'You didn't let any of them touch you, did you?'

I shook my head quickly, glancing away fast. I had a horrible vision of myself colliding with Caleb back in the crowd. I swallowed, my mouth going dry.

'Glad to hear it. If their skin touches yours, they get a direct line to your soul. Make you see things. Hallucinate. The visions alone can drive you mad.'

'Visions? You mean of the future?'

I stared at Monster, as he popped open the trunk of the car and started stashing his flamethrower inside.

'You *sure* you're okay?' Monster asked, opening the driver-side door as two cop cars raced past the end of the alleyway, making a beeline for the two wrecked Hummers. 'You've gone white as a ghost.'

I shook my head quickly as I remembered my dream of the Apocalypse last night. I'd been getting them more and more frequently lately. My mouth was too dry to speak. Monster broke into a broad smile and opened the passenger door for me.

'Glad to hear it, Kayster. You're a pain in the ass but it'd suck to have to kill ya. Come on, hop in before the cops find us. If you wanta stop for junk food on the way home it's my treat. Little peace offering, okay?'

I nodded stiffly, trying to forget what Monster had just told me. *It had just been a brush, a brief collision. I would be fine. And besides, I hadn't touched Caleb's skin, just his wings, which were fake.*

*With real wings hidden underneath…*

A cold breeze sprang up out of nowhere, stroking the blood-soaked hair back off my face like an icy hand. Above me, an electricity pole creaked like a ship's mast in the wind, sounding somehow ominous. I paused, one hand on the open car door, glancing behind me with a frown. Something was nagging at the corners of my perception.

*Something bad.*

As Monster started the ignition, waving at me to get in, I turned to survey the alleyway we had just left, now flooded with a wash of whirling red and blue police lights. I cast back and forth for several moments before spotting what it was that had caught my attention.

*There.*

A slim winged figure was standing at the entrance to the alley, watching us, half-hidden in the darkness. *A female Nephilim?* She was barefoot and naked save a long, white oilcloth wrapped roughly around her slender body. A glittering black half-mask covered the left half of her face.

As she felt my eyes on her, she turned and gave me a long, blank look.

I gasped as I felt a sudden, intense sense of pressure fill my mind. It was the same feeling I'd had moments ago when Monster's black magic wave had washed over me, only infinitely, horribly stronger.

I tottered back away from the car with a gasp, clutching my head. The world spun around me, and a black rushing sound sluiced through my temples as the energy swirled through me, searching my mind, tasting me, examining me with an alien intelligence unlike anything I'd ever felt before.

I clutched at the side of the Hunter SUV as my legs abruptly gave out, barely aware that I was falling. It was as if a black hole had suddenly opened up in the street in front of me, a hole that was sucking all the life and energy out of me until all that remained was an empty, dried-up shell...

Just as I was about to start screaming for help, the rushing sound shut off with a neat little click. I hauled myself upright in a panic, turning to shout a warning to Monster.

The words died in my throat. I stopped dead and stared.

Monster was gone. So had the SUV. I was back out in the street with the Halloween crowd, standing in the exact same spot as I'd been in fifteen minutes ago, by the band stage, just after talking to Jack Skellington.

*And all around me, the streets were in flames.*

I stared around me, disorientated. The crackling of fire filled the air, and in the distance panicked voices were starting to scream. The hordes of drunken humanity around me were lit with a ghastly orange light that seemed to come from nowhere and everywhere at once, turning the night as bright as day.

The sound of the blaze grew louder and the costumed crowds milled around in blind, directionless panic as poisonous black smoke poured up into the air, belching out from the ruined shops and houses, which were scarred and pitted with a multitude of craters, as though hit by a shower of asteroids.

I shook my head, blinking hard as I rubbed at my eyes, trying to wake up. I knew this was a dream. It wasn't real...

The ground trembled underfoot as a series of powerful explosions rang out nearby, frighteningly close. A searing blast of heat washed over me and I quickly backed up under the shelter of a nearby shop awning, staring around me in fear. In the apartment block above me the preacher was still in full, frothy-mouthed swing, his burning words drifting downwards on the night air like the hot black ash that still fell from the sky.

'*...and the mountains shall tumble and the seas shall boil, and a plague shall be brought down upon all o' you sinners. God will wipe y'all out, like a plague of lo-kists, as in the time of the pharaohs, and of the Great*

*Flood, and the earth shall be born again in the image of the angels, and be forever clean of your sins…'*

I backed further under the shelter of the closed and barred shop doorway as the Halloween crowd turned and flooded back down the street towards me as though Godzilla was coming, their hands outstretched in panic.

I gasped.

The partygoers' faces were missing, seared off by the blast into pools of molten flesh. Their hair was singed off and their eyes were gone, black blood running down their faces and pooling in the empty sockets. A small child cried, separated from its family, and across the street from me a baby was screaming in its mother's arms. I saw that the blanket that swaddled it was lapping with flame, the fire rushing upwards towards the infant's face.

A number was written on its forehead, outlined in blood.

*3-5-9…*

As I started to run towards it, shouting a warning to its mother, another sound hit my ears, something far more terrible than anything I had ever heard before. I spun around and gaped as the sky above me turned black with what looked like a circling swarm of birds. The flock was immense. There were thousands upon thousands of them covering the entire night-time sky, backlit by the silver moonlight and the ever-present haze of orange light pollution. I blinked, squinting upwards. My jaw dropped in amazement.

Unless I was very much mistaken, those weren't birds.

They were men.

*Men with wings.*

*Thousands upon thousands of them...*

As I watched, one of the winged beings gathered itself and shot down out of the sky in a burning arc, hurtling to earth like a burning meteor. It ignited as it fell, burning with a blue flame which drew white-hot sparks from the massive white sword it carried. A sonic shockwave preceded it, defying the laws of physics, blasting aside people and cars on the ground beneath it up, throwing them up in a fountain of flying debris.

Screams rang out as the burning man struck the earth with an earsplitting *BOOM*, embedding himself in the cab of a nearby gas tanker. I watched in horror as the vehicle's gas tank sparked and ignited, exploding in a burst of flame so powerful the entire rig was flipped up onto its front end, just across the street from where I was standing.

The shockwave of the explosion blasted over me, knocking me and everyone else around me to the ground. I rolled over with a yell on the sidewalk, wiping the hot road dust out of my eyes as I struggled to get up, to run before it was too late.

There was a loud creak, and a huge, horrible, dark shadow fell over me.

I looked up and froze.

The gas tanker loomed directly above me, poised to fall.

Time seemed to slow down as the big-rig hung there right above us, balanced on the front grille of its cab, the giant flammable trailer of gas swinging wildly back and forth behind it like the ass-end of a drunken caterpillar. Everybody around me screamed as it teetered to the left, then the right, suspended in the air like a piece of crazy Dali-esque artwork.

Then, with a creaking, drawn-out groan, the entire

rig overbalanced and started to fall.

*Right on top of me.*

I had no time to move, to think, to even cry out as the giant rig descended, blotting out the light, raining dust and flaming debris down on top of me as it crushed the costumed sinners to death, with me dying as one of them.

And in its dead mother's arms, the burning baby screamed...

# CHAPTER FIVE

I AWOKE WITH a jump and a gasp, my eyes flying wide open in the darkness. For a moment I thought I might be dead, my mangled body burning beneath the wreckage of the supertanker.

Then I saw the familiar green glow of a digital alarm clock burning in the blackness. I slumped backwards in relief, burrowing my head into the soft coolness of my pillow.

'Fuck,' I whispered.

I lay there for a long moment, my mind still gripped by the horror of my dream. I gradually became aware that it was cold in the room. After what seemed like an age I roused myself enough to groggily pull on the blankets, trying to cover myself up.

The blankets were stuck.

I grunted softly and sat up in bed, yawning, groping around me in the semi-darkness till I found the source of the problem. Steady snoring drifted up from the pillow beside me. I gave a wry smile, then leaned down and gently rolled the sleeping form of Karrel over, freeing the comforter from beneath him so that I could pull it over my exposed bare legs.

He always stole all the damn blankets.

I pecked him on the shoulder, and was snuggling up against his back with a contented sigh when it hit me. Something was wrong here.

Very wrong.

*Karrel was dead.*

I froze mid-snuggle, suddenly hyper-aware of the warm, heavy and decidedly male body in the bed next to me. My mind frantically rewound like a broken tape-spool to the previous night as I tried to remember how the hell I'd got here. I drew a total blank. It was as though someone had gone in and completely erased my memory, filling my head full of warm, fuzzy cotton wool.

What the heck had I been drinking?

As though possessed, my hand crept around of its own accord and reached behind me, fingers groping...

I snatched my hand back.

Whoever was in bed with me was also naked.

My senses cranked into overdrive and my pulse sped up. I lay absolutely still, fighting the sudden mad urge to scream and run. Instead I stared pointlessly around the darkened room, trying to figure out where I was. My eyes were starting to adjust to the gloom now, and judging by the nondescript décor, the flowery Seventies-style pull-out sofa in the corner and the little coffee machine on the beaten-up dresser, we were in a motel room, and a cheap one at that.

Why in the blazes was I in a cheap motel room with a strange guy?

That was never a good start to the day.

I almost jumped out of my skin as a warm, heavy arm curled around my shoulders as my unseen bed-mate rolled over onto his back and drew me in closer. He—whoever he was—sighed contentedly, nuzzling warm lips into the side of my neck.

That did it. I flung the arm off me and leaped out of bed with a cry. Or I would've done, had my legs not been trapped beneath my bedmate's. I fell forward awkwardly onto the bed, then froze as my sleeping partner awoke and shifted, licking dry lips.

'Suzy?' said a husky, sleepy voice.

I relaxed, although not much.

'No,' I said, then cleared my throat and said it again, louder. 'No. It's me. Kayla.'

The mattress shifted and creaked as the muscular form of the Demon Guy from last night— Niki—rolled over to fully face me, breathing lightly in the darkness. His other leg remained locked over mine, my bare legs pinned under the crook of his knee.

By now my night vision was good enough for me to make out the faint highlights and shadows in the room, to see the expression on Niki's strong, if somewhat angular face. I could see the black shock of his hair sticking up like porcupine quills, silhouetted faintly against the curtained window behind us, a dark contrast to his pale skin. It looked like someone got bed head worse than I did.

I swallowed, my eyes quickly flitting to the motel-room door. This guy wasn't human, and I was in bed with him naked. Oh, wonderful. I was sure my mother would have a few choice things to say about that. I wondered if Niki would kill me if I made a sudden break for it, then instantly regretted thinking that.

'Mind explaining why I'm here?' I asked, as casually as I could.

'Why are any of us here?' yawned Niki, scratching at his stubble as he trailed a hand lazily over my bare shoulders. I rolled away quickly and he shifted in bed with a twist of his hips, snuggling closer to me.

'That's not what I asked,' I snapped, anger creeping into my voice. Anger was good. Anger stopped me from feeling the bone-deep terror that lurked in my gut. This guy was practically a stranger and yet here I was, naked in bed with him, without a clue how I got here.

I noticed something white on my arm, and glanced down in surprise. There was a fresh bandage wrapped around my upper arm, where I had scraped it on the wall fighting Cyan last night. I poked at it with a cautious finger and was rewarded with a fresh ooze of blood that faintly stained the white bandage. I had no memory of putting it on myself. Niki must have put it on me while I was passed out.

Just how long had I been unconscious for?

'Last night. The guy with the wings…' I stopped, feeling foolish as my anger subsided somewhat at the sight of the bandage. 'You saved me. From the werewolves. You were pretending to be drunk—'

'Werewolves?'

'I mean… the guys who… never mind. And Monster— my friend. What happened to him?'

I stopped, glancing downwards. Niki's hand had crept its way across the pillow to my bare shoulders while I'd been talking, and was now smoothing against the soft, warm skin of my throat as though fascinated by it.

'The big guy? He ran away, like a big baby,' said Niki,

his voice distant. 'Last I saw of him he was running for the hills, yelling something about an angel.' He sighed and propped himself up on an elbow, grinning at me. 'Guess some people just can't take their liquor.'

'You can talk.'

'Likewise, kid.' I tensed up as he trailed a careless finger down my cheekbone, his face just inches from mine. 'You were just lying there on the ground, passed out like Sleepin' Beauty, so I picked you up and hightailed it out of there in case one of those weirdos came back.' There was a significant pause. 'You owe me one, kiddo.'

'There *was* an angel,' I started in Monster's defense, then stopped, unsure of how much I should tell this guy. 'The men with the wings, the ones who—'

I abruptly shut up as Niki's hand grabbed my own under the blankets. His hand was very cold. His cool fingers ran under my hand and flipped it over, stroking the delicate skin of my palm with the backs of his fingers. It was an oddly comforting gesture which at the same time managed to send a tingle shooting down my spine.

I pulled my hand away, breathing quicker. Niki responded with a grin, a flash of white teeth in the darkness. He still hadn't lifted his legs off mine.

'There was no angel, sweetheart. You must have dreamed it,' he murmured, leaning forward to brush his lips over my ear. He dropped his voice to a stage whisper. 'And by the way, I wasn't pretending to be drunk.'

'Oh, great. That makes me feel a whole lot better.'

'It should. I fight better when I'm drunk.'

I closed my eyes and mentally counted to ten. Then

I took a deep breath and looked into Niki's eyes from close range in the warm darkness of the room, waiting until he took the hint and released my legs. I didn't want to resort to actual violence until he made it clear, one way or another, that I had no other choice. It was a strangely intimate position to be in with somebody who was possibly about to kill me, or worse.

Niki gazed back at me through half-lidded eyes, breathing lightly and evenly, then started to lean in closer. I found myself licking my lips, trying without success to slow my treacherous breathing. *I didn't even know this guy. I couldn't kiss him.* I managed to put a hand on his naked chest in time and gently held him back. His chest was very cool beneath my warm hands. He flashed me a wicked grin and his chest shook very slightly with silent laughter, but he didn't move away.

'So,' I said, trying to keep my voice casual, clinical. I couldn't go any longer and not mention this. 'I couldn't help noticing that you're, ah, naked.'

Again the amused pause, the careless shrug.

'So are you.'

'Yeah. That's the problem.' I swallowed carefully. 'How did I... um.' I cleared my throat and tried again, glad that the darkness was hiding my blush. 'I mean, did we, er...?'

Niki laughed at that, a rich, hearty laugh that belied his tough, couldn't-care-less attitude. It went on a long time. When it finished, I was surprised to find that I missed it.

'What do *you* think?' he asked, his intense black eyes seeking mine in the darkness.

I shook my head, my sense of humor slipping. 'I have no clue, buddy. Just tell me who you are, what you are, and what the hell happened to me last night. No more playing games. Did Harlequin send you? Is that what this is all about?'

Niki laughed out loud, as though entertained that I knew the name of the vampire leader. His smile widened as he slowly sat up in an almost threatening move, the cotton covers slipping one by one off his strong, muscular upper body and landing in a wadded pool in his lap. I was glad they did, or I might've bolted right then and there. My night vision was almost at a hundred percent now, and I could see things that I didn't want to see, things that made my mouth go dry.

Niki was stunning. Terrifying, but stunning. What I could see of his naked body was a study in powerful symmetry, an inhumanly perfect human form. Every proud line, every muscle was faintly highlighted by the warm, dim red glow of dawn now shining through the cheap red polyester curtains. He could've been sketched by Da Vinci three hundred years ago, outlined in charcoal and chalk on some ancient parchment sketchbook.

My eyes crept upwards, unable to help looking him over. He had the strong, taut figure of a budding weightlifter, all upper-body strength, bulging biceps and lean curves, although he couldn't be that much older than me. I'd put him at twenty-six, at the most. Twin piercings gleamed in one nipple, and as he turned towards me I could just make out the lines of a winged skull artfully tattooed along the plane of one shoulder blade.

In short, there was nothing about this guy that I didn't like, apart from the fact that he just might be about to kill me.

I suddenly realized that his night-vision had probably

caught up with mine by now, and dived for the covers. I tugged on the sheet but it was trapped beneath Niki's legs. I reached out without thinking and grabbed hastily for one of the dangling curtains from the window beside the bed, suddenly desperate to cover my own nakedness. A wash of pale blue light spilled into the room as I pulled the curtain off its copper rings, wrapping it quickly around my shoulders to cover my breasts.

Niki winced, grabbing the sheets to shield his eyes as the room filled with sunlight. The weak, early-morning light wasn't really that bright, but it was enough to make my eyes water after the velvety darkness of the room.

'Ah,' I said, as I watched him blinking in pain. 'You're a vampire.'

'Are you crazy?' Niki rubbed his eyes, groaning. 'Shut that curtain, woman. I'm not a vampire, just hungover as hell.'

'Prove it. Stand in the sunlight.'

Niki rolled his eyes at me, then climbed out of bed and took hold of the second curtain that half-blocked the main bay window. With a theatrical flourish, he jerked it open. I bit my lip, unable to help staring. His pale, muscular body glowed in the sunlight that streamed in from behind him, haloing him like an angel, and his coal-black hair fell down around his striking black eyes, framing his strong face in an entirely attractive way. He grinned down at me in triumph as he basked in the sunlight, revealing strong, perfect teeth. *Human teeth*.

'Could a vampire do this?' he asked.

I sighed, shaking my head. I watched him closely as he stood there in the sunlight, suspecting trickery, but as the seconds ticked by and he failed to ignite into the customary vampiric ball of flame, I had to admit defeat.

Alright, so Niki wasn't a vampire. But he wasn't human. So what was he?

My mind was running over the various possibilities when my subconscious flared to life and gave me a sharp mental slap. I jerked my head up, finally registering what I had been hearing for the past twenty seconds.

A quiet, almost inaudible beeping was coming from my Hunter Bluetooth headset, which was lying on the nightstand beside me. *The headset that had been dead save for Monster's transmissions since the day the Hunters had been massacred.*

I grabbed the tiny earpiece off the nightstand and turned the volume up to the max, pressing it to my ear and listening for everything I was worth. I could barely hear the signal over the roar of static, but it was definitely there.

*Bip-bip-bip…beep beep beep… bip-bip-bip.*

Nine short beeps, repeated over and over.

A distress signal!

I instantly recognized the beeping as Morse Code. I grinned up at Niki, my worries instantly forgotten. He wasn't a vampire, that much I knew. And I also knew with one hundred percent certainty— I quickly looked away— make that a hundred and ten percent certainty, that he didn't have any weapons on him. I'd have to trust him not to kill me for at least another five minutes while I figured this new dilemma out.

'You hear that?' I asked, holding up my headset.

'I hear that,' Niki said. He sounded distracted. He was watching something outside the window. I heard a car door slam outside, and then footsteps crunched across the stony driveway down below.

Niki swore, then spun around and snatched up a small

block of yellow Post-It notes. He picked up a pen and started writing rapidly, still gloriously naked. 'Shut that thing off, would you. It's flippin' annoying. What is it?'

'*SOS*,' I breathed. I wrapped the curtain around me and sat up in bed, my mind instantly alive with the possibilities. 'Channel one-fifty-nine… that's a localized Hunter channel, a fifty mile radius, tops. Monster's on channel twenty-two, and he doesn't do Morse code. Whoever's sending that signal's gotta be somewhere nearby, and for some reason, they're not able to talk. Why would that be?'

I swept a hand through my sleep-tangled hair, aglow with excitement. 'Someone survived! Another Hunter!'

'That's impossible. All the Hunters are dead.'

'We don't know that for sure –'

I slowly turned around to look at Niki, who had paused writing and was gazing at me across the room with an angelic expression on his face.

'How do you know all the Hunters are dead?' I asked.

There was only the slightest of pauses before he replied. 'You told me.'

'When?'

'Last night.'

'I said no such thing!'

'Did so. How would I know about the Hunters if you hadn't told me?'

It was a very good question. In fact, it was such a good question that I was suddenly out of bed and across the room, the curtain wrapped around me, my back pressed against the door as I stared hard at the dark and suddenly sinister shape of my abductor. I tried the door-handle. *Locked*.

'Who are you?' I demanded.

Niki laughed again, as though entertained by my sudden panic attack. 'You're awesome,' he said through a big grin. 'Can I keep you?'

He put down his pen with a flourish, peeled the top Post-It note off with great care and re-read what he had written, his lips moving as he read. He nodded in satisfaction, folded it in half and held it out to me. 'Here. I got a present for you.'

'What is it?'

'A secret.'

I wrapped the curtain tighter around myself, flustered. 'Read it to me.'

'I can't, or he'll hear me.'

'Who'll hear you?'

'Don't ask. Just read the note then destroy it. Don't show it to anybody.'

'Is this a TV show?' I asked, staring around me in suspicion. 'Am I being filmed?'

Before Niki could reply I heard the crash of an outside door being flung open, rebounding in the hallway right outside our motel room. Footsteps clumped down the hallway. I jumped as someone pounded loudly on the door behind me, knocking so hard that it shook in its frame. I gave a little yip as Niki seized my wrist and pulled me away from the door, still nude, and pushed the yellow Post-It note firmly into my hand.

I closed my fist around it instinctively, curious despite myself.

'Read it,' Niki hissed. 'Now hide.'

I watched him in bewilderment as he strode rapidly around the bed, then dropped to his knees. He slid a black bag out from under the bed, unzipped it and casually pulled out the big, black, ugly shape of a beat-up army shotgun.

Who the hell was this guy?

I yelped and dived behind the nearby sofa as Niki aimed the shotgun at the door and smoothly racked back the slide to load it. The slide was so well oiled it only made the faintest click. The pounding on the door restarted again, making it bounce so hard in its frame that splinters of flaking paint rained downwards.

'Just a minute,' Niki called out in a sing-song voice, his tone light and breezy as though addressing an unexpected pizza delivery guy. 'Be right out.'

The doorway exploded.

Pieces of shattered doorframe whizzed past my head as I threw myself down behind the sofa with an instinct born of long practice. A moment later the entire door *thunked* down across the sofa like a giant wooden tombstone, snapping in half on impact.

A compact, lean man stepped through the smoking remains of the doorway, his golden cat-eyes scanning the room. He wore a scruffy AC/DC T-shirt and black jeans, with his dark hair pulled roughly back into a pony-tail. He had a gun in one hand.

His gaze lit first on the shotgun, then naked Niki, then naked me.

As I opened my mouth to explain, Mutt snarled.

Things got a little messy after that.

# CHAPTER SIX

'You know, you didn't have to actually *shoot* him,' I puffed, as I hurried after Mutt towards the open door of the battered black 1969 Chevy Camaro. The big muscle car sat, engine idling, in the driveway behind my kidnapper's motel room.

Mutt climbed into the driver's side and sat with an exhausted flump in the padded leather seat. He snapped on his harness and unlocked the passenger door, throwing me an ironic look. His forehead was bleeding.

'Get in, Kayla.'

I hesitated, throwing a guilty glance back up at the top-floor motel room that Mutt had just spent the last ten minutes trashing. Two of the side-windows were shattered, and the sofa that I had been hiding behind now lay in the flower-bed, along with part of the bed-frame. Curtains twitched along the length of the motel building and I briefly heard the sound of running feet coming from a side alleyway, and then all was still again.

In the distance, a siren wailed.

I climbed up into the Chevy and slammed the door

in what I hoped was a long-suffering and dignified way, a conflicting mix of emotions welling up inside me. Before the locks had fully engaged Mutt hit the gas, throwing up a rooster-tail of gravel as he sped out of the small parking lot and headed for the highway, leaving burning track-marks on the asphalt.

Mutt narrowed his eyes and glanced over at me as we cut down a side-street and merged onto the 405 freeway, strangely silent for once. It was as though he was trying to see inside my head, to find out what had just happened, but I was in no mood to humor him.

'I was doing fine by myself, just so you know,' I said eventually, to break the almost painful silence. I rooted through the glove compartment until I found a pack of Juicy Fruit. I was starving. I tore into it, popped a piece of gum into my mouth and started to chew.

'Yeah. I could tell.' Mutt snorted, not taking his eyes from the mirror. 'You looked just fine. The way you ran screaming out of that place dressed in some other guy's clothes showed me *just* how fine you were doing, all by yourself.'

I resumed my thoughtful chewing as the early-morning streets sped by. The stolen T-shirt I was wearing had a caricature of Alfred Hitchcock on it. At least Niki had good taste in movies. Presently, my gum became soft enough for a bubble. I blew one, taking my time about it.

'I can handle myself,' I insisted. 'I just need a chance.'

'For what, exactly?'

'To prove myself.' I sat up a little straighter in my seat, smoothed down my ruffled feathers. 'I know I'm just a trainee, but I'm one of the last Hunters left alive in LA, far as I know. There's just me and Monster. If there

were more we would've heard from them by now…'
My voice tailed off, excitement washing through me as
I remembered my big news. I'd picked up a Hunter SOS
signal on my radio! As I opened my mouth to tell Mutt
all about it, he cut me off.

'Sorry, girlie. No more proving yourself on my
watch.' He took a deep breath, then exhaled slowly. His
hands that gripped the wheel were still white-knuckled.
'I know you feel responsible for what happened to the
Hunters, but you can't fix things all by yourself. You're
only human. You should start acting like one.'

I opened my mouth to protest, then shut it again,
folding my arms and slouching grumpily down on
my seat. I fiddled with the bandage on my arm, then
reached down to tighten the black bandana that was
still tied around my wrist. *I hadn't told Mutt about my
wolf bite. It would only make things complicated.*

'But—'

'No, Kayla. I mean that. That guy, he was… I mean,'
Mutt swallowed, flushing slightly. 'He could've…
Yeah. I'm hoping he didn't.'

Mutt snapped up the mirror and gave me a sideways
glance. 'He didn't, did he?'

A small, evil part of me balked at the interrogation.
My life was my business. Mutt didn't own me, even
though he had saved my life so regularly that he'd
recently asked for a small bronze nameplate to be
engraved on my ass.

'I'm still here,' I replied coolly. 'That's all you need
to know.'

Mutt turned away, a muscle in his jaw twitching. I
knew he wasn't happy with this answer, but I knew he
was too proud to try and dig any deeper.

I let out a great yawn as I watched the scenery flash past outside the window. All I really wanted right now was a good, solid meal, a shower that didn't contain any naked possible-vampires, and for Mutt to stop staring at me every two seconds so that I could read the mysterious yellow Post-It note from Niki clutched in my hand.

Niki's note was burning a hole in my palm by the time we pulled off the freeway, but I didn't dare sneak a peek at it. I didn't want to risk Mutt spotting my prize and whisking it away before I'd had a chance to read it. I knew from the look on Niki's face when he'd given it to me that he'd written something important, and besides which, this note was now my only link to my possible kidnapper.

Perhaps he'd been dumb enough to jot down a phone number, or some kind of contact details? I had a feeling that the cops would be very interested in my note, should I decide to press charges.

What a day.

'Where are we, anyway?' I asked, trying to change the subject. We were in a part of town I'd never been to before, all green hills and distant blue mountains.

'Way out in Orange County,' Mutt said, with definite reproach in his voice. 'That son-of-a-bitch dragged you almost sixty miles away from home, Kayla. If it hadn't been for that GPS tracking signal we picked up from your Bluetooth headset thingy…'

'Yeah, well. I'm safe now.'

'For now.'

'What's that s'posed to mean?'

Mutt shrugged, just a hint of a growl rumbling in his chest. 'I'm just glad you're okay, that's all. We've had... something of an issue, back at base. We need your help.'

'With what?'

Mutt paused a moment before he replied. I could see at once that he had news for me, too. But neither of us were telling.

'You'll see,' he replied, ominously.

THE SILENCE IN the car had almost become epic by the time we pulled into the drive of the sprawling, dirty tenement block which was home to almost a quarter of the werewolf community in the city.

I sat up in my seat as we circled the back lot, searching for a parking spot amid the various rusted-out wrecks that belonged to the residents of this particular neighborhood. Living in downtown LA was a bitch for regular folk, who had to deal with the gangs, the cops, the cockroaches, the food, and some of the smelliest, nastiest concrete-covered urban landscape the state of California had to offer.

It was worse for the werewolves, who were only able to lease the most run-down apartment blocks the council had on its books. No regular landlord would rent to a registered werewolf for fear of retaliation from his or her other tenants.

The general public was slowly starting to accept the fact that werewolves existed, although it wasn't very happy about it. It had been over four years now since Bobo 'Ginger' Curtis had forgotten to check his lunar calendar and had changed on live television whilst performing a musical number from 'Cats,' on the smash hit TV show 'National Idol.' He'd eaten three of the more popular judges live on air before they'd managed to cut the feed and evacuate the theater.

But the day still loomed large in the public's consciousness as the day we discovered that we are not alone... although the sheer number of bogus werewolf hunting gangs and groups that had sprung up afterwards made it clear that the general public was soon hoping to personally fix that 'problem.'

Now, things were slowly getting better for everybody, but we still had a long way to go. The wolves lived in the tenement blocks that the humans wouldn't touch with a barge pole, and the LA city council was willing to turn a blind eye to their presence so long as they paid their taxes on time and didn't eat the neighbors. Besides, the more savvy locals knew that having wolves in the neighborhood meant more cops on the beat, seeing as most of the LAPD was run or funded by the vampires, who hated the werewolves more than anybody.

So everybody was a winner.

I was out of the car before Mutt had even drawn the Camaro to a full halt. I slammed the door behind me and started striding down the cracked concrete path that led to the wolves' tower block, trying not to wince as I walked. Everything hurt and my scraped arm stung like a sonofabitch, but I could live with it.

I sniffed as I got close to the building. There was a strange acrid smell in the air, like burnt toast. It made me hungry. I hadn't eaten since last night, and I was starving. The thought of food energized me.

I picked up my pace, putting a few dozen paces between myself and Mutt, then rounded a corner and quickly slid the yellow Post-It note out of my pocket. I unfolded it as I walked, hiding it from Mutt with my body.

Six short lines were hastily scrawled in Niki's angular, untidy handwriting:

> I can help!
> I know where HARLEQUIN lives!!!
> Meet me ALONE tomorrow nite
> @ the Circus Of Sins nightclub,
> Corner of Melrose and Highland, 7pm sharp.
> DON'T BE LATE!

I read the note through twice quickly, burning the words and the address into my mind. The exclamation marks bothered me a bit, but I couldn't work out why. Wasn't three exclamation marks one of the signs of insanity? Who knew. I crumpled the Post-It and shoved it back into my jeans pocket just as Mutt caught up with me, nearly running into me.

'Kayla. Wait.'

'What now?'

'Don't go any closer. We have to wait till it's safe.'

'What the hell are you going on about?'

I stopped walking and glared at him, angry now. I couldn't wait to get inside and have a shower. My hair was in a rat's nest, the remains of last night's makeup smeared across my face like yesterday's tabloid gossip. I opened my mouth to give Mutt a piece of my mind, then shut it again as I finally registered what he was pointing at. I stared up at the five-story tenement block that had been my home for the last month, and immediately knew my shower would have to wait a little bit longer.

'What on earth?' I gasped.

One entire side of the werewolves' apartment on

the top floor was simply gone, vaporized. A massive, smoking hole in the side of the building belched fumes up into the morning sky. Through the gap I could see an awful lot of flame-blackened ceiling, and part of a blown-in-half sofa. All around the building, panicked residents stood around in little excited huddles, staring up at the destruction in dismay and confusion.

I stared, stunned.

'So much for my cleaning deposit,' sighed Mutt. He winced as a large piece of mortar crumbled out of the wall of our top-floor apartment, and smashed with a kind of grim finality on the ash-covered roof of the brand new Lexus parked beneath. *The building manager's car. Ouch.*

I turned to Mutt in a daze.

'Who did this?' I asked.

He turned his cool, maple-colored eyes on me. 'I thought you'd already know.'

'Know what?'

'Your Hunter friends did this. They're back.'

# CHAPTER SEVEN

'COULD YOU REPEAT that, please?' I asked faintly, leaning back on the wall for support.

'We'll talk inside,' said Mutt curtly. 'We got a lot to catch up on.'

I stared up at the smoking hole in the side of the wolves' apartment, slowly shaking my head. How could the Hunters be back? I'd personally visited the exploded remains of the Hunter base just a week ago, hoping against hope that somebody had survived.

*There had been so many bodies…*

I rubbed my eyes as the unwanted memories swept through me in a black, filthy tide. It had been a massacre, pure and simple. Three hundred and fifty-nine Hunters had lost their lives that night, the entire Los Angeles division. Three hundred and fifty-nine bodies. Their base had been hidden deep underground in a disused government bunker in the suburbs of downtown LA, the location of which had been a closely guarded secret.

*Until a week ago.*

I shook my head quickly, trying to dispel the memories

of that fateful night, but it was too late. It had been a tragedy a long time in the making, and it was just dumb luck that I had been there to witness their destruction... and to play my own, terrible little part in it.

After many futile years of searching for the hidden Hunters' base, the vampires had finally gotten wise to the wonders of technology, and had come up with a plan to wipe out their most hated enemies, once and for all. They had begun implanting tracking chips under the skin of decoy vamps and wolves, who then allowed themselves to be 'caught' by the Hunters and taken back to their base for questioning.

Most of the bugged decoys got caught at the screening center twenty miles from the real base, but eventually, one had got through— a young, traitorous werewolf named Dana, who had been masquerading as a prostitute to draw the Hunters out.

The vampires found and breached the Hunters' base less than a day later, ripping apart both men and women in the dead of night in a bloodbath of sport killing. As a finishing touch they had detonated a bomb in the basement, setting off a dramatic chain reaction which destroyed the Hunters' hoarded store of ammo, bringing the entire place crashing down.

As far as I knew, myself and Monster were the only Hunters who had got out alive.

My breathing quickened as I fought against the memories, which pushed up my throat like black lava, threatening to choke me.

It had been partly my fault that the base had been breached. The vamps had found the base by following the signal in the tracking chip, but it had been me who had unwittingly let them into the base. I'd gone out late one night on a mission to save Mutt's life, and left the secret back hatchway propped open with a coke-can…

I came back to earth with a bump as I became aware that Mutt was still staring at me. He was always doing that, trying to read my face as though my feelings were somehow written there in bright red ink.

I turned away, hiding my face behind my hair as I stared at the smoking hole in the side of the building. A new, sick feeling of guilt rose to fill me. I had to find out what had happened here, and fast.

I put my head down and started marching towards the entrance to the building. If the Hunters were trying to find me, then this would be the second catastrophe that I had caused, in as many weeks. The wolves were my friends now, and I didn't want any more blood on my hands. I had to make peace between the Hunters and the wolves, prevent any more killing.

Whatever it cost me.

INSIDE THE WEREWOLF headquarters, I ran upstairs as fast as my legs would carry me, taking two steps at a time. I had to get to the Hunters and explain things before they started killing people. If anyone was going to die over this, it should be me.

I was panting by the time I reached the top. I rounded the corner a good ten seconds ahead of Mutt and walked out onto the werewolves' floor, expecting the worst.

Strangely enough, everything looked normal. The steel apartment doors that lined the corridor were closed, the walls intact. Not at all the war zone I'd been expecting.

I cautiously approached the very end apartment—

the one I'd shared with Mutt and his wolf-pack since I'd fled Karrel's old apartment a month ago in fear of my life. I reached out a trembling hand for the door handle, but the door was wrenched open a split second before I touched it. I cowered back, expecting to see a forest of guns leveled at my head.

Instead, the friendly, pixie-like face of Mia peered out.

I gave a startled cry at the sight of her, then rushed through the doorway to sweep my friend up into a huge bear-hug, almost gasping in relief.

Everything had to be okay if Mia was here.

Mia was a werewolf too, although she didn't live in this particular run-down neighborhood. She worked as an intern doctor on the streets of downtown Los Angeles, and lived about as far away from the area as she could. I didn't blame her. She'd saved my life more times than I cared to remember.

'I see you made it through another week,' she said, reaching up to ruffle my hair. She was dressed in a set of rumpled blue hospital scrubs, with the name-tag from her ward still attached. She'd obviously just got home from her night shift judging by the dark rings under her eyes. Her glossy blonde hair was cut into a sleek bob which was rumpled at the back from her motorcycle helmet.

'So what happened?' she asked, giving me a quizzical look.

'Hmm?'

Mia wordlessly pointed at what I was wearing. I realized I was still dressed in the Hitchcock T-shirt and sweat pants I'd grabbed off Niki's laundry pile while Mutt had been fighting with Niki. My head was cut from where Cyan had thrown me against the wall.

'Rough night,' I muttered, glancing quickly behind me. 'Either I have a huge magnet down my pants that attracts trouble, or everyone I've met I met last night was just really pleased to see me.'

Mia sighed. 'I already warned you to leave the humor to me, didn't I?'

'Twice. I'm sleep deprived.'

'This is your third and final warning.' Mia paused as she took in my preoccupied expression. 'What's up? The nightmares again?' She put a perfectly manicured hand on my arm, her warm brown eyes searching mine.

'Got kidnapped. Last night.'

'Again? That explains a few things.' Mia sighed, looking at me dubiously. 'Remind me again why I'm friends with you?'

'Because I make your life about ten times more exciting.' I tried to peer over her head in search of any stray Hunters who might be lurking in the apartment. 'And because I'm friends with a bunch of super-cute guys who you only wish you had a shot with.'

'Behind you,' Mia muttered. She stiffened as Mutt strode past us, giving her an odd look, then turned and looked up at me, her face glowing a pretty shade of scarlet.

I shook my head. Mia had unfortunately had a crush on Mutt almost from Day One, a fact which—like most things about Mia—Mutt chose to ignore. He was too fixated on me to even notice her for most of the time, and for her own safety I was glad of it.

Mia deserved better than Mutt.

In fact, most women deserved better than Mutt.

Trouble was, I was the only one who seemed to be able to see that…

\* \* \*

I FOLLOWED MIA through into the main room of the apartment, where we dutifully joined the small excited throng of people who were inspecting the huge hole in the end wall. There were no Hunters here, much to my relief, but that was about the only good news.

The usually-neat three-bedroom apartment was trashed. Almost all the windows in the place had been shattered, and the brand-new carpet had been badly scorched by the explosion. Black ash lay in a thick layer over everything near the hole in the wall, and an exposed water pipe cheerfully sprayed everything within a five foot radius with nasty-looking drain water. The back of the TV was on fire.

'Okay, I'll bite,' I said. 'Who let Mutt cook again?'

There was a stir in the crowd. The assembled werewolves parted as the greying, bearlike figure of Motor lumbered forward, scowling at me. Motor was the oldest and strongest of this particular pack of werewolves. He had a legendary bad temper and a face like a bulldog chewing a wasp, but he was surprisingly tolerant when it came to keeping an eye on the pack of over-excitable teen werewolves who lived next door.

'The Hunters happened, that's what,' Motor rumbled, a deeply disapproving look on his broad, freckled face. I sucked in my breath, my mind suddenly racing. I'd wanted to hear those words for what felt like an eternity, but as I heard them I suddenly felt afraid. It was clear that Motor held me entirely responsible for the explosion, despite the fact that I'd been half a city away during the Hunters' visit.

'The Hunters were here?' I asked.

'Aye. Three o' the bastards. They were looking for

you. I woulda ate 'em, but Buck said not to, else you'd get all pissy and stop paying our cable bill.'

'So… they just blew up your apartment when you said I wasn't here?'

'I didn't tell 'em jackshit, kid.'

'But the damage…'

'Yeah, the lady one done that.' Motor snorted, rubbing soot off his arms. 'She was s'prisingly pleasant till we tried to put a bag over 'er head. When we tried to tie her up she went nuts and all this freaky blue fire stuff came out of her hands, set light to the stove.' Motor sniffed, glancing ruefully around the apartment. He didn't seem particularly surprised by any of this. 'She musta melted the gas pipeline, cuz next thing I know there's this huge great bang and half the room fell down. Landlord's gonna go apeshit when he sees this mess.'

I stared at him. A tiny bell in the back of my head was ringing. 'Did you just say that fire came out of her *hands?*'

'Yeah. Spookiest thing I ever seen in my life. Didn't figure her for a wizard, but there you go. Some pretty funny friends you got there, Kayla.'

I gulped. Motor was not the kind of person you wanted to piss off, pretty much ever. The younger wolves had accepted me without blinking an eyelid since I'd arrived here a few weeks ago, but Motor had thrown a fit when Mutt had made his little announcement that a trainee Hunter would be crashing here until the psychopathic monsters who were intent on killing her had given up and gone home.

The fact that I'd previously saved Mutt's life on several occasions seemed to be the only thing that had stopped Motor throwing me bodily out of the window. But judging by the look on his face now, the fine line I was walking had just got slimmer. I cleared my throat, choosing my words carefully.

'Where are they now? The Hunters, I mean?'

Before Motor could reply, a good-looking boy in his late teens with broad shoulders and glossy, waist-length blond hair shouldered his way through the throng towards me, his biscuit-brown eyes brimming with excitement. He was barefoot and clad in a long cream surf shirt with faded jeans. A long, deep, faded scar trailed across his forehead and down the side of his face and neck. I couldn't help but smile at the sight of him.

Buck gave a cry of delight as he ran forwards to sweep me up into a huge bear-hug, almost crushing my ribs as he squeezed me to his chest. I grumbled good-naturedly as he gave me a kiss on the cheek, a huge grin on his soot-blackened face.

'My favorite girl's back! And alive, too!'

He turned triumphantly to the two almost identically blond, brown-eyed teens standing behind him. Buck was one of three triplets, and if it wasn't for his scar I'd have a genuinely hard time telling them apart. Buck winked at his brother and grinned. 'Told you she'd make it. You owe me twenty bucks, dude.'

'Good to see you too, Buck,' I muttered, squeezing his hand. I threw Brad a pointed glance, who gave me a sweet, innocent smile in return. I'd always liked Brad, but now I could see I was going to have to rethink this. *I'd only been gone twelve hours, for Christ's sake...*

Buck flashed his too-sharp werewolf teeth at me in a grin as he happily pocketed his brother's dollar bills.

He was swaying a little, his eyes unfocused. The third triplet nick-named Grids watched us, his solemn brown eyes cautious, hanging back behind his father Motor. He'd always been a little wary of me, and I didn't blame him.

Before I could comment on this Buck grabbed my arm and laid his head on my shoulder, burying his nose in my hair. All the wolves had a problem with respecting personal space, but Buck was by far the worst offender.

'Wanna see something cool, beautiful?'

'You old charmer. You talking to me?'

'Shit yeah. Ain't no-one else in this room who listens to me. Here, check this out.'

Buck lifted his shirt up to reveal his flat stomach. A large, ugly burn mark sliced across his belly, spoiling the smooth perfection of his otherwise flawless figure. The burn was already starting to heal, turning crystalline silver around the edges, but it still looked pretty nasty. He'd be left with yet another scar, when that one was done healing.

I winced. 'That doesn't fit my definition of cool.'

'You shoulda seen it half an hour ago. I took a picture of my own kidney. Wanna see?'

He reached for his iPhone.

'I'll pass, thanks.'

Buck was pale and sweating with the shock of his injuries, but he was practically bouncing with excitement. Clearly, this was the most exciting thing that had happened to him all week. I caught him as he swayed again and almost fell, supporting him in my arms.

'Dude, quit flashing the poor chicklet and tell her what the hell happened,' said Mutt, in a monotone.

'Yeah, tell her,' I said, teasing him.

'I'll do better than that,' said Buck, his eyes gleaming as he planted a huge, sooty kiss on my forehead. 'I'll show you.'

# CHAPTER EIGHT

THE GARAGE DOOR rumbled upwards. As though on cue, everyone gasped.

Two sooty, furious-looking humans sat on an improvised bench made out of orange milk crates. A man and a woman, both tall and athletic. They were bound hand and foot with silver duct tape. As if the tape wasn't enough, thick iron shackles encircled the captives' necks, wrists and ankles, chaining them to reinforced steel braces cemented into the floor of the garage. Clearly, whoever had tied them up had been instructed not to take any chances.

A younger man lay on the floor, also bound, curled up into a groaning ball.

The woman looked up as the garage door opened, blinking in the sudden bright light. Her gaze lit on me, and her face mirrored mine in an expression of shock. The tiny bell that had been ringing in my head turned into a clanging gong.

'*Ninette?*' I gasped.

The spell shattered. I darted forwards, reaching

out to tear off the tape, to free her. Whoever had tied my two Team Leaders up obviously had no idea who they were dealing with here. An icy terror filled me as I contemplated exactly what Ninette would do to whoever had tied her up as soon as she got free. I wondered if I should start running now, or wait for the explosion and just ride the shockwave out of here.

Before I could reach her, two separate sets of hands clamped down on my shoulders, holding me back. I spun around, glaring at the two wolves behind me.

'Knock it off!' I said. 'They're cool!'

Grids and Brad tightened their grip and stared back impassively, not quite meeting my gaze. Out of the corner of my eye I saw Motor nod slightly. The two wolves looked at each other and grudgingly released me, although it was clear from their attitude that I'd better not try that shit again. Everyone was nervous, on edge. Behind them, Motor switched on the garage lights and rolled the steel garage door shut, locking it with a home-made bolting device.

I turned my back on the wolves and stared almost greedily at the three Hunters in an overwhelming flood of relief, mentally removing them from the death toll.

Ninette had been my trainer. She was one of the highest-ranking officers in the Hunters, one of the few Hunters I'd met who knew how to do the Dark Arts... even though practicing any form of the old Magics in public was so far beyond illegal that only the crazy or desperate would dare do such a thing.

Ninette was neither. She had the figure of a Maxim model, the brains to use her looks to their full advantage, and the kind of extensive large-weapons training to level the score should options one or two fall through. Nobody messed with Ninette and walked away with all their body-parts still attached, especially if they were so clueless that they overlooked all of the above and decided to tie her up with duct-tape and lock her in a garage.

I glanced over at the broad shouldered, long-haired guy sitting by her side, and broke into a broad smile of relief. The guy's name was Phil. He was Ninette's partner, and the renegade leader of the infamous Unit D— Karrel's old unit. Phil was one of the coolest guys I knew. I could never look at him without smiling. He wore a dark green camouflage outfit with padded elbows and black lace-up boots, his untamed mane of dark brown hair cascading over his shoulders like a young lion. A steel guitar pick and bottle-opener hung with the dog-tag IDs he wore on a chain around his throat, making him equipped for, he had once joked, 'every kind of emergency'.

He was one of the very first Hunters who'd formed the LA branch and his origins were still something of a mystery to me, but the high-tech black hydraulic brace strapped to his left knee was a daily reminder that even the most highly-trained Hunters were not invincible.

Out of the three humans in the garage he seemed the most at ease, reclining calmly in his makeshift chair and tapping his fingers as though sitting in a doctor's waiting room. Apart from a few minor cuts and bruises the pair seemed uninjured, and my hideous, gut-wrenching guilt over the bombing abated somewhat.

The third figure on the floor I didn't recognize at first. As my shadow fell over him he rolled over with a moan of pain and stared up at me with bulging, half-crazed eyes, dark blood trickling from his nose and mouth.

I leaned forward in dismay, a name coming back to me through the mild fog of sleep deprivation. The guy's name was Billy. I'd last seen him working down in the armory of the Hunters' base. He was a sweet guy who'd shown me around the place on my first day, even shared his lunch with me. He was a tank tech or something, a simple and uncomplicated guy who everyone seemed to like.

Judging by the state of him, he needed help, and fast.

I stood there staring down at the trio of captive Hunters, conscious that a dozen very pissed werewolves were scrutinizing my every move. Every eye in the room was on me, the impromptu ambassador for the human race. A muffled groan filled the air and everyone turned to inspect the prone figure of Billy. He was white as a sheet, gasping and trembling. He'd rolled over and was staring blindly up at the ceiling, blood trickling from his gaping mouth.

I unfroze and moved to Billy's side without thinking, almost daring Motor to try and stop me. I crouched down by the young man's side and gently rolled him over.

Two terrified, bloodshot eyes stared up at me, wide with pain and fright.

'Hey there, buddy,' I soothed. I gently opened his jacket and ran my hands under his clothing, lifting his shirt to search for what I felt sure would be a gunshot wound or a percussion injury. I couldn't find a thing wrong with him.

I beckoned Mutt over, dropping my voice.

'What happened to him?' I asked.

But even as the words left my mouth, I saw it. On the back of his neck, underneath his shoulder-length brown hair, was an ugly half-healed bite wound. A vampire bite, I thought at first. I bent over with a curse, looking closer. But instead of the two classic fang-marks I was expecting, I saw four deep indentations and a mass of purple bruising in between, making an angry-looking dark oval on Billy's neck.

*A werewolf bite.*

My face froze. I sat back on my haunches, the familiar sense of helplessness rolling through me. I checked his pulse— it was pounding like a clapped-out racehorse. *Shit.* Billy's skin was scorching hot under my hands, and a tidal-wave of tremors rocked him every couple of seconds, bouncing his head off the floor even as I tried to still him with my hands.

'He needs help,' I said quietly, staring down at the doomed man. Precious seconds ticked by and I half turned my head, looking over my shoulder. 'Anyone want to help him?' I suggested loudly, as an uncomfortable silence descended on the room.

Motor shook his head, folding his thick arms.

'There's no helping that boy now, lass. Two hours, tops, he'll turn.' He waved a careless hand at me. 'Tell ya what. Untie him. He could really help us out here, even the score a little.' He threw a black glance at the bound figures of Phil and Ninette, his eyes turning dark. 'Know what I'm saying?'

I gave him a dirty look, pretending for his sake that I hadn't understood him. Ninette rolled her eyes and made an urgent noise behind her gag. I looked up at her in hope as she raised her eyebrows and beckoned me over with a quick jerk of her head. *She had a plan!*

Without thinking I reached out and pulled the duct-tape off her mouth, desperate for her advice. I had to help Billy, and leaving him here until he was ready to have the two Hunters as a midnight snack wasn't an option.

The duct tape fluttered to the floor, and Ninette opened her mouth.

A lot of things happened at once, after that.

The line of wolves instantly broke ranks, half of them running towards me, the other half making an urgent break for safety. Motor yelled something at me, but I couldn't hear his words over the sudden ringing in my ears as a giant invisible hand of heat picked me up and lifted me off the ground in slow motion, hurling me through the air. I hit the concrete floor hard and rolled, dimly aware of Mutt's body covering mine protectively as a burst of what looked like giant fireworks went off in the enclosed space of the garage, turning every shadow bright as day. I waited for the sound, for the '*BOOM*' of the explosion, but the massive thunderclap had been completely silent.

And then the world went away for a little while.

SOUND CAME BACK to the room in a slow rush, along with a high-pitched ringing in my ears. It seemed to get painfully louder as I regained consciousness. I lifted my head and opened my eyes. I was lying on the stained concrete floor of the garage, my head nicely cushioned on a pile of fallen bricks. More bricks were strewn across my legs and chest, and an arm was draped protectively over my ribs. As I groaned and started to move it curled slowly around until its steel-ringed hand was gently cupping my left breast.

I shoved Mutt off me with a grunt of annoyance and

sat up, staring around in disorientation.

The first thing I saw was Ninette. My team leader was standing in the exact center of the garage amid a pile of melted, twisted orange crates, her sleek blonde-and-black hair gently fanning out around her as though blown out by a strong wind. The garage floor beneath her was on fire, burning with an incandescent, white-hot flame that danced around her and yet didn't seem to be burning her. Her eyes were closed, her lips moving silently, reciting words I knew only too well. As I watched, the iron shackles around her ankles, neck and wrists began to melt, turning to a silvery liquid that trickled down her skin and made a puddle on the floor.

Mutt yelled as he was lifted away from me as though by a giant hand and dropped carelessly into a pile of electrical goods on the other side of the garage. Ninette turned away, narrowed her eyes and waved a hand at Phil like a mad conductor. There was a muted 'pop' and his bindings exploded, duct tape and iron nuggets showering into the air like burning metallic confetti. Phil stood up, stretched and smiled warmly at me, as though he'd been waiting for her to do this very thing. Ninette nodded to him and turned away, staring thoughtfully at the only person in the group apart from myself who had yet to run—Motor.

The old grey werewolf was utterly silent as he returned their combined gaze, only the curl of his lip and the stiff pose of his body betraying his fury at their escape.

I cleared my throat, started to move, to say something to defuse the situation. After all, both sides were my friends, although they were mutual enemies. But my words cut off as a cold, clammy hand closed tightly on my ankle.

'Help me,' croaked Billy.

I pulled my leg away convulsively, staring downwards as Billy rolled over beneath me, now magically freed from his bindings. Blood ran freely from his nose, and the whites of his eyes turned red with broken blood vessels before rolling up in their sockets.

Then, he started to *change*.

As the man's agonized screams rang out, shockingly loud in the tiny concrete garage, I realized nobody was paying any attention to Ninette.

I only realized this when she calmly leaned over, plucked a piece of broken steel piping from the mess on the floor, wrapped the end in a grease rag to protect her perfect salon manicure, then stabbed Billy the Soon-To-Be-Werewolf straight through the heart with anatomical precision.

# CHAPTER NINE

THE BILLY-BEAST HOWLED, curling around the steel pipe that impaled him through the chest like a human-sized bug on a pin. I stared down at him in shock. There was no way in hell that Mutt was going to get his cleaning deposit back now, I thought, hysteria plucking a merry tune on the one remaining thread of my sanity. I rose to my feet and backed away from the kicking, thrashing ball of fury that only a few hours ago had been a well-respected, highly-trained member of my Hunter team.

I could also see that it was too late to save him.

Billy's body was already half coated in glossy brown fur, his swollen limbs stuck halfway between that of man and beast when he died. Perhaps that was a merciful thing.

The look on Motor's face, however, was not merciful.

Far from it.

Nor were the faces of the other werewolves who now came creeping back, silent as the night, staring with mingled fear and fury at the bloody, twitching remains of what would have been the newest member of their race. Billy's head fell back and his fang-filled mouth gaped open, his eyes fading from the bright gold of the werewolf to a dull, brackish brown, like the last ember of a fire going out.

Billy was dead.

As one, the pack turned to stare in terrifying silence at the two Hunters standing over his still, unmoving body.

I stood absolutely still beside them, my heart pounding so loudly I could hardly hear myself think, clutching at the black bandana on my arm. *The bandana that hid my own werewolf bite from sight.* I reeled as the implications hit me.

Billy had been Ninette's friend and co-worker for almost five years, and she'd just stabbed him to death without so much as batting an eyelid. If she'd killed one of her own highly trained Hunter team-members with such apparent lack of remorse... what would she do to me, the newbie, if she found out that I'd also been bitten by a werewolf?

The wolves fell silent as Motor stepped forwards out of their bristling midst, his brown eyes blazing amber with an ungodly fury.

'You'd better run, lady,' he growled.

'We're Hunters, sir,' said Phil quietly, and I was amazed to hear a tone of respect in his voice as he spoke. Everyone turned to look at him. 'We don't run.'

Motor's rheumy eyes flicked sideways and he glared at Phil, as though seeing him for the first time. He stiffened slightly, then leaned forwards and carefully sniffed the air. His bushy grey eyebrows lifted briefly in an expression of genuine surprise.

'Could it be...?' he murmured.

He stared at Phil for a long moment. I was surprised to feel some kind of power flaring in the air between the two men, as though they were testing each other. After a moment Motor gave a faint nod and stepped back, uncrossing his arms. 'As you wish,' he said with finality, as though in answer to a silent question.

The other wolves hurriedly stepped back as the elderly werewolf pulled his tan gardening pants up at the knees and stiffly bent down, his joints cracking in protest, still staring at Phil as though he was making a point. He leaned over and put his hands on the ground one by one, then rocked forwards to put his full weight on them.

And then...

I can't explain exactly *when* he changed, mainly because by the time his weight had settled onto his palms, Motor was a werewolf. The change just flowed over him like water over a rock, taking place so swiftly that a couple of the younger werewolves did double takes.

I knew of course that the older a wolf got the easier the change became, but before I could process what I'd just seen, Motor gave a loud snarl and leaped at the two Hunters, his yellowing teeth bared.

Phil took the brunt of the impact as he instantly leapt forwards to shield Ninette, disappearing beneath the enormous creature in a flurry of flailing limbs and snapping teeth. I felt Mutt's hand grab my shoulder and pull me away from the fight as I stared in helpless horror, waiting for the inevitable spray of blood and the scream that would mark the end of one of my favorite people I'd met since joining the Hunter-corps.

To my absolute amazement, Motor was the one

who screamed, shrieking in fury as Phil spun around and hurled him bodily against the nearest wall, using the big wolf's momentum against him. Before Motor could fully recover Phil was upon him again, reaching down past his snapping teeth to grab the big werewolf by the scruff of his neck like a disobedient dog. Phil lifted him up and pulled him tightly against his body so Motor couldn't slash at him with his claws, wrapping his strong arms around the creature's throat in a stranglehold.

'Last chance, old man,' said Phil calmly. He wasn't even out of breath. 'Give it up. Call your boys off and let me and my lady leave. We just came for the girl, but your side attacked first.' He flicked a meaningful look down at Billy. 'We meant you and your family no harm.'

Motor gave a wet, defiant snarl that sounded like someone cutting wood with a blunt saw. Phil tightened his grip with a sigh and Motor's snarl turned into a very undignified squeak. His ears laid wickedly flat on his head as his huge back claws scrabbled on the ground, fighting to turn and rip Phil's head off, but he was well and truly stuck.

It had to be another spell, I decided. No human was strong enough to restrain a fully-grown werewolf by hand, and certainly not one as ready to kill as Motor currently was.

As I stood there gawking, Ninette stepped out of her own personal fire-pit and approached Motor, steam drifting lazily off her perfect peaches-and-cream skin. The old wolf grew very still as her eyes flashed with black magic, turning grey, then silver, then white. She held out her hands towards him, like a queen bestowing a favor. Twin balls of steaming blue plasma appeared, one on each hand, super-heated energy jumping and popping.... just inches from the old wolf's whiskered face.

Ninette glanced back to the group as the smell of scorching dog-hair filled the air, speaking in the high, sing-song voice that she only used when she was really pissed.

'Anyone else like to come out and play?' She treated them to a dazzling smile that made the wolves back up hurriedly. 'I brought enough fun for everybody.'

A low, uncertain grumbling came from the group. A couple of the younger wolves dropped onto all fours and started to change, but slowly, as though nobody wanted to be the one to make the first move.

Mutt was the first one to step forward.

'Let him go,' he called out loudly. 'He's got nothing to do with this.'

Ninette blinked, and then peered closely at Mutt.

'*Mathius*? Mathius Corby?' she said, feigning amazement. A slow smile curved on her face but didn't spread much higher, as though it was afraid to be there. 'Look at you, all grown up. Rumor had it that you'd got yourself killed.'

Mutt's eyes didn't leave Ninette's face as he spoke, his voice ringing out with a sharp confidence and command that I'd never heard before.

'Rumor got it wrong. And the name's 'Mutt' now,' he said curtly. His gaze flicked to me and back again. 'If it's the girl you're after, she stays with us.'

Ninette laughed, shaking her head as she turned to wink at me.

'He's a feisty one, ain't he?' she said, as blue flickers

of light crawled over her face, arcing up from the spinning blue plasma that surrounded her hands. 'Did he pick that name out himself, or just look on page one of the Big Book of Dog Names?'

I held her gaze, furious at her for killing Billy, but also truly terrified of the anger that lurked behind Ninette's breezy expression. The last person to piss Ninette off had been sent home carrying several assorted body parts in a jar. I'd heard that with extensive surgery, there was a small chance that he *might* still be able to have children...

There was a yip from Motor as his whiskers started to smoke. I felt my own anger rise and unthinkingly stepped forwards to stand beside Mutt, backing him up. Motor was a giant pain in the ass, but I couldn't just stand here and watch him burn.

'That's enough, guys,' I called out. 'Let him down, or else—'

'Or else what, Kayla?' Ninette snapped back, wheeling around to face me. 'What will you do? Throw a two-inch fireball at a passing squirrel, perhaps? Set fire to your own eyebrows? Isn't that what you usually do under these circumstances?'

I bristled. 'You know that's not—'

'Go get your things,' Ninette said briskly. 'You're coming with us.'

Mutt growled then, an almost inaudible rumble in his throat that made the hair on the back of my neck stand on end. I touched his side to quiet him, unthinkingly reaching down to rub the hard muscle of his lower back, soothing him as I would an angry dog. Ninette's eyes were suddenly on me, registering first surprise, then annoyance, then disappointment.

She shook her head as though in defeat, then pursed her lips and closed her fists to make the plasma between her hands burn brighter. Motor jumped back in Phil's arms as the tip of one ear started to smoke, his yellow eyes rolling wildly in fright.

'Last chance,' she said.

'Enough!' I snapped. 'Phil, put him down. *Now!*'

Phil hiked an eyebrow at me. I'd never raised my voice to him before.

'Kayla,' said Ninette, with an infinite patience that made me want to slap her. 'These are *werewolves*. You're a werewolf hunter. Anyone else see the problem with that?'

'Karrel didn't have a problem with that,' I muttered.

'Yeah, and look at what that did for him. Fifteen years of Special Weapons training, and one misguided friendship later, the boy winds up as the main course in an all-you-can-eat werewolf buffet.'

Ninette's expression softened a little as she saw the look on my face, but not much. 'Sorry to break it to ya, pecan-pie, but that ain't the way it works. You stay here, you'll be next on the menu. Unless you wise up and *do your damn job.*'

'Since when does doing my job include killing my friends?' I asked, unable to help glancing down at Billy's body.

I saw Ninette's face go very hard and cold.

'It's called doing your duty,' said Ninette, so quietly I had to strain to hear her. 'It's what being a Hunter's all about. You might find out all about it someday.' She drew back, looked at me with dark eyes. 'In the meantime, you have one simple choice to make. It's them or us. Pick a side.'

There was a yelp as Motor's black whiskers caught fire.

It was the last straw.

I wheeled around with a cry, unleashing my frustration into a low-level white plasma ball, hurling it at the floor just in front of Phil. He jumped back as the garage floor cracked in a concave pock-mark with the shock of the unfocused blast, as though an invisible cannonball had just struck it.

Motor took advantage of the opportunity to wrench himself free from Phil's iron grip. He dropped to the floor and slunk quickly to the back of the garage. The triplets instantly seized him with cries of relief, smothering their father's smoking whiskers with their bare hands. Buck childishly bared his teeth at Ninette, who took a step towards him, raising one hand.

'Enough!' I cried, stepping between them. 'Get out of here, both of you. I'm staying here.'

'That's your final decision?'

'It is.'

Ninette's lips tightened with regret. She held out her hand towards me, palm up. I flinched back, waiting for the smoking ball of black plasma that would end my life. Several seconds passed and nothing happened. My team leader's eyes flicked to the twin black rubber ID bracelets I wore on my wrist and back to me. I gritted my teeth. She might as well have just hit me in the face.

The bracelets contained my Hunter ID code, rank and name. I hadn't taken mine off since I'd first arrived at the base. Even just wearing them somehow made me feel closer to Karrel.

Angry now, I pulled off the two bracelets and threw them at Ninette. She caught them easily and stashed them in her pocket without a word. She turned her back on me and walked towards the locked garage door. She made a downwards gesture and the door violently sheared down the middle with a scream of superheated metal, revealing a flash of early-morning sunlight.

'Show off,' I muttered.

Ninette strode through the new doorway without a backward glance. Phil looked at me as though he was about to say something, then thought better of it and dropped his head with a sigh, turning to follow Ninette.

The wolves fell back as they passed, letting them through.

I watched them go, a tumult of feelings raging through me. My heart leaped into my mouth as I saw the pair of them vanish into the daylight, and reality started to hit home. The Hunters were my last link to Karrel, the man I had loved and given my word that I would avenge. I had a thousand questions to ask them, and now they were gone.

And besides, I hadn't even mentioned the most important thing of all: that small matter of the world ending on Sunday.

I swore loudly, then turned and started walking towards the destroyed garage door, muttering under my breath.

'Kayla.'

I sucked in a deep, calming breath, then turned unwillingly. Mutt's luminous golden eyes shone in the semi-darkness as he stepped forward, looking me over with concern.

'Need a hand?' he asked.

'I'm fine.' I was trying to convince myself more than

him. 'Gimmie ten. I gotta go fix this mess.'

Mutt's grip tightened on my hand. 'Promise?'

I nodded, then leaned forward to plant a soft kiss on his cheek.

'I promise,' I lied.

# CHAPTER TEN

NINETTE STOPPED WALKING and turned to face me as I hurried up the path after her, a tired but patient look on her face. It was almost as though she'd been expecting me to follow her. I cursed myself for giving in so easily.

I stopped a good ten feet away and folded my arms, sizing her up.

'Just tell me one thing,' I called out, after a few long moments had ticked by. 'What about—'

'The Seekers?' Ninette snorted. 'I was wondering when you'd remember about them.'

My Team Leader pushed her long dark hair off her face, briefly leaning on Phil for support. I saw how exhausted she looked, and remembered again how much doing magic took out of you. Even doing a simple fireball spell made you feel like you'd just run several laps of a baseball field underwater, and the spells she'd just performed were a hundred times more complex.

'So…?' I prompted her.

Ninette glanced up at the bright morning sky, pursing her lips in thought. I thought for a moment she wasn't going to answer me, then she seemed to deflate slightly, all the anger going out of her now she was away from the werewolves.

'Damned if I know. We're in way over our heads on that one.' She paused, rubbing at her face. I was amazed to see that her cheeks were damp and her usually-immaculate eyeliner was running. She wiped her eyes quickly, then breathed out hard and turned to face me, eyeing me in open and slightly hostile curiosity.

I could imagine that she had a million questions she wanted to ask me, as I did with her, but she'd taken my Hunter bracelets away, and my trust with it. I folded my arms and stared back at her, my jaw set. If she was waiting for some kind of apology, she was going to be disappointed.

'We have to stop the Seekers, that much is a given,' I said eventually, just to break the silence, staring at a point just over her left shoulder. 'Whether I stay or go, there's no choice on that one. If we don't stop them…'

'The world will be destroyed in three days, rains of blood, boiling seas, yadda yadda yadda. Yes, I *know,* newbie. You seem to have this wonderful talent for persistently and annoyingly stating the obvious. If you could somehow harness that and turn it into actual original thought, then maybe, just *maybe* you could be of use to us.'

'Just tell me what to *do!*' I cried, frustrated. I strode forward as she started to turn away and put a hand on her arm to stop her from leaving, ignoring the warning flash of her hazel-green eyes. 'Can't we get to a radio station? Call the news, write to the papers or something? Hell, we could even do the thing from that movie about the alien invasion, and drive up to the President's house, get a message through security…'

'And tell them what, exactly? That we just found out about this ancient pre-biblical prophecy that we're almost certain will be triggered at midnight on Sunday, which will call some giant, mythical creatures called Seekers down from Heaven to end the world? Good luck explaining that one on the lunchtime news.'

I sagged, staring at her. When she put it like that, I had to admit that it did sound just a little far-fetched.

Ninette sighed, looking at me with sympathy.

'You can't help us on this one, Kay. One person can't save the world alone. We're gonna head up to Washington, go straight to the Hunter's Council. I hear they've got one or two new tricks up their sleeve.'

'There's a Hunter's Council?' I gaped at her, stunned. 'Why didn't anyone tell me?'

'Kayla, I wouldn't trust you to book a *motel room* online, let alone trust you with the biggest secret the Hunters have.' Ninette's ruby red lips arched up in a smile. 'If I'd have told you before that there was a Council, within twenty-four hours every semi-cute guy within a fifteen mile radius would know. '

'But you just told me.'

'Yeah, now that everyone's dead. Everyone who matters, at least.'

I folded my arms and tapped my foot, waiting for my answer. I hated that she'd known me a month and already knew me too well. Ninette stared at me hard, chewing on her lip, then sighed. A cold wind blew down the path, making the bushes dance and raising goosebumps on my bare arms. She beckoned me closer, lowering her voice so much that I could barely hear her.

'You okay?' she asked.

I nodded unconvincingly, surprised, suddenly unable to speak.

Ninette gave me a long, hard look, then sighed.

'You know you're in big trouble, right?'

I shrugged, swallowed a lump in my throat. Waiting.

'*If* we live through the weekend,' Ninette said. 'And that's a really big *if*, I'm going to come back here and teach that new boyfriend of yours some manners.'

She held up a finger as I opened my mouth to protest. 'And just so you know, I will never, *ever* approve. Anyone who dates a werewolf is officially an idiot.'

Behind her, Phil snorted with laughter.

'I'm serious,' Ninette said. 'You need your head examining for even looking at the guy. Christ, girl, do you have *any* idea how much work it takes to even just—'

Phil cleared his throat very loudly, cutting her off.

Ninette pulled a girlishly grumpy face at him, then jerked her head towards the overgrown path that lead back towards the car park. I fell in beside her as she strode off down the path. Phil trotted along behind us a good ten paces back, giving us some privacy.

'What happened to us?' I asked her quietly, as we walked. 'Who blew up the Hunter base?'

Ninette's frown deepened and she picked up her pace, putting some distance between us and the werewolf's tower block before she finally gave me the answer I had been waiting for.

'It was a coordinated strike, if you must know,' she said, her voice distant, neutral. She grabbed at a passing bush and broke off a sizable branch, spinning it expertly like a cheerleader. She used it to swipe at every bush we passed, sending showers of leaves fluttering to the ground in her wake. 'We lost every main base from here to Canada, and a bunch over in Europe. Not many people know about the HQ in Washington, or else that would've been hit too. The vamps must've been planning this for years.'

She paused, looking wryly up at me.

'Turns out our base wasn't quite as unbreachable as everyone claimed. Apparently we had a rat on the inside, and high up. We smoked a vamp nest last week and found a blueprint of our base in the nest. Gave us all a nasty shock. The blueprint must have been smuggled out weeks ago and sent out to every vampire nest in the city, presumably by whoever the rat was consorting with.'

A rhododendron bush exploded under an angry swipe of her stick. Purple flowers filled the air, making me sneeze.

'The weak points of the base were all marked on the blueprint. Along with load-bearing walls, all emergency exits, and the location of the high-explosives store. Whoever came up with the plan sure as hell did their homework.'

I stopped dead as I watched her take out an aloe plant, feeling a huge weight lift off my shoulders. *It wasn't my fault that the Hunter base had got hit. Thank Christ for that.*

The relief was almost overwhelming.

'Any guesses at who the rat might have been?'

Ninette shook her head. 'I got a few suspects, nothing concrete. All our witnesses died in that explosion. Makes it a bit hard to go around asking questions.'

She stabbed a small dead fir tree with her stick like a swordsman, impaling it right through one of the soft dead branches. With a twist of her wrist the whole rotten branch came off, crashing to the ground with a loud thud. Ninette jerked her big stick free and walked on, a renewed spring in her step. I trotted obediently at her heels as she strode onwards up the path, hungry for all the news she could give me.

'We lost almost a dozen bases in ten days,' Ninette went on. 'Detroit went first, followed by every major Hunter base across the nation. LA was one of the last to go down. Each and every one was an inside job.'

My eyes were huge as I digested this new information.

'Were there survivors?'

'From our base? No.' Ninette shrugged, her gaze instantly become guarded. *People she loved had died in that explosion.* 'Just us, far as I knew. Then I picked up your tracking signal, bounced you an SOS back. Thought it might be a trap, so we came prepared.'

She hurled her stick violently into the mud and dusted off her hands. We rounded the corner and she nodded over the top of the hedgerow.

'This is us. Check it out.'

I STOPPED WALKING in surprise. An outdated Hunter SUV was parked up behind the wall. The left wing was pitted and burned, and I realized they must have dragged it out of the ruins of the base before the cops had sealed the area off. The striking decals on the back and side jumped straight out at me— a stylized grey wolf's head in a black circle. *Grey on black.* Just the sight of the Hunter branding was like a beacon of hope in a cold, dark world.

But what could we do with just four of us left?

I was surprised to see Monster sitting behind the wheel, his massive form crammed into the tiny cab, one arm hanging nonchalantly out of the side window. He gave me a little wave as I approached, turning down the radio program on finance he'd been listening to.

'You found her, then,' he said, with a yawn. 'What took ya so long?'

Ninette gave him a sideways glance that had daggers in it. I saw his warm orange eyes take in the red chain-marks on her wrists and throat and travel with interest over the tiny blood-spatters that stained her clothes.

'I won't ask,' he said, settling back in his seat with a creak. A thought occurred to him and he sat up abruptly, scanning the pathway behind us with worried eyes. 'Billy….?'

'Just start the Goddamned engine.'

'Ah, shit. Told ya I shoulda come in with you. You never listen to me…'

Monster's sorrowful eyes followed Phil as he strode up behind the vehicle and popped the remote lock to open the trunk. I raised an eyebrow in interest as I saw the veritable arsenal of weapons stashed in the back. Phil rooted through a pile of taped-together guns and firearms, then paused awkwardly and drew back.

'A little help, honey?' he called.

Ninette reached in past him and withdrew a huge rack of silver stakes. She started loading them expertly one by one into a miniature rocket-launcher. She handed the weapon to Phil, who gingerly carried it around the side of the SUV like it was a primed bomb, stashing it under the seat on his side. I felt a prickle of unease take root in my stomach, although I couldn't figure out why.

'So what can this Hunter Council do about things?' I asked.

'Maybe zip. We'll see. But we need some serious manpower to defeat the vamps, else we're screwed. This whole thing's got Harlequin's name written all over it. I personally wouldn't wanna face that motherfucker alone without a whole army of big brawny men armed with flamethrowers behind me to back me up.'

'I could take him,' muttered Phil, slamming the trunk.

Ninette winked at me, and for a moment I saw a trace of her old self shine through. 'Men are great, aren't they? The eternal optimism of the male mind continually astounds me.' She blew Phil a kiss and opened the back door. 'If only we could find a way to channel all that self-destructive macho energy into something practical like doing the dishes, we wouldn't need war. Just a whole new way to stockpile vast quantities of soap, in case the other guy claims he's getting his saucepans cleaner.'

She gave a cheery snort of laughter, tossing a SIG Sauer carelessly onto the back seat. I saw it land just inches away from a large pile of plastic explosive and backed up quickly.

'She's had a lot of late nights,' said Phil by way of explanation, glancing up from his work. 'Don't make any sudden moves and you'll get to keep all your fingers.'

'I'll cut to the chase, newbie,' Ninette clapped me on the back and propelled me towards the car. 'You're an enormous pain in the ass and practically worthless as a fighter, but I sure as hell could use another gal to dilute the testosterone in the car on the way to

Washington. We're getting signals from a few Hunter stragglers dotted here and there, a few survivors. We'll stop to pick 'em up if we have time, but even if we find a couple hundred people that won't be enough to stop Harlequin. We need an army, and those damned vamps just killed our General.'

I nodded, my face darkening as I remembered. Sage Griffiths, the leader of the Hunters, had been killed just a week ago under suspicious circumstances.

'And Harlequin will be expecting us. It's just his style.'

'Right, said Phil, opening the back door of the SUV. 'That cat's got some wicked security. Just getting to him's gonna be like pulling lawn furniture out of our asses.'

I stared at him.

'Very difficult, and probably very painful,' Phil translated. He grinned at me, a devilish look coming into his eyes. 'You in?'

I shook my head, trying not to smile. I'd missed Phil, too.

'Just tell me what I can do from here.'

'Nothing, by yourself,' said Ninette, as she hopped into the passenger seat of the Hunter SUV. 'As a Hunter, you're about as useful as a fart in a diving suit. If you come with us then at least we can try and keep you out of trouble.'

'What if I like trouble?' I asked, glancing back at the smoking remains of the wolf base.

'Then we can't help you.'

I heaved a huge sigh. Then I stepped back away from the car and folded my arms tight across my chest. I half-hoped Ninette would argue with me, try to talk me into coming. She merely shrugged, as though she couldn't care less what I did.

'Your funeral, kid,' she said, slamming the door and winding down the window. 'Just sit tight and pray we get to Washington in time. All the radios are down and the old guys in Head Office aren't exactly known for checking their email regularly. Last time I was up there I caught the Head of the War Council trying to make toast in the CD drawer of his Apple Mac.'

'So glad the world is in good hands.'

'They're great guys, just a little in the dark ages where tech stuff is concerned. They still think that Yahoo is what you shout when you get a free trial of Viagra in the mail. But they're the only hope we've got left. Far as I know, we're the only ones who know the Seekers are coming. The country's wide open if we don't get to Washington ASAP.'

'Then get going.' I thumped the hood of the car 'What are you waiting for?'

Ninette opened her mouth to reply, then suddenly stiffened, glaring over my shoulder. I had no need to look to know that there were wolves behind me.

I hesitated, then stepped back to join them, feeling the warm, sinuous shapes of Buck, Grids and Brad wind themselves protectively around my legs, now in full wolf form. I reached down for them instinctively. My hands glided across silken backs and shaggy manes as they flowed past me to form a living blockade between me and the Hunters, grumbling and chirping and giving me meaningful glances as though they thought I could understand what they were saying.

I glanced down at them, hiding a smile. The young werewolves were blond as the sun and big as half-grown lions, with the feathered ruffs of juvenile werewolves ringing their necks. I knew that there are as many different breeds of werewolf as there are nationalities of humans, their size, strength and color varying from region to region, country to country. I had seen three or four distinctly different breeds of werewolf so far, breeds that as yet I had no names for, ranging from small, shy creatures the size and shape of pet dogs to massive, shaggy-haired beasts with the strength and bulk of a full-grown bull. The diversity of the species is incredible, and makes even modern day werewolf movies look very, very lame indeed.

I didn't know the official name for my pack's breed, but I'd once heard my boys called *Lobo Guará* by a misguided and now-deceased Mexican werewolf executioner who'd come calling on us late one night, shortly after I'd moved in with the pack. *Lobo Guará* meant Maned Wolf, and looking at them now, I couldn't help thinking how appropriate the name was. The young wolves slunk around my legs, their lean rangy bodies packed with muscle and sinew, their honey-colored manes glowing in the bright sunlight as they childishly bared their teeth up at the Hunter's SUV— teeth more than big and strong enough to rip the door off the vehicle if they so wished.

If they weren't on my side, I would've been running by now.

I reached down to stroke Buck's sleek head as he pushed his snout into my hand with a faint *whuff* of defiance, feeling suddenly and irrationally invincible. If the Hunters couldn't use me, then the Wolves would take me in. Finally, I would belong somewhere. The wolves would look after me, and somehow, together, we'd beat this thing.

We'd save the world, prove Ninette wrong.

We were a pack now, after all.

The Hunter's SUV started up, and I glanced up just in time to see Ninette's silver-tinted window snap shut. Monster revved the engine and a cloud of blue smoke belched out of the back, enveloping the wolves. Moments later, the three Hunters were gone, accelerating off towards the interstate highway. I knew without asking that I'd probably never see them again, even if I begged them to come back and get me. Once Ninette gave up on someone, that was the end. You got one shot with her, and that was it.

I sensed a presence behind me, and turned to see Mutt was standing a short distance away, an apologetic look on his face. He folded his arms tightly across his chest as he watched the three younger wolves cavort around my legs, stamping their feet and running back and forth in excitement as though dying to chase the departing SUV.

'Don't worry, they're cool,' I called out to Mutt, bending down to pet the angelic doggy faces that surrounded me. Buck licked my hand, then sneezed and grinned up at me. 'Don't be mad at them. They were just trying to help.'

There was no reply.

I looked up at Mutt as his silence deepened, concerned. It wasn't like him not to crack a joke at this point, or at the very least make fun of my hair. He had plenty of material, after all.

'Everything okay?' I asked, after a moment. I wiped wolf slobber off my hands and stood up, dusting myself off.

'Not really. It's Motor.'

'Is he alright?' My heart sped up. 'No lasting damage, I hope. Except to his ego.'

'Oh, he'll be fine,' said Mutt, and my heart fell at the bleak look on his face. 'But we're not.'

He took a deep breath, jamming his hands in his pockets.

'Motor wants you out, Kayla. He says you can't stay with the wolves anymore.'

I stared at him as the bottom fell out of my world.

# CHAPTER ELEVEN

THE FIRE DOOR clicked shut behind me as I began to climb the two flights of creaky wooden stairs that led up to my old apartment, the home that Karrel and I used to share. I hadn't been back to the place since Karrel had been murdered, and wasn't quite sure what to expect.

Familiar smells crept into my nostrils as I climbed—cigarette smoke, floor wax, the sickly-sweet scent of old candles and incense sticks that the beach-dwelling ex-hippies that lived here liked to burn. I had so many memories in this place, all of them good up until recently. All of them involving Karrel.

Now that Karrel was gone, it just felt weird being here.

The old brick building was quiet for once, and I was alone as I turned the corner at the top of the staircase. Pure habit made me glance through the low door to the laundry room as I walked slowly past. Deserted. No washing tumbling in the dryers, no neighbors dawdling over the rinse cycle, exchanging gossip and occasionally bodily fluids over the top of the big, old-fashioned washer-dryers.

I shook my head and moved on.

My steps slowed as I reached the top of the heavy wooden stairs, my stomach knotting with worry. I didn't even know if I had a place to go back to. Our building manager was notoriously harsh on tenants who missed a payment, and most of the furniture in my place had been acquired as a result of his heavy-handed and extremely practical eviction methods.

My apartment looked fine from the outside. I stood outside for a good ten minutes, listening hard, before I dared to go inside. My key slipped easily into the lock on my front door and the door swung open, whisper-quiet. I paused just outside the threshold, waiting. I didn't know what to expect. A dungeon-like creak maybe, followed by the cackling of killer vampires lying in wait for me. Perhaps even the crack and *zzzip* of a specially-rigged crossbow bolt flying towards my head, ready to pierce my brain and send me tumbling, lifeless, to the floor...

As it turned out, I was disappointed. The only sound that greeted me as I entered my darkened one-bedroom apartment was a deep, cold, empty silence. No noisy guitar-solo from Karrel, practicing his riffs in the bedroom like he used to every night before a gig. No happy greeting from my black cat Koosh, whose preferred method of welcoming me home each night was a loud mewl followed by a sharp, loving bite in the back of the ankle.

The living room was also unnaturally empty of random black-clad guys dressed in AC/DC T-shirts who would happily cluster around my TV set, analyzing the guitar-wielding, head-banging moves of Zakk Wylde as a long-forgotten pizza burned away merrily in the kitchen, so it looked like Karrel's buddies weren't here either.

I sighed, counted to ten, then quietly let go of the illusion like a burst balloon. Koosh was gone, staying with my friend Wylie while I fixed my screwed-up life.

And Karrel was dead.

You'd think after a month I'd have accepted it, but no.

I didn't like the silence. It unnerved me, so I crossed the bare wooden hallway with brisk, businesslike steps and fumbled for the lamp switch, flooding the front room with a wash of white light.

I gasped, frozen by the switch, staring around me in horror. Part of me had expected as much, but seeing the reality was infinitely worse.

Our cute little apartment had been trashed. But this was no smash-and-grab by opportunistic thieves, no enforced eviction by our money-grubbing building manager.

This was malice, pure and simple.

I slowly shook my head as I turned in a full circle, taking in the full extent of the devastation. The few electronics I owned— the old analog TV, the thrift-store stereo, my battered Sony VAIO laptop covered in surfer stickers— were all still there, relatively untouched by the cyclone of destruction that had apparently touched down in the room, so this mess wasn't the result of a robbery.

But that was about the only thing that had been spared.

The carpets were shredded. The furniture was

smashed. The walls were daubed with my expensive multicolored oil-paints and what I hoped was stale beer. The sofa had been torched, and the fire had apparently been put out with every bottle of wine I'd had left in my modest pantry. The refrigerator door hung open on one shattered hinge, and most of the food inside had been dumped on the carpets and smeared up the walls. The one piece of original art I owned— a Malibu seascape painted in oils by a local beach-dweller down in Venice— had a carving knife sticking out of the sun, while the sunset was almost obscured by the hardened remains of most of a bottle of ketchup.

I sank to the floor, staring around at the stricken remains of my apartment. It was only then that I noticed the gaping, fist-sized holes in the plaster of the molded ceiling, the claw-shaped slashes on the walls. Someone had really done a number on this place.

As I sat there shaking my head, my Bluetooth earpiece blipped on, making me jump.

'You still alive?' Mutt asked over the radio, in our customary greeting.

I nodded wearily, my eyes pressed tight shut. 'Sure. Why not.'

'The apartment?'

'Trashed. I can't stay here.'

'Oh.' Mutt was silent a moment, and I heard the engine of his truck rumbling behind him, along with a snatch of rock music. 'I'm turning around. How long do you need?'

'Gimmie twenty. I'm going to try and salvage some stuff.'

'Fine. I'll park out back. Grab what you need and we'll figure something else out.' Mutt sounded distracted. A horn honked in the background. 'Look, I gotta go, the parking guy's on my ass already. Try to stay outta trouble for at least fifteen minutes.'

'You too,' I said wearily, then paused. 'Hey, just do me one last favor before you—'

There was a thump and an oath as Mutt abruptly switched off his set. The radio cut to static.

'Nice talking to you too, pal,' I muttered.

As I put down my radio, a gust of wind flowed over me. I frowned, looking up. The main window was shut, as was the front door. Where was the wind coming from? The hairs on the back of my neck prickled. I could've sworn I heard a floorboard creak. I had the weirdest feeling that someone was watching me.

I got to my feet, padded silently from room to room, checking every closet, poking behind every door, my hand resting on the hilt of the gun Mutt had lent me to protect myself with.

There was nobody there.

I shook my head. I had to be imagining things, made paranoid after the drama of the day. This mess had been here for weeks. Whoever had trashed my house was long gone.

I returned to the living room with a sigh and gingerly skirted around the worst of the mess. It was only midday but I felt an almost overpowering urge to just crawl back into bed and stay there, let the world take care of itself for the rest of the day. But first, I had to clean up the place a bit before I headed out, try to salvage what supplies I could. Already, the smell of rotting food was so strong I was surprised nobody had come knocking on the door by now looking for the bodies.

I cat-stepped over the big puddles of paint that overflowed from the ruined fish-tank, trying not to notice the tiny sad bones and bits of chewed fish-fin on the floor. *They'd done that on purpose. I'd loved those fish.* I turned on the tap in the kitchen, wet a sponge, and turned to bravely face the mess.

It was only then that I noticed the end wall.

The sponge fell from my hand. I stared, stunned.

I seemed to float across the carpet and halted, lost for words, at the far end of the room. The wall over the sofa had been completely covered with taped-up pictures of Karrel. Some had been torn out of larger photos, others burned in half where someone else— namely me— had been in the shot. In every last one of them, Karrel had his eyes scratched out.

I slowly shook my head, at a complete loss. Even a quick glance was enough to see that every last photograph I had ever taken of Karrel had been deliberately and maliciously ruined. There was a kind of meticulousness to the destruction that made me think this was the work of a woman. No man— except maybe for one with severe OCD— would take the time and the effort to do something as artistically evil as this.

'Cyan,' I muttered. I'd be willing to bet my life that this was her handiwork.

The smell of burned plastic dragged my attention to a nearby tin trashcan. I wearily walked over and unwillingly looked inside to see a blackened, melted mess. Not content with just trashing my photographs, whoever had done this had burned all my negatives too, along with my outdated external hard drive.

All our memories, gone.

I reached down into the trashcan and gently extracted

a single, half-melted negative that had somehow missed the conflagration. I wandered over and sat cross-legged on the floor in front of the empty fireplace, holding the negative up to the light.

It was a shot from my recent twenty-fourth birthday party. Two crazy, laughing faces grinned up at the camera, myself with shorter bleached hair, Karrel holding up a can of cheap beer in a cheerful salute. We were both completely covered in shaving foam.

We looked like we didn't have a care in the world.

An ugly, cold feeling began to grow inside me as I sat there on the floor amid the ruins of my life, staring down at the charred negative in my hand. A smoldering anger started to grow out of the ashes of the pain and humiliation of the last month. I felt as though my heart was turning black inside me, consumed by the hatred and mindless horror these monsters inspired in me.

In the space of thirty days, my life had gone from comfortably dull to a living nightmare. Not only did I have to put up with the horror of knowing that the man I loved had been torn apart in cold blood by werewolves, but I also had to come to terms with the fact that things like vampires and ghosts and zombies not only existed, but that for some reason they were all trying to kill me. Four short weeks ago I'd have laughed if someone had told me I'd spend the next thirty days on the run from killer werewolves. But now this was my life, and I had to deal with it.

Right now I didn't want to. Right now I just wanted a hot bath, eight solid hours of sleep, then some good old-fashioned revenge with as pointy a weapon as possible. These monsters didn't know me as a person, they had no clue about all the good and bad things I'd done in my life. Yet they had systematically destroyed my life as thoroughly as if they had sat down and planned the whole thing from the beginning.

I wished that Karrel was here. He'd know what to do.

I scarcely moved as the curtains that covered the smashed window blew open behind me. A chill gust of wind rushed into the room, bringing with it the scent of night-time Los Angeles. Usually, the air had the kind of chemically-treated, over-processed smell that reminded me that the city had over six million inhabitants, and that most of them had toilets. But tonight, something different crept in on the breeze, something pleasant for a change: the faint smell of jasmine.

I lifted my head and breathed in the scent, which seemed to be growing stronger by the second. Helpless tears started to form in my eyes. There had been a jasmine tree in the graveyard the first night I'd ever spent with Karrel. We'd spread our picnic blanket beneath it, laughing as the tiny purple flowers had dropped down around us like rain. We'd lain on our backs in the long grass of the Hollywood cemetery all night long, talking about everything and nothing until the sun rose and the morning dew soaked through our jeans. We'd watched as the star-studded sky above us had turned purple, then blue, then pink as the dawn had finally broken over us.

Karrel's kisses had been as soft as the fragrant jasmine petals, his touch as gentle as the night breeze blowing down off the distant mountains, and I had fallen for him. For a whole year, three hundred and sixty-five precious days, we'd been happier than anyone on earth had ever been. I'd felt like the luckiest girl in the world…

I wiped my eyes and quickly got up to shut the window, the old ache inside me growing stronger by the minute. I'd known it would be a mistake to come back here, back to where my memories of Karrel were the strongest, but I'd thought enough time had passed that I'd be able to handle it.

My mistake.

I pulled the window shut and stood there shivering. I was suddenly freezing, despite the fact that it was seventy degrees outside. The long sleepless nights and the stress of the past few weeks had taken their toll. I realized I hadn't showered in two days, that my hair felt greasy, that my skin was cold and damp to the touch. I felt a bone-deep ache start inside me, almost as though I was getting sick.

I quietly groaned to myself. Coming down with a cold on the eve of the Apocalypse would be the last thing I needed right now. Suddenly, all I wanted was to be warm again. The mess and the drama could wait till tomorrow.

I quickly got to my feet, padded across the room to my closet and rummaged through the unburned portion of it. I selected a fresh pair of jeans and a top, then pulled some clean underwear out of an upturned set of drawers and hurried towards the bathroom, the fresh breeze and the scent of jasmine petals blowing in behind me.

I OPENED MY bathroom door with trepidation, expecting to find a nightmarish tangle of cracked tiles and spurting water pipes. To my surprise, the bathroom seemed to be more or less undamaged.

*Small blessings.*

Offering up a quick prayer of thanks to the gods of hygiene, I quickly closed the door behind me and hopped into the bath. Mindful of Mutt waiting outside in the car for me, I swiftly slipped off my rumpled clothes, tossing them onto the crushed velvet bathmat on the floor. I gratefully drew the white plastic shower curtain closed, remembering at the last moment to pull the Bluetooth headset out of my ear. I laid it down tenderly on the tile beside the washbasin.

At least Ninette hadn't taken my Hunter earpiece back. That much was mine.

The shower warmed up after a couple of seconds and I stepped naked into the full stream of hot, stinging water. A blissful warmth enveloped me, and I felt my tired muscles instantly start to relax as the warm water washed over me, sluicing two full days' worth of sweat, blood and dirt off my skin.

The shower was definitely the number-one best-ever invention of the civilized world, I thought as I blissfully turned my face up full into the water, closing my eyes against the spray. The hot water stung my cold skin, but it was worth it to feel the color coming back into my cheeks, to feel the aching numbness inside me starting to subside under the penetrating heat.

I closed my eyes and tipped my head downwards, letting the water soak my hair, the warm stream trickling down into my eyes and mouth in a delicious torrent. I blew out my breath in a wet blast and groped around blindly for the soap, licking the water off my lips with a sigh of relief. I'd done a half-assed job of shaving my legs two days ago, using Mutt's blunt razor, and was keen to finish the job with my own. Anyone who thought their boyfriend was tough on their razor ought to try living in a werewolf household.

But first, I had one final matter to take care of.

I turned my back to the water, then gritted my teeth and carefully unwrapped the makeshift bandage from my wolf bite. I counted to ten, took a deep breath, and unwillingly looked down at my wrist.

An angry-looking red bite-mark stared up at me, an almost perfect replica of the one I'd seen on poor Billy's neck. Nice.

I lifted my washcloth from the side of the bath, poured a healthy squirt of antibacterial soap onto it, and started gingerly dabbing at the wound. The deep puncture marks had almost completely healed and the bruising that surrounded the bite was already fading. I shook my head with a kind of numb acceptance. There was no way a four-inch bite mark should heal in a week, not while I was still human. I made a mental note to up my dosage of anti-werewolf serum tonight.

Right now, I couldn't risk the consequences.

Ten minutes later I felt almost human again. The water was wonderfully hot and it was a true joy to be back in my own house again, if only for a short time. I was almost humming as I finished lathering up my hair with cheap coconut-and-lime shampoo from the local 99-Cent store, inhaling the fresh and wonderful scent of it. It reminded me almost overwhelmingly of Karrel— he'd gotten me addicted to the stuff while we were dating, scorning the expensive salon shampoo I usually bought.

That was just his style.

Forbidden thoughts of Karrel flitted through my mind as I reached for more conditioner, tipping some onto my hands and slathering it down my legs, using it as a makeshift body lotion to finish shaving with. I'd banned myself from even thinking about Karrel in the few short weeks since his death, not wanting to mope too much, not even knowing what was considered the right amount of time to mope.

That didn't mean he wasn't in my head twenty-four seven, of course, but the knowledge that I definitely wasn't allowed to think about him and make myself miserable was a big comfort when I did.

*And besides, it wasn't like I hadn't seen him since he'd died...*

I didn't move when I felt the presence behind me. I didn't even dare to hope. I slowly put the bottle of conditioner down as the air grew colder around me. The roar of the shower seemed suddenly loud as I listened with all my might.

Long moments ticked by, and my heart leaped with a secret joy as I saw my breath start pluming in the air, even though it was hot and steamy in the bathroom.

I knew by now what that meant.

My legs trembled with excitement as I felt a cool, insubstantial hand trail across my back, tracing a pattern amongst the heavy droplets of hot water that beaded my back. Anyone else would have leaped screaming out of the shower, but I merely smiled for what felt like the first time in years, and slowly turned around.

There was nobody there, of course.

I hadn't expected there to be, but I was still disappointed.

I wiped the water out of my eyes and stood there under the running spray, breathing softly as I listened. I knew I had to be patient, but it was hard. After a few moments an idea came to me. I turned back to face the tile and closed my eyes, my heart beating too fast inside my chest. I put my head down and waited.

Almost instantly a wash of cold air drifted across my skin, scented with the strong scent of jasmine and the salty smell of the ocean, raising tiny goosebumps in its wake. I heard a soft fluttering sound, and opened one eye to sneak a peek behind me.

What I saw took my breath away.

The white shower curtain was slowly floating outwards at a ninety degree angle to the ground, spreading open in mid air and rippling lazily like the ball-gown of a spectral bride. There was no wind in the room to move it. The sight of it as it drifted upwards towards the ceiling in absolute silence was both beautiful and unnerving.

I cleared my throat, almost afraid to speak, to break the spell. But before I could, I was beaten to it.

'Kayla? You there?' asked a soft, hesitant voice.

*Karrel's voice.*

# CHAPTER TWELVE

IT HAS BEEN said that the clinical definition of insanity is doing the same thing over and over again, and expecting different results each time.

I stood there naked in the shower, waiting for the ghost of my dead boyfriend to appear and talk to me, frozen in place by a curious mix of longing and fear.

Let me make one thing completely clear at this point. I don't believe in ghosts. That was one thing I was completely, one hundred percent certain about. I'd been brought up to believe that science was God, that chemistry, biology and physics could explain anything and everything. I could just about get my head around the fact that lycanthropy and vampirism were real— some kind of genetic mutation, maybe? It hadn't been properly explained to me yet and I was almost afraid to ask, although I'd heard that several major universities were starting to introduce classes on the subject.

But not ghosts.

Forget horror stories told around the campfire. Forget Patrick Swayze and the Hollywood baloney trotted out like clockwork at movie theatres every Halloween. For I was a child of The Discovery Channel, of the investigative prowess of Mulder and Scully and *CSI*, of the constant daily joys of Wikipedia and the Google search engine. No-one in their right minds believed in ghosts.

Right?

However, not believing in ghosts hadn't stopped me from seeing one.

I stood absolutely still, my pulse beating lightly in my throat as the levitating shower curtain drifted back down and settled around the bathtub like a shroud. I remembered the last two times I'd seen Karrel's ghost, or spirit, or whatever the hell you wanted to call it— two painfully short encounters which had raised more questions than they'd answered. I couldn't believe I was going to get another chance to talk to him.

I was beginning to think I was losing my mind when I felt ghostly ice-cold fingers run up my back, like tiny puffs of freezer-air. I smiled and let my eyes slide shut as the ghostly touch moved lightly over my shoulders, smoothing over my skin in an achingly familiar way. I stood there with my eyes closed, water pouring over me as the icy hands began to gently trace the outline of my shoulders, brushing over every inch of skin as though checking I was still whole.

I tensed slightly as the shadows shifted, as though something had passed over the bathroom light. Then a cool pair of lips touched my shoulder, pressing reassuringly against my wet skin in a soft kiss. I let my breath out hard, turning my head slightly to lean into the kiss, making the illusion last as long as I possibly could. *There were no such things as ghosts,* my rational mind told me. *I was imagining things, driven crazy by grief and stress and exhaustion.*

*Yeah, that was it.*

I sighed, then turned around.

The ghost of Karrel was standing behind me in the shower, gazing at me with crinkled, adoring eyes. He looked so incredibly young, much younger than I remembered him being when we'd been dating. His shoulder-length dark hair fell in a ragged fringe over his handsome, intelligent face, and his skin was smooth and very pale, like ice. His sculptured physique seemed harder, leaner, making him look like a beautiful statue, but his sea-green eyes were how I always remembered them— warm, loving, adoring.

Alive with love for me.

I smiled in wonder, drinking him in, the sight of him as refreshing as a long cool drink of water to a man stranded in the desert. I didn't want to move, to breathe, in case the mirage shattered into a thousand pieces.

'Is this a dream?' I asked finally.

'No. You're just drunk. I told you not to drink those Jagermeister shots that night,' Karrel said with a hint of reproof, his voice as soft as the winter breeze. 'You never listen to me.'

'That's my line,' I replied with a smile.

I gazed longingly at the dead man I loved. There were so many things I wanted to say to him, but the words stuck in my throat. The aching void inside me was already beginning to fill in his presence, leaving me absolutely calm, absolutely content.

Unable to help myself, I lifted a hand and reached out towards him. Karrel stepped forwards and slipped his spectral fingers through the empty gaps between mine. I felt the faintest tingling in my fingertips. Fresh tears welled up in my eyes as I looked down at his ghostly hand in mine, trying to convince myself that I was imagining this. At least that would mean I was still sane. But even as the thought went through my mind Karrel's hand seemed to fade, until my fingers seemed to be grasping empty air.

'Don't go,' I whispered.

The spectral hand seemed to waver, and I looked up in panic. The vision of him was so faint that if I half-closed my eyes he seemed to disappear, becoming no more than a pattern of highlights and shadows on the tiles. I blinked and he snapped sharply back into focus. I realized my vision had been blurred by the tears that I hadn't even felt slipping down my face.

I wiped my eyes and tried to smile, to be brave. There were so many things I wanted to ask him, to say to him, but for now I settled for the most unoriginal.

'I miss you,' I said. It was the understatement of the century. 'I wish that—'

'I know.'

Karrel reached out with a cool finger to lift my chin. It felt more like a tiny gust of cold air brushing my skin, but I lifted my head anyway and gazed at him as he looked into my eyes. 'You're in big trouble, kiddo,' he said, for once looking serious. 'The Seekers are coming.'

'I know. I was just talking to Ninette about that.'

'You want to know how to stop them?'

I nodded and laced my fingers through his, a muscle twitching in my jaw. *I missed him so much.* Karrel was silent a long moment, then he turned his green eyes towards the door, as though listening intently. As I started to speak, he turned around and put a finger to my lips. The corner of my mouth twitched up and I kissed his finger, as I'd done when he'd pulled that dumb move on me when he'd been alive.

Karrel took a deep breath, let it out hard. It had to be from habit, because as far as I knew, ghosts didn't need to breathe. 'The person you need to find. Her name is Doll. If you want to stop the Apocalypse, find her and rescue her. She's an angel.'

'An angel,' I repeated. 'Wonderful.'

'Don't complain. Things could be worse. In fact, they will get a helluva lot worse if you don't find Doll quickly. She's the key to all of this. You see, Harlequin plans to kill her tomorrow night, in order to bring about the end of the world.'

I stared at him, shaking my head. His words were ringing a definite bell in my head. Something Ninette had been telling me last month about an angel we had to rescue to save the world?

'Hey, is she this fallen angel that everyone's been talking about?'

'Who's everyone?'

'Ninette.'

'Ah.' The ghost of a smile crossed Karrel's face. 'That sounds like her. She never could keep a secret, especially if it's an illegal one.'

I nodded unhappily. I remembered how things had gone this morning with Ninette, and felt fresh tears seeping into my eyes. Dammit!

Karrel looked at me, and his face softened.

'Come here, you. It'll all turn out alright. Give us a squeeze.'

He stepped in close to me and wrapped his ghostly arms around me, although I felt nothing. I laid my head as best I could along the angle of his insubstantial chest, feeling chills race across my skin as I touched his spectral form. It was like trying to hug a cloud. There was nothing there to touch but cold, damp air with a tingle of electricity to it, but I had to at least try.

I felt a chill breeze rifle through my hair as Karrel's ghost stroked my head, his expression turning serious. 'Please listen to me, Kayla. We don't have much time. If we're going to stop the Apocalypse, we gotta find Doll immediately, before Harlequin kills her. If we don't, the consequences for the human race could be catastrophic.'

'Why?'

Karrel narrowed his eyes and stepped back from me. I felt the air around us grow colder, and felt suddenly afraid.

'How much did Ninette tell you about angels?' he asked.

'Er, that they exist. And that you don't mess with them.' I swallowed. 'Ever.'

'Why?'

'Because they're the oldest race that exists.'

'And why should you never, ever kill an angel?'

'Because, er…' I shrugged, guessing. 'All the angel's friends will get mad and come looking for you?'

'You're half right.' Karrel threw a quick look towards the door and dropped his voice, as though he was afraid of being overheard. 'Actually, the murder of an angel by a non-angelic entity is pretty much the worst crime anyone can commit, ever.'

'Says who?'

'Says other angels. You have to understand something about angels, Kayla. These guys have existed since The Beginning. They have a very primitive, tribe-like culture, and a very definite pecking order. The ones at the bottom are always bickering and squabbling, trying to get higher up, get closer to God.'

I gave a disbelieving smile. 'Which God are we talking about here?'

'Pick one, they're all the same one anyway. The point is, they all worship Him. They believe He made them, and so their entire lives revolve around worshipping Him. Sometimes they'll accidentally kill each other with their petty squabbles, trying to get closer to Him, and then of course the killer gets Cast Out of heaven, sent to Earth in a mortal body.'

'That's all that happens to them?' I snorted. 'Doesn't seem so bad.'

'You don't understand. To an angel, getting Cast Down to earth is like a human getting sent straight to hell. They don't get to hang out with God any more, to bask in His glory and love, and so God, Mr. Egocentric, figures that's punishment enough.'

'I still don't think that's much of a punishment.'

'Oh, and they also lose their immortality and all their crazy super-powers. You remember what powers angels have?'

'Angels can see into the future, right?'

'And she nails it! They can see a short way. They can't see as far ahead as Big Boss God. But they can see far enough ahead to guide Little Miss Lost Sheep out of a snowstorm, or stop Farmer Barley's tractor from crushing a cute little baby in a runaway pram. That's what angels tend to do at first, when they come to earth.'

I gave a small smile, wringing out my wet hair as water continued to patter down around me. 'You mean that's what those crazy people in those late-night TV specials claim they do.'

'Not all angels are like that, Kayla.' Karrel's tone turned serious. 'Those angels are the good ones. The sane ones. We've already been over this. Angels on earth are here either because they've been Cast Down for committing a crime, or because they've cast themselves down on purpose to check out the human race.'

'Why would they cast themselves down?' Now I was confused. 'I thought you said getting thrown out of heaven was like hell, for an angel?'

Karrel's ghost shrugged, leaning against the shower wall. The illusion was only slightly spoiled by the fact that his shoulders were actually starting to slide right through the wall.

'Even angels get bored, I guess. Floating around on clouds all the time, playing their little golden harps, singing God's praises… I figure a century and a half tops and they'd be slitting their wrists through sheer fucking boredom. I know *I* would.'

I grinned and reached for the conditioner, poured a generous squirt into my hand, started working it through my tresses. Getting clean was the last thing on my mind right now, but I needed to do something with my hands, to give myself time to think.

'So… I'm guessing this Doll angel got bored in Heaven, cast herself down.'

'Correct. Now, Harlequin's caught her and he's going to kill her, to complete some dumb prophecy which he thinks will wipe out humanity.'

I snorted. 'How's *that* one going to work?'

'I already told you,' said Karrel, running his transparent fingers through the shower spray. 'You kill an angel, all that angel's friends come looking for you. And not just its friends. Oh no. In the olden days, the rule was that if a non-angel killed an angel, the person's whole family would be killed by Avenging Angels. An eye for an eye, and all that. Killing an angel was considered the sin to end all sins, and so the whole of Heaven's armies would be mobilized to deal with it. Only when the murderer's personal bloodline was erased was the sin considered wiped clean.'

'Jeeze.'

'But that was back then, when there were only a few thousand human beings on earth. That's when all this crap started, when that rule was made.' Karrel paused, staring at me hard. 'Can you guess what would happen if a human killed an angel now, in modern times?'

'Er... that person's family would get wiped out?'

'Not just their family would die, Kayla, but their every living relative.'

'So?'

'So, we're not just talking about the twenty-odd people on their Christmas card list. There are six billion people on earth now, and they all sprang from just a handful of original human 'families.' Look, try to understand it this way. If one person kills one angel nowadays, under the old rules, it could lead to the systematic slaughter of *every single one* of that person's far-distant relatives, now living in all corners of the world and interbred with countless other 'families' of all creeds and colors. Nobody can track their own bloodline back to pre-biblical times... apart from the angels.'

Karrel stepped forwards, looking at me seriously.

'Millions could die, Kayla. That is why we have to save Doll.'

'That's dumb.' I shook my head, putting down the conditioner. 'How could God allow that to happen?'

'He let it happen before. Think of the Great Plague, Kayla, the biblical Flood. Hundreds of thousands of living human beings killed and the sonofabitch didn't even blink.'

Karrel shook his head, a sorrowful look coming into his eye.

'Some people say that He has a Plan for us all, that everything happens for a reason. Me, I say the big guy's lost it big time, all those millennia of living up there alone, hearing nothing but good things about Himself. The guy sends us hurricanes and typhoons and what do people do? Rush to the church like frightened sheep to praise Him. To suck up to Him so He won't kill them next. What kind of a message do you think that's sending Him?'

I started to smile, swatting at him. 'Stop it. You're joking, right?'

'I wish I was.'

'Okay, fine.' I wiped water from my eyes and turned up the temperature knob on the shower. It was getting chilly in the shower as the hot water started to run out. 'So to sum up, the angels get mad at us for killing one of their own... and then what? Where do these Seeker guys come into it?'

'They start the whole process off, and also finish it. Their one job in heaven is to count the angels, and tell God if any are missing. Every Sunday, it is said, they count all the angels in heaven and on earth. It's supposed to take them twenty four hours, exactly. If they find out one angel's gone missing, God sends them out at midnight on the dot to look for it. Think of the Seekers as heavenly bloodhounds.'

'Great. What happens next?'

'If they find out it's been killed, they take out the killer themselves, right after sending for help.'

'Then the angels come down and whack us?'

'So to speak. But not just regular angels, Kayla. Warrior Angels. Hundreds of thousands of them. All on edge from millennia spent sitting around in heaven, polishing their armor and dying for a good rumble.' Karrel rubbed his eyes, looking pale, which for a ghost was saying something. 'When Harlequin has Doll killed, all those Warrior Angels are gonna have a field day.'

'What do you mean, 'has her killed?''

'Oh, he'll use a human to kill her, for sure. If he knows anything about the prophecy then he knows the rules. If a human kills an angel, the human race gets attacked. If a vampire kills an angel, the vampires get attacked. Notice a pattern here?'

'And so *blam*, the Warrior Angels come to avenge Doll's death, find out that a human murdered her in cold blood, and that's the end of life as we know it?'

'Precisely.'

'Oh, balls.'

'Balls indeed. And because Harlequin's a vampire, he'll get off Scot-free. The angels will know that he started all this, but unless he kills Doll with his own two hands they're powerless to punish him.'

'The Overseers?' I stared at him hopefully, grasping at straws.

'...will have no idea what's about to hit them, thanks to Harlequin. The Hunters are like their early warning system. With the Hunters out of commission, the Overseers won't get the warning about the angel's death until it's too late.'

'So that's why Harlequin blew our base up. Well, shit.'

The hissing of the shower grew very loud as I stared at Karrel in silence, my mind whirling on overdrive. I was dying to call Ninette on my Bluetooth Communicator, tell her everything Karrel had just told me about Doll.

But how would I explain where I had got this information from? Would I really tell her that the ghost of my dead boyfriend appeared to me in the shower, and told me that they should turn around and drive for fifteen hours back to LA in order to help me find an angel I'd never met and save her life? Even if she believed me, she'd never get here in time. And even if she did, what good could three extra Hunters do? Ninette had said it herself. We were outnumbered. We'd need an army to fight Harlequin.

Who else would believe us, let alone stand with us?

I reeled a little, putting a hand on the tiled shower wall to steady myself as the implications hit home. If what Karrel was telling me was true, I was now the only one left who had the chance to save the human race from annihilation.

'Um,' I said, in a small voice. 'Help?'

'Close your eyes,' whispered Karrel. I did so, my heart pounding. I felt sick. The air moved and my skin prickled as the spectral form of Karrel leaned in close. I could've sworn I felt the cool press of lips against my own.

I reached out, desperate to touch Karrel, but my hands just met empty air. I felt a shock of heat as the dragon pendant around my neck caught light as Karrel blew on it gently, making it burn with a ghostly blue-hot fire. The heat seemed to pour through me, settling in my bones, coursing through my bloodstream. By all rights my skin should've been melting in magical heat like that, but it didn't so much as scorch me.

'As long as you love me,' whispered Karrel. 'You're never alone. Remember that.'

'I know,' I whispered, frustration boiling through me. 'But you have to help me. I can't do this on my own. There's so much I need to know.'

I sighed, pressing my eyes tight shut, not knowing where to begin.

'This necklace you gave me, for instance,' I started, touching the tiny iron dragon pendant on its frayed black string. 'You told me to never take it off. But how does it work? You said that you gave me your power, put it into this necklace somehow.'

I closed my fist around the small embossed pendant, feeling the heatless fire spread to engulf my hand in a blue wash of ghostly flame.

'But how do I control it? Is there some kind of technique? It only seems to work when my life is actually in danger… not that I've been trying to take pot-shots at road signs or anything.'

I paused for breath, my eyes moving behind closed lids. 'And how come I picked up the Dark Arts so quickly? Is that something to do with the necklace too, or am I just naturally talented?'

No reply. I paused, listening to the echoes of my words in the shower.

I opened my eyes, and sagged in disappointment.
Karrel had gone.

# CHAPTER THIRTEEN

THE FOLLOWING DAY dragged by on wings of lead. Seven PM tonight might have been seven PM in fifty years, judging by the frantic whirling of my mind as I prepared for my first proper date with Niki.

It wasn't an actual date, I told myself firmly, as I unpacked my suitcase in Mia's guest room, where it now seemed that I was staying. Real dates involved flowers and chocolates, and pretty much depended on both date-ees knowing it was a date.

Both parties being human also helped, too, or so I'd heard.

And that was another mystery I hoped to unravel tonight, if things got that far...

I blushed and tried to put all thoughts of Niki out of my mind for now, so I'd make it through the day without going nuts with impatience, waiting for my date-that-wasn't-a-date. I tried to focus on the details of the room around me, on getting through the morning.

Mutt had dropped me off at Mia's house after I'd retrieved a suitcase of clothes from my trashed apartment. So far, it had been quite an experience. I'd never been to Mia's house before, a small condo located in the heart of the prestigious Beverly Hills. She'd never invited me over, and now I saw the reason. Everything was painted pink, and she also had more teddy-bears than anyone, adult or child, should ever have.

One of them was shaped like a werewolf.

But that was just Mia for you.

After killing a couple of hours putting my stuff away, then taking it all out again and putting it back exactly where Mia had told me to put it, bad girl that I was, I sat on my neatly-made bed in Mia's guest room, staring at the clock as it crept slowly around the dial, waiting for seven o'clock to arrive and put me out of my misery. Despite the early hour I had already changed and was raring to go out, but doubt was starting to creep in around the edges as my mind worked on overtime.

Was this really a good idea, going out by myself tonight to meet a guy who everyone around me suspected was a vampire? Did he genuinely know where Harlequin was, or was that just a line he'd made up so he could see me again?

If it was true, and he could lead me to Harlequin, then I was almost certain that I could get enough werewolves together to storm his place and take the master vampire down.

And if we found Harlequin, Doll couldn't be very far away. It was Doll's blood which when spilled would supposedly trigger the end of the world, in less than two days and counting.

I had to prevent this at all costs.

To sum up, I was almost obliged to go on this date.

I sighed and rubbed my eyes, considering my options.

First things first. Despite the message Mutt was constantly trying to drum into my head, I knew that it was better for everyone if I kept this one to myself. I couldn't explain it, but I felt intuitively that I could trust Niki. He'd had two chances now to kill me, and had resisted both of them. If he really was a vampire, that was practically a marriage proposal.

My second concern was getting into the club he'd mentioned with a weapon. I knew the place he was talking about very well, mainly by its reputation. The Circus of Sins club was one of those places in Hollywood which was famous for simply being famous. So I'd bet my life that security at the door was probably heavy as hell. These days you literally had to have a bag-check, a body-scan with a handheld metal detector and a full-body pat-down by security just to get into a dive-bar to see a no-name band. Most of the larger clubs on Sunset Strip had greater security measures than some major airports, what with the bomb-threats and the gangs and the everyday fights that could quickly turn into riots in the celebrity-packed underground rooms.

So that would be fun.

Finally, I had to work out how to get out of the house without Mia asking awkward questions. Even though she was two years younger than me, she'd always acted like my big sister, tried to protect me from things she thought were dangerous or inappropriate, a list that was at least three times longer than the list of things Motor disapproved of.

But truth was, telling her that I was going out on a date with a possible vampire would cause major drama. She'd probably insist on coming along to protect me, or even worse, she'd tell Mutt, and then he'd probably get jealous and nix the idea, or worse, he'd want to come along to chaperone me.

No way was that happening. Quite apart from the fact that it would ruin the date and probably spook Niki so he wouldn't talk to me, my new friend's safety was now my number one concern. The wolves had stepped in to help me because I had saved Mutt's life. They'd asked nothing in return but my friendship. It was bad enough putting myself in danger without risking the lives of my new friends. I'd tried asking for help once before, and people I cared about had wound up dead.

That wasn't going to happen again.

As I lay there on the bed staring out the window at the darkening evening sky, an idea popped into my mind. It was so simple that I was surprised I hadn't thought of it sooner. I felt myself smiling as I got up, grabbed my car-keys, and reached for my cellphone.

It was perfect.

I only hoped that if we lived through tonight, Mia would forgive me.


EIGHT HOURS LATER, I was beginning to doubt the wisdom of my plan.

Getting into the Circus of Sins nightclub had proven easy enough. There were no metal detectors on the door, after all that. I'd simply walked right through the front entrance. The surly sleep-deprived doorman had let me in after a brief bag-check and a quick but sharp glance into my eyes, which surprised me.

What was he looking for, dangerous contact lenses? *Weird place.*

I wished now that I'd brought silver stakes rather than the wooden ones I had strapped to the inside of my thighs. He hadn't even glanced at the twenty-dollar bill I'd offered him in place of my ID card, which I'd forgotten in my rush to get here in time.

I hid a smile as I glanced up at the security camera. I'd always thought it funny that at age twenty, the US government would let you drive a car, have kids and buy a gun, but it wouldn't let you drink a glass of wine until you were twenty-one.

The second doorman waved me through the high-tech folding glass doorway without looking up from his battered porno magazine or altering his terminally bored expression by one muscle. I stepped through with a nod of thanks, and he pulled it tightly shut behind me.

I stepped inside, looking around with trepidation. The opulent mirror-walled entry hall was littered with dozens of burned-out guys and girls in various stages of undress and intoxication. I paused just inside the doorway as every pair of eyes in the room turned on me, inspected me and instantly dismissed me. The looks on their faces said it all. I was a nothing, a nobody, not even slightly famous. I was invisible to them. Bunch of star-chasers. I could smell the thick, sickly scent of money in the room, even above the incense burners that burned along the walls of the oval room, and instantly regretted not wearing my one and only designer dress.

*Ah, well.*

The Circus of Sins was one of the most famous, or rather, *in*famous 24-hour clubs in LA. I'd read about this place in a dozen nightlife magazines since it opened up a year ago, but I'd never been here myself.

It was the place that the well-to-do and the soon-to-be-famous staggered or crawled to at the end of the night's revelries, to come down from whatever drug they were on and to relax amongst others like themselves, well away from the prying eyes of the public. It was said that if you sat long enough on one of the sticky, pearl-encrusted barstools of its multi-million-dollar function room long enough, every fallen major motion-picture star from the last twenty years would come by and try to steal either your drink, your date or your car, depending on how broke they were at that particular moment.

Judging by the look of the place, I could well believe it. I was surprised Niki had asked me to meet him here. This was about as far from a secret meeting place as you could get. I would be about as conspicuous here as a nun in a brothel.

But I was free for the evening, and I was going to make the most of it. I'd set Mia up on a blind-date with my Goth friend Wylie, who was the only person in this city who I trusted enough to take care of her for the evening.

I also knew that he hadn't had a date in at least as long as her, maybe even longer, so I figured they'd make a lovely couple.

After sending them off together, I'd sent Mutt out on a bogus mission to find some leads on Harlequin, just to get him out of my hair. I'd given him specific instructions to search the more fashionable end of Main Street in the nearby Santa Monica, paying particular attention to the stretch of road between Ocean Park Boulevard and Pier Avenue, where I knew all his favorite bars were.

He'd jumped at the chance. For the first time ever he hadn't even asked to borrow money from me before leaving. He'd left skid-marks in the driveway.

Put simply, neither of my two werewolf baby-sitters were coming home tonight.

I was free. The evening was mine.

I smiled and glanced sideways at myself in the reflective door, trying to relax, checking myself out before I met Niki. I was dressed simply in a form-fitting black rocker-style skirt, matched with a red satin corset with a sexy lace-up back. My hands were sheathed in delicate black fishnet gloves, complete with lacy cuffs and a matching black choker. My long chestnut hair was neatly curled, hanging in loose, bouncy ringlets down my back. A silver-studded belt completed the outfit, along with the customary crucifix around my neck and the only pair of long black boots I owned that I was sure I could run fast in.

I took a deep breath, smoothing my hair out of my eyes as I launched myself out into the room.

*Here went nothing...*

A movement from the end of the room drew my attention as I drew near. A pair of long-limbed, gazelle-like black girls turned to face me, an expectant look on their faces. They were twins. They were sprawled on a plush sofa lined with white fur and silver trim, their bodies hung with black satin and golden silk. They were watching me with the same predatory expression as the men.

As I began to stride purposefully towards the end door that led to the main lounge, they rose to their feet, silent as a pair of jungle cats, and quickly moved to block my path. They stopped opposite me and folded their arms, wearing matching expressions of sullen petulance.

I drew to a halt, sizing the pair up. Neither of them looked any older than sixteen, but their eyes were much older, seeming to glow a watchful orange in the smoky darkness. Their gold-painted fingernails matched their golden lipstick and dramatic golden eyeshadow, and their long pure-white hair hung in loose garlands around their shoulders. I felt instantly old and unfashionable compared to them. They looked like they should be on the cover of Vogue. I looked like I should be on the cover of What Not To Wear, as the 'Before' photo.

I nodded a brisk greeting to the pair.

'You girls seen a restroom anywhere?' I asked brightly.

The first girl glanced at her sister, who sniggered.

'You new here, chica?'

Her voice was a soft hiss; the warning tones of a snake made human. The diamond stud in her tongue clicked as she flicked it lightly against her too-sharp teeth, giving me the once-over. Judging by the look on her coldly beautiful face, she didn't think much of what she saw.

'New?' I gave a little laugh. 'Nah. I practically live here. Got a buddy who works down at the bar.'

'Which bar?'

'The one downstairs. You know. The long one. Got drinks on it,' I breezed. *Please, Lord, let there be a bar downstairs…*

The girl held my gaze for a second longer than was comfortable, then broke into a broad, lazy smile. 'Oh, you'll mean the Kerouac Lounge, then.'

'Never heard of it,' I replied instantly, on a hunch. I saw the first girl glance slyly at her sister, who gave the barest of nods. The two girls moved forwards, stepping on either side of me. Two small, strong hands slid down my biceps as the two girls linked arms with me, like high school buddies.

'We'll show you downstairs,' said the first girl, grinning like a cat. 'In case you get lost.'

'No, I'm fine thanks—'

'We insist,' said the second girl. Her tone was cool, amused. 'If you've been here before, you'll know what this place is like. I would hate to see anything untoward happen to you.'

I saw the second twin's face light up with a spark of mischief, which instantly vanished as soon as I glanced in her direction. A spotlight wheeled over her, and I instantly tensed up. Her pupils were open way too wide to be human, her irises a bare sliver of orange around their edges, like the flare around the edge of a solar eclipse. There was a flash of greenish silver at the bottom of each pupil, like cat's eyes.

I knew right away what that meant.

*The girls were vampires.*

I bit my lip, trying to tactfully slip from their grip, which instantly tightened on me. Out of the corner of my eye I saw several black-clad guys rise to their feet and begin moving casually towards us. *I was busted. Shit!* My pulse sped up and I stepped back quickly to keep them in view, wishing to God that I'd dared to defy security and bring a gun with me.

''S okay,' I said as I backed off, tugging futilely on the first girl's arm. 'I'll go find another restroom. I'm not that *that* drunk.'

'Would you like to be?' said a soft voice in my ear.

I jumped. Niki had magically appeared beside us, a dark shape silhouetted against the flaring blue spotlights which stabbed down from the ceiling on all sides. He was dressed in expensive black velvet Destroyer jeans and a tight-fitting black muscle shirt, unbuttoned at the waist to reveal the smooth perfection of his toned figure. I felt an instant spike of desire go through me and smothered it hurriedly, trying to keep my mind on the mission. His powerfully muscled arms were decorated with a number of leather straps and rocker chain bands, and his mop of black hair was newly dyed with fiery streaks of red, like slashes of blood.

All in all, he looked great.

As Niki turned to face us, the two girls hurriedly stepped back from me, their entire demeanor changing in a heartbeat. Whereas before they had been predators intent on the kill, suddenly they looked like two naughty schoolgirls caught smoking in the restrooms.

'Demara. Demelza,' said Niki, in a gentle, almost shy voice. 'Are you bothering my clients again?'

The two girls immediately set up a storm of denial. Niki silenced them with a glance before turning his attention back to me. In the silvery light of the club his eyes were different to before— intense, almost regal, a brilliant shade of sky blue. He must have been wearing black contacts before, for Halloween.

I grew very still as his gaze finally met mine, and a flash of something very much like anticipation passed between us. My heart gave a dizzying little thump, and my breath caught in my throat. I knew right there and then that he knew how much I'd been looking forward to seeing him again.

And that this wasn't just a business date.

*Shit.*

I gave him a tight little smile as adrenaline pumped through me, making my heart pound and my breathing speed up. I secretly cursed myself for not bringing a friend with me, or at least telling Mia where I was going. Just in case.

But I hadn't wanted to blow the deal. And after all, Niki *had* told me to come alone. I had to get that information about Harlequin and Doll, whatever it cost me…

I sighed, giving up the pretense.

I was out on a date with a possible vampire, on the eve of a probable apocalypse.

I was an idiot. I could see that now.

Before I could reconsider, Niki pressed a knuckle to his lips, considering me from beneath the shadows of his choppy bangs, a hint of a smile on his face.

'Wanna come check out the basement club?' he asked. 'It's pretty neat.'

The girls sniggered, then fell silent as Niki's gaze cracked across them like a whip.

'Well,' I started. 'Funny thing. I was actually just on my way out—'

'Oh, don't be a wuss. You'll be safe with me. I don't bite.'

The girls giggled and I hung back, glancing back at them for reassurance. A moment ago I had been afraid of them. Now they seemed like trusted friends compared to Niki. I dug my thumbnail into my palm to stop myself from running as Niki reached out and pushed a lock of hair off my shoulder, looking at me sideways as though he was laughing at me. I jumped as Niki slid his cool hand into mine, twining his fingers together with my own like a lover, in a gesture of over-familiarity that seemed gauged to unsettle me, to find out what I was made of.

I flashed him a warning glance and Niki grinned back at me, delighted.

'Sure you can handle this?' he asked, lowering his mouth to kiss the back of my hand.

'No problem.'

'So lead the way.'

Taking a deep breath, I made my way past the crowds of drunken clubbers and headed towards the end door that led to the basement lounge.

What was I getting myself into?

THE STAIRWELL TO the underground club was cool and dark. I silently followed Niki down a winding set of stone steps carpeted with black velvet, twisting and turning as we descended a surprisingly long way into the earth.

'So much for earthquakes,' I muttered, pressing close to his side.

'Hmm?' Niki seemed distracted.

'Earthquakes.' It was as good a conversation topic as any. Just the sound of my voice in the menacing black darkness was reassuring. 'This is LA. One good five-pointer and you're picking bits of ceiling-tile out of your drink.'

Niki gave a strange smile. 'There are worse things in LA than earthquakes.'

I had no reply to that.

My steps slowed the deeper into the earth we went,

and my breathing sped up. Before long, a low pulsating, growling sound became audible beneath us. It grew in volume as we moved quickly through the plushly upholstered darkness, the tiny blue lights cut into the edges of the curved steps lighting our way.

Niki stopped before a set of silver-plated double doors at the bottom of the steps, which were lit with a wash of red light. He swiped a black membership card in the reader by the door and the light turned green with a beep. 'Ready?' he asked, his bright blue eyes sparkling.

'I was born ready.'

Niki chuckled, and pushed the club doors open into a vision of carnal Hell.

# CHAPTER FOURTEEN

I BLINKED, STUNNED, as we entered the huge oval room. There was almost too much going on to take in all at once.

The supremely opulent basement club was packed to capacity. I'd never seen anything like it, and certainly not at quarter past seven in the afternoon.

I stared around me in wonder as we made our way across the room. Despite the early hour the place was packed solid, as though every rock and punk club in town had turned out for the night, disgorging a torrent of hot, sweaty, jubilant revelers into the club.

Impossibly beautiful young girls spun and waltzed in intricate patterns around their partners, all lean tanned thighs, glossy lips and gracefully arched tanned flesh. Their blonde hair and pearls whirled like flashes of forbidden sunshine amid the velvet darkness, contrasting with the feline cool silks of their daringly scanty attire. The young men dancing with them were mostly bare-chested and longhaired, grinding themselves against their stunning partners with an abandon that was nothing short of hedonism. The air was thick with a pall of cloying red smoke which hung at head-height in the room. I took one breath of it and immediately felt dizzy.

I had the strong feeling that most of these people had been here for days, if not longer.

The central feature of the oval room was the raised band-stage. It sat in the very center of the room, towering over the revelers. The base of the stage was made to look like a massive coil of giant carved steel snakes, hundreds and hundreds of them, all winding their way around in a tapering pile. At the very top sat a round band-stage, half-buried in the metal snake-coils.

Atop the stage, four pale young men wearing spiked dog collars and not a whole lot else sweated and thrashed behind white ivory guitars, which were slicked with what I hoped was fake blood. The stage top was covered in a thick carpet of red rose-petals, which gave off a heady perfume as the band's boots crushed them underfoot. The band's blindfolded faces were turned up to the heavens as they pumped out a punk version of an ultra-heavy club stomper. I saw metal glinting in the red-tinged darkness, and noticed that silver chains of varying sizes tethered the band to the stage by their collars, as though to stop them leaping offstage and running for their lives.

Judging by the freaked-out looks on the sweating band-members' faces, the chains probably weren't there for decoration.

Niki's hand squeezed mine. I blinked and snapped my mouth shut. I hadn't been aware that I'd been gaping. Niki stepped up beside me and lazily slung one arm over my shoulders as he looked around the club with a proprietary air.

'Not bad, huh?'

'It's very... The band is very... there are some beautiful people here,' I said in a daze. 'I feel about fifty.'

'You don't look a day over forty-nine.'

'Ha, ha.'

Niki stepped behind me and twined his arms around my waist, smoothing his lips over the bare skin of the back of my neck in a soft kiss. The nearness of him instantly made me tense up. I was already having second thoughts about all this, and the further I got from the outside world, the more wound up I became.

There were no handles on the insides of any of the doors, I'd noticed. That was never good.

I couldn't figure out why I was so on edge... until a slender, outrageously dressed couple brushed past us. The guy's head turned as he passed me, quick as a snake. He gave me a hungry look before he disappeared into the crowd, his eyes flashing cat-eye silver in the whirling disco lights. I quickly glanced at the next couple, then the next. My hackles instantly rose.

The room was crawling with vampires.

Niki's hand tightened on my shoulder as I tensed up, ready to run. I was all for turning and hightailing it out of here, right now. Only the strength of Niki's fingers clasped around my own reminded me that I had my own personal bodyguard... or so I hoped.

'Like the place?' he asked, casually adjusting my bra strap.

I absently swatted him away, too distracted to speak.

'You should do,' he said. 'I own it.'

I turned to him in surprise. 'What're you, Donald Trump's son?'

Niki just smiled. 'Let's go grab a drink, then I'll tell you everything you need to know.'


THE CROWD SEEMED to magically part as we made our way past the stage, through the sweating crowds of dancers to the other side of the room. The room was so big that the far wall was barely visible in the reddish gloom. I let go of Niki's hand and found a safe spot by the wall while he cut into the line at the bar. Nobody seemed to mind, and I noticed that he got served immediately. The barman even put down the drink he had been making to serve him first.

I raised an eyebrow, impressed.

Who was this guy?

Now that my eyes were accustomed to the gloom, I noticed a number of big circular windows inset into the walls around the outside of the oval room at regular intervals. The windows were lit from within by a soft pink glow. I threw caution to the wind and dared to move two steps away from the relative safety of Niki to peer through the nearest one.

I blinked, surprised. On the other side of the window was a fully-functioning shower-room, shaped like a bubble with a wall-to-ceiling round window on both sides, so that people in the two adjoining clubrooms could see in. The shower room looked like a scene out of a typical teenage boy's wet dream. Gleaming golden faucets poured shining fat drops of bubbly water over a half dozen of sleek young women. All six of them were gloriously naked and soaking wet, their long hair winding in sodden curls over their perfect, slender forms, while snowdrifts of bubbles slid down over their pert pink breasts and flat stomachs.

They all seemed blissfully unaware that their every movement was on display to drooling club patrons in the two rooms on either side of them

I raised an eyebrow. I'd never seen anything like this before in a club. I stepped back from the glass, feeling an unaccustomed surge of protectiveness for the young girls. Okay, so they were obviously vampires, but so what? Did the management know nothing about women's rights? It made a change from the strip poles you found in the basements of most LA clubs, but there should at least be a guy or two in there too to even things up a bit... Oh.

As though answering my prayers, the door to the shower room slid open and a tall, graceful and indisputably male figure entered. He stepped into the shower with the girls, carrying a huge pile of fresh fluffy white towels. He was completely naked. Depending on your morals and your gender, it was either a really good job or a terrible shame that he was carrying all those towels in front of him.

I glanced furtively around me, aware that the group of giggling girls who had been peering into the exhibit beside me had gone very still. On the other side of the glass, the newcomer made his way along the line of nubile naked women, handing them each a fresh towel and exchanging a smile and a personal joke with each one. They all seemed to know him very well indeed. I wondered just how well they knew him, then wished I hadn't thought of that.

Reaching the end of the line, he stepped under the

spray of water beneath the empty end faucet. Now, he was right in front of me. I stepped back quickly and glanced away, but he didn't seem to be aware of my presence. Either the walls were made of one-way glass or he was a very good actor. He turned his face up to the spray and shut his eyes, reaching for the shampoo himself. I couldn't help but stare.

The man was quite simply stunning. After living near Hollywood for a year I was more than used to the endless succession of wannabe actors parading around the streets at all hours, serving my coffee in teahouses and slicing my pizza in restaurants while they earned enough money to survive until they were 'discovered.'

I had grown almost jaded to male beauty, overdosed on the tanned, perfectly-maintained physiques that paraded up and down on Muscle Beach, jamming the leafy boulevards of Rodeo Drive in their rented Porsches and packing the streets on Hollywood Boulevard on Oscar night in the vain hope of getting notice by a big-time director or producer. They wore fake designer outfits, sported fake tans, and wore big fake smiles.

This guy, however, was something different. He was quite simply and naturally beautiful. Through the crystal clear glass of the shower-room window I could see every detail of his tall and elegant figure.

If I'd thought that Niki was regal-looking, this guy was positively kingly. He was well over six foot and perfectly proportioned. There was a quiet dignity to the way he held himself, in the way he moved. His long black hair was perfectly straight, hanging in silken cords over his broad, strong, naked shoulders, reaching almost halfway down his back. Unlike every other man in this movie-star tan-obsessed town, his skin was pure white, the color of freshly-fallen powder snow, gleaming softly over layers of lean muscle. He reminded me a little of a muscular white panther. Every inch of his body was perfectly defined, what the bodybuilders called 'ripped'— every muscle was clear-cut beneath his skin, with not an inch of fat anywhere to be seen on him.

It made my head swim just looking at him.

I was aware that my mouth was moving. The sounds seemed to come from a long distance away, as though I was drunk.

'That guy,' I was saying to the nearest watching girl above the buzz of music and voices. 'Is he, I mean... do you think he works here?'

'Yeah. I seen him before. Lots of times.' The girl nodded sagely, sipping her green apple martini without taking her eyes off the guy. 'Why else d'you think I just paid forty bucks to get in here?'

I shook my head, still staring. I hadn't paid a penny to get in here, and I immediately wondered why. *Paranoid, moi?*

I swallowed, blushing slightly. 'I didn't realize this was a strip joint.'

The girl turned to look at me then, her orange eyes laughing. *Vampire eyes.* I took a quick step back, my hand going to my belt for a stake, but she waved her hand at me dismissively. She knew that I'd pegged her, and didn't care.

'This ain't a strip joint, girl. And chill with the *Buffy* shit, we're all friends here. This your first time at the Circus of Sins?'

I nodded, unable to speak as in front of me, the man

poured a long squirt of shampoo down his bare chest and started soaping himself in a leisurely fashion.

*Work brain, work.*

'Man, are you in for a treat,' said the girl, nudging me. 'This is just the warm-up act. Believe me, you ain't lived till you've seen the main show.'

'Huh?' I looked at the girl and raised my eyebrows in polite incomprehension, aware that she'd just said something to me.

She looked at me sidelong, and sighed. 'You too, huh?'

'What?' I asked, distracted. My whole attention was riveted on the Towel Guy, as if the world around me had faded away like a big dumb cliché. *I shouldn't be standing here gawking at this big hunky piece of eye candy. I had to get back to Niki, find out if he knew where Harlequin lived, rescue Doll, save the world...*

My heart skipped a beat as the beautiful guy turned around in the shower.

He was no longer holding the towels.

'Oh!' I quickly spun away, covering my eyes with my hands. I was no prude and it wasn't as if I'd never seen a guy naked before... I'd just never seen *that* kind of guy naked before.

I was vaguely aware that the vampire girl was laughing at me. I snapped a blushing glance sideways to see that she hadn't moved an inch, openly watching the guy lather himself up with a small smile of contentment on her face. I was surprised that she didn't whip out a camera and start taking photos.

'Look, I gotta go. I'm here on a date. I shouldn't be watching this,' I whispered, fighting the almost overwhelming urge to turn and stare through the glass again. *He* was still there, looking in the girl's direction now. Perhaps he could see us after all, and the thought made me blush even harder.

'Go in five minutes,' sighed the girl. 'You won't believe what he does with that bar of soap.'

'Huh?' I was staring at the guy again, unable to help myself.

As though sensing my eyes on him, the newcomer suddenly turned around, the big white bar of soap still in his hand. He was standing right in front of me, less than a few feet away through the glass, his face lit up by the lights that spun and wheeled on the stage. For a brief, razor-sharp second my eyes locked with his through the glass of the shower room wall, and everything else faded away.

He had blue eyes, I noticed with a sigh. But not just any blue. There was a kind of unearthly, primordial beauty in them that stilled my heart, made the hair rise on the back of my neck as my gaze drifted over his face like a warm summer breeze. His full lips were sensuous, curved like ripe dragon-fruit on the vine, his features strong and almost predatory in their beauty. Even in the bright lights of the exhibit he seemed to carry his own personal shadow with him, like the special lighting in a sculpture gallery, as though to highlight the exquisite perfection of his features.

He was the most beautiful man I'd seen in my whole life.

I noticed suddenly that Niki was staring at me from over by the bar. I turned away quickly, pretending to examine the drinks menu, which was framed on the wall nearby. I flicked a brief, guilty glance up at my date. Nick was a good-looking guy, but even he paled into insignificance beside the fiery beauty of the man in the glass shower room. I saw his eyes go to Towel Guy and back to me again, as though gauging my reaction. I had to clear my throat several times before I could speak

'Did you get the drinks?' I asked, a little huskily.

'I did.' Niki motioned with his wine glass towards the shower-room window, a strange smile stealing over his lips. 'You know you can watch if you want.'

'I've seen quite enough, thanks.'

I peeked over my shoulder, unable to help glancing in again. In the shower I saw the Towel Guy casually put down the soap and stroll up and down the line of girls, as though measuring them up. He stopped in front of one of the youngest ones, a pretty twenty-something with blonde hair down to her waist. He beckoned to her and she broke into a shy, hesitant smile, as though unable to believe her luck. She started to move towards him, seductively swaying her hips.

Aware of Niki's eyes burning into my back, I turned away fast and flashed him a bright smile, hoping the low lighting hid my blush.

'Let's get out of here,' I said.

Unable to help myself, my gaze darted fleetingly to the reflective black marble wall behind Niki, which was directly opposite the backlit shower window. The man's shadow was easy to pick out, and there was no confusion whatsoever about what he was doing with the woman. I was glad I'd turned away when I had.

But there *was* something strange going on here.

'What the…?' I turned half around and peered back over my shoulder at the steamy action playing out through the glass. Around the gasping woman's feet, the running water had turned pink. 'Is he...?'

'Nope. You're just imagining it.'

I shook my head in dismay, folding my arms. I might as well just say it. 'Nick. You could've *told* me you were bringing me to a vampire club.'

The music chose that exact moment to stop. My words hung in the air, too loud for the sudden silence. Several patrons near us turned and gave me a look of wary amusement, before turning to roll their eyes at Niki. He took my hand in a very easy, natural gesture and walked towards a door at the end of the room, pulling me in close to him so he could talk quietly in my ear.

'Do me one favor. Don't talk like that around the clients. You'll just encourage them.'

'But your clients are vampires!'

Niki shook his head, mouth twitching as though suppressing a grin. 'They wish.'

'Excuse me?'

'You heard me. Come inside and I'll explain.'

Inside where? Niki led me onwards. I unwillingly followed him, wondering what new kind of trouble I was getting myself into.

And surprisingly, I couldn't wait to find out.

# CHAPTER FIFTEEN

WE LEFT THE main room and walked down a wide corridor deeply carpeted with thick red shag pile. More of the round windows I'd seen in the main room lined the corridor.

I took great care not to look through any of them, staring straight ahead as I walked. White alcoves were inset into the wall every ten feet or so, and beautiful young couples lounged on black satin recliners under colorful art canvases depicting angels and devils. Some of the booths had the curtains drawn, and the unmistakable sounds of passion drifted out from underneath. As we passed by the open booths the half-clad couples' eyes seemed to follow us, watching us with a speculative interest, the girls nudging their partners. Some of them even jumped up to shake Niki's hand and snap pictures, shirts and pants hanging open with no trace of embarrassment or shame.

Niki was obviously a big deal in this place.

The mystery deepened.

A doorway slid open at the end of the corridor and

I reluctantly ducked through, my bravado evaporating rapidly the further I went from the outside world. I was deep in vampire central now, and was already beginning to heartily wish that I'd brought some kind of edged weapon with me, or ideally a flamethrower.

Niki slung an arm around my waist as we walked down the short corridor on the other side. He smelled like bourbon and cigarette smoke, with just a hint of something underneath it that reminded me of gunpowder. He paused at a large mahogany door at the very end of the hallway, and swiped his black ID card through the card-reader beside the door. The door swung open and he clicked on the light, motioning me to go through ahead of him.

I peered inside, and raised an eyebrow. I'd thought that Mia's decorating skills were a little on the extreme side, what with her whole apartment being pink, but extreme didn't even come close to describing Niki's room.

It was black. That was the first thing I noticed. Black and... expensive looking. Every item of furniture in the room looked as though it had cost at least four or five grand, from the dark marble flooring covered in giant black-dyed mink rugs, to the black carved mahogany walls and elegant stone fireplace with carved roses and swans climbing up the sides. Even the enormous iron-framed four-poster bed was black, its two-foot thick mattress groaning under the weight of a ridiculous number of heavy black velvet blankets, red silk sheets, and more black silk throw-pillows than I thought was strictly necessary. A red silk drape hung in elegant folds around it, screening it off from the rest of the room. The bedroom ceiling above it was domed like the inside of a temple and covered in glass, so it looked as though we were inside a big glass bell.

Niki glanced at my stunned expression and shrugged.

'I like black. Deal with it.'

He slipped past me, slyly brushing his hand over my hip as he passed by, sending a shiver up my spine. He walked over to the end wall and briefly turned his back on me, fussing with the fireplace.

I took a deep, careful breath, reining in my hormones, then surreptitiously poured the drink he'd given me out into a potted plant, being as quiet about it as possible. I held the glass up to the light, checking for the tell-tale specks of dissolved pills at the bottom. The glass was clean, but I knew I still had to be careful. I'd known Niki for a couple of days now but that didn't mean I could trust him.

I carefully set the glass down on the bedside table, just as Niki lit a long match and tossed it through the bars that framed the fireplace with casual flamboyance.

There was the soft *whumph* of igniting gas, and my eyebrows shot up as a long column of fire belched up the deep glass-fronted channel in the wall in a long, tall stream, flowing upwards to the ceiling. The tongue of fire split in two at the top of the channel and raced away in opposite directions, left and right, flying around the charred pathways cut in the ceiling before joining up on the other side, forming a circle of fire that ringed the entire dome-shaped glass ceiling. Niki turned a knob beside the fireplace and fingers of fire fanned out from the ring to dance up into the glass bell in the center, giving the impression that the entire ceiling was made of fire.

Niki smiled at my expression. 'And yes, I am trying to impress you.'

'You could've just bought me flowers.'

'I'm an old fashioned guy. Does that bother you?'

'No.' I scowled, confused. 'Actually, yeah, it does. I think I'm just having a weird week in general.'

'How so?'

I shrugged. 'It's long story.'

Niki sat down on the bed and patted the mattress next to him. I shook my head slightly, circling him cautiously so that my back was to the door. I felt the sensual warmth of the flames licking down from above, and unconsciously turned my face up to it. The heat felt good, and I felt myself relaxing a little. I was cold in my short-skirted outfit, and hadn't thought to bring a sweater.

'C'mon, girl.' Niki smiled disarmingly, patting the bed again. 'You've been wound tight as a spring since the day I met you. Wanna tell me what's up?'

I eyed the bed. It did look temptingly comfy, and my high-heeled boots were already killing me. I edged over towards him and gingerly sat down on the bed, taking care to put at least a couple of feet of space between myself and Niki. Niki leaned over and grabbed my hand, squeezing it encouragingly. His fingers were very cool. I shivered, trying not to pull my hand away.

'Not really. It depends how much you already know.'

'I know everything.'

'Not likely.'

'Try me.'

I frowned, confused, wondering what I could say to test him. He obviously knew a lot about vampires, and he claimed to know where Harlequin lived, too. I had to broach the subject of Harlequin without being too obvious about it, but where to begin without giving everything away?

I remembered the kids back in the crowd the night we'd met, the guy dressed as Jack Skellington who'd known my name. Perhaps Niki could help me shed some light on that?

'I'm just having a crappy month, that's all,' I started, fiddling with the bandana on my wrist. 'There's a ton of stuff happening right now that you really, really don't want to know about. But the weirdest things have been happening to me lately.'

'Like what?'

'Like dreams. Strange dreams about the end of the world. I know that everyone has those... but there's more to it than that. People seem to want to kill me for no reason. Complete strangers know who I am. The way they look at me... it's like, they're waiting for me to do something. Save the world. Grow an extra head. I don't know.'

'And can you?'

'Grow another head?' I shrugged. 'I could try.'

'These people you're talking about.' Niki leaned forwards and pulled what looked like a blackened jousting sword out of the nightstand. He poked the base of the fire-pit with it, flipping a hidden switch which seemed to turn the fire down. 'These were human people?'

I shrugged, avoiding his gaze. He had to spill the beans first.

'Only...' he went on. 'If they were non-human people, they *might* know something you don't know. Conceivably. Those of us who are more... *unusual* in origin can often sense things that normal people can't. We can see things, hear things that a normal human can't. Even things that haven't happened yet.' He paused, giving me a meaningful look. 'It's like dogs barking before a hurricane, or cats hiding before an earthquake. Know what I mean?'

'Define *unusual*,' I managed. My throat was so dry I could barely speak. Was Niki talking about the Apocalypse? I hadn't even dared tell my own best friend about all this stuff, not wanting to worry her, and yet here I was, pouring my heart out to a guy I'd known a grand total of twenty-four hours.

Sometimes, it was easier that way.

Niki looked at me sideways, sliding his hand across the space between us on the bed and resting it lightly on my knee. We were both being deliberately vague, but I had a strong feeling we were on the same page here. 'You go first. What do you think I mean by unusual?'

I took a deep breath and lowered my voice. I wasn't usually the first one to crack, but time was a' ticking and I needed the lead on Harlequin as fast as possible. 'I mean… supernatural creatures. Vampires. Werewolves. And possibly zombies.'

'Ah.'

'And that's another thing that bothers me,' I went on quickly before I changed my mind. 'All those people upstairs, in the club. Your club.' I paused, twisting my hands together as I tried to think of how to put this. 'The… vampires. Those girls in the shower upstairs, I mean, the whole shower-exhibit thing…' I pulled an eloquent face, my cheeks flaming helplessly pink as I fumbled for words. 'And you say you run this place? How can you let them get treated like that?'

Niki laughed, long and loud. I glared at him, outraged.

'You think that's funny?' I protested. 'That one poor girl in the shower... she was really bleeding after what that guy did to her! I mean, I know she's a vampire and she'll heal, but the health-insurance bills alone—'

'They're not real vampires, sweetheart.'

'Huh?' I was thrown.

'They're role-players. Hobbyists. Even the girls in the shower.'

Niki flopped back on the bed with a sigh of contentment, propping himself up on the pillows so he could watch me with those startling blue eyes of his. His hair seemed to have escaped its customary torture of gel and backcombing tonight, and it spread out beneath his head in a soft dark wave, like a raven's wing. I had to fight the urge to touch it, to see if it was as soft as it looked.

'Don't worry about those folks upstairs,' he went on, reaching out to idly stroke up and down the length of my leg. 'They pay us a ton of money so they can come down here and make-believe they're in a real vampire club. Bunch of rich bitches from Hollywood, looking for the Next Big Thing. More money than sense, most of them. They buy a set of fake vamp teeth and some orange contacts and they think they're the shit. And of course vampires are so fashionable right now, what with all those big summer movies coming out lately.'

Niki shifted closer to me on the bed, stretching his legs out with a sigh of contentment. 'Nobody's complaining. It's good for business.' His smile grew wider as he slipped his fingers beneath my knee, playing with the soft skin there. 'What made you think they were real vampires?'

'They looked real to me.' I felt immediately braver, although to tell the truth a little disappointed. I had to fight not to pull my legs away as his hand stroked over my upper thigh and squeezed lightly. 'All that blood…?'

'Fake blood. We sell it in bottles at the bar.'

'Ah.' Now I just felt stupid. 'But those guys in the booths we passed on the way up here. They were really—?'

'Having sex? Yeah.' Niki's head slid down into a shadow, his eyes bright with laughter as he watched my reaction. 'What our clients do in their own time is their own business. We charge two hundred bucks an hour for those booths.'

'So you basically run a brothel.'

'Not a brothel.' Niki looked hurt at the word. 'Those are real couples. Nobody's forcing them to do anything they wouldn't normally do in the privacy of their own homes. Our club just adds to their fantasy. Besides, I like to think of us being more high-class than that.'

I wasn't convinced. 'How so?'

Niki sat up, his face growing animated. 'This is a top-dollar operation, my sweet. Big players and big money are involved. Everything at the Circus of Sins is top of the range. We've got a million dollar sound system up there. That band? We fly them in from England twice a week. They seem to like the weather here. I introduced the lead singer to Kat Von D last week. I hear they're opening her twentieth tattoo parlor together on Melrose next month.' He grinned. 'We got every Hollywood gossip magazine foaming at the mouth for a feature, but we don't do press passes. They can all kiss my ass.'

'Huh.' I wasn't sure I believed that, but it sounded more plausible than the alternative. 'So you're not a real vampire either, then.'

'Oh no, I'm a vampire alright.'

I gave Niki a skeptical look. Without thinking I leaned forwards and laid my head on his chest inside his half-open shirt, listening for a heartbeat. I heard the deep *thud-thud, thud-thud* of his heart thumping in his chest, loud and strong, and instantly relaxed.

'Bullshit. You're human.'

'Not human. Way cooler.'

'What are you?'

'Same as you. Part monster, part huge pain in the ass.'

'Pull the other one.'

'I'm serious.' Niki grinned again. His teeth were human-looking. No fangs there.

'But I saw you out in the sunlight!'

'It's complicated.'

'Prove it.'

'What do you want me to do?'

'I don't know!' I sat up and waved a hand around vaguely, already tired of this game. 'Do something vampiric. Vampire-like. Whatever. Then tell me whatever you were going to tell me about Harlequin so I can stop wasting time and get out of here, maybe save some lives...'

I winced. I hadn't meant it to come out like that, but Niki didn't seem to be in the least bit offended.

'Wasting time, huh?' he said, studying me with bright eyes. 'Like this?'

He rolled over and crawled up the bed towards me, grinning like a Cheshire cat. I folded my arms and raised a sardonic eyebrow at him. I wasn't moving an inch. He put a hand on my chest and gently pushed me down backwards onto the big pile of throw-pillows. I felt my breathing speed up as he trailed his closed lips up the side of my neck, and turned sideways awkwardly, glancing at the door. I wasn't scared of him any more now that I had decided he was human, but he was getting a little too close for comfort.

'Nick,' I said, a warning tone in my voice.

He lifted his head to gaze into my eyes for a long moment, then grinned and leaned in towards me, his lips parting...

Ah, so he expected me to fall for that old trick, did he?

I stared at him crossly, refusing to take the bait. I hadn't come down here to fool around. I'd come to find out about Harlequin, to do my job and save mankind. Niki grinned as he leaned over me, his breath cool on my cheek as he stared longingly at my lips.

'I should probably warn you that I'm a biter,' I murmured as he moved closer, trying to make my breathless words sound like a threat.

'Funny. So am I,' Niki whispered back.

Then he leaned forward the final fraction of an inch and kissed me, his lips soft against mine, his breath as sweet as cut grass in the sun. I held myself absolutely still, my brain stalling with surprise, amazed at how good his lips tasted. It was as though he'd just been eating honeyed, ripened fruit dipped in butterscotch and chased down with a glass of red wine. His kiss was so incredibly soft, so gentle, so hesitant, that I automatically leaned forward the barest fraction of an inch, tilting my head slightly to nudge his lips apart, drinking in the taste and the sensation of his lips on mine, as delicious as cool, sweet water.

This was heaven, sudden and unexpected. Before I could make up my mind what to do about it, he broke the kiss and leaned closer to me, sliding down my body to press his lips gently to my throat, just above my collar bone. I immediately tensed up as one hand touched my shoulders, rolling me over onto my back on top of the pillows. His touch was feather light, but something in his attitude warned me that resisting it would probably be a really bad idea.

And the strangest thing was, I didn't want to.

It was funny. I'd known all day that this was what he really wanted, what *I* really wanted. This was the reason he invited me down here, away from the protection of the wolves... and the reason I'd let him. I also knew that this was the absolute worst thing for me to be doing, and at the worst possible time.

The world was at stake, after all.

But somehow, it felt right. *We* felt right.

Before I could think about it too much I rolled him over on the bed so that I was lying on top of him, propping myself up on my arms. I'm not really a 'guy-on-top' kinda girl. He didn't resist me as I leaned over him, pressing my lips to his in a harder, deeper kiss. He cupped my chin in his hands, gently surfacing from the kiss to nip at my lower lip as he pulled me down fully on top of him, his arms twining around my back, his hips lazily arching against mine as though we'd done this a thousand times.

All my troubles and worries suddenly seemed to vanish, fading away in a white haze of bliss. Niki continued unhurriedly kissing me, his body relaxing against mine, sighing into my mouth as he shifted expertly under me, molding himself to me so that I could feel every last inch of him pressing against me. And when I say every last inch, I mean... never mind.

It was as though he'd been made to fit me perfectly. He felt incredible, so strong and warm and... *safe*.

I hadn't felt safe in a long time.

My fingertips found his face, stroking and exploring the planes and contours of his features. Beneath strong, well-shaped brows, his cheekbones were a gently angled swell down to the firm line of his jaw. Short, almost invisible stubble roughened his lean lower jaw, lengthening to a slightly longer patch beneath his chin. I ran my fingers through it while his lips feasted on my throat, tilting my head with one hand so he could kiss under the angle of my jaw.

This wasn't what I'd expected from him at all, I thought with a touch of unreality. Niki was a predator, a killer. I could feel it in my bones, despite his behavior towards me so far. Every last inch of him radiated danger and pain and harshness. I could read it in the wary lines of his body, in the dark glint of his eyes.

Yet his hands were gentle on my face, his lips almost hesitant on mine, and every practiced touch of his body brought about an exquisite reaction from me, like a violinist playing his favorite fiddle.

I shifted my weight on top of him, my hand cupping the back of his head to pull his lips back up to mine, then rolled over a second time to draw him down on top of me in a spur-of-the-moment gesture of trust. He seemed a little surprised at the move, but he didn't complain. He leaned his weight on me just a little too hard as his tongue explored my mouth, sighing in pleasure, and I slid a hand around the back of his neck, locking my legs around his thighs and arching my back to press him up against me.

*This was more like it.* I gripped a handful of his dark

hair as I kissed him back harder, deeper, losing myself in the rapture of sensation, blocking off all thoughts about where this might lead. This was so good I didn't want it to stop. I didn't want to move, or think, or feel anything but the incredible softness of Niki's velvet lips on mine, his cool fingertips exploring my cheekbones as his hips ground against mine.

He finally broke the kiss to shuck down my body, dipping his head to lick a long, slow line down the side of my neck, making me squirm. His honey-sweet mouth continued moving down my throat, one soft, slow kiss at a time, veering off to one side to claim the sensitive skin beneath my ear as I turned my face away from him with a grin, trying to catch my breath.

My gaze wandered aimlessly around the room as he briefly leaned in close to lick the hollow of my throat, searching for a clue to his identity, for a sign that I could trust him. I focused on the nearest painting, squinting against the firelight crackling down from the false ceiling. If I half-closed my eyes, the painting looked a little like a black demon fighting a giant white werewolf...

I glanced hurriedly away. I didn't want to be thinking about werewolves right now.

I buried my head in the cool pillow and gave the softest of sighs as he moved onwards, gently biting and licking as he went until goosebumps flashed across my skin. A glowing warmth flooded over my skin in the wake of his mouth, setting my blood on fire and warming the places inside me that had been so achingly empty since Karrel had died and left me alone in the world...

And there was another thought I didn't want to be having right now.

I closed my eyes and cautiously relaxed my body against his in a bid to stop thinking, shutting my mind off to everything but the warm, wet sensation of his lips moving unhurriedly over my skin. He gave a sigh and pressed his hips harder against mine, as though testing the water, and desire swept through me in a dark surge as I opened my eyes and gazed up at him.

A spark of electricity seemed to crack between us and I felt like I was suddenly drunk, drifting down deeper and deeper in a warm sea of pink champagne, tiny fizzy bubbles bursting all over my skin and trickling over my scalp. The sensation was so real it brought me out in goosebumps. It was as if I was floating, looking down on myself lying there on the bed kissing this perfect stranger, watching events unfold as though they were nothing to do with me.

Niki's movements grew more confident with every touch, every caress, and as he lifted his head to look up at me a wave of longing swept through me that was so strong, so sudden, that it was almost too much to bear. I tangled my hands in his hair and pulled his head back with a hard sigh, locking my lips over his and letting myself sink into the kiss, letting it be everything he wanted it to be. I clamped down tightly on the old ache in my chest, the jagged, bleeding hole in my heart left by Karrel's death. It was still just as raw, just as painful, but strangely enough, it didn't hurt quite so bad as the last time I had tried this, with Mutt....

*And it was really time for me to stop thinking now. Seriously.*

A surge of guilt flooded through me even as I tried to push it away, to turn my stupid brain off and just enjoy the moment. Why *shouldn't* I be doing this, after all? The man I loved was dead. Things with Mutt were... complicated. My Hunter bosses were pissed at me whatever I did, and everything I did these days, no matter how hard I tried, seemed to be wrong.

In fact, it seemed that the harder I tried, the worse things seemed to get.

And besides, there was a very good chance that the world itself was going to end in two short days' time, if I didn't turn into a werewolf before then.

Why shouldn't I let myself have this last little bit of fun?

Niki let his breath out hard as he tangled his hands in my hair and pulled me roughly closer, pressing himself against me with an urgency that left me no doubt whatsoever about his intentions. His hands were suddenly in my hair, clutching my skin, all over me. I tensed up, gripping his wrists as I kissed him back fiercely, almost overwhelmed by my own need. A shock of adrenaline scorched through me as Niki collapsed his body and settled his weight fully on top of me, pressing against me with a very masculine groan that betrayed how much restraint he was using to keep his touch this gentle. He ran his hands down my body, growling low in his throat with a sound so primal it made every hair stand up on my body. He reached down, and started to undo my belt.

Alarm bells went off in my head as I realized he wasn't going to stop. I bit my lip, staring up at the flames licking across the ceiling as Niki continued hungrily kissing me, letting me feel a hint of teeth as his control started slipping. I thought I'd wanted this, but now that it was actually happening, I was suddenly afraid. I wasn't ready for this yet, I realized. Not so soon after Karrel. I'd thought things would be different with someone who wasn't a werewolf, who was at least slightly closer to human, but it wasn't just that.

It had barely been a month since Karrel had died, after all. Just thirty short days... it wasn't nearly long enough to wait.

I needed more time.

'Nick. Enough,' I gasped.

I started to sit up, suddenly panicking, but Niki's lips seized mine and he pushed me back down onto the bed, his grip tightening on my wrists. I started to struggle, to fight back. My pulse was too loud in my throat, my blood too hot in my veins. I felt like I was drowning, suffocating under his weight. I couldn't breathe, couldn't catch my breath in the unexpected tide of panic that slammed through me.

Before I could draw a breath to tell him to stop, his hand tightened in my hair and he tore his mouth from mine, gasping like a drowning man coming up for the third and final time. In the flickering firelight his eyes opened wide, flaring with a sudden flash of silver fire. He turned his head away and bared his teeth, grimacing as though in pain.

I stared up at him uncomprehendingly, then froze, my mouth opening in surprise. His eyeteeth had grown a good quarter inch while he'd been kissing me, forming two saber-like points that peeked wickedly from between his lips. I stared at him in shock.

Niki really was a vampire.

His eyes were unfocused as he clenched his fists and shoved himself up off the bed, deliberately putting some distance between us.

'Believe me now?' he grinned.

# CHAPTER SIXTEEN

I REMAINED FROZEN for a long moment, lying on the bed beneath the beautiful, svelte figure of Niki, too stunned to even scream. Of course I'd seen a vampire before—I'd killed several myself not two weeks ago during my first mission with the Hunters, one on purpose, one purely by accident.

But I'd sure as hell never kissed one.

There was a first time for everything, I guess.

My entire body tensed as I stared up at him, ready for fight or flight. My neck burned with a burst of heat as my protective dragon amulet flared to life, ready to defend me if need be. Niki stared down at me, through me, the sculpted planes of his body strong and proud in the crackling firelight that bathed us from above. My hand slid down to my garter belt, surreptitiously groping for the small wooden stake I kept clipped there. But then Niki did something so unexpected that it made me jump.

He laughed.

I stared at him as he abruptly rolled to the side,

letting me get up. I slid quickly off the bed and turned to face him, my eyes wild, breathing just a little bit too fast. Niki's breathing was uneven, his pupils dilated with desire, but his smile was genuine as he stood up and unhurriedly crossed to the wall. He ripped a large silver cross off the front of an iron cabinet, snapping the thick melded metal as easily as if it were made out of balsa wood. He graciously offered it to me.

'Need this? I hear it's traditional in situations like these.'

I hung back, waiting for his skin to start burning on contact with the silver cross, but nothing happened. After a moment I snatched the cross from him, peered at the back to see the little engraved hallmarks that identified pure silver. I flicked the cross with a finger, listening to it ring out with a clear, bell-like sound. It was real silver, alright.

'What the hell are you?' I asked, eventually.

'I already told you. You know what I am.'

'But—you can't be a vampire! You just touched silver. And I saw you in the sunlight!'

'You believe everything you see in the movies?'

'No, but...'

'You should do,' said Niki, sitting down on the bed and rubbing at his teeth with his forefinger as though they itched. 'It's all true. Every last word of it.'

'No need to be sarcastic,' I said. I couldn't take my eyes off those glittering fangs of his. I'd never been this close to a real vampire before and not been fighting or running in the opposite direction screaming. It took some getting used to.

'I'm not,' Niki replied. 'The sunlight thing's true, at least. Most vampires are severely photosensitive. But not me.' He gave me a funny little look, then grinned impishly. 'I'm just… special.'

'Special's right,' I muttered. I risked a glance towards the door to see if it was locked. 'As in short-bus special— hey!'

I yelped in alarm as Niki suddenly lunged at me and snatched me up in his arms, moving too fast for me to react. He pulled us both over backwards onto the bed, rolling on top of me and pinning my arms down beneath his knees. I wriggled and fought and twisted my way upright, cursing up a storm as he beamed down at me from beneath the dark curtain of his hair, his face just a few inches from mine.

'And this is why you should never kiss a vampire,' he said, grinning down at me with a wicked look in his eyes. 'You really, really don't want one as a stalker. Get my drift?'

He bared his teeth and pretended to snap at my throat. I yelled and tried to tear myself free, then scowled in fury as he burst out laughing.

'Not funny!' I cried. 'What the hell is wrong with you?'

'Apparently, I'm seriously starved of entertainment,' Niki admitted, settling down into a comfortable position on top of me. 'Or I was, till I met you.' He rested his chin on his fists, like a little kid, looking down at me with a lopsided grin. 'Can I keep you?'

'No!'

'Why not?'

'It's… complicated.'

'Why? Just because you've got a horny werewolf hot on your tail and your old Hunter buddies treat you like crap.' Niki shot me a searching look, his eyes glinting with merriment. 'Oh yeah, and I think there's something big happening on Sunday night that you should be taking care of right now, instead of ditching your best friends to hang out with your sworn enemies.'

He grinned at me, blowing a strand of hair out of his eyes.

It was several moments before I could speak again. 'You've been spying on me!'

Niki shrugged, looking inordinately pleased with himself. 'So?'

'How long have you been watching me?' I demanded.

'Long enough,' said Niki, chewing on a fingernail. 'To tell you the truth, I'm fascinated.'

'By what?'

'By you. It's like watching a car accident, drawn out over a period of weeks. It's terrible, heartbreaking, but almost impossible to look away.'

'Like your life is so perfect,' I snapped. I wriggled beneath him, trying to get some leverage to throw him off me. Niki immediately rolled his hips around and trapped my thighs inside his own, squeezing lightly, letting me feel the incredible strength that lurked inside his muscular body. I growled and relented, but I hoped that the warning look in my eyes told him that he was in really big trouble.

'I'm almost done making my point here, sweetheart,' he assured me. 'Just listen for a minute. I'm trying to save your life here. I'm on your side, or at least I hope I am.'

'But you're a vampire!'

'But not just any vampire. I'm a white vampire. That's what I wanted to tell you.'

'A *what?*'

'A white vampire. The offspring of a human and a vampire.'

My expression must have looked truly scary at this point, because Niki rolled off me and finally let me get up. I sat up quickly on the bed, ready to run but too curious to leave yet. This was something new. I'd rather be talking about Harlequin, but the Hunter in me needed to know what he meant.

'Nick, if you're making all this up…'

'We're very rare,' said Niki, his expression darkening. 'I'm one of the few that survived.'

'Survived what?'

Niki half-turned away from me and drew his knees up to his chest like a small boy, picking at a loose threat on the plush silken blanket. 'You don't wanna know, but let's just say that it's not pretty. There's a reason you haven't heard of us. There's not very many of us around. Our mothers usually don't survive the birth, and those who do… they usually wish that they hadn't.' He looked up at me, serious now. 'He seduced my mother, knowing what would happen to her when she… That's why I have to stop him.'

'Stop who?'

'Harlequin. He's breeding white vampires. On purpose.'

*Finally. The topic I had been waiting for.* I smoothed my hair back, trying not to show my intense interest. 'Why?'

'He hates all vampires. Even though he's a vampire himself. Despises them. It's the ultimate irony, or so he claims. He can't stand what he is, what he's become. He hates his own weaknesses— the vampire thirst, the sunlight phobia. Even the way he looks.'

I sucked in a breath, then asked the million-dollar question.

'Any idea what he's planning?'

'Plenty. He's using all his power, his money, his technology, to literally build a new race of vampires from scratch. Vampires that don't need to drink blood to survive, that can go out in sunlight, like the humans do. His babies, he calls them. He wants to use some ancient prophecy to cleanse the world of the weak humans and the flawed vampires.'

'Why bother getting rid of the humans?'

'He just wants them gone. He got picked on in high school or something, I don't know. But when the prophecy is complete and the number of humans in the world has been reduced, he plans to fill the world with a new, perfect race, built from scratch in his own image. Beautiful, immortal, telepathic...'

'*Telepathic?*'

'Once again, it pays not to ask. And telepathy's no big deal. Everyone always goes on about how great it would be to be able to read minds, but believe me, it ain't pleasant. Having someone else in your head all the time, seeing every little thought you have...' Niki shuddered. 'Takes a lot of time and a hell of a lot of will-power to learn to block it. Fire blocks it, for some reason. Hence the roof.' He nodded upwards at the bell-shaped ceiling. 'If you don't block it, then they see everything. *He* sees everything. It's how he controls us...'

He stared into the fire, his expression unreadable.

'So he wants to use telepathy to control his new race,' I prompted.

Niki nodded, a flash of pain passing over his face before vanishing again.

I sat back, taking all this in. I'd heard parts of this before, in a more garbled form, so I wasn't as surprised as I should have been.

Ninette would just die when she heard all this new info…

'How's Harlequin building this new race of his?' I asked, after a while.

Niki was silent a long time. When he finally spoke, he sounded like the admission was costing him more than he made out.

'A mixture of high-tech genetics, and good old fashioned breeding. With his new race, he's splicing in a gene from another species to fix each fault in the vampire gene.'

'Why doesn't he just use humans and vampires to breed an army of white vamps? You guys seem pretty indestructible. I saw you get shot in the chest the other night and it just healed right up again. And you're immune to sunlight. Or does he want more?'

'Ah, little girl.' Niki laughed softly. He reached out and touched my face, running his fingers lightly over my cheekbones, down the bridge of my nose, softly tracing my lips. 'He wants *way* more than that. Just you wait till you see these ugly bastards he's breeding. You think regular vamps are scary?' He shivered, pulling a face. 'It takes a lot to freak me out, but those little shits scare the living crap outta me.'

'Great.' I pushed his hands away, sitting up on the bed. 'So how are we supposed to stop them?'

'We can't. I've got an insider in his lab and he says these things are hardcore. Harlequin's basically crossed every supernatural being that can't be killed with everything that lives forever. They're about as far from human as you can get. If even one of these things ever gets out, we're fucked on a scale you can't even imagine.'

'Do they have big teeth?'

'They have *really* big teeth.'

'So why add human DNA to the mix?' I couldn't let it go. 'Won't that make them weaker?'

Niki shrugged and reached down to unlace his boots. 'Elementary, my dear Kayla. Human DNA is the key to gene splicing. I don't want to get all technical on you, but vamp genes are just pure evil. You try to mix two breeds of vamp gene, you get a big bloody mess. One gene will always eat the other and the baby will be one species or the other rather than a mixture of the two. It's like trying to breed a black dog and a white dog to produce grey puppies. It just doesn't work. One gene will always win out, so you'll get a mix of black or white pups.' He pulled off his boots with a grunt of relief and pitched them into the corner. 'With me so far?'

'Kind of.'

'Cool. So each new creature has to be first interbred with a non-vampire race to produce a half-blood offspring. In other words, Harlequin's using human DNA like a painter uses water to mix two paint colors. Human DNA dilutes the two warring genes, waters them down to the point where they can co-exist. Mixing the genetic colors to make something new, so to speak.'

'Like you.'

'Like me,' nodded Niki, rolling over on the bed so that his hair flopped across his face. 'I'm half human, half vampire.'

I risked a smile. 'So which bits of you are human?'

Niki smiled at that, snapping out of his somber mood, and I was secretly relieved. 'No bits that you have to worry about right now, young lady. But yeah, using white vampire genes is the big 'fix' to the vampire race's aversion to sunlight. It makes us resistant to sunlight, but one problem we have left is that we're mortal. I'm warm-blooded, and I have a heartbeat. I just heal really, really fast, and live for a very long time. The next step would be to mix my genes with those of an immortal species, to lose the mortal heartbeat and make the next generation one hundred percent perfect...'

Niki stopped there and gave me a sharp look, as though worried he'd said too much.

'And there's such a thing as a black vampire?' I asked, curious.

Niki nodded, grimacing. 'A black vamp is a vampire crossed with a demon. Even harder to breed than a white vamp.'

'Why?'

'Vamps are blood-drinkers. Demons are flesh-eaters. Combine the two, you're in for a real headache, but that's what happened all the time back in the bad old days. It's said that demons ruled the earth before humans arrived. Some even say that demons are God's first attempt at angels. But He screwed up, made an immortal, all-powerful being with free will. He had no way to control them, and they all went bad. So He cast them down, wiped His hands of them and started again.'

'That's not good parenting.'

'I don't think He cared. Out of sight, out of mind and all that. Some of these demons then interbred with the very first vampires, made a hell of a mess. Most of them died out, and the ones that lived only did so by getting very good at hiding. That's what black vamps do most of the time.'

'So are these creatures still around today?'

'Not many. But they're there, if you know where to look for them. They don't do well in modern societies as they tend to change back to their elemental demon form when you make them mad. They also have an almost uncontrollable urge to eat human flesh. Makes it kind of hard for them to hold down a full-time job, if you know what I mean.' He gave a strange smile. 'Harlequin is a black vampire, you might like to know.'

'I see.' I tactfully slid away from him on the bed. 'How do you *know* all this?'

'Let's just say it's complicated.'

'Nick. Please.'

Niki stared at me a long moment, then sighed, gazing wistfully at my lips. 'I'll tell you if you kiss me again.'

'I have two words and a hand gesture for you, to answer that one.'

'Fine, fine.' Niki sat up on the bed, rubbing his eyes. 'Just stay with me for a couple more hours. I have something else I wanna show you tonight.'

'Niki. Is this 'something' inside your pants?' I asked, trying not to smile.

Niki blew his hair out of his eyes and looked up at me, his eyes shining. 'Just say yes. I promise I'll make it worth your while.'

I lifted up my shoulders, sucked in a breath, then let them drop in defeat. Right now, it didn't seem like such a bad idea. I was learning a lot, and the guy hadn't actually tried to eat me yet. *What the hell.*

'Fine. You got till midnight, but then I gotta get going. And this had better be good or you're in big trouble. I'm kind of pushed for time right now.'

'I'm already in big trouble. I'm dating a human, aren't I?'

I opened my mouth to correct him, then thought better of it. I had enough to worry about without figuring out how to tell him that I was actually days away from turning into a werewolf. I knew that all vampires hated werewolves, and with this good a source of insider information, I didn't want to push my luck and risk scaring him off.

Niki's grin grew wider as he gazed at me thoughtfully. Before I could move away he leaned across the space that divided us on the bed and planted a feather-light kiss on my lips, letting his warm, sweet mouth linger on mine. The kiss went on a long time.

I was breathing hard by the time he pulled away, almost dizzy with desire. It took everything I had not to simply push him down backwards onto the bed, strip off his clothes and finally let myself give in to temptation.

'And if I stay till midnight, you'll tell me where Harlequin lives?' I asked, a little unsteadily. I was feeling braver now. 'That's why you invited me here, after all.'

Niki nodded, waving his hand dismissively. 'Of course. And I have one last thing to tell you.'

'What?'

He sat back on the bed, glancing around as though we might be overheard. He leaned forwards again, dropping his voice as he stroked a finger down the curve of my cheekbone. 'I told you I owned this club, right?'

'Right.'

'I do, but it's part of a new franchised chain. There are clubs like this one springing up all over the West Coast, and all the money they earn goes into one central bank account. You want to know who owns that bank account? Who owns us?'

I stared at Niki in sudden understanding, as the pieces finally clicked into place. When he reached down to lift up his shirt, I didn't even need to look to know what he was about to show me.

The letter 'H' was branded into Niki's left hip, outlined in raised white scar-tissue.

*A cattle-brand. A mark of ownership.*

I didn't have to ask to know what that letter stood for, or who Niki worked for.

*H for Harlequin...*

'Just know one thing,' Niki said, as he tucked his shirt back in, glancing around as though embarrassed. 'I want Harlequin taken down as bad as you do. My mother was human, too, and he killed her. I'm on your side, I promise you that.'

I narrowed my eyes, sizing Niki up. 'Prove it to me.'

'How?'

I decided to go for broke. 'This angel Harlequin's planning to sacrifice tomorrow night. Her name is Doll. Do you know where she is?'

Niki's eyes flickered, his gaze becoming guarded. 'Maybe. How did you know her name?'

'I'm the one asking the questions,' I replied, getting to my feet. Playtime was over. 'You got ten seconds to tell me where she is, or I'm out of here.'

'Why do you want to know?'

'Because I think I can stop him.'

Niki gave a small, roguish smile. He lounged back

on the bed and let his free hand creep down his body, toying with the buttons on his shirt. He licked his lips, his voice becoming husky. 'How bad do you want to know?'

I folded my arms and tapped my foot. Waiting.

'Spoilsport.' Niki's gaze flicked down my body and I shivered at the look in his eyes. A slow, lazy smile spread over his face as he saw my reaction. He had me and he knew it. 'Fine, fine. Just let me change. Then I'll show you.'

I nodded as Niki got up and headed for his cavernous closet. I watched him as he started to change his clothes, and a frown stole over my face. A terrible thought was dawning on me.

'One more thing,' I said finally. 'You said that Harlequin deliberately breeds these half-and-half creatures, to use for his gene transplants. What happens to those creatures, once he's done with them?'

Niki grinned at me, smoothing his hair out of his eyes in barely suppressed excitement.

'Wanna come see?'

# CHAPTER SEVENTEEN

THE INSIDE OF the below-ground level of the Circus of Sins was warm, heated by hundreds of bodies. I looked around in surprise as we entered a vast set of double doors and emerged into a giant underground auditorium half the size of a football stadium, complete with tiered seats and central arena.

This place was certainly bigger on the inside than it had looked when I'd seen it from the outside. If Harlequin really did own this place, he had to be filthy rich just to get the permits to build underground in earthquake-prone LA. I was guessing he'd bribed someone high-up just to make the permits go away. He was a vampire, after all, so I was guessing that safety wasn't real high-up on his list when it came to building his latest cash-cow.

Niki guided me through the crush like a true gentleman, holding tightly onto my hand as people of all ages and nationalities swarmed past us, all excitedly chattering. There was an air of barely-subdued excitement and expectation in the hall, and everyone we passed seemed to know Niki. He must have stopped to shake hands with a dozen people as we slowly made our way up to our seats. I wondered again who this guy was, why he was so popular.

I hoped he wasn't popular for the same reason the Towel Guy was popular.

I turned back to Niki and looked him over while he talked to a group of giggling girls by the hot-dog stands. He had changed his entire outfit for the evening, and was now dressed casually in dark blue jeans studded with a multitude of silver rivets and sequined skulls, the legs of which were artfully ripped and scrawled with random quotes in White-Out marker pen. Judging by the various four-letter words I could see capitalized here and there, I assumed these were lyrics from his favorite rock songs.

Very Hollywood.

The scruffy designer jeans were matched with scuffed black cowboy boots and a soft white velvet vest top which seemed cut to show off his stunning figure, accentuating the powerfully curved planes of his chest and the soft swell of his biceps. He wore a dark red bandana that hung loosely around his throat, and his shoulder-length black hair was spiked up into a textured mane which flowed over his shoulders, showing off random streaks of dyed red and flame-orange. He looked like a young rockstar on his way to a rodeo.

My eyes flicked up to Niki's face, and saw that he'd caught me checking him out. *Damn.* His spiked-out forelocks slid forwards over his face, hiding his eyes from view. Only the upturned quirk of his mouth from beneath the shaggy curtain of his hair gave me a clue that he was watching me from beneath. He reached out and touched my hand as we walked away from the girls, idly stroking the skin of my inside wrist with his warm fingers while his smile grew wider. I cleared my throat and glanced away, my heart speeding up.

*Focus, Kayla. Think of the mission.*

'And you're not going to tell me what I'm letting myself in for here?' I asked.

'Uh-uh. It's a surprise.'

'Oh, goody,' I said, without much enthusiasm. 'I like surprises.'

Niki handed me a pair of yellow foam earplugs. I took them and looked at them in curiosity as we casually strolled past a very long and impatient-looking line, straight to the front. Everyone was watching us, I realized, secretly enjoying the jealous stares of the other girls in the line. We were handed big gold tickets by a stern-looking security guard. I couldn't help but notice the disturbingly large gun clipped to the man's belt, and glanced around me quickly. The crowd was mostly teenagers and young Goth couples dressed in black. They didn't look very dangerous.

I bit my lip as the guard pushed aside a heavy gate, and guided us through into a fenced off private area.

'Where are we going?' I asked the guard.

He grinned at me, revealing pointed vampire teeth.

'To see the greatest show on earth.'


NIKI GUIDED ME up to the very top of the stands, which were topped by a series of rounded velvet-lined private boxes.

'Showoff,' I muttered, as I glanced at our box with

apprehension. The box was an inverted 'U' shape, almost like a love-seat, completely screened off from prying eyes. Inside it contained a black velvet couch covered in yet more throw-pillows and a half dozen loose silk blankets. A black tasseled canopy rose overhead, enclosing the box and screening it from the overhead floodlights.

It looked very... private.

Niki sat down on the love-seat and threw his arm over the back, beckoning me to join him. I sat down with trepidation, leaving as big a gap as was polite between myself and Niki, then sat back and turned to study the venue.

The circular dirt ring in the center was surrounded by tiered rows of velvet-cushioned seats, currently packed by a good five or six hundred spectators. Judging by the looks of excited expectation on their faces, most of them had been waiting for this show— whatever it was— for a long time. Some of them even had sleeping bags with them.

The ring itself was enclosed by a ten-foot tall thick glass wall. It was filled with freshly dug brown earth, which was mounded up into a huge mountain in the center. The mountain was almost twenty feet high and just as broad across, ringed by about a dozen carved earthen pathways which wound up the miniature mountain.

A giant, man-sized silver birdcage sat on the top.

Impressed, I craned my head back to look up at the ceiling. The entire place was lit with four great star-shaped spotlights. The lighting over the audience had the same intense pinkish-red tint as the lighting in the club. I almost instantly felt warm and sleepy again, and

I had to shake myself to snap out of it. I felt as though I'd been here before, and it took me a few moments to identify why.

I'd been to a place like this before, on a much, much smaller scale. The circular dirt ring, the glass box... it was all very familiar. There had been a ring just like this one in the basement of a corrupt police station, which was acting as a front for illicit vampire activities, most of which involved hunting and killing werewolves for sport.

Mutt had been one of those werewolves. They'd almost killed him...

I shuddered. If this was what we'd come here to see, I couldn't stay. Werewolf baiting was not yet illegal, but if the new laws went through this year that gave werewolves human rights, it would be reclassified as GBH or even murder. Anger rose inside me as I thought of my new werewolf 'family' back home. If any of them ever got caught by the vamps and ended up in a place like this, there would be hell to pay...

Niki leaned closer to me in the box, rubbing my arms as a sudden rush of goosebumps flew over my skin.

'I'm fine,' I said, a little too sharply, and he looked at me strangely. 'What time does the show start?'

'It starts when I say so,' said Niki, not taking his eyes off me. I quickly looked away, busying myself with arranging my purse on my lap to cover the bandana-bandage on my arm. If this was a wolf-baiting ring then I could be in even worse trouble if Niki saw my werewolf bite. He'd probably think I was a spy, come to shut this place down. To distract myself, I opened the leather-bound show program and read the first few lines, checking to see if I was right before I headed out of here. My eyebrows flew up.

'Don't read that! You'll spoil the surprise!' Niki grumbled, making a grab for the program. I held it up away from him, out of reach. I couldn't read it fast enough. I twisted my body away from Niki, my eyes flying over the page.

'No way. It says here...' I read a few sentences more and dropped the program in alarm. 'I don't wanna see that!' People in the next booth turned to stare at me, whispering and grinning at us in a way that I didn't much like.

'Close your eyes, then,' Niki said, winking at me.

'Around you? Never?'

Niki chuckled, his eyes crinkling with appreciation as he looked me over. I glared back at him in a silent challenge, and the sensual pout of his mouth quirked in a grin that was just a little too evil for my liking. I folded my arms and turned my back on him with a huff as he leaned over and started to nibble my neck, a grin rising to my own lips in direct defiance from the orders coming from my brain. Oh, this was just great. Two hours into my 'mission' and we were already acting like a pair of school-kids.

God help me.

Niki licked his lips and sat back with an expansive sigh, throwing an arm carelessly around my shoulders as he waited for the show to start. We didn't have to wait long. Before I could come up with a plan to get away from the horrors I was apparently about to see, an echoing fanfare sounded. Despite myself, I sat up straighter in my seat and peered into the ring, clutching at the metal barrier in front of me. As the fanfare reached a peak, a cheer went up around the stadium.

People started chanting and yelling, stamping their feet on the wooden boards.

Their cheers turned to rapturous applause as ten-foot-tall fireballs shot up from the banks of giant pyro-machines that ringed the arena, crashing up towards the ceiling in a blast of black smoke. JumboTron screens flared into life on all four sides of the ring as the in-house camera crew took up their positions, dutifully zooming in on the action for the watching crowd. Before the flames had fully died down, the giant silver doors at the far end of the ring flew open with a loud BOOM and an armored female figure on horseback galloped into the arena.

'Ladies and gentlemen,' cried a female voice over the PA. 'Welcome to the Circus of Sins, LA's premiere entertainment destination. Let's hear it for our performers tonight!'

The audience exploded into applause, then started chanting a name over and over.

'Who's that?' I asked, having to shout to be heard over the cheers of the crowd.

'Libitina,' Niki replied, leafing through the program. 'In Roman mythology, she was the Goddess of Death. She would appear as a dark robed figure and hover over the dying on the battlefield. When the moment came, she would seize their soul as it departed the body, and take it to the afterworld.'

'Teacher's pet.'

'I Googled it, bitch,' Niki grinned.

I sat back anxiously and watched as the woman galloped around the ring on her horse, tailed by a number of dark-robed figures who went into the audience bearing large silver pans. I saw people depositing large rolls of dollar bills into the pans.

'What are they doing?' I asked, craning to see.

'An ancient tradition,' said Niki. 'When someone died back in olden times, it was traditional for their family to leave a silver coin in Libitina's temple, to thank her for carrying their soul to safety. If they didn't, Libitina would pay them a visit soon after to take their own soul instead, as payment.'

He reached into his own pocket and withdrew a slim roll of what I took to be dollar bills. He peeled ten of them off before I realized they were hundreds. I couldn't help but stare, wide-eyed, as he rolled up what was easily twice my monthly rent, secured it with a rubber band, and tucked our numbered seat-ticket inside. I jumped as a dark robed figure leaned into the top of our little booth, holding out his pan and barking a command in a language I didn't recognize. Niki responded in the same strange flowing language as he dropped the roll in. The figure's eyes lit up beneath his cowl.

I could've sworn he winked at Niki before he left.

Down below, the action was in full swing. The arena doors opened once again and a dark stream of horsemen rode into the ring, circling the arena to the accompaniment of a heavy metal anthem, played at ear-splitting volume. I was already glad of the ear-plugs.

The horsemen's faces were obscured by silver masks, and they each carried a fearsome-looking grappling hook: a four-foot-long steel pole with a pair of reversed spiked prongs on the end.

I swallowed. Already, I didn't like the look of this.

'Ever read *Dante's Inferno?*' asked Niki casually, leaning his head on my shoulder.

I shook my head, my gaze riveted to the show.

'Dante Alighieri,' Niki explained, idly stroking my knee. 'Italian poet, lived in the middle ages. Big inspiration to us in creating this club. He wrote a book called *The Divine Comedy,* a couple hundred years back. It was about his pilgrimage through Hell to Purgatory, ending up in Paradise.'

'Niki. You read a book? I'm impressed.'

'Do you want to hear the story or not?'

'Fine, fine. So this show is based on his book?'

'Correct. The act is a theatrical interpretation, in three parts. This week, we're doing 'Purgatory.'

My vampire friend gently traced the seam of my lacy fishnet tights with his fingertips, not even bothering to watch the show. I guessed he had seen it many times before.

'Now, Dante had some very specific ideas about Hell,' Niki continued, almost deliberately avoiding my gaze. 'He divided Hell into seven different levels, one for every kind of sin.' He drew his fingernail up my knee, just pressing hard enough to leave a raised white scratch on my skin. 'The first four levels were Upper Hell, which contained people who had committed what he called sins of Incontinence.' His fingernail moved down my leg, drawing a second line until it hit the top of my calf-length boots. 'The last three levels are Lower Hell, which contained people who'd committed what he called sins of Malice.'

Niki turned to direct my attention back into the ring.

'See the horsemen are forming two ranks over there?' He pointed. 'They represent the two halves of Hell that Dante envisioned, Upper Hell and Lower Hell. Now. Incontinence—' he cuffed at me as my mouth twitched in amusement at the word, '—the *old* meaning of the word, means the human refusal to moderate a natural instinct, like desire or hunger. The gluttons, the adulterers, the drunkards, the scoundrels.... these people are said to have committed the mildest of the seven different kinds of sins, so they're punished accordingly.'

'Punished?' I didn't like the sound of that.

Down on the stage, the armored riders dismounted and danced around the mountain as they acted out the various sins, falling down, drinking, tearing off each other's clothing and chewing on enormous turkey legs in a parody of gluttony. The audience roared with laughter. Niki looked up at me, his eyes dark.

'Someone committing an act of Malice, on the other hand, has no intention to do good in the first place, and is thus immune to reason. The murderers, the rapists, the bribers, the swindlers... their punishment is the worst, and they're forced to spend Eternity in Lower Hell.'

Down in the ring, a dark stream of robed assistants returned to the arena and led the armored 'sinners' up the winding dirt track which surrounded the giant mound of earth in the center of the arena, positioning several people on each of the seven levels with jabs of their spiked poles. One by one the 'sinners' ripped off their horseriding armor to reveal...

The crowd gasped. Beneath their armor, the riders were naked.

And they were all female.

'Vampire riders,' said Niki, winking at me. 'They don't need insurance.'

'I'm sensing a theme here,' I muttered.

I watched as the beautiful women turned to face each other, their long dark hair flowing around them, backlit by the jumping flames from the pyro machines. A smattering of unsure-sounding applause and hoots from the men rang out as they started climbing the giant mountain of earth. Once at the top, they turned to face the cameras and began to kiss and embrace one another, twining their bodies around each other.

Down below the giant flames blazed higher, sending a curtain of flame boiling up both sides of the mountain. Spectators— mostly the men — rose to their feet, whooping and yelling with approval.

'You might have heard of the seven deadly sins,' Niki went on, not taking his eyes off the spectacle. 'In Dante's vision of Hell, each sin is punished on a separate terrace of a giant mountain of earth on a remote island— Mount Purgatory. Dante believed the island was created with earth taken from the excavation of Hell.'

I jumped as an almost comically large red warning beacon begun flash overhead. A set of oversized sprinklers went off, putting out the flames that ringed the mountain. The riderless horses formed a ring around the mountain and turned outwards, snorting and pawing at the earth, as though guarding the circle of writhing female flesh which formed a pale pool in the top of the muddy mountain of earth. The water from the sprinklers had already turned the earth around them to mud, and the naked vampire women slipped and slid around on it as they exchanged lovers, gleeful hands clutching at one another's pale flesh with unholy abandon.

Every camera in the room zoomed in for a close-up, flashing X-rated images up onto the four great JumboTron screens.

The audience applauded, although a little hesitantly. I saw at least several girls elbow their boyfriends sharply in the ribs, who were staring with just a little too much enthusiasm at the live vampire porn show going on beneath them.

'Now,' Niki went on. 'In *Dante's Inferno*, if a sinner genuinely desires to repent, they are escorted to the mountain of Purgatory by an angel, to begin penance for the crimes they committed in life. Once they are put on the correct level, they must then accept their punishment, in order to stand a chance at one day getting out of Hell.'

'How do they repent?'

'Each sinner is punished in a fashion according to their sins. You see, Mr. Alighieri was very big on poetic justice, on allegory. Thieves have their hands cut off so they can't steal again. Those who commit crimes of Lust or Wrath are set on fire for all eternity, as their passions and anger burned them up in life. Those who commit crimes of Rape or Murder are perpetually torn apart by thousands of hands, just as they tore their victim's lives apart with their own sinning hands. And those who Covet are condemned to haunt the earth as spirits, unable to feel or touch, forever separated from the object of their desire.'

'I bet that Mr. Alighieri was popular in high school.'

'I'm sure. Now, to save their souls, the sinners must gradually make their way up to the top of Mount Purgatory, purging a sin on each of the seven levels, before they can pass through the Garden of Eden and ascend to Heaven. When they're at the top, the angel that guards the gate uses two keys to open the gates: silver for Remorse, and gold for Reconciliation.'

Niki paused, scanning the ring.

'Ah. Here she comes now.'

But I was no longer listening. All I'd heard was that one magic word.

*Angel.*

No. It couldn't be. Surely not even Harlequin would be that arrogant...?

I sat bolt upright as the auditorium's ceiling parted, breaking into two halves along a mechanical fault-line. There was a scream loud enough to wake the dead, then a pale, naked, female figure was rudely dropped from the very center of the ceiling, plunging downwards through a vortex of stunt-smoke.

She flailed around helplessly as she fell seventy feet to the ground, her jet-black hair spooling around her like smoke.

My heart stopped. There was nothing to break her fall, and the ground beneath her was solid packed dirt. I leaped to my feet along with half of the crowd as the screaming woman fell headfirst towards the ground...

A second before impact, a bright white light snapped on around the woman, almost like an aura. She thrust her arms out before her and screamed again as two furled skeletal shapes burst out from between her shoulder-blades, lengthening and broadening into two feathered wings. A gasp went up as she flapped them downwards once, breaking her fall. A second mighty flap righted her and lifted her up into the air.

And then she was soaring, flying, circling the ring to the accompaniment of slightly shaky applause. As she passed by us at a low altitude I distinctly heard the torrent of breathless, furious curses pouring from the naked woman's lips as she flew, and realized that not all the performers in this circus act were voluntary.

I clutched the metal barrier and gazed up at her as she flashed past overhead.

*A winged woman. Could it be…?*

I hardly dared to hope.

I frantically seized the show program and began thumbing through it. At the very back of the book, among a dozen biblical illustrations showing Mount Purgatory, was the usual list of cast and crew. My finger flew down the list of unfamiliar names, and stopped dead beneath one particular name, overlaid with the picture of an angel.

'Doll,' I breathed.

# CHAPTER EIGHTEEN

MY HEART POUNDED. *I'd found Doll!* My vision swam a little as I stared down at the name printed beneath a picture of a Greek angel. I lowered the program and looked up at the pale, naked winged figure slowly circling the arena, shaking my head in wonder. That was typical Harlequin, so Goddamned arrogant that he'd put his prize on display for the whole world to see rather than hiding her away.

I had to hand it to the guy. He had one hell of a nerve.

I rose to my feet, staring in fascination as the cameras zoomed in for a close-up on the big screens.

Doll was beautiful. Her body was almost the definition of human female perfection, all tight curves and ivory-white skin. Her limbs were long and clean, her black hair silken, her breasts full and round. I couldn't see her face from this distance, but I was sure it was as gorgeous as the rest of her. A collective sigh went up from the mainly male portion of the audience, earning itself another mass punch-on-the-arm by a dozen annoyed girlfriends.

But the angel's beauty was marred by the way she held herself as she flew. She looked so tired, so defeated, so *human*, dipping almost halfway to the ground between flaps of her long, feathered wings, a dainty, almost breakable figure compared to the vampire women still merrily cavorting at the top of the mountain. She gave a last great flap and alighted on the top of the earthy mound, folding her wings. I sat up in my seat, leaning forward in excitement. I needed to talk to Doll ASAP, to warn her of the danger she was in. But how?

I sensed eyes on me and turned to look at Niki. He was lounging back in the love-seat, watching me intently. He couldn't have looked more smug if he'd tried.

'See anyone you know in there?' he asked, picking his teeth with his program.

I tried out several responses in my head, trying to keep my face as blank as possible. Niki was a vampire, and from what I'd been taught, vampires were notorious tricksters.

How safe would it be if he knew everything? What if he knew that rescuing Doll was the key to saving the world? And more to the point... how had he known that I'd been looking for Doll at all?

I didn't like this at all.

Before I could voice my suspicions, a spotlight stabbed down on me from on high. I lifted my arms to shade my eyes from the blinding light, then groaned as I saw myself appear up on the two huge screens that flanked the arena.

Great. Public attention was all I needed right now.

I turned to direct a withering glare at Niki as two robed helpers materialized out of nowhere beside me.

I remembered Niki tucking our ticket into the roll of hundreds. Had that been a bribe? What the hell was he thinking? Yes, I needed to talk to Doll, but not out in public like this!

The robed men seized my arms and started hauling me down the steps towards the arena. Niki's smile radiated innocence as he gave me a happy little wave.

I already wanted to kill him. So much for my covert operation.

'Ladies and gentlemen,' boomed Libitina, over the speaker system. 'We will now be taking a short fifteen minute break before the main act— the trial of the Sinners! Till then, sit back and enjoy our half-time show. Please welcome our first human volunteer of the night, and put your hands together for the legendary Tommy Tombdigger!'

The audience rose to their feet cheering as the main doors were blasted open in a spray of green glitter. A giant monster truck flew out, engine revving. It was painted a bright neon green, with glowing green strip-lights welded beneath. Even my unwanted abductors paused to watch as it landed on its huge front tires and rebounded in a spectacular spray of mud. Flashes went off all around the arena like glittering limelight as cameras went off *en-masse*. The monster truck flew to the middle of the ring and spun in a crazy circle like a mad dog, smoke pouring out from its huge engine.

The crowd went nuts.

I stared up at the man-sized cage balanced on top of 'Mount Purgatory,' and I groaned as I realized what was about to happen to me. Even when the world was at stake, I'd rather die than be a willing volunteer in audience participation.

I turned away, tried to break free from the robed helper.

'Calm down, Kayla,' Niki was suddenly behind me, following us down the steps. He dropped his voice and leaned in close. 'You wanna talk to Doll or not? That woman is locked away like Rapunzel for twenty-three hours a day. Not even I can get close to her. This is your one and only chance to meet her, say whatever you need to say to her.'

'Fine. What do I do?'

Niki pointed to the arena, where Doll was standing at the very top of the mountain beside the cage, as though waiting for me. 'Smile for the cameras,' he said in a low voice, his face carefully blank. 'Don't pick your nose. And for God's sake don't tell anyone your real name.'

One of the robed assistants touched a finger to his two-way headset. 'Stunt-guides in position?'

Niki nodded briskly. 'All clear.'

'You'll burn for this,' I growled, taking a swipe at him. 'I'll flambé you myself.'

Niki grabbed my hand and kissed it.

'Just trust me. You'll be fine.'

'That's just the problem. I don't trust people.'

Niki shrugged, his eyes bright with secrets. 'Your loss.'

I MUTTERED DARK things under my breath as I was propelled down the steps and through the two-foot-thick door that led into the ring. It was hard to stay calm as the two robed assistants led me through the mud to one side of the arena, opposite the mountain of writhing female bodies, which I tried my best to ignore.

I looked upwards as I felt a cool downdraft brush over me. Doll was hovering overhead, staring down at me. One of the assistants had thrown her a white satin robe to cover her nakedness, and she was buttoning it up with slow dignity as she hovered, waiting for the half-time break to end and the next part of the show to begin.

I cleared my throat, throwing a furtive look up at the cameras. I had to talk to her, warn her that Harlequin planned to kill her at midnight on Sunday night. Even earth-bound angels were incredibly powerful, Ninette had once told me. If she knew what was about to happen, I was sure that she'd have no difficulty escaping.

But how could we talk with all these people watching?

Before I could come up with a plan, Doll gave a flick of her wings and banked steeply away from me, circling the mountain of earth. She returned moments later carrying the giant silver birdcage, which she carried like it was made of lightweight foam. I saw that the cage had no bottom. I looked down with a sigh to see that I was standing on a raised concrete circle marked with a big red 'X'.

Story of my life.

I stood very still as Doll hovered above me, blasting my hair into my eyes with the downdraft from her great white feathered wings. She expertly lowered the cage around me as though she had done this a thousand times. The robed helpers hurried over to lock it into place, snapping iron rings closed around its base. I noticed the cage had no door, and wondered just what exactly this little 'audience participation' trick would involve.

As the guards ran for cover, I gripped the bars and craned my neck upwards to peer at Doll, who had landed on top of the cage and was perched there like a giant bird.

'Hey!' I hissed, practically dancing with excitement. 'You're Doll, right?'

Doll didn't reply. Instead she shifted, stretching out her wings until they quivered, each wing-blade poked through slits cut in her white satin robe. She sat down and swung her perfect feet over the side like a little girl, chewing on her nails.

I couldn't help but stare at the wing that hung in front of my face. Each flight feather was nearly as long as my arm, and glowed with a pearly whitish-blue sheen.

I shook my head. I'd just kissed my first vampire, and now I was getting to meet my first real angel.

*Amazing.*

Doll leaned down to glance listlessly into the cage, her black hair sliding half over her face as she looked down at me. I noticed a cryptic-looking black tattoo scrawled up the side of her neck, like a cattle-brand. Other similar marks were inked onto her forearms, shoulders and wings. I was about to comment on the brands when Doll pushed back her hair and turned her head casually into the light.

I recoiled as though I had been slapped. One side of her face was perfect, radiating light and life, the roundedness of her cheeks and brows betraying just how young the angel was. She looked barely into her teens.

The other half of her face was scarred, ruined. White razor-blade scars criss-crossed each other from her chin to her hairline in a shocking, almost deliberate-looking pattern of 'X's.

I hadn't noticed her face before now. She'd been too far away, and besides, when a naked flying woman goes past you, her face usually isn't usually the first thing you notice. I'd bet that not one of the men in the arena had noticed her face, either.

I stared at the ruin of her beautiful face, stunned, before finally looking upwards to meet her gaze. I shuddered when I saw the look in her eyes. Doll's mirror-like silvery blue eyes were empty, uncaring, drained of all warmth and life. They were the eyes of an automaton, a zombie. She peered in at me, looking through me, then slid a delicate hand down to touch one of the silver bars that imprisoned me.

'God loved the birds and invented trees,' she said softly, at length. She stroked her hand down the bar, then squeezed lightly. When she lifted up her hand, I saw a perfect impression of her fingers. She'd dented the solid silver. 'Man loved the birds... and invented cages.'

Her lower lip began to tremble, very slightly.

'But you're not in the cage.'

Doll rolled her eyes at me, then stood up fast and disappeared from view. I heard her moving around restlessly on top of the cage, pacing back and forth, muttering what sounded like Latin under her breath. I cleared my throat and tried again, glancing behind me anxiously as the green monster truck started to circle us.

'Doll, please! I need to talk to you about Harlequin. He's going to kill you!'

Doll's face reappeared briefly, her black hair hanging down over her pixie-like ears. 'I know.'

'You know?' I couldn't believe what I was hearing.

'Why the hell are you still here, woman? You have to get out of here!'

No reply.

I stared up at Doll for a long moment, then ran around to the other side to thump her wing through the bars, where it draped down over the side of my cage. She flicked it away from me and tucked it behind her back as though irked.

'Hey! I'm talking to you!' I hissed, trying to keep my voice down so that the black-robed helpers who stood nearby wouldn't overhear. They were leading the naked female 'sinners' out of the ring, and I wasn't sure I wanted to know why. 'Did you hear me? I just told you that you're going to die, and you just sit there—'

'It is the plan.' Doll stared straight ahead as she spoke. Her face smooth, emotionless. 'It is destined to happen. No mortal can change their destiny.'

'Are you mortal, then?' I asked her, then slapped at her wing again. 'Do you have any idea what's at stake here?'

'I know,' Doll said again, lowering her head even as she half-raised her wings as though to strike back at me. 'It is a price I am willing to pay to destroy the abomination.'

'What abomination?' I hissed back. 'We're talking about the human race here! They'll kill everyone if you don't—'

A loud thump shook the arena, followed by a blare of music and a bloodcurdling snarl.

'Showtime,' said Doll.

I turned to look over my shoulder, and froze.

A team of five burly vampire security guards had entered the arena through a side-door, each dragging a steel animal wrangling pole behind them. Each pole was as thick as a tree-trunk with a springy steel ring on the other end, like a noose. They tugged and pulled on their poles, but whatever was on the other end of those nooses was apparently reluctant to perform tonight. Three more security guards ran over to join them and they all pulled as hard as they could, dragging into the ring…

My hands tightened on the bars of the cage. A giant male werewolf was pulled through the door, bigger than any wolf I'd ever seen before. The half-time crowd leapt up, yelling and stamping their feet while I watched in dismay. I knew that werewolves never stopped growing throughout their lives. This old boy had to be over sixty to have reached that size.

That wasn't fair…

The heavy metal music kicked in and the creature spun around, frightened by the noise, dragging the heavyset vampire guards around with him as though they were children. One by one, the guards opened their nooses, dropped the poles and fled for the safety of the stands, leaving me alone in the arena with the werewolf.

But the wolf wasn't interested in the guards. The giant creature spun around and snapped wildly at the flashing lights, at the crowd, at the dry ice curling through the air, his hackles raised in rage. I heard doors slamming all around the arena, and realized that we were now alone in the ring. Everyone else had gone. My blood turned to ice as the wolf lifted his nose to the breeze and gave a single, sharp sniff, before slowly swiveling around to home in on the one human target that remained in the ring.

*Me.*

# CHAPTER NINETEEN

I YELLED AND pressed myself back against the bars as the werewolf spun around and charged me, tearing across the arena like a flesh and blood freight train. I was protected by the silver cage— in theory— but I'd seen first-hand the devastation these creatures could create. I knew right away that the cage didn't stand a chance.

Before the scream had left my throat I heard the roar and leap of an engine, and my heart leapt with it. Mud flew as the green monster truck hurtled across the arena and cut across in front of the charging werewolf, causing the wolf to switch target.

The werewolf spun on a dime and charged after the monster truck instead of me, drawing a smattering of polite applause from those still watching the half-time show. I held my breath, clutching the bars with a white-knuckled grip as the truck effortlessly jumped and leaped over a series of muddy troughs and ditches, the enraged werewolf hot on its tail.

People started laughing at the spectacle, throwing popcorn into the ring.

I pressed myself back against the bars, wiping the sweat out of my eyes with a shaking hand. I wanted out of here, right now, before the werewolf came back. What the hell was Niki thinking, putting me in danger like this? If he really did own this club, why hadn't he just taken me backstage after the show so I could talk to Doll... unless either he was lying about owning the club...

A sudden gasp from the crowd drew my attention. The monster truck was in trouble. Big trouble. It had misjudged a jump and come down too hard on the packed-earth ramp, snapping its rear axle. One back wheel spun crazily in the mud while the other turned inwards at an angle, acting as a brake. Smoke poured from the overheating engine as the frantic driver hit the gas again and again, trying to rock the truck to the safety of the arena doors... just a few dozen feet away from the charging werewolf.

The huge creature streaked towards the truck like a hairy brown bullet, barking and snarling. I could see right away that the monster truck wasn't going to make it. Shouts rang out and the main arena door flew open. Uniformed guards ran out, wielding huge tranquilizer guns. But before they could get anywhere near the truck, the pony-sized werewolf bunched his muscles under him and sprang, slamming into the side of the truck with such force that the entire rig was knocked sideways, rolling over and over through the mud...

*Heading straight for me.*

DOLL TOOK OFF with an alarmed whir of wings as the monster truck catapulted across the packed earth

towards me, spraying mud and water in all directions.
I yelled with all my might and pressed myself against
the back of the cage as truck and wolf rolled over and
over...

*Three times...*

*Four times...*

*Five times...*

I cowered back as it finally rolled to a halt on its
roof with a loud thump, its huge front balloon-tire just
tapping the bars of my cage, making it ring out like
a bell. Smoke hissed out from the engine and then all
was still.

My lungs started working again. I was alive. I lunged
to my feet, trembling, and stared at the stricken remains
of the crashed monster truck lying just feet away from
me on the other side of the bars. Its wheels were still
spinning at full speed, the gas pedal smashed and stuck
in gear. People in the stands were running, yelling,
flooding down towards the ring as the enormous wolf
shouldered his way out from under the wreckage. His
ears flattened against his skull in rage as he shook his
coat off and circled the wrecked truck, snatching and
tearing at the spinning tires like a hungry dog with a
giant chew-toy.

I pressed myself back against the bars. I could plainly
see the driver inside the smashed cab, hanging upside
down from his strap harness. The man was staring in
dazed horror out at the giant furry monster who was
tearing at his stunt truck as though it were a giant
can of lunchmeat. He yelled in fear as the werewolf
scrambled haltingly up on top of the truck. The huge
creature started digging at the undercarriage, his nostrils
twitching, his sharp claws easily tearing through the

lightweight fiberglass bodywork beneath to get to the driver. The buckled chassis creaked and started sinking into the mud under the giant creature's weight.

The strength of the werewolf was incredible.

I eased away from the bars, trembling, and looked quickly around me. Weaponless as I was, I couldn't just stand here and watch this guy get eaten. Guards with tranq guns were shouting and running towards the truck, but they were moving too slowly, hampered by the thick mud underfoot. They'd never make it in time. I muttered a quick prayer to the gods of idiocy, grabbed a piece of broken-off metal from the truck and started banging on the bars of my cage, trying to distract the wolf until the guards got here.

The wolf dropped the back tire of the truck and turned around to face me. His ears pricked forward with sudden interest as he lifted his great furred head, tossing his chin as he sniffed the air, homing in on my scent.

That was when I noticed that the big werewolf was blind. Two dark sockets stared back at me from under a shaggy curtain of matted brown fur.

I backed up a pace, feeling a stab of sympathy for the creature, but my pity was short-lived. As the wolf stepped towards me, snuffing at the air, the monster truck beneath it creaked alarmingly. With a horrifying creak the whole rig rolled slowly over onto its side, the lightweight stunt cab crushed down into the mud by the werewolf's shifting weight. I stumbled backwards as one of the great wheels slammed down into my cage, snapping the metal locks and knocking it sideways into the mud, exposing the open underside of the cage... with me still inside.

*Oh, crap!*

My heart was thundering as I pushed myself up out of the thick, cold, gritty mud that oozed up through the bars of the broken cage. I was out of the cage and on my feet in record time as the blind werewolf jumped down off the stricken monster truck and trotted towards me, nose lifted high to follow my scent, rumbling low in its throat. Werewolves have an incredible sense of smell, I knew. I'd also bet that being blind had sharpened this creature's nose like there was no tomorrow.

There was no way I could run. I could barely take two steps without falling over in the thick mud. I had to fight every screaming instinct to force myself to stand still as the huge creature approached me, step by halting step, his rumble hardening into a growl. I lifted my right hand, getting ready to throw a fireball. It would get me in deep shit to do magic in this public place with all these people watching, but my life was in danger here. They'd probably think it was part of the show.

I clenched my fists as the dragon-pendant around my neck heated up, waiting for the perfect moment to strike.

The wolf stopped five paces from me and lifted his great wet nose, blowing out his nostrils in a sharp blast. Close-up, I saw that the werewolf was going grey around its muzzle. He must be even older than I'd thought. He had a wiry patchwork coat that looked like it had been sewn together out of scraps of soiled shag-pile carpet. His blunt, intelligent face screwed up in concentration as he neared me, ears pricked up and whiskers pointing forwards in interest, chirping under his breath like a dog looking forward to a special treat.

I stood absolutely still, hyper-aware of the figures

running towards me from all sides in my peripheral vision. They were almost close enough to fire. Maybe I wouldn't have to kill him after all. The wolf was blind, I told myself. If it charged me, I'd just step to the side, like a matador with a bull in the ring. All I had to do was stay absolutely still until one of the guards with the tranquilizer guns reached me…

Too late.

The werewolf sprang.

# CHAPTER TWENTY

MY MIND WAS a white-hot blaze of fear as the three-hundred-pound werewolf hit me, knocking me back into the mud, its weight pressing me down into the black slimy ooze. I yelled as loudly as I could as gunfire sounded in the arena, as the guards peppered the ground around me with tranq darts. I fought and squirmed in the muddy slime and grabbed handfuls of the wolf's wet fur, trying to lift it off me.

The wolf growled and a hot blast of fetid air enveloped my face. I turned my head away, getting ready to fight for my life, trying to somehow shield my throat with my arms...

After a moment I realized that nothing was happening. There were no gouging claws, no jaws locking around my neck, no shark-sized teeth trying to chew my head off. The wolf was just standing there, one huge paw on my chest, looking down at me. I blinked filthy water out of my eyes and turned my head to cautiously glance up at the creature.

Had someone got lucky with a tranq dart?

As my vision cleared, I saw that the pony-sized head of the werewolf was hovering directly above me, muzzle pointed right at my throat like a sword poised to drop. I yelled in fear and seized it by the ruff, trying to lift it off me, but it was like trying to bench-press a full-grown horse. Ignoring my shrieks, the wolf delicately lowered its wet black nose to my hair and carefully sniffed me over with great interest, once again making that strange chirping sound of excitement deep in his throat.

I gradually became aware that a sizable portion of the crowd had returned from the hot-dog stands. The half-time break was over, and now hundreds of rapt faces were watching me. Some were munching popcorn. I realized they probably thought that this was all part of the show. I could see a corner of the JumboTron screen hanging above me, and had the curious out-of-body experience of seeing myself from above on camera, just a pair of kicking legs trapped in a tight black miniskirt sticking out from beneath a creature the size and shape of a brown bear.

I hoped to God that they weren't videotaping this.

As the sounds of running and shouting got closer, the wolf suddenly barked in what sounded very much like frustration and shoved his wet furry forehead against mine. I yelled out loud… then grew still with amazement as a voice, muffled but distinct, sounded in my head.

'…*stupid dumb broad. Do you have a death wish, little lady?*'

The wolf lifted its head and appeared to listen intently for my response.

'Huh?'

I stared up into the creature's creepy blind eyes, then shoved his great paw off my chest and scrambled to my feet, trembling. The wolf didn't try to stop me. I carefully began to back away, trying not to make any sound. The wolf followed me, step by step. On the monitor above me the camera zoomed in, showing a mud-spattered young girl with long, wet brown hair facing off against a giant wolf almost as tall as she was. I'd never seen a werewolf so big.

The wolf finally huffed in annoyance and pushed his face against my chest. The vampire guards were almost upon us.

'*...got to get out, now!*' The werewolf's voice rang out again in my head with a clear note of authority, making me jump. '*They kill us both!*'

I cleared my throat, feeling faintly foolish.

'How do we get out?' I asked it, as loudly as I dared.

'*Guide me.*'

I yelled as the werewolf suddenly shoved his strong snout under the small of my back and gave a mighty flick of his bulldozer-like head, tossing me into the air like a human pancake. I came down hard across his great hairy back, the breath hissing out of me in a bruised rush. I barely had time to seize a handful of the wolf's wet shaggy hair before he took off at full speed, pelting towards the ten-foot-tall glass wall of the arena, with me clinging onto his back.

'*Hold on tight!*' cried the wolf's voice in my head.

I hauled myself up into a semi-prone position on the giant creature's back, holding on for dear life as the creature headed at full speed towards the entrance gate. The crowd was by now on its feet, yelling and cheering. I saw a bunch of guys in the front row start laughing and taking pictures as we neared the wall, picking up speed. This was obviously much greater entertainment than they'd been hoping for.

I had other things to worry about, though. We were fast approaching the thick glass side wall of the arena, and the wolf showed no sign of stopping or turning.

'Turn! Turn!' I yelled, hauling backwards on his ruff and wishing desperately for some reins. The werewolf banked sharply right, almost spilling me off.

Doors around the outside of the ring burst open and a dark stream of new vampire guards in black armor ran into the ring. They did not look amused. They leveled sleek-looking weapons which they fired at us as we flew past, showering the wolf with tranq darts, but they seemed to have no more effect on him than mosquito bites. I yelped as a stray dart nicked my bare calf, breaking the skin before embedding itself harmlessly in my charge's thick, matted fur. Almost instantly I felt a heavy, drowsy numbness spread through my leg, flooding upwards into my body.

*Oh, that just made things so much more fun.*

More by luck than design we ended up heading towards the side entrance where I had originally entered the ring. I yelled a warning to my ride and threw myself flat on his back as the door flew towards us. The wolf put his head down and sped up. I realized he was going to try to smash his way through it. I put my own head down and braced myself for the impact. If I jumped off now I'd be dashed against the wall. We were seconds away when shouting erupted from the other side and the wooden doors abruptly swung open.

We thundered through the doorway in a storm of mud and flying fur. As we emerged from the other side,

I was startled to see Niki hanging grimly onto the huge door handle, holding the ten-foot-tall door open for me using sheer muscle power.

'Don't mention it,' I heard him call cheerfully in my direction, before he was wrestled to the ground by a dozen vampire security guards. The last I saw of him before he vanished beneath a mountain of angry vampire flesh was his ever-present grin, hanging in the air like a vampire Cheshire Cat. I saw the glint of handcuffs, followed by the blue flash and a sharp snapping sound. They'd just tasered him for helping me escape, but I was too mad at him to care why.

My angry thoughts shut off as we started climbing the steeply sloping stands. I was getting sleepy as the effects of the tranq dart kicked in, and it was getting harder and harder to hold on. The big wolf ploughed through the wooden crowd barrier, smashing it to kindling.

And then we were out, thundering up the steeply tiered seating area, panicked spectators fleeing on both sides of us like rats off a sinking ship as we headed for freedom…

# CHAPTER TWENTY-ONE

We didn't slow down until we were back out onto the streets. When you're clinging to the back of a three-hundred pound werewolf with two-inch teeth and a face like a lion with bad PMS, there're not really a lot of people who will try to stop you.

People had fallen over themselves to get out of our way as we'd bounded up carpeted steps, flown through red-painted lounges filled with panicking celebrities, and ended up in more than one kitchen full of the traditionally-scurrying chefs before finding our way back to the main door of the Circus of Sins. The staff in this place were obviously grossly underpaid, because not one of them even tried to challenge us as we tore through the plush entry lounge like a giant hairy missile. The tattooed bouncer even opened the main door for us, giving us one single, disbelieving look before returning to his porn magazine. He obviously wasn't being paid enough to deal with this shit.

Out on the streets, the werewolf slowed to a fast trot as we reached an intersection, mercifully deserted at this time of night. My entire lower body was tingling and numb by now. I didn't dare release my grip on my ride's shaggy back to look at my watch, but by the angle of the moon I guessed that it was at least midnight.

What a night!

Excitement and adrenaline fought a war with fear inside me as I weighed up my options. My mission had been beyond successful— I'd found Doll, got the inside scoop on the vampires' plans and got a great lead on Harlequin— but for now more pressing concerns came to mind. How the hell was I going to get away from this wolf? I couldn't assume that he was on my side just because he'd saved my life in the ring. What if he'd just picked me up to have as a midnight snack?

Taking a chance, I thumped my new friend hard on the back.

'Okay, old boy,' I said, trying my best to sound authoritative and non-edible. 'End of the line. Slow down there.'

Without ceremony, the werewolf jolted to a halt and sat down bang in the middle of the intersection, tipping me off onto the asphalt. I heard the sound of fast-approaching cars and leapt up in panic as headlights washed over me. My legs instantly gave out. They were completely numb. I pushed myself up and somehow rose to my knees, my legs shaking. I started crawling across the road at high speed to the safety of the sidewalk, which my legs decided would be a nice place for me to sit down for a while.

I sat.

After a moment, the big wolf started whining. He got up and sniffed around disconsolately for a moment before haltingly making his way across three lanes of the highway towards me, completely ignoring the two cars which slewed past him almost at right angles, tires smoking as they desperately braked to avoid the enormous mythical beast strolling casually across their right-hand turn lane. They vanished into the night with an angry blare of horns.

Thank God I lived in Hollywood. Most people knew that werewolves existed, but only on the same level that they knew terror groups and volcanoes existed. You didn't expect to bump into either one, strolling down the street in your safe little neighborhood. I hoped the drivers would assume that this was some kind of TV stunt.

I watched the werewolf approach cautiously, not afraid, but wary at the same time.

'You okay, big guy?' I asked.

The blind werewolf didn't reply, and I wondered if I'd been dreaming before when I'd heard his voice in my head. He stopped a few paces away and stretched out his neck towards me as I sat there on the sidewalk. I fought the mad urge to run as he took a couple of long sniffs in my direction, as though to reassure himself. He flopped down on the sidewalk beside me and gave a loud, nasty-sounding cough.

I looked over at him, buzzing with adrenaline, then gave a yip of fright as he made a grumbling sound and butted me with his head.

'What?' I asked him, shaking in what remained of my boots.

The wolf dropped his head in front of me and waited, giving a sharp *whuff* sound that sounded like a command.

Swallowing hard, I reached out a trembling hand

and scratched the werewolf between the ears in what I hoped was a comforting way. It couldn't hurt to make friends. His fur was so deep and dense that I had to burrow my fingers down a good four inches before I could stroke his head.

I was surprised to hear a deep, rumbling purr start up, low in the creature's throat.

I pulled a clump of mud out of the creature's ruff, my confidence growing, sizing up my chances of getting out of this alive. This guy was huge but aside from his bulk, he didn't seem in any rush to kill me. The feeling was already starting to come back in my legs, and I figured if he didn't eat me in the next five minutes I could try and make a break for it. I wiggled my toes, then winced as a painful rush of pins and needles washed down my leg. Thank God the tranq dart had only scratched me.

Before I could make good my escape my new friend lifted a giant paw and flopped it down across my knees, then put his chin on it and sighed again. It was like having a lion on my lap. His mouth dropped open and he started panting in an unhappy kind of way.

'Tell me about it,' I muttered.

I glanced up as a whir of police sirens sounded nearby. Judging by the speed they were driving at, one of the drivers who had almost hit my new wolf-friend must have called the LAPD. A black and white cop car pulled up beside us with a screech of tires. The wolf didn't so much as look up as doors slammed and two police officers leaped out of the vehicle, guns drawn and aimed at the wolf.

I threw up my hands, startled, shoving at the wolf that lay across my legs.

'Don't shoot! He's just having a nap!' I cried.

The older cop glanced at his partner, a younger blond guy with a crew-cut. 'Only in LA,' he muttered, clicking the safety catch off on his pistol.

The werewolf's head jerked up at the tiny metallic noise. He spun his head in the direction of the gun and snarled, a sharp blast of sound that rang through the deserted late night streets. He rose to his feet as though pulled up by strings, then gave a little hop and rose up onto his hind legs like a brown bear, facing off against the cops.

A howl tore from his throat as he raised a giant paw and poised to strike, his blind gaze locked in on the gun with unnerving accuracy.

The first cop fired out of sheer reflex. I screamed, dropping down into a prone position on the sidewalk as a bullet blew chips out of the stone wall behind us. My legs were still half numb. I couldn't run. I rolled over onto my belly and put my hands over my ears, looking up just in time to see the werewolf's body shorten and shrink down as he changed back to human form, his fur receding and his face flattening.

The cops stared at him in shock, mindlessly firing again and again, the bullets embedding themselves uselessly in the creature's thickly corded muscle.

Next thing I knew, a hulking, powerful-looking man was crouching nude on the sidewalk beside me, down on all fours. I stared up at him, frozen to the spot. He looked oddly familiar, but in the heat of the moment I couldn't place him. The two cops stood in matching poses of frozen disbelief as the man wiped blood from his lips and stood up. His melon-sized muscles flexed in the lamplight as he folded his arms and stared down at the terrified cops. There were two scarred holes where his eyes should have been.

'Is there a problem, officers?' he asked, with a toothy grin.

I watched the younger cop's mouth open and close a couple of times as his sanity wrestled with the plain evidence of his own eyes.

Eventually, he seemed to come to a decision.

'Nudity is not permitted in public in any part of the city of Los Angeles,' he whispered, his mouth apparently moving on autopilot as his eyes tried to flee from his face in two separate directions. He paled dramatically and started to sway back and forth, his gun trembling noticeably as he raised it to sight on the big man's barrel-like chest. 'You are under arrest for violating section twelve, paragraph four of the Californian State Law...'

The werewolf's hand came down in a quick striking motion, and suddenly he was holding the young officer's gun.

'Can it, Five-Oh,' he said without malice, then turned to me and gave me something like a wink. I stared at the scarred mess that surrounded the big man's empty eye sockets and gulped, unable to look away. Running was an option, but not one I would dare try right now.

'Do they have a car?' the big wolf-man asked me pleasantly in the same deep basso voice I'd heard in my head. He popped the clip from the gun and tossed it a hundred feet in the air with a casual flick of his wrist. I nodded mindlessly, still staring at the ruin of his face, then shook myself as I remembered he couldn't see me.

'Uh, sure.'

'That car is California State property!' blustered the first cop, pulling out his own gun and aiming it at the wolf-man as his buddy hung onto his arm and shook his head frantically *no*. 'You can't just take it!'

'Why not?'

My new friend gave an unnervingly broad smile as he calmly walked straight towards the first cop, not stopping until the barrel of the gun was pressed into his bare stomach. The cop blinked frantically, sweating as he tried to decide if he was going to shoot a nude blind man in cold blood for disturbing the peace, and for also possibly being a werewolf.

As he wavered, torn, the wolf-man casually closed his fist around the cop's gun and squeezed, jerking it from the man's grip. The gun went off with a muffled bang and I hit the deck with a yelp. When he opened his hand again, both the gun and the fired bullet were crushed completely flat. The cops stared. The wolf-man's wrist blurred and the disc-shaped chunk of metal embedded itself three inches deep in the wall with a *chink,* three inches from the first cop's ear.

'I'll drive,' I said, as the two cops turned and ran for their lives.


I'D NEVER DRIVEN a police cruiser before, but for some reason it came very naturally, almost like I'd done it before. I wondered whether my newfound Dark Arts powers had anything to do with it, or whether I was just getting used to being a law-breaking fugitive.

At least I could feel my feet again. That was a big plus.

I turned the wheel and headed out onto the midnight roads, my mind racing at a million miles an hour, sorting busily through the facts I knew and trying to ignore the fact that I had a big naked dude sitting next to me in the passenger seat. I was exhausted, and all I cared about now was getting home without getting pulled over. I'd save the world tomorrow, after a full night's sleep and something meaty and greasy for breakfast.

What a night.

The wolf-man sat quietly beside me as we headed away from the bright lights of downtown LA, driving through West Hollywood on our way back to Mia's house in Beverly Hills. It was the only safe place I had left to go right now.

I glanced sideways at my new friend from time to time, trying to place his face. It was too broad and hard-bitten to be a friendly face, but there was something very likeable about it. He reminded me of a mob-boss from an old Hollywood movie, with broad cheekbones, a nose that by the looks of it had been broken too many times, and scrubby brown hair running to salt-and-pepper at the temples.

It was a face you could comfortably bank with, a face that would lend you money when you were in a crisis and demand it back two weeks later along with a down-payment of three of your fingers. A ferocious bell was ringing in my mind, but I couldn't for the life of me remember where I knew him from.

Occasionally the wolf-man would cough with a hacking, wretched sound, then wipe at his mouth and go back to staring blindly out of the window.

'I'll tell you one thing,' he said eventually. His voice was deep and gravelly, with a hint of a Detroit burr to it. 'Mutt was right about you. You're one hell of a woman.'

The police car swerved violently. It was a few moments before I could speak again.

'I wondered why you didn't kill me,' I said, with considerable relief. 'You're one of Mutt's friends, yes?'

The man laughed at that, an ironic, bitter sound that didn't sit well with his friendly-looking face. I shifted uneasily, glancing at him sidelong as he leaned in close as though about to tell me a secret, his face just inches from my ear.

'Tell me something, little one,' he said, his voice rumbling with black amusement. 'How can it be that you're still alive?'

'Pure talent,' I replied automatically.

'That, and the fact that you're a werewolf,' said the big man with a grin.

I actually felt the blood drain from my face.

'How could you tell?' I asked, eventually. 'You're…' I couldn't bring myself to say the word 'blind.' I gestured helplessly towards his empty eye sockets.

'You don't need eyes to see,' replied the man airily, stretching his giant hairy arms until the joints popped. 'I could smell you as soon as I got into the arena.'

'Hey! I showered this morning!'

'I don't mean you smelled bad, dingleberry. I mean you smelled like a werewolf. You're not quite there yet, but you're close.' The naked man settled back on the seat with a sigh, tugging the cop-jacket we'd found in the back across his lap. 'We can track the scent of one of our own from a mile away. We can even hear each other's thoughts, after a fashion. Aw, shit.' His face went blank, and he started sucking experimentally at his back tooth. 'Hold your horses. I think I just screwed up.'

He snapped the metal indicator-lever off the cop car and stuck the sharp end into his mouth. I glanced at him sideways again as he prodded around amongst his overlarge incisors as though picking his teeth.

'Got it,' he said.

He twisted the lever in his mouth and something gave a horrible little crack. He didn't even wince. Blood trickled from his lips as he rooted around inside his mouth and pulled out part of a broken-off tooth. He held it up into the light. I flashed a quick look sideways at it as I drove and grew very still. There was a pea-sized silver device implanted into a channel drilled on one side of it.

The wolf-man wound down the window and tossed the offending molar out.

'Tracking device. You can't be too careful with these sons of bitches. Once they've got you, they've got you for good. Now,' he turned back to me, wiping blood from his lips. 'Where was I?'

'You said werewolves could hear each other's thoughts.' I looked at him in sudden excitement. 'I heard your voice in my head, back in the ring! Was that because I'm a werewolf too?'

The older man smiled. 'I can see you've got a lot to learn about us. Yeah, we can read each other's thoughts at short range, twenty feet or less. It's called the Pack Mind. Helps us co-ordinate as a pack, take down prey. Newbies take a while to tune into it.'

He turned his head to stare at me pointedly.

'What?' I asked, after a moment.

'Less observant wolves might not notice, but I know the scent of someone holding back the change. Tell me, how are you puttin' it off so long?'

I blinked furiously and tried to focus on the road, on the simple and comforting mechanics of driving. I didn't want to be thinking about my impending transformation right now, on top of everything else.

'Best not to ask,' I said, then quickly changed the subject. 'So what were you doing in the ring? Did Harlequin catch you, too?'

The big man stiffened. He slowly turned towards me, the look on his blind face downright threatening.

'What do you know of Harlequin?'

'Enough to know that someone has to stop him.'

The wolf-man nodded gravely at this, sinking back in his seat and touching his thumbnail to his lip. It was a long time before he spoke, and when he did his voice was flat, drained of all emotion.

'You wanna stop Harlequin? You can't. You'll be dead before you get within ten miles of the ugly bastard. Only one guy's got the cahoonas to go head-to-head with the big guy, and he's almost as bad as Harlequin himself.'

'Who is he?' I asked, sitting up straighter in my seat. 'If you could give me a name, some contact details…'

The wolf-man laughed.

'I don't think you'll want to go anywhere near him, sweetheart,' he said. 'You might have heard of him. His name is Harlem.'

My heart sank.

'No good,' I said, deflating. 'I want that guy dead too. He ate my boyfriend.'

I gave a sudden giggle at how that sounded, then coughed my way into silence. Damn, but I needed to sleep. I never giggle unless I'm severely sleep deprived, and once I start it's very hard for me to stop.

'You want the moon on a stick now, don't you, little girl?' the wolf-man said. His smile was a little too wide and nasty. I felt suddenly uncomfortable sitting in the car with him. 'Perhaps you and I have something in common after all.'

'You want Harlem dead too?'

'More so than you can ever imagine,' the werewolf said fiercely. He turned his head away as the city lights flickered across his scarred face. 'Little sonofabitch ratted me up, some weeks back. Turned me in to Harlequin's goons, all for a couple hundred bucks reward money from the vamps. Never thought nor cared 'bout what they were gonna do to me next. I'll see that slime-bag dead if it's the last thing I ever do.' He reached up to touch the scarring over his eye sockets, his hand trembling with anger. 'Or rather, I won't see him.'

'I'm sorry,' I said, with feeling.

'Don't be. I got off lightly, considering. You work for the mob, you die by the mob, that's what I say. If you knew some of the things I done, you wouldn't have gotten into this car with me.'

He laughed softly under his breath, his chuckle turning swiftly to a wheezing series of coughs.

The lights of Mia's gated apartment complex were coming up swiftly on the right. I glanced into my rear-view mirror for the thousandth time, but the road behind us was hearteningly clear. As far as I could tell, we weren't being followed. It never hurt to be too paranoid, not where vampires were concerned.

I carefully turned into the driveway behind the complex and pulled up in front of Mia's empty garage. There were no cars inside it, which hopefully meant she wasn't home yet. I sighed, then killed the engine, put on the parking brake and turned to the big werewolf, taking his big calloused hands in mine.

'Can you help me?' I asked him. 'If you say I can't kill Harlequin, will you at least help me take out Harlem? He's the next one down on my little hit-list, such as it is.'

'I thought good girls didn't have hit-lists.'

'So did I.'

'Fine. It will be tricky, but not impossible.' The big wolf-man squeezed my hands, released them. 'You wanna kill Harlem, you gotta get through his wolf-pack first. Listen good, cause what I'm about to tell ya doesn't bear repeatin'. Here's what you gotta do.'

He settled back in his seat, folding his arms over his belly.

'Now. Skeet is the youngest wolf. He's a baby compared to the rest, but his big weakness is—'

'He's dead,' I said, a trace of smugness in my voice. 'We already got him, a couple weeks back.'

It was true. Skeet had been my first-ever werewolf kill, and the first time I'd ever killed a sentient living being. Actually calling Skeet sentient was like calling a tree emotional, but there you go. I still had nightmares about his death, but they were countered by the knowledge that one of the serial-killing bastards who'd killed Karrel was gone for good.

'You killed him?' The big wolf turned his head towards me in genuine astonishment. 'Well, that sucks. He owes me two hundred bucks. Shit.' He shook his head, moving on without question. 'His brother's name is Jackdoor.'

'The one with the wings,' I said, nodding. 'Another

one of Harlequin's little genetic experiments, from what I heard.'

'Correct, and an ugly one at that. But Jackdoor's a grunt. He should be easy to take down. He's dumb as a post and then some. You'll figure it out.' The wolf-man cracked his knuckles, leaning in closer. 'Next, there's Flame. Kid's an arsonist and a bible-basher to boot. And guess what? He's afraid of fire, if he's not the one causing it. Go after him with a flamethrower and he'll run away screaming like a little girl.'

'One flamethrower, check.' I mimed writing in a notebook on one hand.

'No need to be cheeky. Do you want to know how to kill these bastards or not?'

'Sir, yes sir!'

'That's the spirit!' The werewolf clapped me on the back so hard I nearly choked. 'Well. I guess that just leaves us with Harlem.'

'Right. What're his weakness?'

'That's the doozy. He doesn't have any.'

The wolf-man settled back in the seat, stroking his chin thoughtfully.

'See,' he went on. 'Harlequin engineered Harlem to be the ultimate monster, in the truest sense of the word. And he succeeded.' He looked at me sidelong, the light from Mia's apartment block throwing spooky shadows over his empty eye-sockets. 'You heard how those two freaks met?'

'No.'

'It was all Harlequin's idea. He wanted some grade-A scum to work with, to do his nancy-fancy genetic experiments on. So he busted into one of the toughest prisons in the country, swiped this piece o' work right off the electric chair, just minutes before they were due to throw the switch. Harlem was due to fry for butchering his whole family, from what I heard.'

'Model citizen,' I said, switching off the engine.

'You're telling me,' said the wolf-man, with a grimace. 'He told me his deal once, over a few beers. Back when we was friends. Of a kind.' A flicker of pain shot across the older man's face, quickly hidden. 'Harlem said he lived in South Central for most of his life, just like I did, ran with the same gangs. That was what bonded us. Harlem grew up with no money, an abusive sack o' shit for a father, cops constantly on his ass cuz his mother was a werewolf. They shot her right in front of him when he was twelve. That was what did it, what flipped the switch in him. He got back control in the only way he thought he could: by killing.'

He took a slow breath, turning away from me.

'See, if you're in a gang, killing equals bravery. That equals respect from your buddies, and there ain't no-one else 'cept them that's gonna respect you any other how. Harlem committed his first murder at thirteen, his first rape several years later. Really got a taste for it, from what I heard. By the time he met Harlequin he was pretty screwed up. Harlequin made things ten times worse: he gave him the gift of telepathy.'

'How would that make him worse?' I asked. 'Surely, if he could read people's minds, he could feel what they were feeling?'

'You're missing the point,' snapped the werewolf. 'Harlem kills people so he can feel superior to them, so he can feel in control of another person's destiny. It's basic nut-job psychology. He decides if they live or die, and he gets off on that. I seen a series on TV about serial killers—they got no empathy, says all the experts. Number one red flag. As kids, they kill animals, shoot their pets and walk away—don't feel a thing. They ain't properly human, like. But I digress.'

He licked his lips, stared straight ahead through the front windshield.

'If you want that muther snuffed, the only way you'll ever get close enough to him to kill him is to do a number on his head. Harlem is the biggest, meanest sonofabitch you'll ever meet, and he knows it. He's *proud* of it. He knows that's why Harlequin picked him to be his right-hand man. And that right there lies his only vulnerability. His Goddamned ego.'

'So I act all scared of him, and he'll let me live?'

'No, my dear. Quite the opposite. You wanta kill him, then don't show any fear around the sonofabitch. Ever. And do your Goddamned best not to feel it, either, if you can. That'll drive him abso-fucking-lutely nuts. He likes to make-believe that he's the biggest, baddest, scariest motherfucker you've ever seen in your life. No point in killing otherwise 'cept to get that rush, that boost of fear from his victim.'

'Right.' I was unconvinced.

'See, you don't give him that hit of fear that he craves, he'll hold off killin' you till he gets it, just to feed his Goddamned ego. Make him feel like he's the man. Daddy never loved me, and all that shit. I seen him do it a hundred times. Girls that coulda lived hours longer if they hadn't'a screamed when they did.' The wolf man gave a ghoulish grin. 'Know what I mean?'

I really didn't want to know, didn't want to be sitting in this car with this person having this conversation, but I ploughed on regardless.

'So he hates his father?' I tried to steer our little talk onto a safer track.

'More than you can ever know. He killed and ate him when he turned sixteen. Rumor has it you don't have to be a new-fangled geneticist to make your darling little boy into a monster. Know what I—'

'Yes, yes, I know what you mean.'

I shook myself, tried again.

'So in order to kill Harlem, I just tell him he's not scary, wait till he gets good and mad about it, then insult his father and hit him in the face with a big custard pie?' I shuddered. 'Great plan there, Batman. I'm in. Where do I sign up?'

'You already did, my dear.' The werewolf's broad face split in a horrible smile. 'From what I've heard, Harlem's got his twisted little sights on you. Kid likes a challenge, and boy are you his biggest challenge ever— not only did you survive two of his bosses' hits, but I heard that one of your friends took out his buddy, Rocco.'

The wolf-man shook his head, looking wistful.

'Like two ugly homicidal peas in a pod, those boys were. Used to go out drinkin' and carousing every night that God sent. And now Rocco's dead.' The wolf-man dabbed at his bleeding tooth with a corner of the cop's stolen jacket, grinning now with an unholy humor. 'He's going to take you out, one way or another, and I guarantee you won't enjoy it when he does. You gotta be ready for when he strikes.'

'Thanks for the advice, Pops,' I said with a shudder. 'Can I throw up now or should I wait till later?'

'Don't get cheeky.' The wolf-man leaned forwards and grabbed my arm, shaking me gently. 'If you ain't prepared then get prepared. The guy is a juggernaut, kiddo. I've seen him take a full clip of .45 rounds in the ass and keep going. Keep killing. Human weapons won't kill him. You gotta think smart to defeat him. Think you can do that?'

I suddenly felt very tired. 'Can I take a shower first?'

The nude man laughed and nodded, releasing my arm. I smiled back at him, somewhat shakily, but feeling like I was getting somewhere for the first time in weeks. My sneaky solo mission tonight was really paying off. I had a plan, I had new insider knowledge, and now all I needed was a good night's sleep and I'd be ready to roll.

The world was as good as saved.

'So what about Harlequin?' I asked, gently teasing my new friend. 'I've heard he's immortal. Let's say that I take out Harlem and his wolf pack, leave the Big Boss wide open. How the hell do I kill a two thousand year-old master vampire?'

'You don't. You'll need an army behind you to even touch the bastard.' The big man shook his head, his face grimly humorous. 'Only one man was brave enough to take that mother down by himself, and we put him in the ground. The guy's name was Karrel Dante. He was one o' them blasted Hunters. Killed over three dozen of my men before we took him down, and he died not a day too soon.'

A cold shock ran through me. I suddenly remembered where I'd seen this guy before, and fear poured through me like a sluice of cold water.

'Say.' The big man leaned forward, heedless of my abrupt switch in mood. 'You smell so familiar. I've been trying to place you. We've met before, haven't we?'

It was a struggle to keep my breathing under control as I leaned down to casually unlock the doors of the police cruiser, trying to be as quiet as I could. The lock popped up with a faint *thunk*. I stiffened, then looked up just in time to see the wolf-man's face freeze. I could see that he knew the answer to that question just as well as I did.

And he knew he'd screwed up.

Big time.

I TOOK A deep breath, getting ready to fling the car door open and run for my life. When you're trapped in a stolen police car with a giant naked man sitting next to you who used to be a werewolf, little things like thinking and breathing can suddenly become a problem.

'You're her, aren't you?' said the wolf-man finally, thumping his big fist down on the auto-lock mechanism in the squad car. 'The famous Hunter girlfriend? The one that knows the Dark Arts?'

'I never said that,' I replied, fighting to keep my voice steady. 'And you never told me your name.'

No reply. I popped the lock up again and braced my hand against the door-handle, getting ready to run.

'It was nothing personal, you know,' said the werewolf, after a long pause. He settled back in the leather seat with a creak. 'Your boyfriend was just in the wrong place at the wrong time.'

'That's what everyone keeps telling me.' I bit my lip, scanning the inside of the police cruiser for a weapon. A name finally flashed into my head and I paused. I had to ask, even if it got me killed. 'You're Magnus, aren't you? Harlem's pack leader.'

'I used to be.'

By now I was shaking so hard I had to clench my fists to keep my grip on the door handle. I pulled futilely on the lever a couple of times, then leaned forward and silently opened the glove compartment in the cruiser. I was in luck. An old-style police pistol lay on the gun-shelf. I reached out and wrapped my hand around the grip, popped off the safety catch, held my breath as I carefully lifted it to sight on Magnus's left knee...

'Won't do you no good to shoot me,' said Magnus, in the same easy, conversational tone of voice. 'I'll have your head through that windscreen before you can pull the trigger. Best chance you got to live would be to give me that thing, and run along home to your little wolf buddies. Leave this fight to the big boys.'

As I glanced instinctively up at Mia's apartment building, something hit my hand. I jerked it back and sucked on my finger, then my eyes widened as I realized that Magnus now held my gun.

I held my hands up quickly, staring at the gun. I hadn't even seen him move...

'Now,' said Magnus. 'If you so much as breathe a *word* to any vamps that come looking for me that you know where I am, so help me God I will hunt you down and gut you like a pig in your sleep.' He smiled suddenly, popping the catch back on the gun. 'But if you're anything like your boyfriend, I know that if you set your mind on a goal, you will achieve it. He went down fighting, I heard, your boy. Died a brave death despite being a werewolf-murdering bastard.'

He paused, laying the gun down in his lap. 'Now,

back to important issues. Can you kill Harlequin? Probably not. Can you piss him off? I'm sure you can think of a way. If you want a big hairy army to get in that guy's face and mess up some of his plans, save a few lives, you'll have the support of the wolves behind you. I'll make sure of that. Wolves hate Hunters, but they hate vampires a hundred thousand times more.'

Magnus broke into another fit of coughing. He bent over in his seat, his face contorted with pain.

'You okay?' I asked, after a moment. I meant it sincerely, although the words were like acid in my mouth.

Magnus shook his head. 'Lung cancer. Doctor said I'd be dead in a week, and that was three weeks ago. Shows what the hell they know. Anyway. Least now I get to die someplace other than that damned ring. Thanks to you.' He paused, and for a moment his broad, scarred face softened. 'I don't believe in second chances, Hunter girl, but you've given me something I've never had before. Something I sure as hell don't deserve.'

'Which is?'

'My dignity.' Magnus turned over the gun in his hands. A thought seemed to occur to him, and his mouth quirked up into a grin as he made a pantomime of looking down into his naked lap. 'Or a dignity of sorts.'

He put a hand on the locked police cruiser door and pushed lightly. There was a groan of tortured metal as the door popped off its locks, showering pieces of metal onto the sidewalk outside. Magnus slipped out of the police cruiser and stood silhouetted in the white moonlight outside, still nude, the gun still clutched in one hand. He raised his face to the breeze and took a long, deep breath of the night air, breathing in the smell of grass and mud, of distant woodlands, of the faint scent of the night-blooming jasmine.

He glanced back at me, just once, his empty eyes two pools of shadow in the moonlight.

'Thanks for that,' he said, and vanished into the shadows.

# CHAPTER TWENTY-TWO

THIS WAS GETTING to be something of a bad habit, I thought, as I slipped quietly into the marble entry hall of Mia's apartment complex, being sure to shut the enormous steel security gate behind me. I needed six numbered keys just to get into the place, which was annoying but in a good way. Anything that followed me up here would be no match for Mia's security system.

I grumbled all the way up the draughty steps, heading for the top floor. The feeling had come back into my legs now the effects of the tranq dart had worn off, but my favorite calf-length boots now wobbled as I walked. *Dammit*. My black skirt was torn on one side, and my red satin corset was soaked through with mud from the ring and covered in werewolf-hair.

So much for the glamour of saving the world.

I unlocked the big gate that led to the apartments on the top floor with yet another key from the big bunch Mia had given me, desperate to get inside in the warm. I was freezing cold and spattered with mud from my little romp in the ring, and my back was killing me from where Magnus had knocked me down in the arena.

A nice, hot shower had now become the focus of my entire existence. I only hoped that Mia owned a washing-machine. It was hard enough trying to save the world single-handedly, but trying to do so with no clean underwear would be downright impossible.

I was aching in a million places by the time I shut Mia's mahogany front door behind me, secured it with yet another dead-bolt, and began the slow process of doing up the numerous latches and chains on the inside of the door.

Finally, I could relax.

I couldn't get to the bathroom quick enough, pausing only to grab my meager bag of clothes and supplies from my suitcase in the guest bedroom on the way. Inside, I pushed the bathroom door shut and swiftly laid out my anti-werewolf kit beside the white-tiled sink, ready to take a new dose if I started to change mid-shower. I knew it was risky, but I wanted to put off taking my 'medicine' till the last possible moment, to stretch out the dosage for as long as possible. When it was gone it was gone. Now that the Hunters' laboratories were gone there would be no more meds for me, and pushing back my dosage every now and again there would soon add up.

Enough worrying.

I quickly double-checked that Mia's front door was locked, then ran back into the bathroom, pulled the door closed, grabbed one of Mia's plush pink towels and started sponging the worst of the mud off myself while I ran a hot, deep bath. I'd barely cleaned one arm when the towel ran out of clean bits. I dropped it on the floor and started on a second.

I was so deeply involved in my endeavors that I scarcely noticed the bathroom door creaking open behind me. I did hear the click of the latch, however. Panic knifed my brain and I snatched up the nearest weapon to hand, spinning and dropping to face…

Mutt jumped back, dropping into a defensive pose against the bathroom door.

'Kayla, please!' he cried. 'Not the Scrub'n'Rub! Anything but that!'

I glanced down at the bathroom soap spray in my hand, and tossed it into the sink with a scowl.

'You startled me,' I said, unnecessarily.

'No shit, Sherlock.'

Mutt raised an eyebrow as he saw the pile of muddy towels on the floor. He stuck his hands in his pockets and leaned back against the pink china basin, looking me over in concern. I glanced up at him briefly, annoyed at my date with the bathtub being delayed still further. I was dying to take my ruined corset off, but couldn't with him here.

I noticed that Mutt's hair was rumpled and his white shirt was torn to shreds on one side, revealing a tantalizing flash of his tanned, toned chest. A shiver ran through me at the sight of his bared skin, and I quickly turned away. I'd learned by now not to ask questions when Mutt showed up late at night in this state.

'I always wondered what girls did in the bathroom,' Mutt said with a grin, eyeing up my sorry pile of spare clothes balanced on the top of the toilet. 'I must say, I'm disappointed.'

'Been a long day,' I grunted, turning off the bath taps and reaching for my third towel.

'I can smell that.' Mutt eyed my mud-spattered form

with a touch of incredulity, hiking an eyebrow at me. 'What on earth happened to you? You get in a fight with a truffle-pig over the last pie in the shop?'

'It's just a bit of mud, clown.' I straightened up and looked Mutt over, dabbing at my face with the corner of the towel. Curiosity won out over common sense. 'And you can talk. What happened to your shirt? Get attacked by wild zombie cheerleaders again?'

'We, uh, stopped for a few beers on the way back from our mission.'

'And?'

'And... well, there was this cute girl, see,' Mutt touched my arm, then frowned and wiped his hand on his jeans. 'Funny story really. Buck double-dared me to try for a triple-pointer, but the ice went down this other girl's top by mistake, and it turns out she had a boyfriend who used to sub for the Chicago Bears, and—'

'Stop. I'll *pay* you not to continue.' I dropped my fourth towel onto the floor and turned to face Mutt, trying to control my impatience. My bath was calling to me with a siren's song. I just wanted him out of here. 'Did you even try to get any leads on Harlequin today, or did you just spend the whole night drinking?'

'No, but—'

'No?' I snatched up another towel in frustration. 'Mutt, do you know what's at stake here? I told you to go out and look for leads. You're supposed to be helping me save mankind, not wasting time chasing after girls!'

An image of Niki came guiltily to mind and I swallowed, feeling heat flood my face. I'd sent Mutt out purely to get him out of my hair so I could go see

Niki. But so what? My little ruse had paid off, apart from the whole 'nearly getting me killed' bit. And in my defense, at least I'd come up with a lead on Harlequin and Doll out of that whole drama...

I jumped as I realized that I was staring at Mutt, my head tilted, biting my lip slightly. I tore my gaze away from his bare chest with quite some effort and glanced around the bathroom, trying to distract myself from thinking Evil Thoughts. I seemed to have so many of them right now. I tried to think of how I could tell him about my lead on Harlequin without revealing how I'd got it...

I stiffened as I suddenly noticed my fingernails, which were resting on the edge of the sink. My nails were long and tapered, with the tell-tale pearly-pink sheen of werewolf claws.

My anti-werewolf serum was wearing off!

I quickly dropped my hands to my sides and closed them to hide my nails, cursing feverishly under my breath. I was supposed to take my twice-daily anti-werewolf shot at seven PM each day, but the excitement of my upcoming date with Niki had made me clean forget about it. And now here I was, trying to put it off even further. I was surprised I hadn't turned into a big werewolf pumpkin by now.

I turned quickly to go, all thoughts of my bath driven urgently from my mind.

'Can I ask you a question?' Mutt asked, dropping his arm down to grasp the bathroom door and almost accidentally cutting off my exit.

'Not unless you're about to ask if I want takeout. In which case, yes, absolutely. Get me two Big Macs and a triple order of fries, extra-greasy. And hurry, the place closes in fifteen minutes. Bye bye now.'

'That wasn't my question.'

'Do I look like I care? We'll talk *later*. My bath's getting cold.'

My gaze was fixed firmly on the door, desperate for him to leave. *I hadn't told Mutt about my werewolf bite. I hadn't told anyone.* I didn't want anyone, human or non-human, finding about my little 'situation,' and least of all Mutt. If Mutt somehow found out, within eight-point-five minutes every cheerleader, waitress, bar-girl and schoolteacher in a six mile radius would know. Then all I'd have to do was wait for Ninette to come back from Washington and gun me down in cold blood so I wouldn't tell the Hunters' secrets to the rest of the werewolves.

I had to get Mutt out of here, or I was doomed.

'We'll talk now.' Mutt couldn't seem to tear his eyes off my corset. He moved in closer, staring at me in fascination. 'Just tell me one thing. Why do you keep doing this?'

I folded my arms, refusing to budge. 'Doing what?'

Mutt smiled, that boyish, devil-may-care grin that had made me fall for him in the first place. 'Pretending you don't have any feelings for me?'

*Aw, Jeeze.*

'Uh... can we discuss this another time?' I said, then coughed, doubling over slightly. A fire sparked in my belly as the werewolf virus stirred inside me, yawning and stretching with casual menace. I had the horrible sensation of two red, fiery eyes snapping open inside me— the wolf was awake.

I had to get Mutt out of here.

Mutt watched me in concern, his head tilted as he watched me squirm.

'What was that?' he asked, pointing to my stomach.

'Bad enchilada,' I managed, pressing an elbow into my belly to blunt the pain of my churning insides. 'Look, I don't feel so good. I'm gonna grab a shower, have a lie-down…'

The rest of my sentence was lost because Mutt suddenly swung around and pushed me gently back against the bathroom counter. I leaned backwards in alarm as he put his hands on either side of me on the sink, grinning from ear to ear, his eyes staring quizzically into mine as though trying to actually see the thoughts inside my head. The familiar musky wolf-scent of him washed over me, making my head swim… or maybe I was just light headed with hunger.

'What?' I asked, defensive.

Mutt didn't reply. Instead he tilted his head and grabbed both my wrists as I started to push him off me, his face alight with some secret emotion in the pink-tinged light of the bathroom. He was looking at me in a way he'd started doing more and more often recently, much to my annoyance.

He wasn't actually smiling. It was more like he was trying not to. He seemed to be glowing on the inside, beaming at me with his eyes the way a content lion would survey its pride. That was the best way I could think of to describe it. I wondered what he knew that I didn't. Mutt gave a wry grin, his hands tightening on mine as though to stop me running.

'I'm sorry,' he said, not sounding sorry at all. 'I don't mean to keep doing this. I've just got this little problem I was hoping you'd help me with.' He moved closer, stroking my hair with one hand as his eyes sought mine. 'You see, I just can't seem to get you out of my system.'

'Traditionally, that's what vomiting's for,' I muttered. My stomach heaved and I tore free a hand and pressed it over my mouth, breathing hard. *I wished he would just go...*

'That's a "yes" then?' Mutt's lips brushed my ear.

'Look,' I said, leaning away from him. 'I'm very tired. We've got a long day ahead of us tomorrow, and...' I dropped my voice to a harsh whisper. '*And*, we've got that little matter of the world ending on Sunday night to deal with, in case you'd forgotten.'

I went to pull free then hesitated, glancing quickly outside the door. A nasty thought occurred to me. 'You didn't tell Mia about this Apocalypse thing, did you?' I asked.

'Nah. Figured it was a "need to know" deal.'

'Good. And she doesn't need to know—'

I tensed up as something in my back gave a jerk, as though my spine had suddenly turned into a serpent and was trying to chew its way out of my body. I bent over with a wince, disguising the move by pretending to stretch.

'But what if she could help?' Mutt reached out and touched my upper arm as I shifted in pain, rubbing it gently. 'People can't help you if you don't tell them what's wrong.'

I stared at him, my mouth open in surprise despite the pain of my rapidly mutating insides. I'd been so careful to keep my condition a secret from him.

As I leaned back over the basin, trying unsuccessfully to wriggle out of Mutt's grip, my eyes fell on a square red shape beside the sink. My heart dropped into the pit of my stomach.

I'd left my anti-werewolf kit out!

I quickly looked away before Mutt noticed me staring and worked up my most seductive smile.

'Mutt, be a babe and go grab my handbag for me, would you?' I pushed him off me with a burst of frantic strength and propelled him towards the door. 'It's in the bedroom by my bed.'

'Why?' Mutt's eyes flew around the bathroom. 'Whatcha trying to hide?'

'Nothing,' I lied, thinking fast. 'Hey, where's Mia?'

'Out on another date with that Goth friend of yours, along with all the other diversionary tactics in the book,' said Mutt with a smirk. 'Oh and by the way, I'm staying here tonight, with you guys, so don't try and kick me out like you always do. Motor's still pissed at me after yesterday, and I'd rather not deal with him tonight. You don't mind, do you?' he quickly added, really working the charm. 'If we're lucky, he might eventually forgive you for your Hunter friends trashing his place.'

I winced. It was emotional blackmail, and it worked.

'Was he really that mad at me?' I asked.

Mutt pulled a face in reply. He peered over my shoulder, scanning the sink area with beady eyes. His gaze fastened on the red Medikit case and his face lit up with interest. 'Hey. What's *that*?'

'Girly stuff. Not for the likes of you.'

Mutt's smile got wider.

He pounced.

I got to the Medikit a second before Mutt did. I snatched the kit up and shoved it into the open cupboard behind me, banging the door shut. I turned around to find Mutt standing exactly two inches behind me. I tried to slip to the side but Mutt leaned forwards, pinning me to the cupboard.

'Gimmie,' he grinned, breathing into my face. He grabbed my forearms with one hand and made a grab for the cupboard door with the other. He missed and I cuffed at him.

'No way… *hey!*'

'What?' said Mutt, leaning on me even harder. His hip dug into my stomach, and it hurt. 'I'm not even doing anything.'

'Oh my God, have you always been this annoying?'

I shoved him away from me, angry and flustered now. I was in too much pain to be civil. I ducked my head down and leaned back on the opposite counter in the tiny bathroom, glaring at him, trying not to show my teeth in case they'd grown, too. I was glad the bathroom light was pink as I had no idea what color my eyes were turning right now. My eyelashes felt weirdly longer, and my teeth itched as though tiny black ants were crawling inside them.

Mutt studied me with interest, one eyebrow slightly quirked as he tried to work out what I was hiding from him. As the silence grew between us I suddenly became intensely and uncomfortably aware of the fact that we were alone in the house together. That the front door was locked. That Mia was out for the night with Wylie.

That Mutt was much closer than I wanted him to be…

I caught myself staring speculatively at his muscular chest through the cloth of his torn shirt. I had to force myself to look away. The silence suddenly seemed far too loud. My eyes flicked up to Mutt's almost guiltily to find him already watching me.

You know that guy or girl you always feel awkward with when you're alone together? That's me and Mutt.

No matter whether you're single or married, looking or not looking, reason alone won't stop you from feeling the heat under that casual smile. It won't prevent you from jumping whenever their hand touches yours when they hand you a clipboard, a file, a drink. You know all the reasons why you shouldn't look, shouldn't touch, but you also know that just one simple word behind closed doors would be enough to spill that heat out into a full-bodied fire.

And yet...

And yet you don't.

Because that would be *wrong*...

As I stood there wrestling with myself, Mutt moved forward and stared frankly into my eyes, stroking my jaw with one hand.

'Just tell me what I can do to help you,' he said softly.

I had no answer to that one. Or rather, I did have the answer, but it wasn't one that I liked. Not one bit.

As I opened my mouth to reply, an almost overpowering sensation hit me, and it wasn't something I wanted to feel. The smell of him... the nearness of him... a light went off inside the more primitive, reptilian centers of my brain. I stopped dead in my tracks, staring at him. I jerked slightly, feeling my pupils expand and lock in on Mutt's jugular, which had suddenly became the center of my world.

I reeled backwards as I had a sudden, horrible vision of myself seizing his head, pulling his neck back to expose the soft flesh of his throat and biting down... *sever the spine to stop the struggling...* squeezing with my teeth until the blood flowed freely down my chin and bones clicked aside beneath my teeth, exposing the soft, warm, fresh meat...

I gasped and squeezed my eyes tight shut to dispel the horrific vision. I must be really close to the change. I was horrified to find that my mouth was watering, and swallowed quickly, turning away as my stomach growled. Right now, Mutt truly looked good enough to eat, and the werewolf inside me was screaming for blood.

'Gotta go,' I managed, my voice a hoarse whisper. 'Need to lie down.'

'Can I come with you?' Mutt whispered, his lips seeking mine.

'Not a good idea,' I gasped.

I caught his chin in my palm and pushed him gently but firmly away, fighting the urge to scream. I didn't want to hurt Mutt, but if he didn't get out of my face in the next five seconds flat there was going to be bloodshed.

Mutt tilted his head and grabbed both my wrists as I started to rapidly back up, his golden eyes sparkling as he watched me closely. I cursed his persistence. Any normal guy would've given up on a girl the night she threw him across the room and broke three of his ribs, but not this guy, no. I scowled and he beamed back at me, obviously mistaking my sudden urgency to get away from him as some kind of proof that I was interested in him.

Just my luck.

As I cleared my throat to break that uncomfortable silence, a sharp pain stabbed into my side. I winced as I felt my ribcage start to expand, sluggishly twisting as my chest cavity began to slowly change size, contracting with a ponderous slowness to wolf-size. I pulled one hand free of Mutt's grip and clutched at my back, squeezing down hard to blunt the pain.

'What's up with your back?' asked Mutt, studying me in curiosity.

'Nothing. I must've pulled something climbing over your ego on my way in here.'

'What, before or after you got in the fight with the truffle-pig?' Mutt released me and ruffled my hair with affection, breaking the awkward tension between us. He gave a sigh and looked me over with regret, seeming to finally realize he wasn't going to get anywhere with me tonight. 'You know, you should really speak with someone about these compulsions of yours, Kayla. It's not healthy to chase your dessert down the street like that.' He rubbed his hands together with a smile, eyeing me speculatively. *Oh no.* 'Here, get your shirt off and let me take a look at that back of yours.'

I was speechless for a couple of seconds, which was all it took for Mutt to grab me in a tight bear-hug. He pulled me in close to his body and slid his hands over my shoulders before I could move.

'Here,' he said, digging his thumbs into the muscle of my shoulder blade. 'Turn your head to the side and breathe out for a count of five.'

Without waiting for an answer he pressed down on my shoulder with one hand and pulled my hips sideways with the other, stretching my spine. It made a resounding cracking noise.

'Ow!' I clutched at my back. Magnus had really done a number on me when he'd flipped me up in the air in the ring. It did actually feel very slightly better now, but I wasn't going to encourage Mutt by telling him this.

I needed him out of here, right now.

'No, seriously. It's just a big old knot. I can fix that.'

Mutt perked up and studied the lotions I'd laid out by the sink with sudden interest. 'I've always been very good with my hands. You got any Lubriderm?'

I turned my head away from him quickly as a strange prickling sensation spread over my face. For all I knew I was probably growing whiskers as we spoke. I glanced fearfully at my distorted reflection in the silver edging strip on the shower rail and considered making a run for it.

'I'm not giving you anything with the word "lube" in the title,' I scolded, shooing him towards the door. 'Now scoot. The water's getting cold.'

'Chicken.' Mutt grinned at me, grabbing hold of the doorframe as I pushed him out of the bathroom with a strength born of desperation. 'Just tell me one final thing.' Mutt was silent a moment, still firmly gripping my arm, and I almost screamed. Mutt took an hour to get a thought out. I could practically hear him arranging the words in his mind.

'*If* we get through this,' he started slowly. 'And I know that's a very big "if"…'

'An enormous "if",' I panted, darting a longing glance towards the door.

Mutt looked down at me, his dark eyes unfathomable in the dim light.

'Do you think that there's a chance, even a little chance, that maybe, someday, you and I—'

'Could go out for a beer? Sure. I'd be happy to. I'll buy you all the beer you want,' I gasped. I had no time for this. My hand screamed with pain as I pressed the tips of my overgrown nails into my palm, fighting to keep the wolf inside me at bay. 'So glad we had this little chat. I gotta run now. Bye-bye.'

'Okay, fine. I'll let you take your dumb bath. You get all warm and relaxed...' Mutt wrinkled his nostrils. '... and clean, and then I'll fix your back for you.'

'Out.'

'Fine.'

I'd just started to close the door when Mutt poked his head back around the door, gazing past me thoughtfully. 'Do you have any massage oil? I think I saw a bottle in the cabinet...'

'I said *out!*'


As THE DOOR finally shut, I clicked the lock on and leaned my head against the door, breathing carefully. I opened my eyes a crack and looked down at my nails. They had grown at least another half centimeter while I'd been arguing with Mutt.

I prayed to God that he hadn't seen them.

I blinked in the pink light, fighting the urge to throw up. I double-checked that the door was locked and turned unwillingly to face the washbasin, dreading what I was about to do. I took a deep breath, then slid the small red First-Aid box from the cupboard and set it down next to the sink, moving as quickly as I dared.

Inside was what I'd dubbed my 'Staying Human' tool-kit: a bottle of thick red liquid that seemed to glow in the dull bathroom light, a bunch of single-use diabetes syringes I'd bought at the local medical discount warehouse, a rubber door-stop, and a long straight steel wood-file, like the kind I'd used in woodwork class to rasp down broken edges of wood.

First, the injection. I hated needles, but the alternative was easily a thousand times worse. I thought I'd be used to it by now, but I still had to look away as I slid the cold needle into the flesh of my upper arm and depressed the plunger as quickly as I dared, sending a double-shot of the thick red fluid coursing into my veins.

I'd let things go for far too long tonight, idiot that I was. The change had already gone further than I'd ever let it go before, and I was panicking. Right now I couldn't risk the consequences of letting it go any further, even if that meant using up my precious supply a little early.

I shivered and quickly jammed the doorstop between my teeth, biting down hard to blunt the pain of the burning fluid as it coursed through my veins. I could almost hear the ghostly howl of the caged wolf inside me as the lycanvirus rolled over, doing battle with the serum. It was like injecting myself with liquid napalm, but within a few horrible minutes, it was over.

I picked myself off the bathroom floor where I'd been lying curled up in a ball, spat the doorstop into the sink and rinsed the blood out of my mouth. Next, I lifted a trembling hand to my mouth and touched my lips, pushing them back with two fingers to reveal my teeth. It had been over twelve hours since my last injection and already my eyeteeth had started to grow, as they had every night at moonrise in the ten days since I'd been bitten. They curved downwards into two tiny sharp points a good half centimeter longer than the rest of my teeth. Unlike the rest of the transformation, this was one change that the serum couldn't completely reverse.

I hoped to God that my two friends hadn't noticed my teeth this morning. Mia was so shy she rarely looked me in the eye anyway, and Mutt's eyes were usually glued to parts of me that weren't anywhere near my face at the best of times. I felt confident that I'd escaped detection, this time, at least.

Time to fix that.

I wiped my forehead on the fresh black bandana tied around my left wrist as I steeled myself for the worst bit of my nightly routine.

I took a deep breath, then bared my teeth and reached for the wood-file.

# CHAPTER TWENTY-THREE

I SPENT A long time in the tub. I had a lot to think about.

By the time I got out, both the water and the tub had turned a truly alarming shade of Death-Swamp black. I had to run the shower for a good five minutes until I'd hosed all the clinging pieces of mud off the porcelain, and given myself a second rinse for good measure. The pain from my injection had worn off by now, and I had recovered from my panic attack. My nails had almost gone back to normal now, and my ribs had stopped trying to suffocate me. With my teeth nicely filed down I felt almost human again.

Thank Christ.

I was in the process of gingerly drying myself off on one of Mia's idiotically white guest towels when I heard a soft crackling sound coming from next door. Suspecting hellfire or possibly some kind of slime-demon thing breaking in through the floorboards after the week I'd just had, I hurriedly wrapped myself in a towel, unlocked the door and peeked cautiously through the crack.

I groaned. This was worse than slime-demons.

Far worse.

The gas-powered fire in the living room had been lit, along with a couple of candles on the wooden coffee table. A number of faux-fur blankets from Mia's bed had been folded in half and laid almost ritualistically on the floor near the fire, surrounded by a dozen giant throw pillows and a small pile of towels.

*Oh no. He hadn't.*

I noticed a large bottle of olive oil sitting on the floor at the head of the blankets, and banged my head gently against the doorframe.

*He had.*

As though he'd been waiting for me, Mutt stepped suddenly into my line of vision, rubbing his hands together with relish. He had a small white towel slung over his shoulder, and he'd tied his long hair back with a stolen pink scrunchie.

'Ready?' he asked, a huge grin plastered across his face.

'For what?' I stepped back quickly, pulling the bath towel tightly around myself. I peered over his shoulder, surveying his efforts with horror. 'Hey, that's the blanket off Mia's bed! She doesn't like anyone touching her stuff. She's going to kill you, you realize? And what's with the olive oil? You gonna give me a back rub or make me a salad?'

Mutt grinned at this. Before I could say anything else he'd stepped past me, pulled the bathroom door wide open and let a cloud of steam out into the living room. I pulled the towel tighter around myself and cringed back, feeling horribly exposed and vulnerable as he rooted through the mess I'd made in the bathroom, gathering up supplies from the shelves. He pulled a face at the sight of the bathtub before shooing me through into the lounge.

'Just let me clean the tub first,' I pleaded, turning to face him.

'You can clean up later.' Mutt's voice was soft, persuasive. 'Just relax and let me fix your back.'

'Relax? Around you? Are you kidding me?'

I was too intent on making sure my bath towel stayed in place to offer Mutt much resistance as I felt his strong hands guiding me across the floor to the thick pile of blankets in front of the fire. I looked down at them, feeling wonderfully warm and sleepy after my hot bath. I was exhausted from the stress of the day, my legs ached with the after-effects of the tranq-dart, and by now I was almost swaying with tiredness.

They did look very inviting…

Mutt dumped an armload of oils and sprays down beside the blankets, then dropped to his knees beside the pile and beamed up at me proudly, the firelight painting one side of his face a soft orange. He patted the blanket.

I shook my head. 'Uh-*uh*.'

'Kayla…'

'No way!'

A sly look came over Mutt's face. He glanced quickly behind him, then leaned forwards, dropping his voice. 'Fine. I'll cut you a deal. You lie down here for five minutes and let me fix your back… and I won't tell your little Hunter buddies that you're a werewolf now. Deal?'

He stuck out his hand towards me, clearly enjoying my shocked expression.

My mouth opened and closed like a stranded goldfish. It took me a moment to get some vowel sounds out. 'Does everyone know all my secrets?' I spluttered, eventually. 'Was there some kind of werewolf public service announcement earlier that I missed?'

'So it's true?' Mutt's mouth was hanging open in delight.

'I never said—'

'Haha. Thought so.' Mutt picked up the olive oil and shook it suggestively, a look of triumph on his face. 'On the blanket, bitch. Your ass is mine.'

'Bite me.'

'Fine. Your choice,' Mutt shrugged. He reached up to his ear and fiddled with something. I heard a scratchy crackle fill the air, and realized he was wearing my Hunter Bluetooth earpiece. My mouth fell open in indignation.

'Hello?' he said, finger pressed to his ear. He paused, listening. 'Yes, this is Mathius Corby, Unit D. I'd like to report a werewolf sighting in West Hollywood, at Lat thirty-four-oh-nine, Longitude minus one-eighteen, thirty-eight...'

He spun away as I made a determined grab for the earpiece, covering his other ear to listen. I heard a female voice bark a sharp question on the other end, and groaned to myself. Could this day possibly get any worse?

'Ninette says hi, by the way,' grinned Mutt, covering the mouthpiece.

'You little...' I broke off and glared at him as he extended a middle finger up at me, then revolved his wrist to point down at the blanket.

'You'll die for this,' I growled. 'You really are the stubbornest, dumbest, most self-delusional—'

'Speak up, Ni,' said Mutt, staring straight at me, one finger jammed in his ear. 'Yes, the werewolf's still here. It's in the room with me right now. And *Christ*, is it ugly—'

I took a second to knot the towel above my breasts before I charged Mutt, tackling him and bringing him down on top of the blankets. I sat astride him and made a grab for the earpiece, shoving his wrists aside as he laughingly raised his hands to defend himself. His laughter got louder as I snatched the transmitter from him and pressed the tiny oval silver earpiece up to my own ear, hardly daring to listen. My expression swiftly turned to one of outrage.

'That's not Ninette! That's Directory Enquiries!'

'Got you onto the blanket, didn't it?'

Quick as a flash Mutt shifted his hips and locked his jean-clad thighs around my waist, twisting his body in a perfect wrestling take-down move. I came down hard onto my forearms and rolled, making a frantic grab for my towel before it slid off me. Mutt smoothly shifted his position so he was sitting astride my back, pressing me face-down to the floor. I reached around to take an angry swipe at him as he shuffled further backwards, cackling gleefully, then rubbed his palms together and leaned forwards, laying his hands on my back.

Before I could protest, he rocked his weight forwards and pressed deeply into my muscle tissue several times. There was a wonderfully satisfying click between my shoulder blades, and the pain in my spine vanished.

I frowned, arching my back, then rotated my shoulder blade experimentally. It was pain-free.

'Huh,' I said, matter-of-factly.

'Better?'

'How did you… it's gone.' I twisted my head to look back at him. 'How did you do that?'

'Pure skill. Now lie the hell down and shut the fuck up.'

'Such a gentleman.'

'Not nervous, are we?'

Mutt smothered my growl by pushing me back to the floor again, slightly harder than I would have liked. He held me in place with his knees while he poured oil into his cupped hands, rubbed them together, and lightly stroked his hands up and down my bare back, spreading oil over my clean bare skin in a strangely calming motion. He sat upright on the small of my back and rocked his full weight backwards onto my hips, his lean thighs resting lightly on either side of me. I grunted lightly, wriggling as the sore muscles in my lower back stretched under his weight, releasing the tension that they'd held onto for so long.

'You want the full service?' Mutt's lips tickled my ear as he leaned over me. 'It'll cost ya.'

'Mutt…'

'Relax,' Mutt scolded, stroking my back. He put his fingers into the groove of my spine, feeling for knots, then put one hand on top of the other and pushed downwards firmly between my shoulder blades.

'Kinda hard with you sitting on me like…. *Guhh*.'

My spine popped a second time with a resounding crack, releasing the last kink. A wave of black warmth washed through me as the muscles in my back completely relaxed, and I sagged onto the blankets in relief. I blinked in unexpected bliss as Mutt slid his hands up an inch and repeated the procedure a dozen times in quick succession, pressing down firmly to pop each vertebra in my spine, one by one. When he finished, I felt more relaxed than I had in ages. He sat up over me and dug his thumbs into the muscle on either side of my spine, pressing deeply inwards.

'Good?' he asked.

I nodded, not trusting myself to speak, my eyes drifting shut against my will. It felt so good I was practically drooling.

Mutt worked his way up my back and turned my head to the side with an easy, practiced movement, quickly slipping a faux-fur cushion underneath me in the same move. He cracked his knuckles, and then poised his hands over my back like a pianist about to start a recital.

'Bring your hands up under your shoulders and relax them, palms up,' he instructed me. 'And quit tensing.'

'I'm not tensing!'

Mutt chuckled as I turned my head back the other way, watching him in the large gilt-framed mirror that took up most of the opposite wall. Despite my misgivings, I had to admit that he looked very professional as he sat up straight on my back, a look of intense concentration on his face. I watched him in the mirror as he locked his arms straight and pressed down hard on my lower back until it creaked and finally popped with a loud *clunk* sound.

The tension flooded out of me, washing down to the tips of my toes in a rush of warmth. I sagged down onto the furred blanket with a long sigh. I couldn't believe how much tension I'd been holding in my back. Mutt slid back a little and started massaging my back in slow, deep circles, moving upwards and outwards from the base of my spine to the base of my neck.

A groan slipped from my throat before I could stop it.

This was heavenly.

I lifted a hand to wipe more drool from the side of my mouth, conscious that I was staining Mia's cushions. I settled down again as Mutt leaned sideways with a smile, lifting a bottle of purple massage oil out of the pile. I caught the delicate waft of lavender as he flipped the cap up and tipped some onto his palms, rubbing them together briskly to warm the oil. He paused to quickly lift the shredded remains of his own shirt over his head, fanning himself in the warming glow of the fire, then went back to work on my shoulders. I caught a flash of tanned skin in the mirror and looked away hurriedly.

*Think innocent thoughts. Yeah, that was it. Baby seals lying in the snow-drifts... cold showers at the nunnery... Mutt half-naked and covered in oil and sitting astride me...*

*God help me.*

I swallowed uncomfortably, my breathing speeding up as I tried very hard to think cold, non-naked, non-oily thoughts.

'You're very tense,' said Mutt after a minute, prodding my shoulder experimentally. 'Any special reason?'

I shook my head, not trusting myself to speak. I seemed to have forgotten how to breathe.

I didn't resist as he lifted my damp, freshly-shampooed hair out of the way, then smoothed his hands lightly over my back, from the base of my spine to the tops of my shoulder-blades, generously spreading the massage oil over my skin in a warm slick. He slid his cupped fingers down on each side of my neck in a firm scooping motion, pressing inwards and pulling upwards, kneading my tired neck muscles like dough. Warmth spread over my shoulders like lapping warm water and washed down my arms, leaving my hands and fingers tingling with an entirely pleasant sensation.

My eyes slid shut in bliss and I nestled my face into the cool pillow, enjoying the new and wonderful sensations as Mutt's hands slipped and slid over my shoulders in a steady, rhythmic motion, his strong thumbs digging into the muscles and rolling them into submission.

'*God,* that's good,' I slurred after a few minutes, unable to contain myself.

'You like that?' Mutt's voice was light but I could hear him grinning. 'Used to do this for a living.'

That was news to me, but I didn't want to question him further and find out the answers I didn't want to hear. The less I knew about Mutt's past, the better. I wriggled my hips lightly beneath him to get into a more comfortable position, then grunted in protest as he immediately lifted his hands away from my back.

'Don't do that,' he said, in a curiously expressionless voice.

'Why?' I shifted my hips again, and felt Mutt immediately tense up.

'Just... don't move like that. Trust me.'

He paused to reapply the oil, then slid two strong fingers quickly down my lower spine from top to bottom, pressing firmly. He repeated the movement over and over in quick succession. I groaned again, closing my eyes.

'And don't make that noise.'

'What noise?' I blinked, feigning confusion as Mutt's hands went back to my shoulders and started kneading them, harder this time.

'Oh *God…*' I groaned. 'You got it. *Right* there…'

'Kayla, please!'

I giggled as I slid my arms under the silk pillow and hugged it to my face. I lay back, sighing in contentment as Mutt's wonderful hands smoothed and caressed and stroked every muscle in my back, kneading away every little ache and pain that had built up over the last few weeks. I was amazed to find that I was actually enjoying myself. I couldn't believe I'd never let Mutt do this for me before.

It was a long time before I realized that he had gone very quiet. With an effort I slid my eyes open a crack to peek back at him.

It was quite a picture.

Mutt's strong, lean figure was edged with gold in the light of the crackling fire as he worked on me, leaning forwards slightly, his face intent as he worked. His muscles were pumped from the exertion of the massage, and his arms and bare chest were slicked with oil. He wasn't quite as chiseled as he'd been when I'd first met him now that he was no longer working with Karrel and the Hunters, but he still cut a very fine figure, his hard, lean body bathed in firelight and covered in a gleaming slick of massage oil.

Mutt cheekily poked his tongue out at me as he caught me checking him out, but he didn't stop his work. It wasn't very often that I let him get his own way, and I could see that he intended to make the most of it.

I sighed as I buried my head in the pillow.

What was I letting myself in for here?

*      *      *

'OH GOD, YOU got it! *Right there! Christ* that's good...'

'Kayla!'

'Sorry. I'm really sorry. I didn't mean to—' I sucked in my breath and exhaled hard into the pillow, practically wriggling in frustration. I lifted my head and glanced back at Mutt as he worked on my shoulders. 'Could you just...' I pointed vaguely at my upper back with my warm, limp hand. 'I kind of have this tight thing under my ribs... lower... *oh yeah*...'

A feeling of lazy contentment filled me as Mutt finished working on my shoulders and moved on to my neck, gently turning my head straight so that I was face down on the pillow. I fidgeted on the soft fur blanket, fighting to control my breathing, to lie still as his incredible hands slid over me again and again.

This was amazing. I felt like I'd died and gone to heaven. I felt so warm, so relaxed, so *cared for*. I hadn't felt this good in a long, long time. I stretched out my arms in front of me like a contented cat as Mutt pulled the crown of my head downwards to straighten my torso, before slipping two greased fingers down the tendons on either side of my neck, squeezing and releasing the muscle before massaging it deeply with one strong hand in a slow, circular motion that sent tingles racing up the back of my neck.

It felt incredible.

I closed my eyes and gave myself entirely over to absolute pleasure as Mutt pecked me on the cheek and slid down my body to work on my feet, my mind drifting happily through a pink fog of warmth. I stretched lightly, utterly content, nestling down on the blanket as I fought a losing battle with sleep. I felt like

I could just drift off right here, on the furred blanket by the fire.

I was barely aware through the fog of sleepiness that Mutt had gone silent as he finished up with my foot. He dropped it back onto the blanket, watching me closely. I glanced sleepily at his reflection in the mirror as he shifted sideways to work on my other foot, in the process nudging my thighs a little further apart with his knees as he knelt between them to reach for my calf.

The silence around us thickened as he worked his way upwards with suddenly-too-gentle hands, running his fingers over my ankle, then my upper thigh, in the process lightly grazing the back of my knee with his fingernails. The seemingly-accidental touch sent a shiver through me which I was pretty sure had nothing to do with the draft from the fire.

I swallowed, suddenly wide awake.

'Um, Mutt...' I began, glancing up at the clock. 'It's late. I should really...'

'Just relax. I'm almost done.' Mutt's voice held a touch of laughter as his hands swept down my thigh then up again, squeezing and kneading the soft flesh. 'Don't tense up or I'll have to start the whole thing over again.'

I didn't protest. The silence was so deep that I swear I could hear the ticking of my wristwatch in the bathroom as Mutt's hands swept around the edges of my thigh, his thumbs massaging beneath my knee in a ticklish but somehow sensual gesture. He lingered in the area much longer than he should have done, as though he was aware that he had finally run out of polite things to massage. I was painfully aware that I was naked under the short towel that barely covered my behind. I heard his breathing change pace, speeding up and deepening as he worked on me.

I glanced at him again sidelong in the mirror as Mutt's thumbs dug in deeper, harder, hardly daring to look. He was staring down at the curve of my thigh as if hypnotized. I held my breath as his hands moved onwards, upwards, sliding up and down the back of my thigh with a new boldness, each time moving just a fraction of an inch higher, closer to the edge of the towel.

I swallowed thickly, half-closing my eyes against the sudden, treacherous wash of desire that seeped through me at his touch, like water into the lungs of a drowning man.

*Uh-oh.*

I needed a nice safe conversation topic, and fast.

'You know,' I said, a touch of desperation in my voice. 'I've been thinking. Perhaps we should call Ninette after all. Tell her I'm a werewolf.'

Them there were fighting words. I tightened my grip on the pillow as I waited for Mutt's reply, fighting to maintain control of a situation which was rapidly slipping through my hands. 'Do you think she'd understand, or would she try to kill me, like she killed that... friend of hers?'

Mutt shrugged wordlessly, his expression curiously fixed as his hands crept higher up my thigh. 'Why don't you call her and find out?'

'Because I'm not a wolf yet.' My voice was barely audible. Heat flooded my face as his hand slipped down the lean curve of the inside of my thigh, smoothing oil over the thinner skin there. I was having difficulties keeping my eyes open, pulled under by an almost irresistible current of arousal. My breathing sounded far too loud, my heart was beating far too fast for comfort. 'There's still... time. Perhaps she could... cure me.'

'There's no cure,' said Mutt flatly, fingers slowly circling around the back of my knee in an unmistakably suggestive fashion. 'If you tell her she'll just kill you. Just like she killed her *friend*.'

I willed myself to stop trembling as his thumbs grazed the very edge of the towel, and shut my eyes tightly.

'But I'm still a Hunter. Just like you are... I mean, like you were.' My mouth was by now moving solely on autopilot. I no longer knew nor cared about what I was saying. A delicious heat flowed down my spine in a leisurely fashion and ignited between my legs, sending tendrils of warmth creeping up through my body, tightening around my chest so I could barely breathe. 'Karrel let you stay in the Hunters. Even though you'd...' I caught my breath as Mutt's hand slid still higher, '...got bitten.'

I closed my eyes. I wanted him to touch me so badly that I could barely breathe. The heat inside me intensified as I imagined those talented hands working on other parts of my body. The thought left me practically panting with desire. My fingers tightened in the blankets and I bit my lip hard. I couldn't help it. I desperately hoped that Mutt didn't notice.

*This was still innocent. All innocent...*

'Karrel was your best friend, Mutt,' I went on, hoping he'd get what I was really saying, take the hint. I stared down at the engagement ring on my finger. 'He hid what you were from everyone, for as long as he could. He trusted you, he said. He knew you wouldn't... take advantage. He said you were always there for him, at his side, right up till the end.'

'But I was too far gone, Kayla,' Mutt's voice was as soft as the midnight breeze. 'I'd already turned. It was too late for me.'

I took a deep breath and looked around at him. 'Do you think it's too late for me?'

Mutt's eyes dropped from mine.

'I think it's too late for us to be having this conversation,' he said quietly.

I tried to think of an argument against this, then gave up. My brain shut down as Mutt's oiled hands slid up the smoothly curved plane of my thigh before running back down again, up and then down, each time moving a little higher, his fingers trailing softly against my skin in a way that was anything but innocent. White-hot shivers of pleasure shot down my body at each upstroke, lingering in the juncture between my thighs. Some far-away voice told me this was not a good reaction. I knew that I should just get up, end this massage right now, but somehow, I just didn't have the strength.

I stopped breathing as Mutt shifted position, biting his lip... then suddenly slid his hand up higher, just beneath the edge of the towel, the very tips of his cool fingers grazing the heated warmth between my legs. The sensation was enough to make me shudder, my eyes flying open, my breath stopping in my throat.

Mutt paused, as though waiting for me to stop him, then continued the motion by gently stroking the backs of his fingers over me in a feather-light touch. I felt his eyes burn into me as he waited for me to say something, to end things right here, just as I always had, but my heart was beating far too hard and far too fast for words.

My eyes slid closed and my breath came out in a hard pant as he pressed harder, gently exploring the molten warmth between my legs, teasing me with a cautious finger. My back arched softly as his thumb stroked gently over my most sensitive spot of all, and I moaned low in my throat as I pressed myself back against him, unable to help myself. It was wrong— I knew that much— but I couldn't stop my body responding to his touch, just as it always had.

Mutt's voice was shaky as he drew in a deep, urgent breath.

'Roll over.'

I had no words left. The heat between my legs seemed to intensify as I had a sudden, glorious mental image of him buried deep inside me. My arms were shaking as I rolled over onto my back, and looked up at Mutt. The firelight bathed his tanned skin with a soft golden glow, threw shadows under the curve of his strong chest and illuminated the swirling tribal tattoos that decorated his muscled midriff. I tried not to look down at his hip, at the starkly tattooed 'H' brand that marked him out as a Hunter... meaningless now that he was a werewolf.

Mutt slid a hand under the plush white towel that covered me and lifted it slowly aside to reveal my nakedness. He dropped the edges of the towel on either side of me before letting his eyes wander down the soft fullness of my body, drinking me in, his golden eyes caressing my nakedness just as his hands had done moments before.

I couldn't think, couldn't move. Heat flooded my body in anticipation of what was to come, even as I started to open my mouth, to say something, anything, to stop what was happening, before it was too late…

And then it was too late.

Mutt's mouth was suddenly on mine, demanding, insistent. Shivering, breathless, I reached up to tangle my fingers in Mutt's dark hair, and I pulled him down roughly on top of me, hooking my leg around his to draw him tighter against my naked body. I knew what I wanted now. It was pointless to deny it any longer. I buried my face in the soft warmth of his neck, enjoying the feeling of the firm, slippery muscles of his chest pressing against my stomach and breasts… and another part of him pressing harder against the place where I needed him the most.

Moving unbidden, my hands slipped down between our warm, oiled bodies, and started working on the buttons of his fly.

'This won't end well,' breathed Mutt, his hands tightening possessively on my hips as I wrestled with the three tiny metal buttons which were all that stood between an innocent massage and the two of us hopelessly screwing up our friendship.

Before I could get my thumbs into his tight-fitting black jeans to tug them off, he seized both of my wrists in a tight grip, hauling them back up above his beltline in a surprisingly chaste move.

'Not fair,' I gasped, then caught my breath as he used my bent arms as leverage to slide quickly back down my body, nipping and kissing every inch of me as he went. I yanked away the towel that separated us both, threw him off and rolled over on top of him, aching with a longing that had been building since the day we met. The hardness of him pressed against me through his jeans and I groaned softly, arching against him in a frenzy of need. His hands found mine, our fingers entwining as I pushed his hands down onto the silken pillow on either side of his head, kissing him with an almost delirious passion.

Before I'd got my fill, Mutt broke the kiss and in one quick, easy move rolled over on top of me, gazing down at me with those hard-to-read eyes, his fingers tightening around mine.

I wondered briefly what I was doing here. If my grief and my need for some kind of solace were just feeding the fires of his obsession, whilst driving me into the arms of someone so completely inappropriate that a month ago, I would've laughed at the thought of what I was about to do.

Just because Mutt had been Karrel's best friend didn't stop him being a complete asshole when he wanted to be, after all.

Or a werewolf.

Or a killer.

From the few shady details I'd heard about Mutt's past, he'd done things that would send most women running screaming for cover.

So why did I want him more than anyone I'd ever wanted in my entire life?

Mutt tightened his grip on my wrists and began to kiss me with mounting passion—first my neck, then my cheek, my forehead, then my neck again, tempering the fire inside me with a trail of cool kisses.

'Do you really wanna know?' he asked with a sudden chuckle, his voice roughened with need.

'Know what?' I could barely get the words out, I wanted him so badly. I made a grab for the waistband of his jeans again, but he tightened his thighs around me, holding me still, locked in place beneath him. He didn't reply immediately, gazing down at me with a strange expression on his face. He lowered his head and rested his forehead against mine, closing his eyes in concentration.

I frowned, then my eyes grew wide with shock.

'*Why you want me more than you've ever wanted anyone in your entire life?*' Mutt gave a wry smile. '*That's quite a compliment, by the way.*'

But Mutt hadn't spoken. I was hearing his voice in my head... just as I had done with Magnus.

I stiffened with shock as the implications hit home. Magnus had said that werewolves could read minds, at short distances. I had completely forgotten about that.

Had Mutt really been reading my mind all this time? What the hell had I been thinking about, for this last half hour or so?

I could feel myself blushing already.

Before I could even begin to process this, a new, more worrying sound reached my ears: the click of high heels in the hallway outside Mia's apartment. A bright yellow light snapped on outside, and the sound of drunken female laughter echoed in the hallway outside.

I stared up at Mutt in horror as a key started to turn in the lock.

We both knew what that meant.

Mia was home.

And we were busted.

# CHAPTER TWENTY-FOUR

I'D NEVER MOVED so fast in my entire life. One minute I was lying beneath an oiled, naked, beautiful man by the fire, the next minute I was darting in a panic down the short cold passageway which led to the spare bedroom, with enough presence of mind, *thank god, I didn't need Mia finding out about my condition too,* to grab my werewolf-meds from the bathroom first, my hastily-grabbed towel flying out behind me like an ungainly superhero's cape.

I slammed the bedroom door and turned the lock, then pressed my face against it with a groan.

*Some superhero.*

The panicked thrumming of my heart settled down to a slow, painful thump of frustration as I listened to muffled voices sound in the living room, raised in awkward conversation. Mutt obviously hadn't had the same reaction as I'd had to our friend's sudden arrival, as I heard the sound of his easy laughter drift down the hallway, followed by the sound of Mia's lighter, higher voice, pitched still higher by embarrassment as she questioned Mutt— obviously grilling him about the damp towels all over the floor and why the whole place smelled like lavender oil.

Talk about the world's worst bad timing.

I closed my eyes and gently banged my head against the door in the darkened room. My entire body vibrated with an ocean of longing and need. A dozen conflicting feelings waged a bloody war inside me as I pressed my ear to the door, trying to make out what Mutt was saying, but he was speaking too quietly for me to hear.

But it was okay. I knew exactly what he was doing. He would talk to Mia, pack her off to bed for the night. Then he'd come and find me, finish what he'd started.

I smiled to myself and hopped quickly back into bed, smoothed my hair back, checked my breath, arranged the towel enticingly around my warm, still-naked body and waited.

Then I waited some more.

After some more waiting, the clock on the wall above me struck two AM.

Before long, it became painfully obvious that Mutt wasn't going to follow me to bed. Long minutes ticked by as I listened with bated breath. After what felt like an age, quiet booted footsteps creaked in the hallway outside. I stopped breathing, my heart thumping with excitement... then my face fell as the hallway light clicked out and the front door slammed shut, leaving me in darkness.

Mutt had gone out for the night.

What the hell?

Numb, I sat up on the clean pink sheets and stared at the bedroom door, hoping against hope to hear Mutt's footsteps come creeping back down the hall to join me in bed, delighted that he'd fooled Mia into thinking he'd gone out so that he could stay the night with me. It had to be a double-bluff. Typical Hunter mentality.

Ri-ight.

When the clock struck half past one I had to finally admit I was kidding myself. I drew my legs up to my chest and curled up on the musty-smelling bedspread, my teary eyed gaze never once leaving the bedroom door, my heart thumping with the exquisite pain of need and loss.

Mutt had really gone out. He wasn't coming back.

I closed my eyes and groaned out loud, flopping back onto the bed.

I had no idea how long I lay there on the cold hard single bed, still wrapped in my damp white towel, which smelled cruelly of lavender oil. I must have drifted off at some point, because the next thing I knew the shadows on the wall had moved and I was shivering violently with cold.

I threw the wet towel onto the floor and gratefully slid my chilly legs under the warm, dry blankets, scanning the room for the thing that had awakened me.

There was a mirror on the back of the door, reflecting bright moonlight into my face. My eyes were burning. I wiped at them absently, then blinked and rolled over to stare out of the big window above me at the moon. It was almost full, and it looked far too fat and heavy to be just hanging in the sky like that. It seemed to get closer the longer I stared at it, transfixed, until it almost seemed to be directly outside my bedroom window, its yellow-white surface marbled with bluish veins like a giant, threatening, blind eye peering in at me.

I could *hear* the moon too, I was startled to find out—

something I'd never been able to do before. Perhaps this was my accelerated werewolf hearing finally kicking in. I stared up at it, fascinated, as the cyclical, metallic-sounding '*whumphing*' noise of the moon-rays got louder, whiting out my hearing and pressing down on my thoughts.

Odd.

The moon seemed to suddenly leap through the sky, flying towards me. I almost jumped out of my skin. I lurched upright in bed, trembling violently. It took me a moment or two of disorientation before I realized that the moon hadn't just leaped at me.

I had fallen asleep again, and the moon had shifted across the sky.

I smacked my lips and pulled a face, staring muzzily around the room. My throat burned with thirst. I needed a long drink of nice, cool water. I started to get up, then paused, sniffing. There was a strange smell in the room, almost as if something was burning. I reached up to wipe the sweat out of my eyes... and froze.

Something *was* burning.

It was me.

Smoke drifted lazily up from my right hand as the smell of slowly charring flesh filled the room. I stared down at my hand in horror as the skin on my middle and index fingers blackened and burned beneath the two silver rings I wore. With a yell I tore off both rings and hurled then across the room, then shook my hand and stared down at my fingers in dismay.

A band of perfectly charred flesh surrounded each finger, where my rings had been.

What the hell...?

Okay, that was it. I had to talk to Mia about what was happening to me. Enough was enough with the lies and the secrecy, and besides, wearing that cheap dyed cotton bandana on my wrist every day was bringing me up in some kind of rash.

Mia was a nice person, I told myself as I slid out of bed. She'd understand why I'd hidden my wolf-bite from her. I was scared the pack would reject me, scared someone would rat me out to the Hunters.

Scared that someone would try to hunt *me*.

But Mia would never do that. I realized that now. Out of all the people I'd met since this nightmare had started, she alone had been supportive of me, unquestioningly following me into battle, backing me up and occasionally wiping my blood off the carpet without so much as a squeak of complaint. I would let her help me with this, let her into my life a little bit, see what she knew. Maybe she could help me, maybe not. Either way I knew I'd feel better for telling her.

I knew could trust Mia, unlike certain other people in my life right now.

My plan made, I slid out of bed and padded unwillingly towards my bedroom door. I padded out into the hallway and walked back towards the scene of the crime. I paused as I entered the living room, looking morosely around me. All the lights were out in the room apart from the dying embers of the fire. The entire place still smelled faintly of lavender oil.

There was no sign of either Mutt or Mia.

*Yeah, another great night,* I thought to myself, as I moodily stepped into the kitchen and filled a glass with water. Why was I so damned thirsty all the time? If that bitch she-wolf Dana had given me rabies as well as lycanthropy there would be hell to pay.

I drained the glass, set it down on the spotlessly clean washing-up rack and continued on soundlessly down the hallway towards Mia's bedroom.

The closer I got to Mia's bedroom door, the tighter the knot in my stomach got, until I thought I was going to throw up. I couldn't explain it, but the thought of sharing my troubles with someone else was freaking me out. I'd kept pretty much to myself since I'd arrived in LA a year ago. It was just my personality, how I coped with things.

I knew Mutt would keep my secret for as long as he could blackmail me with it for, but Mia was different. Mia cared about things. Mia divided things strictly into Right and Wrong, and I was a little scared to see which side of the line she'd place me on once she'd found out I'd hidden the truth from her.

What if she got mad at me? Or worse, what if she got Motor involved?

I had to do this right now, before I lost my nerve.

I crept down the hallway that led to Mia's bedroom, trying not to make any noise. I was half hoping that her light would be out so I could put our little chat off till the morning, but as I approached her room I saw a wash of faintly flickering yellow light spilling from under her door.

*Great.* Mia was still awake, no doubt writing a particularly long entry in her ever-present appointment diary about her date with Wylie. I smiled to myself at the thought. Mia was nothing if not predictable.

The bedroom door was open the barest crack. I arranged my terrified features into something resembling a friendly smile, lifted my fist to knock, then paused.

I might have just imagined it, but I could've sworn I

heard a faint groan coming from inside.

The skin at the back of my neck prickled. I listened in alarm, holding my breath. Then… *there it was again,* louder this time, and filled with an unmistakable note of passion. My eyebrows fled to my hairline, and I smiled in a mix of envy, admiration and relief. I hadn't heard Wylie come in with her. It looked like my revelation would have to wait for another time.

'Mia, you dirty old dog,' I whispered, impressed. My pretty young friend was such a quiet, shy little thing that I sometimes forgot that she wasted no time whatsoever when it came to the boys. She knew what she wanted, unlike me, and had no hesitations about taking it. I wished I could be more like her.

I was really starting to like Mia.

I started to leave, then paused, glancing back at the bright crack in the door. I had the sudden, strange compulsion to peek in. I didn't usually go around spying on my friends' love lives, but Wylie had been single for so long that if he had finally got some action, he would be bragging about it for the rest of the year.

I had to get proof on this one. I had to see if it really was Wylie in there, or if she'd ditched him after ten minutes—the usual amount of time it took him before he got drunk on half a glass of Jack and Coke and started explaining Nietzsche's theories on the absurdity of Religion to the nearest waitress's boobs.

Unable to resist peeking, I nudged the door open by a few extra centimeters, grinning, and peered through the crack.

The smile froze on my face. My mouth dropped open as I stared into Mia's bedroom, taking in the scene that lay within.

The main lights were out, and a dozen flickering candles had been lit all around the big pink room. Mia lay on her belly across the stripped-down bed, which had had most of the girlish pink sheets torn off and strewn about the room, covering the watchful glass eyes of a hundred leering stuffed doggy toys. She was topless, still clad in her skirt, bra, stockings and high heels from her date with Wylie. An almost empty glass of red wine sat on the nightstand beside her, within arm's reach of the bed. Her eyes were closed in bliss, her head thrown back so that her cropped blonde hair hid most of her face.

Mutt sat astride her, as shirtless as she was, massaging her back in the exact same way as he'd done with mine. A pair of empty red wine bottles sat next to him on the pink bedside table, drops of spilled wine staining the sheets like incriminating drops of blood. He was so intent on his work that he didn't as much as glance up as the door behind him cracked open, then slowly closed again.

I jerked my hand away from the door as though it had stung me. I silently backed away from the scene, my mouth hanging open in stunned disbelief.

What the hell? Okay, so our little night hadn't ended in quite the way that Mutt had obviously hoped it would. But to then have the nerve to move onto Mia, one of my best friends, while I was still under the same roof?

*Asshole.*

My face twisted in disgust and betrayal—disgust that was largely directed at myself. I'd obviously been fooling myself to think that I was someone special to this guy, that he was here because he cared about me and wanted to help me, despite his better judgment and my own. That a promise to his dead buddy Karrel to keep me safe and alive actually meant something to him.

But no. Mutt was truly an animal, in the most unflattering sense of the word. He'd been preying on my bereavement for one reason alone: to get me into bed. He hadn't got what he'd wanted from me tonight, so he'd simply moved on, not even having the decency to wait a few days or to take his business elsewhere before he tried again.

Well, two people could play at that game. I was going to go and find Niki, and we'd save the world together.

And maybe, just maybe, I wouldn't come back again.

The two of them were welcome to each other.

Abruptly turning away, I walked as quietly as I could back down the hallway to my room. I dressed quickly in the first clothes I could lay my hands on and stalked back through into the front room, seething all the way. Sweeping my purse off the arm of the chair, I pulled the front door open and stepped through into the night, on impulse slamming the door as loudly as I could behind me.

# CHAPTER TWENTY-FIVE

'You sure you can drink all of that, kid?'

'Believe me, I'm sure. Keep the change.'

I dumped a battered twenty on the bar-top and reached for my second triple-scotch in a row with a sigh. It was well past three AM but the long, curving bar of the Snake Pit on Melrose was doing a thriving trade, packed tonight with the usual post-midnight crowd of wannabes, has-beens and burnouts. All around me leather-skinned men in cowboy boots and yesterday's haircuts sat shoulder to shoulder, drowning their uniquely Tinseltown sorrows of the audition that never materialized, the TV show pilot that got cancelled, the script that nearly got sold.

Tomorrow, Hollywood would try again.

I wondered sometimes how they found the strength.

I tossed the scotch back, fuming quietly to myself. I didn't normally drink like this, but after the night I'd just had, I couldn't see how I could *not* drink like this.

The amber liquid burnt in all the right places going down, gradually working on the knots of pain and fury in my chest until they faded to a dull, just-bearable ache. A Faster Pussycat music video blared from the cracked and jumping LCD screen on the wall right above me, further adding to my foul temper.

*How could he?* I was still stunned by Mutt's nerve. To mess around with Mia was bad enough, but to do it with me right next door, just a few short hours after he'd made such a bold move on me... the guy was simply unbelievable.

I knew that drinking probably wasn't the cleverest thing in the world to be doing right now, that drink should be my enemy when I needed a clear head to save the world, but screw it. The words 'Dutch courage' wandered aimlessly through my head as I reached for the scotch bottle again, snatching it out of the bartender's surprised hands.

'Uh... that'll be forty-six fifty, lady,' said the barman, hovering uncertainly. He hadn't picked up my twenty. 'You're short twenty-six bucks.'

I looked at him and curled my lip, letting him take in the half-formed fangs in my mouth, the look of death and destruction in my eye.

'I'll leave the bottle,' he said, wisely backing off.

The woman in red sitting beside me lifted her wine glass to mine as I filled my fourth shot glass. I automatically clinked glasses with her, downing the shot with a shudder and a grimace. It went down a lot smoother than the last one. I didn't know if that was a good thing or a bad thing.

'Booze is great, isn't it?' the woman murmured, in a soft, bell-like voice.

'You're telling me.' I slammed my empty shot glass down on the bar, making the man on the other side of me jump. I felt a storm current of anger building inside my chest as I once again pictured Mutt sitting astride Mia. I abruptly shook myself, rubbing my eyes hard. I had to calm down. Being angry would simply make me careless, which in this particular part of town at this hour of the night would just get me dead.

Besides, I had other things to worry about right now.

I slumped forwards with a groan and put my head in my hands as I remembered that I now had just under twenty-four hours to find Harlequin and foil his plan to end the world… even though right now, all I felt like doing was throwing Mutt through a window, moving to Cuba, and then possibly joining some kind of nunnery.

I thought briefly about leaving the bar, getting a cab to the nearest police station, and… telling them… what? Ninette was right. No-one human would ever believe me if I started babbling on about Avenging Angels. And besides, most cop stations round here were run by the vamps. If I wound up spilling my guts to a vampire-run squad I'd wind up spending the Apocalypse in a body bag.

'You'll survive it, you know,' the woman mumbled into her drink. 'They'll only kill the humans.'

'I can't count on that,' I started, then stopped. I frowned. Slowly, very slowly, I revolved in my seat to look at the woman in red sitting next to me.

My glass shattered on the floor. I flew off my chair and lunged in the direction of the exit. I stopped short a split second later, quivering, as a three-foot-long white blade *thunked* into the wooden bar-siding, trapping my frantic body between the blade and the bar.

'Sit,' commanded Cyan X.

I sat.

There was a frantic explosion of movement around us as everyone sitting within a ten foot radius of us leaped up and hurried towards the second bar on the opposite side of the room. The more knowledgeable ones took off altogether. The rush ended with the front door slamming and the traditional pint glass smashing on the floor. The bartender sighed, then went back to polishing the bar-top.

'Take it easy, ladies,' he murmured. 'Cyan? Third warning, *querida*. I have to scrub brains off the bar-top one more time and you're barred. '

The vampiress looked at him hard. The barman's features blurred for one quick moment, twisting his face into something a whole lot more spiny and shark-like before snapping back to human again. Cyan sighed heavily as she withdrew the organic blade into her wrist with a gory little *schlupp* sound. She gave him a loaded look before backing off, and snatched up her wine glass again. She took a long, un-ladylike chug, draining four fifths of the glass, and then offered the rest to me.

I took it, more out of sheer terror than anything else, and held it trembling above the bar, staring at her. I'd been sitting next to my mortal enemy for a full twenty minutes, and had been so caught up in myself that I hadn't even noticed her.

It was a mistake that would probably cost me my life.

Cyan gave me a single, morose look, her purple cat's eyes smoldering in misery.

'Why are men so dumb?' she asked.

I stared at her, frozen to my barstool, waiting for the bloodshed to start.

'I see. No answer to that one. Ha!' Cyan snatched her glass back from me and drained it in a single long gulp. She seized my scotch bottle, filling her large balloon wine glass to the very top with the honey-colored liquid. She stared at it for a long moment, then abruptly slumped face down on the bar, burying her head in her hands.

'I hate him,' she sobbed. 'Why does he always do this to me?'

My eyebrows flew up in surprise. Here I was, sitting next to Cyan X, scourge of North America, the killer of killers, wanted in every state for mass murder and hundreds of cases of aggravated homicide… and here she was, bawling like a baby over some guy.

I might never get another chance like this.

I rose silently to my feet, glancing around frantically for a weapon. My two-inch Swiss Army knife seemed almost laughably inadequate next to the massive biological swords housed inside Cyan's slender arms. I doubted my pepper spray would do much good either. What I needed was a taser, an army percussion grenade and a whole bunch of muscled men with army rifles. A rocket launcher would also be nice…

I waved frantically at the barman for help. He just gave me a shrug which said quite plainly, *'You're on your own, kid.'*

I rose to my feet, very, very quietly, and started to edge away.

'Tell me something.' Cyan's hand snapped out and locked around my wrist with the speed of a striking cobra. I instantly dropped to my knees and clutched my arm as I felt the bones in my wrist start to bend alarmingly. She lifted her head and stared at me with desolate eyes, her mascara running down her cheeks.

I was shocked to see that she was blind drunk.

'Why do men say they'll call, and then they don't?' she asked.

It was only then that I noticed a tiny silver cell phone sitting next to her on the bar, propped up against an overturned empty Sambuca bottle so that the display was visible. *Ah*. I'd been there before myself, more than once, in fact.

'Um,' I started, wincing in pain.

'I'll *tell* you why,' she growled, her beautiful, exotic face twisting with anger. 'Because they're all *bastards*, the lot of them!'

She seized her cell phone and pitched it into what remained of the crowd behind us. I clearly saw it strike the forehead of a man big enough to be a WWE wrestler. He snarled and whipped around, his orange vampire eyes narrowing in anger... then turned away quickly when he saw who'd thrown the phone.

'What the hell's *wrong* with him?' cried Cyan, slamming her hand so hard on the bar that she cracked the wood all the way along to the end. '*Why doesn't he want me?*'

'Er...' I winced as Cyan's grip on my wrist got still tighter. I had the distinct feeling that my answer would determine how long my hand remained attached to my body. The barman watched me with slightly smug interest, polishing a glass. I got the strong feeling that he'd have been more helpful if I'd tipped him.

'Who are we talking about here?' I managed, breathing steadily to control the pain.

'*Harlequin*, you idiot! Who else?'

'Ah. Well. Let's see.' My throat was suddenly so dry that it creaked when I swallowed. My wrist was in agony. It took all my mental effort to drag my brain out from behind a screaming wall of mortal fear and pain and give the woman I despised most in the whole world dating advice. 'What did he tell you? Harlequin, I mean?'

'What do you mean?'

'Did he say… *ow*… in as many words that he'd call?'

Cyan nodded miserably, blowing her nose noisily on a napkin.

'And what did he say?' I swallowed hard as my face started to pale with shock. I could actually hear my bones creaking under the intense pressure. 'Try to think of the exact words.'

'He said… he said that once I'd tracked you down and killed you, maybe he'd *call me* and we'd go grab a bite to eat before the show,' she sniffed, fiddling with her damp napkin. '*And he never called!*'

'But you haven't killed me yet,' I pointed out, stupidly. My head swam with the unreality of discussing my own impending death with my killer. *I should be screaming, should be running… should have brought a ZipLock bag to carry my hand home in…*

'You don't understand!' Cyan shouted. Her grip tightened still further on my arm and I bared my teeth in pain. 'The show's over! It's finished!'

'What show?'

'The Circus of Sins show! We were supposed to go *together!*'

'But I'm still alive,' I shot back. 'You didn't do your job.'

'But don't you see?' Cyan was getting more and more wound up. 'He *knew* full well that I wouldn't have time to find you and kill you before the show! So he just orders me around, giving me all this stupid pointless shit to do killing stupid pointless humans and bribing me with the promise of dinner with him… and I get nothing in return! I've known him a hundred years. Literally! I do everything he asks me to, everything and more, and he just treats me like his *errand girl!*' She pretty much spat the last phrase, baring her teeth. The drinkers around us who had not yet tactfully moved away picked up their pints and found a new table fast at the sight of her overlong canines. We were now alone at the formerly-packed bar. 'Do you have any *idea* how long it took me to get my hair to look like this?'

'I can imagine,' I said, eyeing up the sleek ringlets in her silky black hair. 'But come on. Really? *Harlequin?* Of all people? Isn't he a bit… you know… scary? What with him being a master vampire and all?'

'Have you ever *seen* him?'

'Not in person, no, but the stories I've heard… the people he's killed…'

'Then you don't know shit.'

'Fine, fine.' I sucked in my breath through my teeth. 'Um, can I have my hand back, please? Still attached, if possible.'

Cyan stared at me, then blinked and released my wrist, like a child relinquishing a favorite toy after a temper tantrum. I reeled it in gratefully, cradling my throbbing hand against my chest. It was badly bruised but nothing was broken. I was lucky.

'Look,' I said with as much kindness as I could manage, given the circumstances. 'It sounds like you're over-thinking things. This Harlequin… he sounds like a very busy guy. You don't think it's possible he got wrapped up in something—' *Like planning the mass-extinction of mankind…* '—and just forgot to call you?'

'You don't understand,' Cyan said fiercely. 'It's *her*. Don't you see? I used to be his favorite. We traveled the world together. Now it's all "Doll this," and "Doll that..." I bet it was *her* he went to dinner with after the show, not me. The *bastard*...'

My heart gave a quick, fierce thump of excitement at the mention of Doll's name. I covered it up quickly, struggled to keep my face blank.

'And the worst thing is,' went on Cyan, really getting into her rant now. '*She doesn't even love him!* Why is he so obsessed with someone he can never have? He's almost as bad as that dog Harlem!'

'Harlem?' Now I was lost.

'Harlem's got a thing for me. Can you believe it? A filthy, stinking beast of a werewolf, and he thinks he has a chance with me.' She gave a dark chuckle, her eyes desolate. 'He follows me everywhere! He's always staring at me, won't leave me alone! Just last week he broke into my room, tried to kiss me when I was asleep. Can you believe it?' She popped out her other wrist blade and crossed it with the first one like claws. Made a violent slashing motion and grinned evilly. 'Gave him a little gift to remember me by. He won't be trying that one again anytime soon.'

'Right.'

'He just doesn't get it. I don't *want* him! *I want Harlequin!*'

Cyan stood up with a quick lunge and flared out her four gleaming blades with a motion like the cracking of a whip. She turned sideways to study her sleek profile in the bar mirror. Even half insensible with drink and red-eyed from crying, she still looked like a Goddess. A very... spiky Goddess, but a Goddess nonetheless.

Every man I knew would kill to get a woman who looked like her, but she didn't seem to notice.

'I'm perfect for him!' she sobbed, looking down at herself, her stunning figure, her gleaming bio-blades. 'I've *made* myself perfect for him! I do everything he tells me to and more! So why won't he even look at me? How can I get him to *notice* me?'

I moved quietly out of range of her blades, praying to God that she would keep talking. If Cyan knew where Doll was being kept, then I had to find out exactly where. I knew Doll worked at the Circus of Sins, but I had no idea if she stayed on site at night or was taken elsewhere.

I'd unexpectedly struck gold, and I wasn't dead yet. That was a good start.

Before I could think of what to say to keep her talking, the front door right between us opened. A human man walked into the bar... then yelled in surprise as Cyan unexpectedly grabbed him by the throat and slammed him face down onto the bar, extending her left blade until it nicked the back of his neck. She turned her violet eyes up to me expectantly.

Her captive whimpered, struggling faintly.

'Advice, please,' she said sweetly.

# CHAPTER TWENTY-SIX

WHEN YOU'RE STRANDED at a bar in the middle of the night, trying to talk a psychopathic love-sick vampiress out of beheading an innocent passer-by just to make a point about how much men suck, you're kind of limited in what you can achieve through logic and reasoning.

Particularly if you've only slept for two hours in the last forty-eight, and have just downed six shots of neat scotch.

Well, shit.

'Take it easy, lady.' I held up my hands, listening to myself talk with mild fascination. I felt unreal, disembodied. 'Gimmie a minute to think—'

The man cried out as Cyan's blade nicked his ear. Bright crimson drops slid down his hairline and Cyan licked her lips in anticipation.

'Quickly please,' she purred.

'I'm thinking!' I cried, wringing my hands as I paced rapidly back and forth. 'Okay, fine. You want to know about men? I'll tell you all about men. But you're not going to like it.'

'I already don't like it,' ground out Cyan, pressing her blade deeper into the man's throat. 'Fix my life for me... and I won't take his.'

'Please fix it,' whimpered the man. 'Quickly.'

'Okay. Now, when it comes to men, if there's one thing I've learned, it's this,' I said, my mind running purely on the hot winds of fear. 'Women are complex creatures. Men are more simple. They have simple needs, simple instincts.'

'Hey!' protested the man.

'Sorry,' I shrugged. 'But it's true. If you really, truly want a man to fall in love with you, you have to learn to appeal to those manly instincts.'

'How?' sniffed Cyan, downing another shot.

'Well... think of it like this,' I said, making it up as I went along. 'A man is a little bit like a dog, when you think about it. He likes three things: food, sex and sleep. Oh, and his very favorite thing in the whole world is to chase things. People, cars, rabbits...'

'Are we talking about men or dogs here?'

'Both,' I said, trying to sound confident even though my knees were shaking. 'A man will chase almost anything that moves, for as long as it's running away from him. He'll never get tired of the chase, even if he knows in his heart that he may never catch what he's chasing. That's all part of the fun of it.'

'Right.'

'But he's not dumb, our man. He's always aware of the danger of what he's doing, because that's a big part of the excitement. The car could stop and hit him. The rabbit could turn around and bite him. The girl with the enormous boobs at the bar could have an ex-Mafia hit man boyfriend. But he doesn't care, because he's having fun now, and now is all that matters to him. He doesn't think very far ahead. He's a man, a hunter. Tomorrow can go hang.'

I moved around Cyan, maneuvering closer to the door.

'So tell me this. What does a dog do if the wonderful thing he's chasing suddenly turns around and starts running towards *him*?'

Cyan frowned. She didn't reply.

'He turns around and runs away from it, that's what he does,' I continued, warming to my subject. 'Being chased is not exciting for a dog. It confuses him, freaks him out, ruins his game. It's only fun when *he's* the one doing the chasing.'

'Is that what I'm doing? Cyan asked, the tears starting to dry on her face. 'Freaking him out? Running him down?'

'Certainly sounds like it,' said the guy pinned beneath Cyan, and earned himself a slap on the cheek for his efforts.

Cyan sighed, her impossibly beautiful face crumpling in despair.

'But why her? Why *Doll*?' She shuddered as she said the name. 'She's not even a vampire! It would never work out! Why put so much effort into chasing a woman he's got no intention of settling down with?'

I shrugged. 'Why do dogs chase cars they have no intention of driving?'

'Enough with the dog analogy!' snapped Cyan. 'I get it.'

The barman wandered back into the room carrying a huge, thick black plastic bag and did a double take, as though stunned to find me still alive. He put down his bag in the corner and folded his arms as he stared at the man who was pinned to the bar top.

'Kitten. Final warning,' he said, in a monotone.

Cyan glared, but she finally released her victim, retracting her blades with a series of grisly little snaps. The man shot upright and fled for the front door of the bar, throwing me a grateful look as he made good his escape. The vampiress heaved a deep sigh as the door slammed, turning her melancholy violet eyes to me.

'So what next?' she asked. 'What the hell do I do now? I've scared my guy off. I get that, even though I might still kill you for your nerve. How do I get him back?'

I looked this beautiful warrior vampire over critically, lightheaded with a heady cocktail of fear and triumph. Something about her looked wrong. It took me a minute to figure out what it was.

'We start by getting rid of this.' I waved a hand at her red silk dress. She looked like a prom queen. 'Is this really you? Or is this who you think he wants you to be?'

'He's royalty, a prince,' she said, with almost religious fervor. 'He deserves a princess.'

'And what about you? What do *you* deserve?'

'What do you mean?'

'Do you deserve someone who loves the pretend you, or the real you?'

'The real me is scary,' whispered Cyan. 'He wouldn't like it.'

'How do you know that?'

I forced myself to sit down beside her, poured her a glass of scotch. Evening the odds a little. I raised my own empty glass to her in a toast.

'You know how I felt when I first met you?' I said, clinking glasses with her. 'Absolutely scared shitless. Terrified out of my mind. But you know what? You made an impression. It was hard to forget you, although the pills have helped a lot since then.'

I gave a little laugh, which faded awkwardly into silence.

'Now... that's the way you should make a man feel, if you want to attract him. Terrified by you, excited by you, raring to chase you. Not bored or trapped or sick of the sight of you.' I paused, looking at her sideways. 'How many times did you try to call him tonight, just out of curiosity? Before your calls started going straight to voicemail?'

'Fifty-two,' Cyan sighed, then abruptly buried her head in her hands. 'I hate my life.'

'Then fix it.'

'Fix it for me,' Cyan demanded, thumping the bar-top.

I stared at her, then shrugged. *What the hell.*

'Let me try something,' I said.

I lifted my hand and gingerly reached out for Cyan, my enemy. She leaned back, eyeing me dangerously as she lifted her blades, but after a tense few seconds she allowed me to reach up and run my fingers through her hair, tousling up her too-perfect ringlets and pulling out the hair pins. The barman made a kissy-kissy noise and I rolled my eyes at him. Why did I even bother?

I hoped she didn't notice that my hands were shaking, that I was fighting the urge to fasten them around her throat and choke the life out of her for what she had done to my life. But I didn't kill her. Instead, I dipped the napkin in my wine, using it as a makeshift makeup remover to clean up the worst of the mascara running down her face.

Job done, I sat back and looked at her expensive, ruffle-heavy silk dress, then screwed up my nose and glanced over my shoulder. A group of wafer-thin girls in ultra-skimpy body-hugging lycra dresses stood behind us, watching us closely. The tallest one curled her lip at Cyan's drunken stance and whispered something to her friends.

They all giggled.

I leaned in close to Cyan, my eye on the girl who had made fun of her.

'I like that girl's dress,' I whispered, pointing to the tall girl. Her dress was black velvet with a red dragon embroidered up the side.

'So do I,' Cyan whispered back, her eyes glinting with sudden mischief. She handed me the rest of her scotch. 'Drink this for me. I'll be back.'

Two MINUTES LATER, Cyan sat back down again on her bar stool and sheathed her bio-blades, adjusting the top of the girl's black dress.

It fit her perfectly.

'You look better,' I said, as the dress's previous owner ran shrieking out of the room in her underwear, followed by her terrified friends.

'I *feel* better, said Cyan, smoothing out her new dress. 'What next, little human?'

I paused, calculating my risks. A plan was forming in my mind. A very stupid, very dangerous plan. A plan that would almost certainly get me killed.

But it would be worth it, to fix things for everybody.

Taking a deep breath, I leant forwards and whispered my plan in Cyan's ear. When I was done, the vampiress slowly reached for the last unbroken bottle on the bar. She popped her left wrist-blade out and absently sliced the top off the bottle as though it were made of Styrofoam. She raised it to her lips.

'Interesting,' she said. 'What do I get in return?'

'You get Doll gone,' I promised her. 'Out of your life forever. You get back at Harlequin for treating you like crap. You get to save a couple million people from dying, which will really spoil Harlequin's night. And you get to blame it all on me.'

Cyan swung her legs on the barstool like a little girl, considering.

'You know I'll just kill you as soon as we're done. You're dumb and short and you annoy me.'

I shrugged carelessly, adjusting the strap on her dress to show off a little more of her incredible cleavage.

'I'll be waiting,' I replied, with my first real smile of the evening. The barman made a noise that sounded like 'Oooh, mama.' I unhesitatingly pitched my empty glass at him. The look he gave me made it very clear that I would not be venturing in here again.

'And what do you get?' Cyan asked me, folding her arms.

'I get to prove a point to a friend,' I said, my eyes not leaving hers.

Cyan stared at me, frowning. I tensed, waiting for the killing to begin. Abruptly, she broke into a wicked, femme-fatale smile. I stared at her gleaming curved incisors and impulsively smiled back, revealing the tips of my own tiny werewolf fangs. Not quite as scary as hers, but it was a start.

'One final thing,' I said, leaning forward in interest. 'Tell me what you meant when you said that they'll only kill the humans?'

Cyan grinned as she started to explain how I was going to save the world. When she had finished, I sat back and smiled. It was a daringly simple plan.

And if I could find Harlequin in time, it just might work...

BY THE TIME the cab dropped me off outside Mia's gated apartment complex, it was close to five in the morning. I opened the gate with the key she'd given me and stole back inside. I'd been gone less than three hours, but now, thanks to Cyan, I had hope again. Now, I needed clean clothes, supplies, and the rest of my anti-werewolf serum. If that meant I had to talk to Mutt one final time before I took off for good, so be it.

Even before I got close to Mia's apartment I knew something was wrong. The faint but unmistakable smell of burning permeated the early-morning air, getting stronger the closer I got to Mia's apartment block.

*Oh, Christ. What now?* The night-time air got thicker and more fume-laden as I unlocked the second high steel gate and headed around the side of the building towards the main entry staircase, dreading what I was about to see.

Mia's apartment complex was on fire.

People were standing around in small excited huddles on the front lawn. A black pall of smoke drifted in a leisurely fashion out of one of the side windows, backlit by the bright white floodlights that lit up the grounds at night. A big red fire-truck was parked out the front, along with the usual paramedics and herds of late-night gawkers.

I didn't even have to look up to know whose apartment was burning.

Mia came bounding up to me as I stood there slowly shaking my head at the devastation. She was barefoot and dressed in an odd assortment of clothes— my black Hustler sweatpants matched with a soft grey sweatshirt three sizes too big for her. *Mutt's grey sweatshirt. Bah.* Her short blonde hair stuck out from underneath a beanie cap, making her look like a dandelion that had gone to seed. She had a large smudge of soot on her cheek.

She let out her breath in relief when she saw me. She gave me a quick, hard hug, then flashed me an apologetic look as she held up a finger and headed back to Mutt. I watched her go, watched the two of them stand awkwardly side-by-side like two naughty children as one of the uniformed firefighters trudged up the lawn to Mia, a disapproving expression on his sooty face. They'd obviously been waiting for his report.

Mia twisted her fingers together as the fireman conferred with her in a low voice, then reached into his pocket and handed her something that looked like the twisted, melted remains of a dog-shaped candle holder.

I watched with infinite satisfaction as Mia blushed.

As the firefighter walked away, shaking his head, I saw Mia pull Mutt aside, lowering her voice so she wouldn't be overheard by curious passers-by. Standing ten feet away, with my new soon-to-be-werewolf hearing, I could hear every word.

'Just tell me one thing, for insurance purposes,' she whispered to Mutt, as she glanced up at the smoking remains of her apartment. 'Did you forget to put out the candles, or did I?'

# CHAPTER TWENTY-SEVEN

'HELL, NO; A thousand times no; screw you Jack; no way Jose; get lost Faust; call me when Hell freezes over; absolutely never in a hundred million years. I think that about covers it.'

'Thanks so much for letting us stay, Wylie,' I gushed, clapping him on the shoulder as I pushed my way past him into his small one-bed cinderblock house.

My best friend stood by the door, looking flustered and wringing his hands as I dumped the small, sad plastic carrier bag which contained the very last of my pathetic earthly possessions down on his sofa. Wylie was wearing eyeliner and the remains of last night's make-up with his Donald Duck PJs, which, being a Goth, were of course black.

Judging by the dark rings under his eyes I guessed he'd just got in from a long night spent in town hanging out at some black painted bar in West Hollywood, paying ten bucks a pop to drink beer with red food dye in it out of a coffin shaped glass. Or something like that. My understanding of Wylie's Goth culture was still a little shaky, but he put up with my bullshit and looked good in tight pants, so I let him hang around me.

He said pretty much the same thing about me.

I looked around me, trying to muster some enthusiasm for our new quarters as I waved Mia and Mutt through into Wylie's modest living room. My plastic bag was still smoldering slightly, and the clothes I was wearing felt gritty. I'd barely looked at Mutt or Mia on the cab ride over here, and they were both wearing identical looks of guilt, although I was fairly sure that neither of them had a clue why I was really mad at them.

I wondered what had happened between them after I left that had wound up with them burning the place down, and my mind shut down. I didn't want to think about that right now, or indeed ever.

But for now, other more pressing matters were weighing on my mind. The only room in Mia's apartment that had escaped the conflagration had been the bathroom, and I'd been lucky enough to leave one single change of clothing and my small toiletry bag in there when I'd had my bath the previous night.

My werewolf meds were gone, burned to a cinder.

I was screwed.

So it had come down to this, then.

I led my werewolf friends through into the main living area, looking around me with sudden doubt, seeing the place as though through their eyes. I'd been here so many times before and was used to the 'student housing' feel of the place, but after the grand if pink luxury of Mia's Beverly Hills apartment and the dead-bolted security of Mutt's place in downtown LA, Wylie's place in the less fashionable end of Venice Beach seemed very low-budget, and painfully exposed. The front door didn't even lock.

I looked around as I dumped my bag down on the sofa. The small entry hall opened out into a small black-painted living room containing a lackluster assortment of mismatched thrift-store furniture. The curtains on the room's one window were held in place by duct-tape obviously stolen from Club Fury, the rock venue we'd both worked at before all this drama happened. Wylie still worked there, but as I hadn't been to work in four weeks now I was guessing I was fired. I'd ask him about that later. His carpet and furniture were threadbare and populated by a rich variety of rather worrying stains, and the whole place in general smelled like fried cheese.

Still, at least we had a roof over our heads. It was better than sleeping on the streets, if only marginally so. Hopefully I wouldn't burn this place down or blow it up in the next fifteen hours before the apocalypse.

I gave a thin smile, eyeing up a particularly alarming hole in the roof, and hastily revised the thought. If the vampires didn't get us, the rats very probably would.

'I still don't get why we have to stay *here*,' Mutt grumbled, brushing past me and eyeing up Wylie with a wary look on his face. 'Don't you have any more financially well-endowed friends?'

'Get over it, *Mathius*,' I muttered, in a voice so low that Wylie couldn't hear me. Mutt gave me a strange look and didn't reply, although I could see that my use of his real name annoyed him. *Good*. He picked the least ugly of the three threadbare orange chairs to sit down in and threw his booted foot over the side, looking moodily around the place.

'Well, this is cheerful. Anyone want some coffee?' asked Wylie, clasping his hands together. He was a barman at Club Fury. Drinks were his forte.

'I'd love an orange juice,' said Mia. I noticed that she didn't meet Wylie's eye either. *Did she feel bad she'd cheated on her new date with Mutt?* I hoped so.

'No probs,' said Wylie. 'Er… could you run to the store and buy me some? I'm kind of out.'

'I'd love to.' Mia was already halfway to the door, relieved to get out of this awkward situation. 'Back in ten.'

Wylie grunted, watching her warily. I notice he stepped back hurriedly as she passed him, as though he didn't want to even touch her. I wondered what had happened on what was supposed to be their first date last night. Why had Mia come home so early? Come to think of it, why had she come home at all? I'd sent them both to the biggest, hottest all-night party in town. I'd been very specific with Wylie in my instructions that he should keep her out as late as possible.

Mia had refused to tell me what had happened after that on the cab ride over, which was always a bad sign.

The front door slammed. An uncomfortable silence fell as my two favorite men in my life eyed each other up. Mutt finally shrugged, dismissing Wylie with a jerk of his head.

'He's too skinny to fight, Kayla, but he might be useful if we need bait.'

'Bait?' Wylie's multiple-pierced eyebrows hiked higher. 'Are we going fishing today?'

'Of a kind.' Mutt's usual good humor was definitely missing this morning. He turned to me, scratching his two-day stubble. 'He doesn't know, does he?'

'Know what?' asked Wylie.

'Figures. Looks like I'm not the only one you've been hiding things from.'

'What's that supposed to mean?'

'Nothin'.'

'Look on the bright side,' said Wylie, squeezing my arm whilst staring at Mutt. 'If the world ever runs out of hair gel, at least he'll survive.'

'If he makes any more lame jokes, can I shoot him?'

'You don't have a gun,' I pointed out.

Mutt regarded me with dark eyes. 'I'm sure I could find one.'

'Ladies, ladies!' Wylie stepped up behind me. 'No talk of guns in here. You'll scare the cockroaches off. What would I do for entertainment then?'

Mutt gave him an irked look. Wylie raised an eyebrow back at him with his usual unflappable calm before leaning forwards to murmur in my ear.

'Kayla, my sweet? A word, if you will.'

I nodded thankfully and stepped around Mutt, who was staring at Wylie with a fixed, pained look on his face as he noticed the easy familiarity between the two of us. He did not look happy, and for some reason that made my heart swell with irrational glee. Maybe he did feel bad about sleeping with Mia after all. I sure as hell hoped so, and wondered again if he'd heard me slam the door when I'd left.

I shook my head and followed Wylie through to the tiny kitchenette.

NEXT DOOR, WYLIE moved aside an overflowing trash can so he could close the kitchen door for some privacy. I couldn't help but smile as I watched him work. Even though it was morning he was still wearing a dozen silver rings, four or five different sized crosses around his neck, and soft leather wrist-guards underneath his PJs. He must have had a rough night last night to have gone to sleep still wearing that little lot. His mid-length brown hair was for once soft and ungelled, hanging in floppy brown spikes into his eyes, and his face was adorably puffy with sleep.

I'd obviously caught him off guard with my early-morning visit.

'See, it's like this,' he said, dropping a tea-towel over the more disgusting portion of the teetering stack of washing-up and leaning back against it to hide it. 'I want to help you, Kayla. I really do. But if you don't want me to kick you and your freaky friends out in exactly two point five minutes, you need to explain some things to me, and fast.'

'Like what?'

'Like everything,' said Wylie, settling back against the kitchen counter. 'Oh and by the way, remind me to never, ever take your advice on women again.'

'You had a good time on your date?' I asked hopefully.

'Oh, sure I did. We had some drinks at my place, planned on hitting the big Saturday night block party up on Sunset. It was all going swimmingly until your friend got so drunk on a single glass of Jagermeister that I had to drop her off at the hospital. It wasn't even nine PM and she was out cold.'

'Mia got drunk?' That was a first. I'd never seen Mia touch a drop of drink before. I decided I wouldn't tell Wylie that.

'My God, you should have seen her. She was so wasted she was stumbling into people and slurring her words.'

'Oh.'

'*Oh* doesn't even begin to cover it, missy. And get this. There was a cop in the waiting room at the hospital. Soon as he got an eyeful of my drunken little friend he called all his mates on the radio, then slapped handcuffs on her before she even got treated. He told me that we had to stay at the hospital till backup arrived, and that my date was under arrest on suspicion of murder!'

'Ah.'

'Kayla! What haven't you been telling me?' Wylie burst out.

A lot, actually. Wylie was one of my last 'normal' friends, and I wanted to keep things that way. I had never told him about my secret life with the Hunters, desperate to hold onto the one last piece of normalcy in my life, to protect him from danger by not getting him involved. I'd been careful to keep him well out of things so far, but I'd felt so sure that he could handle just one little date with Mia...

I sighed, shaking my head. I could see now that even letting him into my life that much had been a mistake.

Yes, Mia was a killer. No, she didn't kill 'good' guys. The murder rap Wylie was talking about was old news, and I'd felt so sure that she'd escaped detection that I'd gotten sloppy, overconfident about allowing her out in public.

Because it was true. Mia had killed a guy. But he'd been a bad guy. His name had been Jax, and he'd attacked us out the back of a club, on the first night that we'd all met. Mia had told me later that he was a vampire, and a really nasty one at that.

I kind of wished she'd told me this before changing to a werewolf right in front of me and tearing his head off with her jaws, but you lived and learned.

'So what happened then?' I asked Wylie, trying my best to look innocent. 'Mia's here now. The cops must've let her off. Must've been a case of, what's it called? Mistaken identity?'

'Mistaken identity my ass,' snorted Wylie, folding his arms. 'Last I saw of her she was being carried away by the cops in a strait-jacket and muzzle like that dude in *Silence Of The Lambs*, which may actually prove your theory about her secretly being a werewolf... a theory, which, by the way you later denied you'd ever mentioned.'

I leaned back against the kitchen counter, biting my thumbnail as I gazed apologetically at Wylie. I felt terrible that his first date in months had gone so badly, but in a way that explained why Mia had been so hammered when she'd got home.

I pictured her again lying on the bed, half passed out, and my anger at her abated somewhat. She must've come home stumbling drunk after escaping from the cops, and Mutt had taken advantage of her.

I didn't want it to be true, but right now I couldn't think of any other explanation.

That also explained another mystery. I'd seen my diminutive friend escape from handcuffs once before when we'd got caught by the vamps, and she'd bitched about how bad it hurt her back. That must've been the first thing out of her mouth when she'd got in, giving Mutt the perfect excuse to strike.

Oh, that boy was in *so* much trouble right now...

Wylie was getting more and more wound up, oblivious to my inner turmoil.

'So yes, my first date in five months sucked. And yes, I am going to blame you. I had to spend the whole of last night down at the cop shop, trying to convince them that I didn't personally know this girl, that I'd been set up on a blind date with her.'

'Wylie, if you'd just calm down and let me explain...'

'And *then*, right after all that crap, you show up at my house at six-thirty in the morning on a Sunday, when I should by all means and rights still be tucked up in bed with a tasteful selection of eighties porn... with the *same* damn whack-job chick and a guy made entirely out of cheekbones, who, by the way, just took a whiz against the side of my neighbor's white Mercedes, out the front of my house.'

I swallowed carefully. 'Did he?'

'He did. I was watching him through the curtains. And to top it all off, you then tell me Crazy Chick's house burned down, and that Cheekbone Boy's apartment was blown up in a gas explosion, and that you can't go back to your own place in case the guys who whacked Karrel are still watching the place, waiting to kill you too... and *then* you ask if you can please all stay with me indefinitely until you find someplace else to live.'

He paused dramatically, panting for breath. 'And you're telling me that *I* should calm down?'

'Wylie, there's a perfectly simple explanation—'

'...that doesn't involve you being on drugs?' Wylie sighed, folding his arms. 'Just tell me this much. What would you do right now, if *you* were in my position?'

I turned around and leaned on the sink beside Wylie, staring straight ahead of me. He was my best friend, and I couldn't talk to him. Couldn't explain.

'If I was in your position?' I thought long and hard. 'Well, I'd give me some chocolate ice-cream and maybe an aspirin or three, and tell me that going crazy isn't a crime.' I glanced at him sidelong, trying to gauge his mood. 'Then I'd give me the number of a good mental health professional and go back to bed. Maybe in the morning all of this would've been a bad dream.'

'Is that all?' asked Wylie, his voice hard.

'Well,' I stole a glance sidelong at my friend. 'I was going to suggest that you lend me your car for the day, if you're not using it...'

'Kayla!'

'I know, I know. I'm a pain in the ass and I use and abuse you and never give you any sex, as is your natural right as the cutest guy in my life,' I said obediently.

'None whatsoever, and it sucks,' said Wylie, without batting an eyelid. He seemed to deflate a little as he turned to face me, looking at me sternly. 'Just tell me one thing. Is this really, truly a case of life and death if there's no room at the inn?'

He pulled the door aside and peered through into the front room, where Mutt was currently scratching himself with one hand and peeling a huge strip of wallpaper off the flaking wall with the other. 'Because at this point, I'm not sure if there's room for you *and* your donkey, too.'

I shuffled my feet, risking a glance up at him.

'Would I be here if I wasn't in some sort of real trouble? You know how much I hate staying in this rat-infested swamp you call a home.'

'Last June you told me that you'd just had all four limbs surgically removed so you wouldn't have to spend the weekend staying here looking after my dog.'

'I'm allergic,' I muttered, but I could see that I was winning. I always won, and he always let me. I had no idea why. I was sure I didn't deserve it. A tiny smile had crept into Wylie's warm brown eyes under his annoyance, and he shifted his position minutely so that his pajama-clad hip was touching mine as we leaned against the sink, side by side—a classic Wylie Reconciliation move.

I decided to go for broke.

'Please?' I added, leaning my head on his shoulder. 'There's a hot chick involved. She's in trouble and we have to save her.'

Wylie folded his arms and looked at me with extreme suspicion. 'Is the hot chick you?'

'Hotter,' I promised him.

Wylie tipped his head back and gave me a long, hard look. 'You cover my night shift for four weeks,' he said, finally.

'Done,' I said fervently.

'And you get me a whole pack of those heavenly caramel biscuity waffle things you stole from that hotel kitchen in Amsterdam and tormented me with all last summer.'

'I'll go straight online and track some down,' I promised.

'And,' Wylie said, holding up a stern finger. 'You never, ever, *ever* tell anyone that I slept with that crazy psycho possibly-a-werewolf girlfriend of yours. Or I'm kicking the lot of you out right now.'

'Sure. Anything you like. I—' My mouth ground to a halt as my brain backfired. My lips opened and closed like a stranded goldfish. I slowly lifted my head from Wylie's shoulder and stared at him.

He glanced down at my shocked face and sighed deeply.

'Yeah, there was a --short delay-- before I took her

to the hospital,' he said, as he reached onto a shelf and handed me a big bottle of aspirin. 'That sweet, innocent little friend of yours moves *fast...*'

At that moment the front door banged open. I heard high heels clomping rapidly on cheap wooden flooring, and then Mia burst into the kitchen, looking extremely pleased with herself.

'Did you get the orange juice?' Wylie asked awkwardly. To my amazement I saw that he was blushing. I stared at him. I'd never seen Wylie blush before.

'Better than juice,' said Mia, practically dancing with excitement, unaware of the revelations that had just taken place. 'I made a quick pit-stop on the way back. Got Kayla a little present.'

She winked at Wylie, making him blush even more deeply, then took my arm in a firm grip and led me through the back door. She practically dragged me down the narrow hallway, picking her way past seemingly endless sacks of garbage and boxes of Wylie's dirty laundry, then opened the back door for me.

'You gonna tell me what's going on?' I asked, wary.

'In a minute,' Mia said, her brown eyes sparkling with secrets as she led me down the garden path towards the road. 'Got a little surprise for you, when you've finished chatting up my new boyfriend.'

'*Boyfriend?*' I stared at her, then decided not to ask. I'd grill her later. I'd already half forgiven her for last night and was too tired to start up any more drama. It was Mutt I was mad at right now. 'Forget it,' I sighed. 'What's the surprise?'

We stepped out onto the street and looked around. Everything seemed normal. Wylie lived in a suburban lower-class neighborhood close to the unfashionable end of Venice Beach. The beach itself had its charms, with the thriving tattoo shops, the daily art markets and the delightfully curving bike paths that cut through mile upon mile of sandy beach. But the housing area behind it had become a kind of beachside storm-drain that collected the human flotsam and jetsam of Hollywood, the washed-up artists and the sunburnt crazies and the drifters who sold woven seaweed charms to tourists and never quite scraped together enough cash to buy a used laptop to write their big feature-film on.

I'd lived here before I moved in with Karrel.

I still missed it.

Mia took my hand, little-girl style, and led me a half block down the patched road towards the parking lot of the nearby Surf Liquor store. The door was barred and the big CLOSED sign was up. I stared around at the empty lot, rubbing my bare arms in the weak early-morning sunshine. There was nothing back here apart from an old set of abandoned tenant garages.

'This had better be good,' I said, looking around, warily. 'I'm in a whole heap of trouble right now, Mia. Those guys who got Karrel are still sniffing around me, and we'll have a tough time defending ourselves now that there's only three of us left.'

Mia's grin widened. 'Not anymore,' she said.

# CHAPTER TWENTY-EIGHT

I STARED AT her in incomprehension, then stepped back in alarm as several sets of random highlights in the darkness of the garages shifted before my eyes and turned into men. There were three of them, and I recognized them immediately.

'Heard you were in a spot of trouble, Missis,' said Buck, ducking down as I flew towards him with a cry of delight. 'Did you miss me?'

I threw my arms around him and hugged him hard enough to bruise. I buried my face into his long blond hair and breathed in, overwhelmed with relief to see him. He smelled like steak tacos and engine oil, familiar 'Buck' scents which made me close my eyes in relief.

His grin widened as I released him and worked my way along the line, hugging Brad and giving Grids a friendly nod. Didn't want to spook him, what with me being a scary werewolf hunter and all. I couldn't help but smile.

I saw Buck glance sidelong at Brad, his gaze mocking, and this time I managed to move quickly enough to snatch the twenty-dollar bill out of Buck's hand. *Ten points to me.* I wondered what they were betting on this time, and if they'd ever get tired of the joke. They were boys, so probably not.

I tucked the twenty into my pocket and looked my pack over with pride, poking my tongue out at Buck. The three young werewolves were casually dressed, sporting their usual surfer outfits of ripped jeans and colorful skin-tight T-shirts that showed off their strong, suntanned torsos. Their waist-length blond hair was for once tied back, their long limbs adorned with assorted brightly colored wristbands and necklaces. Not really tactical, but given the circumstances, I was so pleased to see them they could've been wearing plastic trash sacks for all I cared. I'd need every last man I could get if I was going to go up against Harlequin tonight.

I turned to Mia, my smile fading as I looked her over. I'd have to explain everything to her now if I was going to enlist the help of the wolves. I didn't even know where to begin. 'Um… what are all these people here for?' I asked.

Mia smiled. 'To help you save the world, of course!'

'Save the what?'

I stared at Mia, completely thrown. She didn't even seem fazed. She could've just said 'to help you make pancakes' and her expression would've been just the same.

Mia stepped back to stand with the young wolves. 'It's cool, Kayla. Don't be mad. I get why you didn't tell me. You were just trying to protect me. You're so sweet.'

I didn't even need to ask, but I did.

'Who told you?'

My gaze slowly swiveled until it locked on the figure of Mutt, who had just stepped out of the house a block away. He had an empty crushed beer-can in one hand and he was heading back to the white Mercedes parked nearby.

Mutt's eyes widened in surprise as he looked over my shoulder, back towards the garages. I turned, and grew very still. Standing behind us, looking at me with the usual expression of disapproval on his sunburnt face...

I stepped back from Mia, unable to believe what I was seeing as I stared at the short, grim figure who had been in the shadows.

'Motor,' I said in greeting, folding my arms. I dropped my head a little, not quite a nod, but not quite a bow either. Seeing him here in Wylie's normal neighborhood was weird beyond belief.

'Kayla,' replied the old werewolf. He stayed back, in the early-morning shadows, as though reluctant to join the group. 'You've got a lead on Harlequin, I hear,' he said, without relaxing his tense stance.

I nodded uncertainly, not sure from his tone if this was good or bad.

The old werewolf pressed his lips together, the deep lines on his face creasing. He gave a great sigh, the sound seeming to come deep from the very bowels of his own personal hell. 'You seem surprised to see me here.'

'Just a touch.' It was the understatement of the century.

'I was going to sit this one out, truth be told. Not really my thing. Then a little birdie told me what you did for one of us. I felt it was my duty to come here tonight and offer you the service of my boys.'

'You hear that, monkey pants?' cackled Buck, giving me a wink and a nudge. 'You get to service us all tonight.'

I kicked him in the shins to silence him. I couldn't tear my eyes from Motor.

'Not following you,' I said. 'What do you mean, "What you did for one of us?"'

'He means, you saved my life, little lady,' said a deep and very familiar voice from the shadows, as the giant shape of Magnus stepped from the darkness.

Buck, Grids and Brad all immediately bowed their heads in respect, glancing sideways and nudging each other frantically, like little boys before visiting royalty. Motor was the only one who stood straight, unbowed. He gazed at Magnus with a curiously immobile expression, then turned back to me and removed his hat, holding it between his clasped hands.

I stepped back, looking the old werewolf leader over. Magnus was dressed simply in an expensive-looking grey woolen jacket and cowboy-style jeans. His boots had silver buckles on them, and he'd had a shave and a haircut. Far from the beat-down refugee he'd been not twelve hours before, he now looked like an in-the-money movie producer. He wore sunshades to hide his missing eyes, but his body language radiated an immense amount of power.

'We have a saying where I come from,' said Motor, touching my shoulder. 'By taking revenge on one's enemy, one is even. But in passing it over, he is superior.'

He moved to take Magnus by the arm, leading the blind man gently forwards. To my surprise Magnus grinned and threw an arm over Motor's shoulders, as though the two were old friends.

'I know you've had a touch of trouble with this old bluffer,' Motor said, holding up a hand as I started to protest. 'But believe it or not, this fool and I used to go hunting together, back before his life went one way and mine went the other.' A ghost of a grin twisted his lips. 'He had his empire, I had my boys, and never the two shall meet... or so I thought.'

'That's right. Rub it in,' rumbled Magnus. 'Nice and slow.'

'With pleasure.' Motor's eyes twinkled with a radiance I had never before seen on his face. For a moment he looked like the fearless surfer of his youth. I'd seen photos. 'Never thought I'd see the day when Mr. Hoity-Toity would get down off his big werewolf throne and come banging on my cheap-ass Home Depot door, beggin' *me* for help. This is a great day.'

'*Asking,* old man,' said Magnus mildly. 'Not begging. And it's Kayla you got to thank for me showing up at your door at two in the morning, scaring the crap outta you in your Mickey Mouse jammies.'

'They were Pluto PJs, you daft beggar.'

'Whatever.'

I shook my head in wonder, wondering, briefly, if Motor shopped for pajamas at the same store as Wylie.

'Madam, we are at your disposal,' said Magnus, giving a formal little bow that was only a few degrees in the wrong direction. 'I heard you had a project of some urgency for us to attend to? Something about the end of the world?'

'Er... yeah.' I glared at Mia and ran a hand through my hair, trying to factor this new development into my plan. My world had just turned a one-eighty on me in three minutes. My brain was starting to ache with the possibilities. 'If you're not busy, of course?'

Magus smiled, baring enormous lion-like teeth. He waved a hand towards the back of the liquor store garages, where I saw the familiar battered shapes of Buck and Grid's two black cars waiting, engines idling.

'Lead the way, Captain,' he said.

# CHAPTER TWENTY-NINE

MY NEWFOUND CONFIDENCE in my plan seemed to have evaporated by the time I neared the spot where I'd promised I'd meet Cyan, eight hours of preparation later: the secret back load-in entrance to the Circus of Sins club.

Seen from outside, the nightclub was much bigger than it looked from the inside. It sprawled three blocks in either direction and a good fifteen stories up, all mirrored windows and cutting edge trendy architecture.

In other words, the exact opposite of a place you'd expect to find a crazed madman secretly plotting to destroy the world. I'd heard volcano bases were more traditional.

The club was the underground bit, I was fairly sure, while the building on the top was some kind of corporate offices. During our little talk at the bar Cyan had told me that Doll was housed in the penthouse suite on the very top floor of the office building. She'd promised that there would be no security to stop us.

Yeah, right.

It went without question that I couldn't trust her. However, I also knew that there was no fury like the proverbial woman scorned. I'd been there myself on more than one occasion, and I was ready to bet that if there was honor among thieves, Cyan was about the most honorable vampire out there right now.

Harlequin had taken down the Hunters by bribing a rat in our midst. It made perfect sense that we'd take him down the same way. We'd both agreed that.

So this was my plan. Cyan would let us all in, and we'd follow her upstairs and save Doll. We'd have plenty of time. It was nine PM right now, and according to Cyan, Harlequin wouldn't be here for at least another hour. Right now he was in the next town, picking up some vital last ingredient that would help him fulfill the Prophecy. When he was done he'd swing by the club and collect Doll. Then he'd begin the rites that in just three short hours would end with him calling down heavenly vengeance upon the world.

I had to stop him, whatever the cost.

I looked down at my tightly closed fist, took a deep breath, and opened it. A simple iron key lay in my palm. I tilted it into the light, letting out my breath through my teeth. It was an insignificant looking key, hastily cut out of cheap silver metal, but right now I was quite literally holding the key to the future survival of Mankind in my hand.

It was the key to Doll's room. Cyan had given it to me.

*Three hours to go.*

I picked up my pace as I rounded the corner of the darkened building, wolves in tow, praying that nobody would try to stop us before we reached our destination.

Despite my confidence in my plan, I wished that the wolves would let me go and check that Cyan was really here before bringing them in as backup.

These were people I cared about. I didn't want them winding up a lunch-time snack for a vampire guard. If anything went wrong, I'd have more at risk than just my pride.

I reached the spot Cyan had described to me behind the club: a long, red-painted wall opposite a large ring of flagpoles, bearing flags from all around the world. I stopped under one I wasn't familiar with: an entirely black flag bearing a pattern of white stars at its center. It was also the largest of them all.

I blinked, frowning up at it. Seen from a certain angle, the stars formed the shape of the letter 'H'.

And I'd thought that Mutt was big-headed. *Ha.*

This had to be the place. I shoved aside an empty dumpster on wheels that had been blocking the wall and peered into the darkness. I could just make out the sloped edges of a hidden doorway. If I hadn't been told it was there I would never have been able to find it. I glanced triumphantly behind me, almost glowing with satisfaction.

'So what happens if Cyan and Harley-boy kiss and make up before she comes to meet us?' Motor grumbled from the darkness, making me jump. 'You still think she'll let you in so you can steal her lover boy's pet angel and ruin his life's work?'

I tried to think happy thoughts, but dammit, it was in my head now. Could it happen? Possibly. Knowing what I knew about Cyan, I knew she was crazy enough and obsessed enough to turn on me if he got down on one knee and begged her to take him back.

But would she let that happen, after what she'd told me about the terrible way Harlequin had treated her?

I felt the sudden heat of the other wolves' gazes burning into me, and glowered at Motor. He had a point, but he could have brought that up before we came here, preferably in private.

'I guess we'll deal with that *if* it happens,' I said as coolly as I could manage.

I stepped back in alarm as a loud cracking noise came from behind the disused door as it was slowly levered open. I smiled in triumph, quickly recovering my composure. *Right on cue.* The door was so secret it probably hadn't been used in many months. It sounded like Cyan was having to pry it open with her wrist blades.

The door finally gave way with a resounding crash, brick dust billowing up in a cloud. I stepped forwards eagerly, squinting into the light.

My welcoming smile froze on my face.

A solid mass of vampire security guards packed the doorway. More spilled into the brightly lit hallway beyond. There must have been two dozen of them, all dressed in the characteristic black and red uniforms of Harlequin's royal guard.

Cyan was nowhere to be seen. Either she'd ratted us out, or she'd been busted herself.

Their guns were all pointed at us. The sound of safety catches being removed and rounds being chambered seemed very loud.

Motor slowly leaned in behind me and cleared his throat in the sudden silence.

'Start dealing,' he whispered.

\* \* \*

So THIS WAS the end. We were royally screwed.

I sat back on the cold concrete floor and watched as the braver members of my hunting party took it in turns to attack the solid wall of metal bars which was all that stood between us and freedom.

I caught Buck's eye as he stepped away from the door, sweating. The echoes of his kick rang out through the dimly lit room, but the steel door wasn't even dented. The fourth wall of the cell was a thick glass window, overlooking a fifteen-story drop. There was no ledge on the outside, just the slick, mirror-like marble of the side of the building.

'Look at it this way,' I said with a shrug. 'At least we're in.'

'Told you Cyan can't be trusted,' said Motor, from the other cell. He looked almost pleased to be proven right. 'Why does nobody listen to me?'

'Easy, Pa,' said Buck. He shot me a sympathetic look. 'He gets crabby when they take away his prune juice.'

I heaved a deep sigh and turned to look for the twentieth time in as many minutes around the big concrete room we were being held captive in.

There were eight of us in the long, high-ceilinged room. It was split into two separate cells which faced each other across a narrow passageway, with four of us in each cell. The back wall of my cell was a giant window, which looked down at a dizzying fifteen-story drop into the car park of the Circus of Sins, far below. Escape was, as far as I could make out, impossible. I wondered briefly what had been kept in these pens before us, then instantly regretted it.

Mutt sat with his back to me in the opposite cell,

staring at the wall that backed his own cell. He was currently ignoring me. The others were arranged in sulking, bleeding groups up and down the two cells. Only Motor looked in any way cheerful, and only then I guessed because he now had a great excuse to bitch at me for the rest of my life, of which I had about— I glanced again at my watch— an hour and a half left.

Buck noticed my pained expression, and came to sit beside me on the floor.

'How're you holding up, love?' he asked, sliding up close to me to warm me up. It was cold in the cells, and I'd lost my jacket in the scuffle when they'd been bringing us up here.

I tried to look cheerful. 'Nothing a submachine gun and a visit to the Cheesecake Factory wouldn't fix.' My stomach growled and I gave him a half smile, which faded slowly as I caught Mutt's eye in the opposite cell. He was now staring across at me with a look of open accusation on his face.

*He blamed me for this. Of course he blamed me. I had trusted the word of a vampire over his, and now look what had happened.*

I turned away, deliberately ignoring him.

'Everyone's staring at me,' I whispered to Buck. 'I hate this.'

'Look at it this way, pumpkin,' said Buck, rubbing my shoulders. 'Sure, they're staring. But look around. What do you notice?'

I unwillingly looked from face to face. Every wolf met my gaze without looking away. There was a curious immobility to the group, a breathless tension, as though they were waiting for some kind of instruction.

'They not looking at you, they're looking *to* you,'

murmured Buck. 'They're your pack now. Sure, they're mad at you, but there's only one way out of this. You brought them here, so you're the one who has to lead them out again.'

'Me? Lead *them*?'

I looked around at the assembled faces, trying to imagine this. The other two triplets Grids and Brad were leaning on the wall by the door in my cell, and watching me eagerly, as though expecting me to pull a rabbit out of my ass at any minute. The lean and muscular shape of Mutt had gone back to sulking, but with his head turned slightly back towards me, as though listening. Motor was standing with his back to the light in the center of the big window, talking in a low voice to Mia. But he glanced at me from time to time, watching me over her shoulder, his expression a mixture of disapproval and expectation.

My pack was waiting for me. It was my move.

I hesitated, then leaned in closer to Buck, butterflies dancing in my stomach.

'Don't we have the *real* werewolf leader in here?' I said, nodding at Magnus. The older werewolf sat in the far corner of Mutt's cell, staring blindly at the wall. His dark glasses had been smashed by the vampires, and his empty eye-sockets looked horrific under the stark overhead lights. Everyone was avoiding him.

'Sure,' whispered Buck, dropping his voice still further. 'But face it, Kay. It's kind of hard for him to lead the victory charge if he can't see where he's leading us.'

Buck looked up at me, his eyes shining.

'Just try. I know you can do it.'

I nodded to myself, then squeezed his shoulder in

thanks and stood up, looking around me carefully. The captive wolves all turned to face me, watching my every move with sullen, expectant eyes.

Screwing up my nerves, I circled the room, trying to look confident and decisive as I examined the walls for a weak spot. What would Ninette do in a situation like this? Probably melt a hole in the wall and go out looking for someone's balls to put on a stick, that's what. The thought made me smile. Realistically, I wasn't quite strong enough yet to blast through two-foot-thick concrete, but if I could find a place where the wall was a little thinner, perhaps I could use whatever remained of my Dark Arts powers to burn through it, get us all to safety.

Or maybe there would be a loose brick somewhere...

Buck grabbed my hand and squeezed it tight for reassurance. I glanced at him as he briefly leaned his slender body against mine, burying his head in my hair. I gave him a half-hearted hug, and was shocked to feel the frantic beating of his heart through his textured cotton top. His slim, lithe frame shook with some unknown emotion as he pulled me tight against him, letting out his breath in a hard sigh.

I realized then that he was terrified out of his mind.

I shook my head in wonder, gazing down at Buck as he pushed his face against my shoulder like a frightened puppy, not quite meeting my eyes. After meeting all the other big, tough wolves who hung out with Mutt, I'd just assumed that all werewolves were automatically bad-asses who fought vampires for a living. I'd forgotten that these guys were surfers, not fighters. I wondered if Buck had even seen a vampire before, let alone been captured by one.

'It smells like vampire in here,' he said quietly, picking at a loose thread on my top. 'If they eat me, you can have my Star Wars action figures.'

'They're not gonna eat us,' I promised him. 'I'll get us out of here.'

Buck looked at me hopefully and I felt the stirring of protectiveness deep within me. I reached out to rub his back, wondering where the hell Cyan had got to... whether she had really betrayed me, or if Harlequin had found out about her defection and killed her too.

Either way, we were pretty much screwed.

'Buck,' I whispered, trying to keep my voice from trembling. 'We're in some really deep shit right now, and we can't fix it stuck in here. Do you think you can help me get us out of here?'

It was only then that I became aware of Mutt's jealous gaze burning into me from across the hallway. He slowly got to his feet and gripped the bars of his cell in white-knuckled hands.

'You should be asking *me* that question,' he called out loudly. He sounded angry and confused. 'And yes, I can get *us* out of here. Surfers aren't much good at doing anything that requires using their brains.'

'Like you're any better,' I snorted. 'I don't see you doing anything to get us out of here.'

'I'm on it, girlie,' Mutt promised, stretching his arms above his head so that his lean muscles stood out, gleaming in the moonlight. 'No sweat. Just gimmie a minute to warm up...'

'Maybe I don't *want* you to get me out,' I muttered under my breath, turning my back on him. Buck leaned his head on my shoulder and I started stroking his silky hair to calm myself.

'What's that supposed to mean?' asked Mutt, a veiled threat in his voice. I saw him look hard at Buck, as though reassessing him. I could tell he didn't much like what he saw or the way that I was touching Buck, innocent enough as it was.

*As though Mutt knew anything about innocence.*

'I think you should stay right where you are,' I said quietly. 'You got what you wanted. You two are finally together. Why would you need me anymore?'

'*What?*'

Mutt was staring at me like I'd just spoken to him in Cantonese. I saw Mia dart a quick, guilty glance in my direction, seeming to shrink inside herself as she sat on the cold metal bench. She'd always been quicker to catch on than Mutt.

Hell, a *chimpanzee* would be quicker to catch on than Mutt...

Mutt cleared his throat, drawing himself up. 'I have no idea what you're talking about,' he declared, his gaze still fixed firmly on Buck. His tone turned almost patronizing. 'But come on, Kayla, did you really think this would work? Making deals with vampires? I swear, I can't leave you alone for five minutes...'

'Maybe I want to be left alone,' I snapped.

'And going out by yourself after dark?' Mutt still wasn't getting it. 'Mia told me how you got your little 'lead'. You're lucky you didn't get yourself killed. You shoulda let us know if you wanted to go out. We'd have come with you, protected you....'

'Yeah, right,' I snorted. 'I would've asked you to come out with me last night... if the two of you hadn't been *otherwise occupied*.'

I hadn't meant to bring it up, I truly hadn't, but my

anger pushed the admission unstoppably out of me, as though shunted through my lips by a freight train of jealousy.

I bit my lip, breathing hard. There. It was said now.

I saw the slow light of comprehension dawn in Mutt's eyes. He stared at me for a full five seconds, then quickly blinked and shook his head in instant dismissal. 'What are you talking about?' he blustered. 'I didn't do anything last night. I stayed over in case you needed me—'

'In case *I* needed you…?' I laughed out loud at that one. 'Oh, come on! I'm not stupid, Mutt! I *heard* you both… well. I heard *her*, at least.' I gave a quick, tight smile, avoiding Mia's suddenly-horrified gaze. 'Sorry, Mi. But it didn't sound like either of you did much *sleeping* last night.'

Mia was on her feet instantly. She slipped her hands through the bars, looking vulnerable and cute in her mix-and-match clothing.

'Kayla,' she started, her voice soft and sincere.

Mutt hushed her.

'Heard us doing what?' he asked, angry now.

'You know *exactly* what I heard!' I exploded. 'Mutt, I can't believe you!'

I held his angry gaze for a long moment, furious, then swung around to face Mia, shaking my head. 'And Mia, you of all people. You know how I feel about—'

I broke off, ashamed into silence.

Mutt was the first person to speak up.

'How you feel about what?' he asked softly.

'Forget it,' I said, turning away from him.

'No. Tell me.' Mutt's hands tightened on the bars of his cell, his amber eyes seeking mine. He looked very serious all of a sudden, like I was seeing beneath some kind of mask that he'd been wearing. 'What were you going to say?'

'Nothing. Absolutely nothing. Forget it. Forget I ever existed.'

'Easier said than done,' came a horribly familiar voice from the dark end of the corridor. 'But please do forget the lady. All the more for me.'

Beside me in the cell, Buck stiffened in terror, his slim body pressing hard against mine. I saw Mutt and Mia react instantly, tensing up and getting to their feet in their separate cell.

Two giant vampire guards came into view in the dim fluorescent light, dragging a tattered, stumbling shape with them.

*Niki.*

I IMMEDIATELY TENSED up. Mutt's eyes never left me as I backed away from the door of my cell, watching as the guards jammed the key in and unlocked it. They threw Niki in with me and Buck and slammed the door, locking it behind him.

Oh, great. My life was now complete.

I hopped back in alarm as Niki rolled over on the floor, giggling. He was wasted out of his mind, still clad in the same outfit that he had been wearing last night at the Ring.

Buck stared at Niki, tentatively sniffing the air. His face went slack with fear. He edged around the giggling vampire before I could stop him and ran to the door of the jail cell.

'Hey!' Buck yelled after the retreating guards, frantic,

rattling the bars. 'Get me out of here! He's a vampire!'

The taller and uglier of the two guards turned and gave him a single morose look.

'So?'

'Are you crazy?' he yelled. 'He'll kill us all!'

'So kill him first,' yawned the guard as he reached the exit door. 'Help me out with my paperwork.'

The end door slammed with a sound like the doors to Hades closing. A pair of hydraulic bolts rammed shut, locking the pens down for the night.

In the echoing silence I couldn't even bear to look across at Mutt, who was by now gripping the bars of his cell, staring at me a little too hard for my liking. Instead I turned back to Buck, to reassure him. He was standing with his back pressed against the bars, frozen in place. His eyes were huge as he stared at Niki.

I instantly moved towards him, focusing on calming his fear. It was far easier to deal with than my own. Before I could reach him, Niki was suddenly standing between us without seeming to pass through the intervening space.

I sized him up as we locked gazes, as though preparing to fight. I tensed in surprise. Niki looked as though he had been badly beaten and then some. A livid series of bruises blossomed across his cheekbone, and dried blood caked around his eye socket and on his lip. His friendly smile was for once missing and his face as he looked at me was cold and hard.

What had happened to him, after I'd left the ring with Magnus?

'Spying on me again?' I asked with a smile, trying to make light of the situation.

Niki grinned, although his black eyes held zero

warmth. I suddenly felt afraid. His voice was flat and hard when he replied.

'It's always such a beautiful view. From any position.'

He made the last word sound like something dirty. Mutt's growl was just audible above the metallic creaking sound which suddenly filled the air. I glanced out of the cell to see the steel bars beneath Mutt's hands start to whiten with strain. They bent fractionally as he pulled steadily outwards on them, not one other part of his body moving, his black gaze locked on Niki.

'Touch her and you're dead, leech,' he growled.

Niki turned around, stared at him.

'I'm already dead, then,' he said, with a grin.

The sound of creaking metal grew louder. I heard Mia gasp, and my face flushed red with humiliation and anger.

I opened my mouth to protest. Niki's hand blurred as he put a silencing finger to my lips, letting it linger just a moment too long.

I glared at him. His eyes shone with malicious laughter as his gaze flicked back to Mutt, reading his tense body-language like a book. In the short time I'd known him, I'd seen that Niki was the kind of guy who loved to mess with people, to rattle the monkey-cage and see what came out. He'd kick Beelzebub himself in the balls just for giggles, even if it meant a longer stint in the pen.

Right now I was praying to God that his sense of self preservation kicked in before Mutt got to him, because from the look on Mutt's face he was about to find out exactly how good at killing werewolves were, bars or no bars.

Niki turned back to me then, and smiled broadly.

His eyes flicked left and right, taking in and instantly dismissing the other three wolves in our cell. If I thought he'd looked human before, he looked considerably less so now. His eyes were a glossy crimson-black, glinting out from under a wild tangle of jet-black hair that now put me more in mind of porcupine quills than human hair. He moved in too-quick, sinuous bursts as he closed in on me with the deadly grace of the predator, forcing me to back up quickly, every inch of him radiating a kind of effortless vitality.

He walked right up to me and stopped directly in front of me, his gaze steely. The triplets growled. Niki didn't appear to hear them.

'So you're hanging out with werewolves now,' he said, folding his arms.

'Yeah. So what?'

Niki's gaze flicked quickly to Mutt and back and his lip curled. His voice only trembled the tiniest bit as he replied.

'How's that working out for you?'

'What's it to you?'

Niki gave me a tight-lipped smile, something shutting off in his eyes. He flicked a loaded glance at the other wolves in the cell. As he made eye contact with Grids, the young wolf's face twisted with pain. He backed up a step, reaching up to grab his head, shaking it as though it hurt him. Buck watched his brother in fear, backing off along with him. Something was wrong here. Very wrong.

'Nick, what's up with you?' I asked, getting angry now. 'Why are you acting like this?'

'I just heard all about you,' Niki breathed, taking a drunken step closer to me. 'And I mean *all* of it. Who you are. What you do.'

'What do you mean?'

'The doorman at the Ring is a vampire, Kayla. Vamps can read minds, in case you missed the memo. It's his job to check people's thoughts as they enter, make sure no-one's thinking about blowing the place up or starting trouble. He asked me afterwards why I'd brought you of all people in as a date.'

He paused and clenched his fists, fixing me with a morose stare.

'Why didn't you tell me what you are, Kayla?'

'What, you mean a Hunter? I thought you already knew.'

Niki stared at me, long and hard. I stared back, trembling very slightly, willing him with my eyes not to give away my secret, not to out me in front of my friends. I wanted to tell them in my own time, to pick the perfect moment. To explain why I hadn't told them before.

I could see right now that I wasn't going to get that chance.

'I didn't mean a Hunter, Kayla.' Niki hiccupped loudly, waved a hand in front of his mouth. 'See, it's like this. Me and *werewolves*... we don't get on so good. They killed my... they destroyed my...' He stopped, weaving, fixing me with an accusing look. 'You don't care. Of course you don't. I thought that you were human, that you were *normal*, that we had a chance of one day... never mind. But then they told me who you are, what you are...'

'Nick, I think you've had way too much to drink—'

'No.' Niki shook his head hard, a muscle in his jaw twitching. 'No such thing as too much to drink. Forget it. You'll never understand. I let your little friend live because I liked you, by the way. I thought it was kind of cute. A Hunter keeping a pet werewolf. Fancy that.'

He glanced at Mutt with dark eyes and his smile faded. 'But werewolves don't belong in the house, Kayla. They belong in the yard, on a chain, with the rest of the animals. I thought you should know that.'

The hostile silence in the cell finally got through to Niki. He released the bars and shut up, looking up into eight pairs of accusing golden eyes, every muscle in his body coiled as though ready to attack.

But instead of attacking, he gave a sudden mad smile and reached into his back pocket for a pack of cigarettes which obviously wasn't there.

'I get that. But I don't agree with it,' I snapped, my anger rising. 'Niki, what did they do to you? Why the hell did you let me go in the Ring, take part in that dumb act when you knew what was going to happen? I could've been killed back there!'

'What ring?' asked Mutt. His voice had teeth in it.

'Because the act went wrong, dumbass,' snapped Niki, sweeping a hand through his tangled hair. 'The angel was s'posed to rescue you, take you up in the cage. Thought you girls could get a little chit-chat time in there during the half-time show. Thought that would make you *happy*.' Niki sniffed, his tough mask slipping for a moment. 'Didn't know they were going to send *that* wolf out tonight. Boy, he was a mean one. Blame my father for that. Ha.'

In the cell on the other side of the room, Magnus started softly growling.

'What wolf?' Mutt rattled the bars. 'Kayla, what's he talking about?'

Niki shot him a dark look.

'When those guards jumped me for helping you escape, they took me back to *him*. He asked me why in the name of sweet Jesus I'd brought a Hunter spy to his club as a date. And that wasn't all he told me.'

Niki focused on me, the hard mask slipping back into place. 'Lemmie tell you, kid. If I'd have known you were a werewolf when I met you, last night might have gone a whole lot differently.'

*Ah, crap. He'd got me.*

'Kayla. What's he talking about?' Mia called out, glaring at Niki.

I jumped as Niki stepped forward without warning and ripped the bandana off my wrist, exposing my half-healed werewolf bite. 'I'm talking about *this*, little miss. How do you explain this?'

There was a long, shocked silence. I saw Motor get up and move closer, staring at me with a strange expression on his face. There was anger there, and of course disapproval… but also a weird kind of hope.

'You should have told me,' said Mia quietly.

'She should have told all of us,' said Motor, his face set like stone. 'You're in big trouble, little girl. Hunters who get bit are tracked down and shot, if they're lucky. You know that as well as we do. They got too many secrets. Do you have any idea how much danger we're all in, now, even if we get out of here?'

'Whoa, back it up a step there,' said Mutt, gripping the bars. 'Just how *did* last night go, Kayla?'

'You mean she didn't tell you guys about the best night of her life?'

Niki stepped closer, ignoring Mutt's growl. He stopped a hand-span away from me, as though making a point. I tensed up as the heat of his body washed over me like the pulse of radiation from an atomic bomb. Despite the fact that we were in a jail cell, despite the fact that everyone was watching us, the scent of him was still as intoxicating to me as ever. It had to be a vampire thing. The delicious scent of him washed over me, filling my senses, silencing my mind. I felt like a starving man standing before a rack of crackling, frying bacon.

Niki leaned forwards, breathing out hard. I felt my mouth start to water involuntarily as I gazed at his lips, remembering the sweet, warm taste of his mouth on mine....

I realized I was looking into Niki's eyes again, and tore my gaze from his with some difficulty. I backed up two steps, my hand going reflexively to my necklace. Niki bared his teeth and mock-hissed at me, then threw back his head and laughed uproariously.

I'd never seen him this drunk.

Then his smile faded and a dark light came into his eyes. I saw him shift his position and lock his muscles as he stared hard at my throat. He looked for all the world like he was about to attack me, for no reason other than he'd just found out that I was a werewolf.

So be it, then.

I focused on channeling my emotions into a bolt of magic that would protect me, and felt my dragon charm start to warm up. He was just drunk. I didn't want to hurt him, but if he attacked me I'd have to try and knock him out. If turned down the voltage, hit him at just the right angle...

I backed up, getting ready to fire, then froze as my vision suddenly flashed with black, as though someone had punched me in the back of the head. I gasped as a bright, terrible image flashed into my mind…

*Me and Niki, writhing on the furred blankets in Mia's front room right where I'd been with Mutt. My head was thrown back in bliss as his hands moved softly down my naked sides, his fangs tearing through his gums as he started to lose control… an image of what things could've been like between us, had I stayed human…*

'Knock it off, Nick!' I snapped, shaking my head. 'That's not funny!'

'It wasn't supposed to be.'

Niki's eyes shone with the effort not to laugh, even as a tear glinted on his cheek. I backed up two steps, breathing heavily, my hand going reflexively to my protective charm. His eyes darkened as he moved in closer to me, ignoring the warning growls from the rest of the pack. I knew I had maybe seconds left before he jumped me. He bared his unnaturally sharp teeth in a grin, and I raised a hand before me and focused on channeling my emotions into a bolt of magic that would protect me.

I'd never killed anyone using magic before, but if I hit him at just the right angle…

'Oh, yeah. Right.' Niki eyed me with studied indifference. 'So you do black magic. Big flippin' deal. I could take you down in a heartbeat.'

'Why don't you try?'

Niki's eyes narrowed.

He boldly stepped right up to me, breathing into my face, so close that his hips were almost touching mine. I clenched my fists as I waited for my dark magic to fire and drive him off, but nothing happened. The growling increased in volume from the rest of the pack, but no-one seemed to want to be the one to make the first move.

'See?' said Niki, grinning like a little kid. 'Achilles heel of black magic. It's all in the mind. That shit don't work if you don't genuinely want to kill someone.'

'I genuinely want to kill you after last night,' I whispered, although my voice sounded a lot more uncertain now. 'I could've been killed in that ring.'

'Bull. You had a great time, admit it. You'd do the same again if you got half a chance. Lemmie demonstrate.'

Niki grinned, and then leaned in to kiss me.

A massive crash rang out, reverberating through the room. My head snapped around. A giant silver werewolf was lying on the floor of Mutt's cell, shaking his huge head as though dazed. After a moment the creature scrambled to his feet, kicked off the remainder of Mutt's clothes and limped up to the intact bars. He stared up at them, inspecting them intently. His growl of frustration turned to a frenzied whine as he transferred his gaze to me.

I took advantage of the distraction to break free of Niki's grip. I shoved him roughly away and danced back out of reach, warning him with a glare to stay back.

'Cool it, Mutt,' I called out, my throat tight. 'The bars are too thick. Don't dent your big dumb cone-head. I'll deal with this jackass...'

My voice tailed off as I stared up at the white-painted walls right behind Niki. My mouth fell open in horror. Close-up, I saw that what I'd thought was an artistically textured surface was in fact hundreds and hundreds of hastily-painted-over claw-marks, long fork-shaped slashes which scored almost a half inch deep into the surface of the reinforced walls. It looked like the wall of a lion-house. I swallowed as I came to a sudden and horrible realization.

Something bad had been kept in here before us.

Something that had wanted, very badly, to get out...

My pulse sped up as a new and horrible idea came to my mind. They hadn't manacled us when they'd put us in here. Hadn't chained us to the walls. They'd just left us loose... loose in a freshly-painted room with giant claw marks all over the walls.

We weren't prisoners here, I realized.

We were lunch.

But what could possibly be big and bad enough to eat a full-grown werewolf, let alone eight of us?

I reached out to touch one of the slash-marks, watching Niki's eyes narrow in confusion as he turned to check out what I was looking at. We both froze as a scream of pure animal outrage echoed through the wall. I jumped and spun around as a warm hand descended on my shoulder, pulling me backwards, away from Niki.

It was Buck. He looked as freaked as I did.

'Please tell me that was your stomach,' he said.

Before I could reply, the main door to the cell rattled and the loud *clunk-clunk* of a dozen locks being disengaged rang out. The door was flung open with a crash, letting a blinding flood of white light into the room.

I groaned as my eyes adjusted to the light.

Harlem stood in the open doorway, grinning in at us. He was dressed casually in a tight black-and-red T-shirt paired with semi-destroyed black Junker jeans with legs so slashed up they were more hole than jean. Two thick dog-wrangling arm-guards were strapped to his strong forearms, and a set of mirrored cop-style motorcycle glasses protected his eyes.

And beside him, straining against a ship-sized chain, was…

Silence slammed across the room. I couldn't believe my eyes.

'What the sweet holy *fuck* is that?' cried Motor.

# CHAPTER THIRTY

I STOOD FROZEN as Harlem took two steps into our cell, dragging the hideous *thing* in with him. I couldn't tear my eyes off it as it strained away from him on the end of its lion-snare; a thick metal pole with a noose of inch-thick chain attached to it.

*So this was what Harlequin had been breeding.*

I took a step forward and stared, fascinated despite myself.

The creature reminded me a little of a giant, hunched, man-sized bat, all fangs and claws and snapping teeth, but the proportions were all wrong. Its limbs were compact and insanely muscular, and its two front claws were grotesquely overgrown, hanging down like a pair of foot-long twin scythes.

Thick webs of skin stretched from the tips of its giant claws to the backs of its legs in a set of primitive wings, carpeted with grey, spiny feathers and bound tightly to its back with a series of silver clips and straps. Its teeth were curved and needle-like, stretching a good three inches from its lips in either direction like a bulldog gone wrong, and it had a fearsome array of spines and bone-spurs that ran up its spine in a waving frill that tapered off to a thin, almost delicate crest on top of its head. Its naked skin was so white it hurt your eyes to look at it under the bright lights

It was blindfolded, its eyes covered by a thick strip of silver duct-tape.

The creature's clawed hind feet scrabbled on the floor as it fought to get to us, screeching and yowling, its overgrown front talons raking at the chain around its neck as its nostrils twitched and flared. It could obviously smell us, even though it couldn't see us. The creature lifted its bat-like nose and scented the air, then opened its mouth and screamed. It looked half-starved.

I swallowed, the blood rushing from my face. Now I knew what had been kept in this room before us.

Harlem jerked it back sharply, both hands on the snare-pole.

'Grey. *Heel!*' he snapped, scolding the freakish beast as though it were a dog at the park. The creature turned its snubbed, bat-like face up to the ceiling and howled, squeezing its prehensile hands together in an unmistakable expression of misery.

Harlem saw the look on my face and grinned.

'I know what you're thinking,' he said, as a stunned silence fell over the group. 'There's two of us, and eight of you. Oh, and look. I've left the door wide open behind me. What a silly boy I am.' He turned to face Niki, handing him a pair of silvered glasses and nodding towards the door. 'Your dad wants to speak with you, Nick. Bring the girl and quit fucking with the prisoners.'

'Your *father?*' spat Mutt, eyeballing Niki.

'Oh yeah,' I said, as offhandedly as I could manage. *I had forgotten to mention that little fact. I may as well break the news and secure my place in Special Hell.* 'Everyone, meet Niki. Niki is Harlequin's son.'

The effect of my words was electric. I'd thought that it wasn't possible for the pack to move any further back in the room. They somehow managed it, pressing themselves against the walls and looking between me and Niki in shock. Mutt just stared at me, slowly shaking his head. Even Magnus looked alarmed, which from a guy with no eyes was pretty impressive.

'Yeah,' said Niki sadly, taking in the suddenly-frozen atmosphere. 'I get that a lot.'

Enough already. Time to put an end to this freak-show.

I stepped quickly forwards and raised my hands, as if to cast a fireball at the bat-creature. Harlem flinched back and took one hand off the snare, as though preparing to release it.

'Careful, my sweet,' he purred. 'You take me out, I let go of this little guy.'

As one, everyone moved back. Even Niki backed up a step, staring at the creature with a kind of pained distaste.

I smiled faintly, studying Harlem as hope flared inside me. He thought I was much stronger than I was, that I was a properly trained Dark Artist.

That meant I suddenly had a hell of a lot more bargaining power.

I made a big show of considering his words, then nodded and stepped back, folding my arms high up on my chest like a wizard taking a break from a duel.

'Very well,' I said, as though it was a big effort for

me not to magically incinerate him on the spot. 'One condition. I let you live, you let my friends go. They have nothing to do with any of this.'

'The wolves?' Harlem's voice was bright with interest, and I could see that I'd picked the wrong way forwards. Now he looked twice as interested in them. 'Uh-uh. We're all in this together, sweetpea. No deal.'

He put his other hand back on the chain and hauled Grey backwards, his huge muscles bulging under the strain. The creature's claws left deep gouges on the concrete floor as it flailed and snapped, fighting to get free.

'Now. Which one of you pampered pooches thinks you can take my boy Grey, here?' Harlem's gaze flitted around the group. 'C'mon. Surely one of you gotta have the balls to save your friends?' He spread his arms wide, gesturing behind him. 'Look! Door's wide open! You could all be outta here in two minutes!'

He gave a wide, mocking smile, enjoying the fear on my friends' faces.

I decided then and there to call Harlem's bluff. Screw it. Harlem was way too confident, too smug. I had to try, had to protect my new pack. I flexed my arms and concentrated hard, feeling the first faint stirrings of magical power awaken in me. I was tired but I could do this.

Time to put my money where my mouth was, and...

Buck stepped forwards. 'I'll fight him,' he said bravely.

'No!' I shouted, but it was too late. Harlem grinned as he nodded to Buck, accepting the challenge. He leaned over to grab the snarling beast's chain collar. Getting a tight grip on it, he reached around its snapping fangs and tore its duct-tape blindfold off.

The effect on the creature was immediate. It instantly calmed down, the tortured heaving of its chest slowing, the tension in its muscles relaxing. It gulped and slowly rocked back upright onto its hind legs in a kind of defensive half-crouch, furling its leathery wings behind it with a curious dignity, like an old man tucking his cape behind him. Its newly-revealed eyes were squeezed tight shut.

It wasn't angry, I realized.

It was terrified.

Harlem sighed, baring his teeth. Leaning forward, he slapped the creature hard on the rump, as though it were a stubborn horse refusing to leave the starting blocks.

Grey's eyes flew open with a flash of blue fire, and focused on the first thing he saw.

*Buck.*

The young werewolf screamed as he made eye contact with the creature. He instantly dropped to the floor and started rolling over and over, tearing and beating at his skin as though he were on fire. I was barely aware that I was yelling as I ran towards him, along with half of the wolf pack.

What the hell? The creature hadn't gone near him, hadn't touched him. All it had done was look at him, and he'd gone down like a sack of bricks.

I dropped to my knees and grabbed at Buck's flailing limbs as he thrashed around on the floor beneath us, managing to seize his wrist. The blond werewolf's eyes were open wide, staring sightlessly at the ceiling, his face frozen in an expression of unholy terror. Grids grabbed his other wrist while Brad fell across his legs, pinning his lower body down.

'What the hell have you done to him?' I yelled, wrestling his wrist to the floor. Buck subsided briefly, until a spasm ripped through his whole body and he threw all of us off with a burst of frenzied strength. He resumed clawing at his skin, screaming bloody murder. Foam started to pour out of his mouth.

I went tumbling backwards and landed on my ass, but I couldn't tear my eyes off the live-action horror-show happening right in front of me. Buck's tall, lean body was changing, morphing, ripping itself apart as claws and spines and things that didn't belong on the human or werewolf body tore their way out of him. His tanned skin changed color right before my eyes as though he were bleeding from the inside, all the pigment bleaching out to be replaced by a deathly white hue, like a corpse.

Buck screamed as his hands snapped backwards and welded themselves to his back, the skin liquefying and reforming around them to hold his wrists tight, like wet cement. He yelled in fear and tore them free, ripping a sheet of wing-shaped skin off with them. The raw flesh beneath instantly healed up, stretching outwards to form wings. His body jerked as long spiny scythes burst out of his fingertips, the white tips so long and fine that you could see the light through them.

His eyes flashed open, blazing with an internal blue fire.

He looked as terrified as Grey did.

A second later he lurched to his feet with a bloodcurdling howl and pelted at full speed towards the wall-sized window. Before any of us could stop him he deliberately leaped through it headfirst, crashing through the glass at full speed.

He didn't even scream as he tumbled fifteen stories to the ground, vanishing into the darkness below. It was so far down that I couldn't hear the final impact.

There was a brief, stunned silence. Cold wind whipped into the room, sending chills down my spine. Behind me I heard a wail of despair from Motor, followed by the sounds of a scuffle as Grids seized Brad by the arms, holding his brother back as he tried to throw himself at Harlem and his pet, howling for vengeance.

Slowly, very slowly, I turned to look at Harlem. He smiled an evil smile, toying with the ends of Grey's chain as he smoothed the duct-tape back over the creature's eyes.

'Anyone else wanna try?' he asked.

# CHAPTER THIRTY-ONE

THE DOOR SLAMMED behind us, remote control bolts clicking into place as we made our way down the blue-painted corridor.

Buck was dead. I still couldn't believe it. My sweet, funny, handsome young friend was gone. Buck had been barely eighteen, a lifetime of living and laughing ahead of him.

All gone, because of Harlem.

Anger swelled in my chest, threatening to overwhelm me. I clenched my fists and breathed hard to keep the tears that were budding in my eyes from spilling down my cheeks.

Somehow, some way, I'd make Harlem pay for this.

I completely ignored Niki as I walked. The young vampire kept pace with Harlem a few feet behind me, arguing with him in a low, angry voice. He seemed to have sobered up a great deal, and I wondered how much of his drunkenness had been an act. I could feel the heat of both of their gazes burning into the back of my head, and shivered at the double menace. I would give anything for a weapon right now. I still wasn't so sure whose side Niki was on, but after what had just happened, I was fairly sure he was no longer on mine.

The muscles in Harlem's arm bulged as he dragged Grey down the corridor behind the three of us, using sheer muscle-power. Wherever we were going, Grey didn't want to be going. He kept up a continuous caterwauling of complaint as he was pulled down the corridor behind Harlem like a misbehaving dog. He constantly tried to flare his bound wings for balance as his overgrown claws slipped and slid on the polished stone floors.

The creature had to be some kind of telepath, I decided, eyeing him warily as we turned a corner. His powers had to be some super-magnification of the vampire Thrall, gone horribly wrong.

'What have you people done?' I asked Harlem quietly, unable to tear my eyes from Grey. Harlem's pierced lips curled in a smile.

'We've made the world's most perfect killer. Apart from me, of course.' He jerked sharply on the chain as Grey tried to grab hold of a metal stairway, curling his claws around the side with a shrill howl. A piece of metal railing was sliced free as Harlem yanked him onwards, grumbling and growling.

'What breed is it?'

'Fuck knows. Young Grey here is the first of his kind—a vamp who makes more of himself telepathically. Tele-morphism, Harlequin calls it. Just one look into its eyes, and—boom! We have a new convert, praise the lawd. As your little friend back there just found out.' Harlem's smile grew wider at the look on my face. 'And this little guy's just a baby. In a few more months

he'll be all growed up. Check out the size of his paws.'
He waved a black-gloved finger at Grey's overgrown
clawed feet. 'He's gonna be huge!'

'I'm so happy for you both,' I muttered.

Harlem curled his lip at me, his white fangs flashing
against his dark stubble. A gust of air from an overhead
vent swept through his black hair, briefly lifting his
forelocks off his face. I was surprised to see a set of
new, deep 'V'-shaped scars ripping across the side of
his forehead before he quickly pushed them back down
into place.

I was impressed. Not many things could go up against
Harlem and live to tell the tale. I wondered whether it
was Grey or Cyan that had given him those scars. Ten
bucks said it was the latter. The beginnings of a very
evil plan began to take shape inside my head.

'Hey, check it out, chickie.' Harlem stopped at one of
the heavily-barred doors and pressed a button on the
wall, retracting the steel shutters on the large police-
style viewing window. 'Wanna see our factory floor?

I stared through.

An enormous low-ceilinged room stretched hundreds
of feet in either direction. It was divided into two parts.
On one side was what looked like the entire right
wing of LA County Penitentiary. At least sixty heavily
barred jail cells like the one we'd just been in were
lined up. Dozens of white tails and giant clawed limbs
hung through, idly scratching at the bars and restlessly
shifting around.

On the other side of the room, a lab was laid out,
white-tiled and modern. Hundreds of glass baby-cribs
were lined up in orderly rows, topped with the bright
red lights of heat-lamp incubators. Blue-clad vampire

techies moved slowly up and down the rows, checking on each one, making notes, changing food-bags. A high-pitched yowling sound filled the air, like hundreds of young kittens crying all at once.

And in the cribs...

I stepped quickly back from the door, pressing my hand to my mouth. Harlem grinned at my reaction as he let the shutter fall and shoved me forward, flicking his head to indicate I should walk on.

'We've been trying to think up a name for these guys,' Harlem went on, jerking on Grey's chain. 'We've been calling them Tele-vamps. But perhaps you could come up with something better.'

'I'm not naming your dumb pet,' I snapped, my mind still on the horrors I had just seen. *It had looked like a human baby with a bat's face. Soft pink mittens had been fitted over its pudgy hands. The protruding inch-long fore-claws had been blunted with strips of duct-tape.* 'Just tell me why the hell you made so many of them, so I can get on with killing you. Or are you just going to stand there and gloat all day?'

'Oh, but gloating is my second-favorite thing to do,' Harlem murmured, letting his fire-colored eyes dip slowly down my body. 'Tell me something. If I cut off your hands, could you still do that little fire-trick of yours?'

I shrugged, turning to regard him with a smile. 'Dunno. Could you still do your favorite trick if I cut off your—'

'Alright, that's enough,' snapped Niki. 'Both of you.'

Harlem raised an eyebrow but said nothing, his eyes fixed on me with black intent. I waited for his reply, but instead the big wolf shook himself and turned away, muttering something that sounded like Spanish under his breath. I looked at him in surprise. The last person I'd seen raise his voice to Harlem had been sent home in three separate body bags. They'd never found the head.

Another porthole loomed at head height. I darted a glance through it as we walked past.

Another lab. Hundreds more glass cribs.

*Cribs filled with baby Televamps.*

*Hundreds and hundreds of them...*

I glanced back at Grey, taking great care not to look at his face just in case that blindfold of his slipped. It didn't take a genius to put two and two together. If just one Televamp could 'convert' a thousand humans or werewolves into vampires, just by looking into their eyes, then if even a few hundred of the creatures escaped, they could potentially take over the entire world... or repopulate it.

I looked at Grey with fresh eyes, mulling over my options. I noticed that the creature was digging in its claws, its body tilted sideways at an almost forty-five degree angle as it leaned away from Harlem, trying to get as far away from him as possible. Its slit nostrils were wrinkled as though in disgust, as if it was trying not to breathe in the smell of him. I blinked as I suddenly deciphered the alien creature's body-language.

That creature wasn't just scared of Harlem. It actually hated him.

It hated him because he was a werewolf, and because it was part vampire.

All vampires hated werewolves. It was genetic or something.

Right?

The spark of an idea started to form in my head as I watched the creature slide and scrape its way forwards, pulled along the floor by Harlem. The smell of Harlem was obviously freaking the Televamp out. But Niki hadn't been able to 'smell' that I was a werewolf, because I hadn't yet been through the change. Grey didn't seem that bothered by my presence either.

Huh.

The spark turned into a solid plan. I couldn't outrun Grey, but Grey hated Harlem more than he hated me or Niki. Ten bucks said that if he got free, Harlem would be the first thing in the creature's sights. I was either about to do something really clever, or really spectacularly dumb. Some days even I didn't know the difference.

Here went nothing.

I took a few careful breaths and concentrated hard, drawing the last vestiges of my magical power up into the pit of my stomach, channeling it up to my chest like a tide of hot lava, letting it smolder and burn there. I pictured the look of blind terror on poor Buck's face as he took a swan dive out of the window. The look of disappointment on Ninette's face when she'd taken my Hunter stripes away. The sight of Mutt, half-naked and drunk as he bent over Mia's smooth tanned body...

The fire in my belly flared up brighter, hotter. *Good*.

Pain wasn't always a bad thing. You could either drown in it, or you could learn to channel it until it formed into a towering, shining wave that you could ride out of Hell on. It had always worked for me.

As Harlem turned away to mutter something to Niki, I reached out and touched the metal pole of Grey's snare chain, whispered two short words, and released every ounce of magical power I had in my body. A surly snap of orange electricity spilled from my body and grounded itself on the pole, shooting down towards Grey. The Televamp leaped back, more frightened than hurt, wrenching the pole from Harlem's hands.

'Oops,' I muttered. 'Damn those nylon carpets.'

All three of us exploded away from Grey as the big bat-like creature swung around and shot towards us in an explosion of pent-up muscle power, flying forward so fast he hit the wall. Still blindfolded, Grey spun around and locked his teeth with a snap onto the first thing his snout touched—the lion-pole. He shook it back and forth vigorously, like a dog worrying a stick, then dropped it with a *clang* as he discovered his freedom. The Televamp gave a snake-like hiss as his blind head swiveled around and locked in on Harlem with alarming accuracy.

Harlem froze. 'Oh shi—'

Grey pounced.

I was already running before the screaming started. I didn't look back, putting everything I had into running, putting some distance between myself and the furious creature. My muscles started burning almost immediately but the adrenaline in my belly was more than enough to keep me going as I flew down the corridor, slammed through sets of steel fire doors, and darted round a blind corner before hitting a stairwell.

I caught myself on the edge of the door and stared backwards, my head spinning around in a quick, panicky circle, but the corridor behind me was reassuringly empty. There were no sounds of pursuit. I wondered briefly if Niki had got away or if the Televamp had got him, too.

Right now, I didn't much care either way. *Jerk.*

I glanced down at my watch and relaxed a little bit. It was only nine PM. I still had three hours left to find Doll and save mankind before Doomsday. I knew I should go back and try and release my wolf friends, but not until after Grey had gone. I was the only one in the pack who was free right now, and I couldn't risk getting recaptured by Harlem or killed by Grey. Unless the creature could chew through three inch steel bars, they would be safe for now. I hoped.

It was a start.

Then my brain kicked in, and my heart stalled in my chest as I finally registered what my eyes had just seen. I snatched at my wrist, ripping back my sleeve to expose my watch. It was nine PM. How could it still be nine PM? It had been nine o'clock when we'd first been captured, and we'd been locked up in the vampire pens for at least an hour.

Unless…

I madly shook my wrist as I raced down the stairs. The second hand wasn't moving.

*My watch had stopped!*

Karrel had given me that watch. I'd worn it every day for over a year with no problems. To have it stop working now, right when I needed it the most, was a pretty cruel thing for Fate to do to me.

I was glad that Mia wasn't around to hear the torrent of swearwords pouring from my mouth as I pounded up the stairs, no idea where I was heading, only knowing that I had to keep going. I had no idea what the time was. I had no *time* to go and find out what the time was. All I knew was that Cyan had said that Doll was being housed in the penthouse suite of this place. So right now, my only choice was to go up.

\*   \*   \*

I REACHED THE top floor panting and out of breath. I was really starting to regret giving Karrel's BowFlex exercise machine to the thrift shop as I hauled myself up the final flight, fighting the urge to just drop to the floor and crawl on my hands and knees until my lungs started working again.

Ye Gods I was out of shape.

I pulled myself to my feet and jogged down the length of the hallway, frantically peering through the glass windows of the doorways lining it as I ran. This was the very top floor. Unless I had been lied to, Doll had to be up here somewhere. She *had* to be...

It was much darker up here, with an odd, metallic taste to the air, like the scent of the wind before a storm. The lights in the corridor were out, and the whole floor was lit purely by the dim blue emergency lighting. I rounded the corner of the curved corridor, looking around me in the half-light. Judging by the position of the bright stars I could see through the windows it had to be close to eleven PM, if not later.

'Doll?' I called out, as loudly as I dared. 'Are you here?'

I was staring through the window of the locked end door, trying to make out if the dark shape huddled in the corner was a woman or a pile of rags, when I heard the sound of someone tactfully clearing their throat behind me.

I whirled, instantly on guard.

Someone was standing behind me, halfway down the corridor, blocking the exit. I squinted in the dull blue light and my eyebrows shot up. A tall, elegant and very pale man was watching me. The details of his face were lost in the shadows, but he was at least six-two, dressed in expensive black slacks with a white ivory belt buckle, black motorcycle boots and very little else. His luxuriant spill of jet-black hair was backlit by the moon, which hung large and heavy in the end window behind him. A black steel cross hung around his neck on a black chain, resting lightly against his gloriously bare chest.

'Can I help you, madam?' The stranger's voice was rich and musical, lightly tinted with a rounded European accent. His voice slid straight down my spine like warm honey. He stepped into a patch of moonlight from the rooftop skylight, straightening his belt.

I sagged in relief, clutching my chest.

It was just the guy I'd seen earlier in the fake shower-room exhibit. The Towel Guy. *Thank Christ for that.*

'You scared the crap out of me,' I gasped. I moved quickly away from the door before he saw what I was doing, and worked up a winning smile. 'What are you doing up here, cutie-pie? Shouldn't you be working?'

The man stopped a short distance away and put his hands in his pockets, watching me closely. He seemed half-amused, half-curious to find me up here. A mop and bucket rested against the wall a few feet behind him. I wondered if all the workers in this club were contracted to work shirtless.

'Apologies, madam. We are closed for the night.'

The stranger hesitated, then moved cautiously closer with a sensuous, flowing motion, his intense blue eyes focused on me. He looked unarmed and seemed extremely surprised to find me here. His mane of silky black hair slid over his face as he pushed it out of his eyes, looking me over with an openly curious expression.

Wow. I'd forgotten how gorgeous this guy was.

I wavered, torn between the drive to get the hell on with my mission and the strong urge to just stand here and stare at this incredible specimen of manhood, and perhaps drool a little bit. I bit my lip as I looked him over, hyper-conscious of time ticking away. Towel Guy was every bit as beautiful as I remembered him being, if not more so, from his exquisite sharp cheekbones to his full luscious lips, to the obvious strength in his lean, muscled body which lay just beneath the soft fabric of his perfectly tailored clothing... what little he was wearing of it.

Every girl in the club would just *die* when they heard that I'd actually talked to this guy in person. I cursed myself for not bringing a camera, to get proof. Despite my dire circumstances, I grinned at the thought.

The beautiful man tilted his head to the side as he looked me up and down.

'I don't mean to intrude on your night, little one,' he said with a small smile, the bass in his voice sending shivers down my spine. 'I was just curious. You seem to be looking for something. Is there anything I can do for you?'

I gave a short, involuntary laugh, startling myself.

'Uh,' I said, trying to keep a dozen somewhat obscene images and thoughts out of my head. I fanned myself quickly with my hand, trying to smother my completely inappropriate bout of hysteria. I was definitely starting to lose it. 'Not now,' I said, darting a look on each side of him. 'Maybe some other time, if I ever get a night off. I'm kind of busy right now.'

'Oh.' The man packed a lot into that one small, short sound.

'And yes, I know I'm not supposed to be up here,' I added quickly, wishing he'd take the hint and leave me in peace so I could go back to trying to break into this room. 'I'm just looking for a friend. She's very important to me, and I have to find her before midnight. Wish me luck.'

I turned away, glanced over my shoulder. The man was still watching me.

'You can go back to work now,' I said, blowing him a little kiss. 'I'll be out of your hair in ten minutes.'

The man just looked at me. I could almost see the big question mark hovering over his head. I wondered how good his English was.

'Okay then, bye-bye,' I prompted him, making a vague shooing motion that usually worked with the sweet if monolingual waiters that worked at the bars in town. 'We'll talk some other time. It's nothing personal. I'm sure you're very nice, I just have to find my friend now.'

*Very nice?* demanded a little voice in my head, as I hurriedly walked away. *The guy looks like freaking Fabio, the male model who was on the cover of every romance novel ever published... and you just told him he looked very nice?! What is wrong with you?*

I mentally squashed the voice and turned back to the locked door, chiding myself for my weakness. An hour and a half left to save mankind and I'd just wasted a precious thirty seconds drooling over some Random, as Mutt would put it.

I had to move, now.

I peered through the glass viewing window of the end door and tried the door-handle again, no longer caring that the man was watching me, leaning my entire weight on it. Of course, the door was locked. I quickly slipped the key Cyan had given me out of my pocket and tried it in the door.

The key turned.

I stepped back from the door, steeling myself. Now that my big moment was here, I felt oddly afraid. But I had to be brave. Whatever was behind this door could be no worse than the horrors I'd faced in the last couple of weeks. I had to do this. I had no other choice...

'We all have a choice,' whispered a male voice in my ear, startling me. I spun around to find the beautiful man standing right behind me, so close that his hair tickled my exposed shoulders. I made a startled sound and backed up a quick pace. Didn't they have personal space in Slovakia, or wherever this guy was from? Despite his boundary issues I couldn't help but notice that the guy smelled incredible, a mixture of ambrosia and molasses, with a touch of something exotic and luscious that reminded me a little of ripe honeydew melon....

I gulped as I came to the obvious conclusion.

He had to be a vampire. No human guy smelled this good.

I turned around completely, taking Towel Guy seriously for the first time as he moved in closer to me, closing the space between us. His eyes drifted in a leisurely fashion down from my lips to the pulse that was suddenly beating frantically in my throat.

'Yes, that's nice,' I muttered, as he backed me around slowly towards the door, grinning now. I couldn't seem to let go of the word. '*Nice* vampire. Hey, you know what? Go down about four floors and you'll find a whole bunch of blood all over the floor. You'd better hurry before it gets cold.'

'Madam.' The vampire's voice held a faint note of disapproval. 'I can see that you have a lot to learn about our species. We don't eat dead blood.'

His soft, cold fingers gently closed around my wrist. He lifted my arm up, cradling it like a baby between his strong, long-nailed hands. My breath caught in my throat as he leaned down and softly brushed his lips over the soft pale skin on the underside of my forearm, his electric blue eyes never once leaving mine.

'We prefer our food fresh,' he whispered.

'That's... nice,' I choked out.

An involuntary shiver swept over me as he tightened his grip on my arm. His touch seemed to flow down my spine like molten lava, igniting things deep within me that I didn't want ignited right now. I had to call up resources that I never knew I had to pull my arm away, as tactfully as I could manage. The vampire seemed surprised at the move, that I had the power to resist. A richly ironic smile lit up his face, making his blue eyes crinkle in an astonishingly attractive way.

I stared up at him, unable to help but mirror his smile with a goofy grin of my own. *I wanted to swim in that smile, roll around in it like a dog in a hay-field, smother myself in it until I drowned...*

I blinked and shook myself.

*Think of the mission. Think of the mission...*

'And what is the mission?' the beautiful vampire whispered, moving in closer, so that the incredible scent of him wafted over me. I stepped back out of reach, swallowing hard. There was already a door-handle sticking into my back. It hurt. I couldn't move any further back than this, and still the vamp was getting closer. I didn't feel any sense of threat from him and the scent of him soothed me like a lullaby, but my hackles were up, my skin covered in goosebumps at his touch.

Maybe my body knew something that I didn't.

I held my breath and pressed myself as far back as I could go as the vampire leaned in close to me, lips parting as though he was going in for a kiss. He raised his eyebrows as he waited for me to answer him. I caught another gust of his wonderful, mouth-watering scent. My head swum a little, my eyes drifting out of focus.

'Uh,' I said, blinking hard. 'What was the question again?'

'Just tell me what you need,' Towel Guy prompted me, his breath a gust of honey-scented air as he traced velvet-soft lips up the side of my neck. My eyes slid half closed against my will. 'And I shall oblige.'

I swallowed hard, not daring to speak. Ever since I'd started turning into a werewolf I'd found myself becoming increasingly... needy. That was the polite way of putting it. And it wasn't just every so often. It was *all the time*. Even when the fate of the world was resting in my hands I still felt the incredible, heady pull of temptation like a red-hot strait-jacket under my skin. *Jesus*.

I wondered if this was what Mutt felt like on a daily basis, whether the old-wives tale was really true, that the wolf that bit you decided what kind of werewolf you were going to be.

Unable to help myself, I felt my eyes drift helplessly downwards, moving over the gorgeous vampire's exposed upper chest, dwelling on the Celtic cross which hung in the cleft between his well-developed pectoral muscles. The skin around the cross was scarred and slightly blackened, but he didn't seem to be in any pain. I frowned. This guy was a vampire. How could a vamp be wearing a cross? The spark of curiosity died away seconds later, and I strangely felt no urge to think about the subject further. I had other things to occupy my mind right now.

I peered closer, fighting the strong urge to run my hands over those muscles, trace their outline with my tongue, smear them with molten chocolate and lick them... I wanted to touch him so badly, just to see if he was real...

'Baby! *There* you are! I've been looking all over for you.'

I snapped back to awareness at the sound of the familiar, infuriating, mocking voice. I glanced over Towel Guy's shoulder, cursing under my breath.

Niki was standing at the end of the corridor, staring at me. His chest was heaving, his muscles pumped from his fight with the baby Televamp. His shirt was torn in multiple places and spattered with blood that I already knew wasn't his. His gaze flicked to Towel Guy and he pulled up short, his eyes widening in surprise.

'What are you doing here?' he snapped, glaring at my sexy new friend. 'Don't you have *work* to do?'

This was my chance. I quickly turned to Towel Guy and leaned in to him as Niki prowled closer. 'You gotta help me,' I whispered urgently into the handsome vampire's ear. 'See that guy? He just told me that he wants to kill me. It would be real nice of you...' *Stop saying 'nice'!* '... if you could keep him busy while I go find my friend.'

I paused, then decided to go for broke. 'The fate of the world may depend on it.'

To my surprise, the beautiful vampire threw back his head and laughed, the movement making his thick hair shimmer like a black waterfall in the moonlight.

'I'll do my best, little one,' he said with a wink, his eyes sparkling with mirth.

I looked at him in bemusement before shifting my gaze to Niki, wondering why he hadn't attacked yet. I knew how fast Nick could move and how strong he was. This new guy would probably be no match, even if he did decide to try and defend me.

Niki stopped a short distance away, glowering.

'Are you even listening to me?' he snapped, stabbing a finger at Towel Guy. 'What the hell is wrong with you? We're behind on the schedule, we've got prisoners running around all over the shop, and you're just standing there like a big overstuffed lemon. This place is starting to look like a Goddamned petting zoo! And put your shirt back on, for the love of God. You look ridiculous.'

'Relax, little one,' said my new friend, turning to wink at Niki. 'Everything is under control.'

'That's what you always say, *Dad*,' muttered Niki.

I stared at Towel Guy, then back at Niki. I started to smile, waiting for the joke.

No joke came.

I turned back to look at Niki, an eyebrow raised in a question. Niki wasn't even looking at me, all his attention fixed firmly on my own personal Fabio. Niki had a look on his face I'd never seen there before; a sulky, petulant scowl.

Almost like a little boy...

'*Dad?*' I prompted him, as the silence lengthened. I folded my arms, staring at Niki. 'I thought you said that your father was Harlequin.'

Niki didn't reply, his eyes locked with the other man. Realization suddenly slammed into me as Towel Guy turned around and winked at me, baring his white, pointed teeth in a smile.

'I *am*,' he said.

# CHAPTER THIRTY-TWO

I STOOD FROZEN, my heart racing, my trapped gaze
flitting back and forth between Niki and Fabio— no,
Niki and… *say it!*

I couldn't say it. Not yet. My brain had gone bye-
byes.

I stared up at the beautiful vampire standing beside
me, and shook my head.

This gorgeous guy couldn't be… *him.*

A hundred images flashed through my mind. Every
grisly, blood-soaked tale I'd heard about this murderous
psychopath, this immortal tyrant slammed into my
brain, the gruesome stories crashing into one another
like a deadly pile-up on the freeway.

*Ten thousand dead in Russia, bound in chains
and marched off the edge of a cliff. An entire village
butchered in Poland, the villagers' intestines found
hung from the trees like gory Christmas decorations.
Whole armies slain the length and breadth of Europe,
their bodies found sucked dry and beheaded, the legs
of their horses gnawed to the bone as though by flesh-*

*eating locusts…*

I'd been expecting a scale-covered demon, an alien monster with red eyes and spines and blood dripping from his mouth. Not a guy who looked like every fantasy I'd ever had in my life put together and then some.

Whatever I'd been expecting Harlequin to look like, it was never like this.

There had to be some mistake.

The silence between the two men deepened as the seconds ticked by. Niki glanced at… at… at his father, and folded his arms defiantly.

'Just go. Start the Prophecy. I've got this one, Dad,' Niki said at length. He gave an angry smile, reaching out for me. He must be just dying to kill me, traitorous werewolf-loving beast that I was. His father's hands tightened on my shoulders, pulling me back out of reach.

'Do not concern yourself with this one, child,' Harlequin said mildly, an undercurrent of steel to his voice. 'You have enough to do tonight. I will take care of this.'

Niki's whole body tensed up. He stared at me, a strange, almost desperate look on his face. What was up with him? A minute ago he wanted me dead. Now he looked like he was about to cry. As Niki stood there wavering Harlequin smiled again, a flash of perfect white in the darkness above me. I looked back at him over my shoulder. Close up I could see that his teeth were pointed and very slightly hooked at the ends, like rattlesnake fangs. I'd never seen a vamp with teeth like that before, and the sight made me dizzy with fear. Teeth like that did not look normal in a human mouth. Period.

'Do not allow me to detain you, Nicholas,' Harlequin said pleasantly.

Niki didn't move. The silence thickened between the two men as they stared each other down. Neither man spoke, but the air took on a very heavy, greasy feel, as it often did when one of the more advanced Hunters performed a Shield-spell. I was sure I felt the floor tremble beneath my feet. Either that or it was a small localized earthquake. Niki winced as tiny blue sparks spat from the piercings in his eyebrow and the steel rings on his fingers, burning his skin like miniature fireworks.

Harlequin narrowed his eyes sharply and Niki's face twisted as though he was in pain. He took a slow, unwilling step back, then another, as if he was being pushed backwards by an invisible hand. He finally broke eye contact with his father and looked away, squeezing his eyes tight shut. He wiped his face, sweating. When he took his hand away, there was blood on his cheeks.

He stared at his bloodied hand in horror, then leaped back in shock as his hand suddenly ignited, the blood burning with a bright white flame. He gave his father a look of stunned betrayal before turning on a dime and taking off down the corridor, moving so fast that he was almost a blur. I heard the end door slam hard, making the whole hallway shake.

And then I was alone.

Alone with the King of the vampires.

I didn't dare looked behind me as Harlequin's hands slid down over my shoulders, lightly gripping my upper arms as though I was some kind of prom date. The only sound in the deserted corridor was the noise of my panicked breathing as a shiver of pure horror went through me. My head was ringing. I was lightheaded with fear. I couldn't say that things could be worse, for they couldn't be.

I was all alone, and quite literally in the hands of my greatest enemy.

I had only one option left. My small burst of energy to scare Grey downstairs had magically exhausted me, so I did the only thing I had left to do. My left hand crept downwards, inch by excruciatingly slow inch. My fingers slid softly into my pocket, tightening on the hilt of my tiny Swiss Army knife.

With a cry of defiance I unfolded the blade and spun around in one sharp, violent movement, my knife slashing through the air towards Harlequin...

Who was suddenly no longer there. My knife swooshed through empty air and glanced off the wall behind me, embedding itself in the brick with such force it made my arm go numb. I dropped it and spun around, backing up so fast that my shoulders hit the opposite wall a second later, winding me.

An eerie whisper echoed behind me, flying down the length of the corridor. My head spun around and I glanced both ways, but there was nobody there.

Harlequin was gone.

Before I could decide which direction to run in there was a loud buzz of electricity. I almost jumped out of my skin as the lights clacked on in every room, running down the length of the corridor in quick succession until they reached the end door. Bright light spilled through the porthole windows. I jumped again at the loud clacking sound of multiple sets of heavy locks disengaging, apparently by themselves.

Slowly, as though in a horror movie, the very end door creaked open.

My eyes flicked back to the wonderfully inviting exit door at the other end of the hallway. I might be able to get to it if I ran fast enough...

And then...

All thoughts of escape instantly vanished as my eyes adjusted to the bright light. The door at the end of the corridor gaped wide open, to reveal what looked like an observation deck. I squinted into the light, peering into the room. All three end walls of the room were made of thick glass like a giant fish-tank, revealing a breathtaking view of the glittering lights of Hollywood in the distance.

In the exact center of the room sat a man-sized silver bird-cage. The bird-cage from the auditorium. My heart gave a great thump of excitement at the sight of it. The lights in the room were so bright they hurt my eyes, but I could just make out the unmistakable shape of a pale, slender winged woman standing up inside the cage, clutching the silver bars, staring out at me in fear.

My heart slammed into my rib-cage in triumph.

*I'd found Doll!*

# CHAPTER THIRTY-THREE

I'D BEEN THROUGH a lot in the last forty-eight hours. I'd been chased, shot at, attacked by five different werewolves and almost set on fire at least twice.

I was not, let me point out at this juncture, thinking particularly clearly.

Before my brain had even kicked in I was halfway down the corridor, sprinting towards the open doorway like a kamikaze moth dive-bombing an open flame. I covered my head as I ran through, fully expecting something horrible to happen to me—a guillotine dropping from the top of the doorway to slice my head off, perhaps, or Harlequin leaping out with a Freddy Krueger-style cackle to sink his teeth into my neck...

Nothing happened. I made it through the doorway alive. I rushed across the room and grabbed hold of the bars of Doll's cage, breathless with relief.

'You're alive!' I gasped.

'Am I?' whispered Doll. 'I wasn't sure.'

She seemed confused, possibly drugged. My eyes flew over her, checking her out, but to my relief she seemed unhurt. She looked even frailer than I remembered her being, and seemed much weaker. She was barefoot and dressed simply in a flowing white robe of creamy silk, held together with ornate silver clasps. Several of the clasps had inexplicably melted and were stuck in oily clumps to the material, and her silken gown spilled open in random places to reveal glimpses of her fragile ribs and pale slender thighs. Her eyes had faded even further, from the metallic blue I remembered them being in the ring, to a dull silver, like the scales on a dying fish.

Was Doll dying? God, I hoped not.

I reached out for her... then hesitated, my eye drawn to her neck. A thick iron collar ringed her delicate throat. I leaned in closer and saw with relief that it was a simple iron collar, not one of the bulky remote-controlled radio-collars that had almost blown Mutt's head off the last time we'd crossed paths with Harlequin.

Small blessings indeed.

I wondered if iron did to angels what silver did to werewolves. I seemed to remember Ninette saying something along those lines, a few weeks and a hundred years ago. No sooner had the thought gone through my mind when I smelled something burning. Pain blazed through me and I let go of the bars with a yelp, frantically shaking my hand. It was smoking. When I opened my fingers, a vivid red burn-mark slashed across each palm.

The bars were solid silver. And I was close to turning into a werewolf. Wonderful. How the hell was I going to bust Doll out of there if I couldn't even touch the bars?

At that moment, the lights shut out.

*Crap.*

I ducked down fast and darted away from the cage, backing off in the semi-darkness until my back was pressed up against one of the glass walls. My eyes gradually adjusted to the dim light and my breathing slowed. I heard a gasp from behind me and turned around quickly, dread etching itself onto my face.

*Fuck.*

The unmistakable, devastatingly handsome shape of Harlequin was standing in the corner of the room, facing away from me, having apparently materialized out of thin air. His hands were clasped behind his back as he stared out of the giant observation window at the bright lights of LA, apparently lost in thought. His long shadow fell over Doll, blacking out her face so all I could see were two white wings, flaring and closing anxiously in the darkness.

I reached out and grasped the door handle, pulling it down. *Locked.* Shit! I started to fumble in my pocket for the key. It was gone.

I swallowed. I was locked in a room with a homicidal killer and his not-so-human sacrifice. If I ran away then I just might save my own life, but for what? As soon as Harlequin killed Doll the human race would be doomed, anyway. So long as I was still part human, the avenging angels would get me, too.

I flicked a glance over at Doll, begging her with my eyes to tell me what to do. She shrank back, staring at me, as though surprised by my lack of fear. I noticed a carriage wall-clock behind her, and peered up at it.

It was exactly eleven PM.

I breathed a little easier, but not much.

Before I could say anything, Harlequin cleared his throat and spoke without looking around. 'Tell me,' he said, speaking quietly. 'When you look at me, what do you see? Do you see a man, or a monster?'

He half turned to look at me, a stray beam of light from the next building illuminating his face with a terrible dark beauty. I rubbed my chilly arms, wishing I'd brought a sweater. I was coasting purely on adrenaline right now, and it was wearing off fast.

'I see a man,' I said, as loudly as I dared. 'A man who acts like a monster.'

'Do *you* think I'm a monster, little one?'

'I don't know you,' I said, surprised by the turn in conversation. To my credit my voice only shook a little bit. 'But I know what you've done. If a person is defined by their actions, then yes. I think you act like a monster.'

Harlequin turned around then, studying me more closely as though surprised by my answer. I felt something cold take hold of my mind and squeeze it like jelly inside a giant fist. I stood my ground as the master vampire ghosted towards me, making no sound save a whisper of silk in the darkness. He stopped before me and narrowed his eyes, brushing his hand lightly over the ends of my hair as though waiting for me to react.

'If you tell me you've traveled across oceans of time to be with me, I'll smack you in the mouth,' I whispered, willing my legs to move. They stayed obstinately still.

Harlequin tilted his head. 'You are not afraid of me?'

'Should I be?'

Harlequin stepped around in front of me and peered into my eyes, licking his full, luscious, kissable lips. I felt an instant spike of lust explode in the pit of my stomach. I couldn't help blushing as he stared into my face with those exotic blue-green eyes, fighting the urge to let my gaze drop lower. In the dim light of the room his eyes were almost hypnotic, magnetic in their impossible beauty.

I found it hard to look away. I could understand now why Cyan was so besotted with this guy, why she'd had major cybernetic bone surgery just to try and increase her chances of getting a date with him.

The things we did for love.

Harlequin sighed, gazing down at me in sorrow. He took my unresisting hand and laid it against his perfect cold cheek, cradling it there. His skin was cool and smooth under my hand, like the white alabaster used for Greek sculptures. I stared in amazement at my limp hand, inviting it to move and claw this murdering bastard's eyes out.

Any minute now would be nice...

'I am physically attractive, yes?' he asked, as though unable to let the subject drop.

'You're not bad looking,' I grudgingly conceded, in the same way that Michelangelo's foreman at the Sistine Chapel might have said he did 'a good job' of painting over the cracks in the ceiling.

Harlequin nodded, unsurprised by my answer.

'This face is both my blessing and my curse,' he said, stroking my embarrassingly willing hand along his cheekbone. I had to fight to control my breathing, to tear my eyes from his soft lips. 'I am a demon who wears the skin of an angel. Everything about me is attractive to you. We do not fear that which we desire, and so of course you do not fear me.'

'So why do I get scared every time I walk past the Ben and Jerry's ice-cream store?'

Harlequin gave a faint smile at my dumb joke. I always made dumb jokes when I was nervous. He pressed a thumb into my palm, turning my hand to kiss the back of it. I remembered why I had come here and concentrated, gathering all my willpower, then pulled my hand away. Harlequin's chest heaved with a sudden flare of emotion, as though distressed by my unwillingness to touch him. Before I could look away he touched my chin with a forefinger to tilt my head up to him, and looked straight into my eyes.

I gasped as an almost blindingly powerful wave of buzzing hypnotic power spilled over me like a blast of heat from the desert. I reeled, gritting my teeth as I felt the earthshaking power of his vampiric Thrall blast through me, like a shot of napalm straight into my bloodstream. What I had felt before with Niki was nothing compared to this, a mere ocean breeze compared with the hurricane force of the desire that blasted through me now. I had to fight with everything I had to overcome the sudden desperate urge to rip every last shred of clothing off Harlequin's body, before tearing off my own and...

I threw out my hand in desperation and grabbed one of the silver bars of Doll's cage. The sharp hiss of pain as my hand burned cut through the overwhelming wave of desire which threatened to swamp me, bringing me back down to earth with a bump. I subsided, panting. *Thank Christ.*

'So that's how you got Cyan to fall for you,' I said through pain-clenched teeth, glancing behind me for an escape route. *Nothing but foot-thick glass and then two hundred feet of empty air before I hit the ground. Crap.*

'Cyan?' Harlequin frowned. 'What of her?'

'She said you guys were an item, or something.'

Harlequin chuckled darkly, the sound raising the hair on the back of my neck. His eyes lit up when he laughed, and I had the overpowering urge to make him laugh again, to devote my life to making him smile. 'She is a naughty kitty. Telling stories, as always.'

'So what did you do with her?' I asked. 'Did you kill her?'

'Cyan? No.' Harlequin looked shocked at the thought. 'She is too valuable an experiment to kill. But she had to be contained. She had become... unstable. A danger to herself.'

I thought of the sobbing, drunken mess I had seen scaring customers at the Snake Pit, and couldn't help but agree with him. But I was on the right track here. I'd noticed the flash of reaction on Harlequin's face when I'd said her name. Perhaps there was a weak spot here that I could use.

'You know she's in love with you, right?' I babbled as I moved further back, trying to rile him, to make him careless. It had worked with Harlem, so maybe it would work with Harlequin. Behind me, Doll flared her wings in terror as Harlequin approached her, backing me towards her cage. I felt the downdraft of air as she beat her wings several times, as though trying to get my attention.

I ignored her.

'Cyan... is a complication,' sighed the master vampire, stepping closer to me. 'She was my greatest triumph, my first successful surgery... but she has become a liability. A man in my position cannot have any ties. He cannot!'

'Perhaps you should tell *her* that.'

Harlequin shrugged, an eloquent gesture. 'I cannot say I am indifferent to her,' he mused. 'The hand must love what it creates, for the necessity of creation. But now I have a new love, a new masterpiece. I believe you have already met her.'

He extended a gracious hand towards Doll, looking at me with a sudden blaze of almost boyish excitement. 'Would you like to see her perform?'

Before I could reply, he clapped sharply twice. A side-door opened and a small, squat man with a shock of ginger hair entered. He was wearing blue overalls and carried a clipboard. He didn't look particularly dangerous. He looked up at Harlequin expectantly.

'Demonstrate,' the master vampire said, gesturing at Doll's cage.

The little man paled and bowed, a little shakily. Turning away from me, he surreptitiously crossed himself before vanishing in an almost comical puff of oily orange smoke.

I looked at Harlequin in surprise. What kind of creatures were being bred here?

However, when he rematerialized inside Doll's cage, there was nothing comical about the two large silver butcher's knives he pulled from a sheath on his back.

He raised the knives and charged at the angel, screaming like an Indian warrior.

Before I could move to help her, Doll spread her wings in fright and rose to her feet, spinning to face him. The first knife hadn't even finished descending before Doll had stepped into the defensive pose I knew so well from watching Cyan fight.

I guessed what was going to happen next.

Doll's eyes flashed with white light, as though someone had just taken a photograph inside her head. She flung her arms out as solid silver oiled spikes slid smoothly out of her wrists and elbows, just as Cyan's bone-blades did.

But there was no blood when they came out, no tearing of flesh and skin as there was with poor Cyan. As soon as they touched they fused together with a burst of heat, making two long diamond-edged silver-white swords. It was the perfect weapon.

The lab tech didn't even have time to cry out before Doll lunged at him, screaming in fear and fury. One light stroke of her blade and the little man's head bounced off the bars and rolled across the floor of the cage. Doll hit the barred cage wall and shielded her body with her wings as the man's body caught light and started burning with a white-hot, magnesium flare of flame.

Ten seconds later, it was all over. All that remained of the little vampire was a small circle of smoldering embers on the floor. Doll's wings parted and she stared out at the dead lab tech, sobbing. Her blades retracted so smoothly she didn't even seem to notice them vanishing back into her arms. She scrambled backwards away from the pile of ash, huge tears rolling down her cheeks.

I rounded on Harlequin, angry now. 'That was unnecessary!'

'No such thing when you're in love.'

'Said like a true monster. Congratulations.'

Harlequin walked around Doll's cage, gazing in at

her adoringly as she recoiled from him in fear.

'Most monsters only wish to be understood,' he sighed, lightly gripping the silver bars. Smoke rose from his fingertips, but he didn't release his grip. 'As do I. I am over two thousand years old, my dear. I have lost too many great loves. Wonderful woman who stood by my side, only to be stolen from me by time and by those who seek to overthrow me, to wound me.'

Harlequin looked up at me sharply, and the expression I saw in his blue eyes was haunting. 'My love is my only weakness. I admit that freely. One with as many enemies as myself cannot afford to be weak. I cannot!'

'And making the women you love into monsters is better?'

'I give them the gift of protection,' snapped Harlequin. 'I can make my women immortal, like myself, but I cannot make them wise. The weapons I give them are a gift of love.'

'Bullshit!' I kicked the bars of Doll's cage, making them ring. 'A gift is something you can refuse. What you did to Cyan was just wrong. You love a woman, you give her flowers, you take her to the movies. You don't implant freakin' bone spikes in her arms!'

Harlequin sighed, looking at me in sorrow.

'Tell me,' he said, his voice sharpening. 'What else does Cyan say about me? Perhaps she told you why I summoned you here?'

Once again I felt a strong pressure inside my head, as though a giant was squeezing my brain with both hands, wringing it for information. I shook my head in irritation. 'You don't have to do that. Get out of my head. I'll tell you the truth.'

'Which is?'

'The truth is, you didn't summon me here. I came here to kill you. You ordered Cyan and the wolves to kill a Hunter commander called Karrel Dante. He was my boyfriend. I just want to know why you had him killed.'

'The Hunter boy? Is that what all this is about?'

'Why the fuck else would I be here?' I asked, clenching my fists. 'I heard you had him killed because he knew something about you, something to do with you and the Hunters. Are you going to tell me what that secret was, or do I have to beat it out of you?'

Harlequin threw back his head and gave a weird soundless laugh, his blue eyes sparkling. 'My dear,' he said, moving towards me, his hand graciously extended. 'A thousand years ago I would cut out your tongue for your flippancy.'

'But for now you need it in my head, right?' I stood my ground, gaining courage. 'Let me tell you what I think. I think you aren't going to kill me now. I think you need me alive, for some weird reason. I should have been dead a hundred times over by now, but I'm not, so I'm guessing that you've let me live this long for a reason. And that reason has something to do with this secret that Karrel found out. Am I right?'

As Harlequin opened his mouth to reply, a loud pounding rang out on the window behind us.

'*Father?*' screamed the voice.

At first I thought I was imagining things, hallucinating with fear. Could it be Niki?

No. It was worse. The glass wall behind us suddenly rang with a sharp impact, making the glass shimmer and vibrate. The sound so loud that even Harlequin turned and stared over his shoulder at...

'Harlem?'

The big werewolf's face was pressed up against the inch-thick glass wall, his burning amber eyes locked on Harlequin with malevolent intensity. He'd obviously just been running, because the glass around his mouth steamed up, cleared, and steamed up again.

Harlem was out on the roof. How the hell had he got out there?

An instant later he vanished from my line of vision, darting backwards toward Doll's cage. I'd barely begun to shout a warning to her when Harlem pelted forwards like a charging bull and struck the window from the outside with awesome power, blasting through the inch-thick glass into Doll's penthouse suite.

Time seemed to move in slow motion as the wall of glass directly behind us started to topple over, falling inwards and downwards, right on top of us...

# CHAPTER THIRTY-FOUR

BEFORE THE FIRST shards of glass had got halfway to my unprotected head, Harlequin braced his arm and flung me ten feet sideways with incredible strength, away from the falling glass. There was a horrible moment of vertigo as I flew across the room and landed in the far corner. I hit the ground hard and rolled, wincing as something sharp stung my shoulder. A moment later two steel-heeled motorcycle boots landed next to my face as Harlequin leaped across after me, landing safely in a cat-like crouch.

I glanced up, then ducked down with a yelp and covered my head with my hands as the other half of the glass wall collapsed, sending a snow-drift of glass flying in my direction. The whole thing hit the ground with a crash loud enough to wake the undead and snowballed towards me, the outermost nuggets bouncing harmlessly off my back with a sound like a chandelier coming down.

And then all was still.

I raised my head cautiously, grimacing as my bruised

ribs protested. The entire side wall of Doll's penthouse suite was gone. The night wind whipped into the room, raising miniature snake-like coils of glass-dust, like mini-cyclones. The middle of the pile of shattered glass burst outwards and the broad shape of Harlem surfaced with a growl. He lunged to his feet and turned to face us, tiny pieces of broken glass bristling from his thick brown leather jacket.

I flicked a small piece of glass out of my shoulder and wiped the blood off on my dress with a groan, getting ready to once again run. I only realized that I'd screwed up when I heard a bloodcurdling hiss coming from behind me. I turned slowly, clutching my bleeding shoulder. The cut stung but it was superficial, barely more than a scratch. I was lucky.

I took one look at Harlequin and recoiled with a gasp.

Okay, maybe I wasn't quite so lucky.

The master vampire's gaze was fixed on my bleeding shoulder with the intensity of a half-starved tiger spotting wounded prey. All trace of humanity was gone from his eyes, which were suddenly focused on me with an intensity that made me shudder. He blinked, and his pupils snapped wide open like those of a hungry snake and focused on the blood.

Harlequin snarled at me, dropping back into a cobra-like attack position.

Oops.

I could only stare as the smooth surface of Harlequin's high-cheekboned face rippled and blurred and *something else* emerged from beneath. It was black and scaly, and it was certainly not sexy. It seemed to have far too many teeth, and the thin, multi-pronged spines that jutted out of its forehead and swept back from its sharp cheekbones were like nothing I'd seen before on anything in the animal kingdom.

He looked almost alien.

A second later I was on the ground, my head ringing from the sudden hammer blow which came out of nowhere. I didn't even have time to draw breath to scream as Harlequin's teeth punched down into my shoulder as the vampire mindlessly bit down on the small smear of blood on my glass-cut. A blazing, red-hot pain shot down my arm and I gasped, twisting my body beneath him in an effort to throw him off. I might as well have tried to throw a house off me.

I was barely aware of the sound of booted footsteps scrunching across the glass-strewn ground towards me. Two seconds later Harlequin howled and ripped his teeth from my flesh, swinging around to snap at someone who had just grabbed hold of his leg.

Harlem was looming over us. Even though the haze of dull queasy pain from my bitten shoulder I could see that there was something very wrong with Harlem's eyes. They were foggy, a dull, cloudy grey, and stared sightlessly ahead like the eyes of a zombie. As though he was enchanted, or maybe possessed.

I remembered how one glance into Grey's eyes had turned my poor Buck into a Televamp. Had Harlem looked into Grey's eyes? If so, why hadn't he instantly become a Televamp, as Buck had?

The big werewolf's face was filled with mindless, animalistic rage as he hauled Harlequin off me and directed a vicious kick at his prone body. I distinctly heard the vampire's ribs snap and suddenly I was alone again, rolling up into a ball of pain around my bitten arm. I watched with pain-blurred eyes as Harlequin sprang to his feet with a hiss of rage and eyeballed Harlem, stalking around him. I swear his eye-teeth grew an extra half inch as he coiled his body like a snake and flew at the werewolf, his bloody teeth bared.

What the hell was going on here?

I scrambled to my feet and crept around behind a broken section of wall, anxious to get away from the fight. I leaned out just in time to see Harlequin's fangs retract, the scales slipping beneath the surface of his skin like ripples on a pond and the horns and spines on his cheeks and eyebrows vanishing as though they had never been there in the first place. There was no anger in Harlequin's eyes as he looked down at his attacker, only a cool, faint puzzlement, as though he'd just been scratched by his favorite kitty-cat and was now curious about what had spooked it.

'What is this foolishness?' he snapped, rubbing his jaw which now bore a long, bloody scrape. 'I am not your father!'

'I killed you once already, Padre,' coughed Harlem, bracing both hands against the master vampire's leg as his boot ground down on his throat. 'No big. I can kill you again.'

Harlequin's perfect brow wrinkled in confusion.

Before I could think much further, Harlem locked his gloved hands on Harlequin's leg and gave a vicious twist. Something in the master vampire's knee crunched and he released Harlem with a howl.

Dazed, I watched as the pair tackled each other, smashing outwards through what was left of the biggest glass wall and landing on the huge flat rooftop outside. They rolled over and over on the glass-strewn roof, claws and fangs flying, coming perilously close to the edge of the roof with its yawning fifteen story drop. Harlequin was superhumanly fast but Harlem was built like a tank and just as unstoppable. Harlequin recovered quickly from the surprise attack and launched the big werewolf up into the air, throwing him sideways through the second glass wall of the room as though he were a foam mannequin rather than a two hundred and fifty pound werewolf.

Harlem sailed clean across the room. He slammed upside-down into the side of Doll's cage with a force that made the whole room shake and the silver bars ring out like a giant bell. The cage must have weighed a good half ton but it went down like a giant skittle, the thick pure-silver bars bending and tearing open like tin foil.

I peered in through the hole Harlem had punched in the side of the cage. As the dust settled I could just make out the shape of Doll crouching against the bars. Her eyes were wide with fear as she stared down at Harlem, who lay on the floor beside the cage, unmoving.

She lifted a delicate hand and waved me over. I needed no further encouragement. I rolled to my feet and staggered across the room, almost falling up against Doll's cage. My heart was pounding like a jackhammer from the pain and the shock of Harlequin's bite. I risked a look at it and winced. It was a really deep wound that would probably need stitches. I thanked my lucky stars that vampirism wasn't contagious, like werewolf bites were. Vamp bites hurt like hell and made you groggy for a few minutes, but there had to be a massive exchange of blood for you to become a vampire. At least I wasn't about to start sprouting extra fangs and craving blood on top of my werewolf symptoms, because that would really suck.

'Kayla?' Doll hissed, reaching out to me. 'Take my hand. Quick!'

I was now in so much pain I could barely see straight. The bars of Doll's cage swum and crossed before my eyes as I tried in vain to focus on them. I felt like I was drunk, as though I was moving in slow motion. The world was spinning, twisting, slipping away from me...

A small, cool hand slipped out between the bars and caught me before I fell. Doll pulled me back hard against the bars. I felt the vampire bite in my shoulder connect with the burning silver bars with a pain like nothing else I'd felt before in my life. My legs gave way in agony as steam squealed up from the wound, flash-frying it shut.

I stared at the blackened, burned bite in wonder, noticing with a faraway relief that the heavy bleeding had stopped. Then the world went black, turned sideways and smacked me in the head.


WHEN I WOKE up I was on the ground, slumped a few feet away from the twisted remains of Doll's cage. Doll herself was crouched over me, outside the cage, checking my pulse with her small cold hands. There was a loud roaring sound in my ears which I couldn't at first identify. It sounded like the engine of a taxi. I wondered what a taxi was doing up here on the rooftop.

I shook my head in an effort to clear it. If anything, that made the noise louder. I could hear the cab driver shouting at me to wake up.

'But I didn't order a taxi,' I mumbled.

Doll gave me a strange look, then did something to my shoulder which hurt. I pulled away from her, sitting up with a wince.

'You're free,' I managed, gingerly touching my wounded shoulder. Already, the pain was subsiding. It had turned a strange crystalline silver color, but at least the bleeding had stopped. 'How…?'

Doll straightened and flicked her silver-grey eyes to one side. I followed her gaze. The entire side of the room was missing, the two remaining glass walls shattered by the battle between the two titans. The room was open to the night air, a long stretch of glass-strewn flat rooftop stretching off to our right, bordered by a low wall. Harlem's bloodied, semi-conscious body was sprawled beside the upturned, crushed cage. Harlequin was nowhere to be seen.

*But Doll was free.* And we were both alive.

That meant we still had a chance. I felt almost lightheaded with relief.

'Where's Harlequin?' I asked.

'Gone. He took off after Harlem broke my cage. Guess he figured I wasn't going anywhere. The inside door is locked and there's no way off this rooftop.' Doll looked at me. 'Can you unlock it?'

I shook my head. 'Lost the key.'

Doll tapped me on the shoulder and pointed down at the ground. 'You mean that key?'

I snatched it up, pressing it against my heart in relief. 'Why didn't you pick it up?'

'I can't. Angels can't touch iron,' said Doll, twisting her hands together. 'It drains our powers, hurts us like silver burns a vampire.'

'Good to know,' I muttered.

We both turned to stare at Harlem. He was lying on his back on the ground beside the cage, dazed, staring blindly up at the ceiling. He was muttering something about his father. His eyes were still that spooky, ghostly shade of white. 'What's wrong with numb-nuts down there?' I asked.

'I performed a binding.'

'A what?'

'A kind of mojo.' Doll cocked her head like a bird and stared down at the dazed werewolf. 'If a mind is simple enough, I can sometimes control it, bind it to my own. Use it for my own purposes. I escaped from every cell Harlequin locked me up in, till he figured out that I was simply willing the guards to unchain the doors for me. That's why he locked me up here, away from everyone.' She gave a small, roguish smile. 'I've been trying to crack Harlequin's mind for weeks, with no luck. That man has a mind like an iron trap.' She nodded down at Harlem, smiling now. 'But with that guy, it was like taking candy from a baby.'

'Why did he think Harlequin was his father?'

'It's simple. Harlem hates his father—a priest. He killed him when he was a teenager. I saw it in his head. One of the many perks of being an angel.'

I glanced down at Harlem as he made a violent punching movement in the air, eyes now shut, muttering obscenities under his breath. His black spiked hair quivered like porcupine quills.

'So what did you do to him?'

'Simple. I enchanted him, made him believe that Harlequin was his father. Every time he sees him from now on, he's going to feel an irresistible compulsion to kill him. He won't be able to help himself. An ordinary werewolf can't kill a master vampire but it may buy us some time.'

I was impressed. 'Nice shootin', Tex.'

She grinned at me as she helped me to my feet, her eyes bright despite the pallor of her skin. 'I'm a Goddamn genius, even if I do say so myself.' She blushed and put a hand over her mouth like a child, as though she had just said something bad.

I rubbed my bruised head, ran a hand through my hair. My left arm was a wonderful bruised yellowish color, and I had bloody claw-marks on my left wrist. When the adrenaline wore off, that was really going to start to hurt. I shook my head ruefully and broken glass fell out of my hair with a series of little tinkling sounds. 'So what next?'

Doll nodded to the door, starting to move towards it.

'Um, didn't Harlequin just go that way?' I asked. 'Shouldn't we wait a few minutes till the coast is clear?'

Doll nodded to Harlem. 'You want to be here alone when he wakes up…?'

Her eyes widened suddenly as she stared over my shoulder. I took in her horrified expression, and groaned.

'Too late,' she said.

A few feet away from us, Harlem stirred, groaning loudly as he opened his eyes. His face shone in recognition when he saw me, and his lips parted in a savage grin.

'Hunter,' he growled. The way he said made it sound like 'lunch.'

I looked at Doll as she darted across the glass-strewn floor to stand beside me.

'I'm going to run like hell now,' I said, in a surprisingly matter-of fact voice. 'Want to join me?'

# CHAPTER THIRTY-FIVE

THE TOP LEVEL of the Circus of Sins nightclub was dark now, a nightmarish maze of corridors crossed with hallways seemingly designed to confuse us and random sets of steps ready to trip us. We pelted through the corridors, bumping into each other and bouncing off the walls as we ran, forcing every last ounce of speed out of our aching legs. Doll spread her wings in alarm as she ran, the stiff tips of her flight feathers scraping along the walls, knocking down pictures and clattering over windows.

I didn't have to look to know that Harlem was hot on our tail. The sound of the werewolf's labored breathing seemed to fill the air as he slammed through fire-door after fire-door, snarling threats at us as he pursued us through the industrial corridors. It was like something out of a nightmare, and my brain was too stunned to think of a clever way to shake him off.

So I ran.

'Stop him!' I gasped as I ran. 'Get into his head! Make him think... we're his friends!'

'I'm trying!'

'Try harder!'

I snapped a glance back and saw Doll's eyes spluttering with little bursts of blue light, like a shorting fuse board.

'No good,' she cried. 'Harlem… doesn't have any… friends. The only person he likes enough not to kill is… himself.'

I banked sharply right as we rounded a blind turn, shoving the set of double swing doors wide open before ducking back through them, reversing direction. I grabbed Doll's arm and hauled her with all my might in the opposite direction, doubling back and slamming open the women's restroom door with my elbow. I practically threw Doll through the door and spun her into the room, hauling it shut behind us.

'Hide!' I hissed. Doll was already way ahead of me, leaping six feet into the air with a single flap of her wings and disappearing into the trick alcove above the door. I ran to the very end toilet stall and leaped up onto the toilet seat.

I started to pull the door shut behind me then stopped, staring through the open door. No good. We weren't in high-school here. Harlem would find me in a second.

I spotted a bag-hook on the back of the door, about three feet from the top. A really dumb, desperate idea struck me. As the sound of running feet approached the toilet door I pulled it shut, then climbed up on top of the stall walls with a mad surge of adrenaline and lowered myself down backwards, my back to the door, hooking my thick leather belt onto the hook, hanging myself from the back of the door like a giant girl-sized purse.

I slid down the inside of the cubicle door, praying I

didn't rip my dress, until all of my weight was hanging from the bag-hook.

The belt dug into my ribs, squashing them painfully, but my odd perch held firm. I pulled my knees up to my chest and linked my fingers firmly together beneath my knees, holding my legs up. The weighted cubicle door creaked open a few inches and stopped, with me, the human counterweight, hanging from the bag-hook. It hurt like hell, but I could hold it for at least a few more minutes, and the position made me completely invisible unless the door was pushed all the way back.

I'd no sooner tucked my legs up when there was a tremendous crash and the restroom door flew open so hard it came partway off its hinges. I closed my eyes and sunk my teeth into my lip to quiet my nerves as footsteps entered the restroom, thudding with appalling loudness across the floor.

They marched back and forth a couple of times, and the stalls shook as Harlem viciously swiped a bunch of them open, running down the line. I almost yelled out loud as he pushed my door open with so much force that my head cracked against the wall. I saw a big star and bit back a cry, but my little ruse seemed to have worked, as the footsteps immediately stamped away again. I was just starting to let out my breath in relief when they paused, and marched back up towards my stall.

They paused just a few feet away from me, and I distinctly heard Harlem sniffing the air. He took another two steps, and paused right in front of my stall.

*Listening.*

It was only then that I realized the fatal flaw in my plan.

I couldn't breathe. With all my weight on a two-inch section of my belly, and with my legs curled up to my chest, compressing my ribs still further, there was no way I could take a full breath.

That hadn't mattered a second ago, when I'd been deliberately holding my breath. But now, with Harlem standing still right outside my stall, maliciously and deliberately *listening*, the mad, frantic urge to take a deep breath hit me. I tried to squeeze my throat shut to keep from gasping, but I suddenly felt like I was drowning. The harder I tried to hold my breath, the more panicked I became.

I opened my eyes and caught a glimpse of Doll's pale face poking out almost invisibly from a shadowed recess among the cleaning supplies, watching me in alarm.

As my lungs slowly started to combust, I realized that the footsteps were going away. Heading for the door. *Thank Christ.*

I heard a creak as Harlem grabbed the restroom door, jerking it open to leave. That was the exact moment my life-saving bag-hook chose to give way, spilling me onto the ground with an almighty crash.

I hadn't even recovered from the shock of my head hitting the hard tiled floor when Harlem was upon me. His huge hands clamped around my ankles and he yanked me out backwards from under the stall door like a striking shark. I rolled over onto my back and stared up at him in that peculiar moment of buzzing silence that follows a really well-executed head injury.

You'd think I would be used to it by now.

Harlem released my foot as I slid to a halt, staring down at me gleefully. This guy looked like my worst nightmare made real, a flesh-and-blood Grim Reaper. His hands slipped inside the thickly cut modern leather jacket he was wearing over the whole ensemble, and reappeared holding an ugly set of custom throwing knives.

'Didn't I kill you once already?' snarled Harlem, tossing the first knife into the air and catching it again with a snap. His strong-jawed face twisted into a smile as he sighted carefully on my throat.

I watched in a concussed, unreal daze as he drew back his arm to strike.

White feathers exploded on the edge of my vision. Doll flipped out of her hiding place among the cleaning supplies and struck Harlem in the back, feet first. For such a tiny little thing she must have hit him with incredible force, for he went down like an oak tree, sprawling on top of me.

The three of us fell into a tangled pile on the restroom floor, kicking and yelling as Harlem rolled over and tried to grab us both at once. Doll instantly sunk her tiny blunt teeth into Harlem's thumb and he released her with a howl. He cried out a second time as I fired a Shield spell, sending a sharp jolt of natural electricity through his body. Probably not the smartest move, because I'd forgotten about Doll's bionic 'enhancements.'

Doll screamed as her body convulsed, cracking the back of her head on the hard tiles, and I remembered a second too late about all that conductive metal buried deep within her. I swore and wrenched myself to one side, breaking contact with her and Harlem to shut off the spell, but it was too late.

Doll's head lolled to the side, her eyes fluttering up to

white and closing. She was out cold. And now I was on my own with a killer werewolf in a deserted restroom.

Do you ever have a day that just keeps getting better?

# CHAPTER THIRTY-SIX

'You know, you really need to get a hobby,' I gasped, as Harlem bent over me, threading the stained rope expertly between my crossed wrists and the pipe which ran up the wall behind the toilet bowl, hanging me from the cistern like a pig at the slaughterhouse. Blood streamed freely over my face and down my throat as I tipped my head sideways, trying to redirect the bloody flow so that it stayed out of my eyes. I was sure that at least three ribs were cracked, if not broken.

So this was it. I was going to die.

To tell you the truth, I was surprised this moment hadn't come a lot sooner. I'd done well to get this far. The thought should have made me feel better, but it didn't.

I watched Harlem work with a kind of numb acceptance, trying to distract myself from the pain that burned through my tightly-bound arms. There was something just a little too practiced about the way he tied the ends off and rotated my wrists around so that my bodyweight pulled the knots tighter, almost cutting off my circulation. My shoulders screamed with the strain, and I wondered how many times he'd done this before.

Then I remembered who he was, and wondered how many *hundred* times he'd done this before. I bit my lip to keep from screaming as my mind ran at a hundred miles an hour, trying to think of a way to get out of this.

I drew a complete blank.

I'd already tried a couple of small fireballs when he'd first tied me up, trying to free my hands, but the miniature blasts hadn't reached the ropes which bound me. Instead, they'd burned small holes in the wall in front of me and set fire to the flimsy remains of my black club dress. I'd managed to put the flames out by dint of some frantic rolling against the one remaining wall of the restroom stall before Harlem had seized me. He was still laughing at my apparent attempt to flambé myself as he sealed his mouth over mine, forcing his tongue between my teeth to pry my mouth open, kissing me so hard he left my lips bruised.

The moment he touched me, I'd hit him with everything I had. I'd waited for him to leap off me as the jolt of electricity shocked through him, but he hadn't even broken the kiss. I was half-suffocated by the time he pulled away, blood on his lips from where I'd bitten him, a look of smug triumph on his face.

I knew at that moment that I was dead.

I watched him now as he crouched down before me, staring down at me with a deep hunger in his dark eyes.

'You know, they put me on the chair once,' he said, smiling at the memory. His fingers traced the multitude of holes that had been scorched in my dress by my abortive efforts to electrocute him. 'Did wonders for this little knot I had in my back.'

I fought the urge to scream as he put his hands on my hips, thumbs lightly resting on either side of the largest rip, and dipped his head to lick experimentally at the small circle of my exposed skin, sending shivers crawling up my belly.

*Don't panic. Don't react.* I lay back on the lid of the thankfully-closed toilet bowl and closed my eyes, trying to calm myself, to focus on thoughts of escape. With my hands tied I couldn't use my Dark Arts powers, couldn't do the motions needed to conjure up even a small fireball.

But I had one small gem of hope left.

I remembered what Magnus had told me, back in the cop car. Unlike the other killers I'd run into in the past few weeks since this nightmare had started, Harlem got no satisfaction or joy out of simply killing someone. Harlem needed to feel like he'd actually beaten someone, both mentally and physically, to feel relief from whatever twisted mental pressure drove him to kill. He needed me to be afraid of him, and until I showed him that fear, he wouldn't kill me.

That was the key to surviving.

Harlem backed off a step, his eyes scanning my face with fierce interest. I gritted my teeth and glared at him, pulling down hard on the knife with all my strength. All I succeeded in doing was pulling the leather strap tighter.

'*Stood up,*' Harlem whispered, tilting his head to study me. '*The strongest and fiercest spirit that fought in heaven, now made fiercer by despair.*'

'Still on the Milton kick, are we?' I asked in a jovial

fashion, as I tried with all my strength to pull my hands free. I looked down at the top of Harlem's head as he dipped down my body again to lick and nip at my bare belly, moving steadily downwards, and a sudden realization hit me.

Aside from the rope around my hands, he wasn't even hurting me. There was no sport in taking down a relaxed, calm victim, I guessed… and from the increasingly irritated look on Harlem's face, he *knew* that I knew this. I just had to figure out how to push him further, make him careless… and then take him down.

*I could do this…*

I jumped as Harlem knelt up and slapped me lightly across the face, just hard enough to sting. My eyes flew open and narrowed dangerously.

'Wake up, little kitty.' He leaned forwards to lick a spot of blood off my lips. 'Wouldn't want you to miss the show.'

'Only thing you're missing is a brain,' I muttered, and earned myself another, harder slap for my troubles. I grinned despite that, then opened my mouth and laughed out loud. It felt good to laugh. It made me feel stronger.

I noted the way Harlem's eyes flared dangerously at the sound of my voice. I was surprised by it myself. I sounded… different. More powerful, somehow. I wasn't scared of him now I knew what his one weakness was, and I could see from Harlem's face that this infuriated him.

This gave me an idea. I decided to throw salt in the wound.

I smiled at him.

Harlem snarled and lunged at me, moving quicker than I could follow, knocking me back against the wooden wall behind the cistern I was tied to. His two knives were suddenly buried in the wall behind me, pinning my hair to the wood on either side of my skull. I gasped as my scalp blazed with pain and I felt a tickling line of blood run down my cheek from where one of the knives had nicked my scalp.

Harlem stared at the blood running down my face and exhaled hard as though the sight of it excited him, tracing his hand up my cheek as his eyes scanned mine. *Waiting for me to fight back, to try and pull free, to give him the fear he needed.*

But I didn't want to play that game. I wanted to play *my* game.

I planted my feet on the ground and curled my lips very slightly up from my teeth, exposing my longer-than-human eyeteeth.

Harlem's smile grew wider, his eyes flaming with a challenge. He put both hands on the wall on either side of me as he bent slowly over me, breathing hard as though he were about to kiss me. I licked my lips, setting the bait, waiting for him to take it. I knew that he could sense my emotions, and didn't care. He knew full well how repulsed I was by him, how deep my utter hatred of him ran.

I was counting on that.

'C'mere, baby,' I murmured, forcing a seductive smile onto my lips. Harlem licked his own lips in anticipation and eagerly rose up on his knees, his fangs seeming to lengthen as he did so. He planted his hands on either side on my head and slowly lowered himself on top of me, crushing me between the cold closed toilet seat and his hard, leather-clad body.

'Tell me what you want,' I murmured.

'You don't wanna know what I want,' Harlem whispered back, his fanged mouth lightly ghosting over my neck.

'And what if I do?'

'I don't think you're in a position to argue, my pretty,' murmured Harlem. There was a scrape of metal as he reached down to slide off his belt. He folded it in two and lightly brushed it across my lips. It smelled like rich fresh leather. I'd always loved that smell— until now. He stroked it down my cheek, then smiled. 'You like that?'

I shrugged, licking blood off my lips.

'It's made from the skin of the last girl who argued with me.'

A cold spike of fear shot through me as Harlem sat up. He smiled as he slid his fingers beneath the ruins of my dress and ripped it clean across the stomach, baring my belly.

'I took a slice from here…' His warm finger touched my aching ribs on the left hand side. 'Cut right round to here…'

His finger traced around the circumference of my waist. He grinned like a broken pumpkin, tilting his head so that his black spiked hair flopped down over one eye. 'Took me several goes to get it out in one strip. Like peeling an apple.'

He gave a horrible laugh at the look on my face.

'Is that the best you got?' I asked, secretly working the rope above my head back and forth as I tested it for weak spots. *I wasn't going to panic. No panicking, now. I still wasn't panicking.* 'You know you don't scare me, Harlem.'

The big werewolf smiled as he reached behind him into his back pocket and pulled out his throwing knives, wrapped in an oilskin cloth. He laid the cloth on my exposed belly as though I was a table. He unwrapped them, one by one.

'I know. But I think that perhaps you should be scared of these.'

Harlem's eyes remained fixed on mine as his hand slid seductively down his body and dipped into the side-pocket of his leather jacket, as though he was about to do a strip-tease. His fingers reappeared holding another, smaller knife, so curved it was almost an 'L' shape.

He breathed hard and weighed it in his hand, his eyes glittering furiously.

Before he could decide what to do with that knife I put all my weight on my bound wrists and snapped a savage kick out at him, trying to knock the blade from his hand. Harlem swayed aside, easily avoiding my wild blow, then flicked the knife towards my belly with a sudden sharp movement. I yelped as an ice-cold burn of pain opened up on my left flank, followed by a well of hot blood.

He'd sliced me clean across the ribs.

Growling, I hauled myself upright on the leather binding which held my wrists and glared at him, gauging his next move, although with a little more caution this time. He tossed the knife to his left hand and got to his feet, stepping back as though to get the full picture.

He prowled around me, his lips parting as he licked his lower lip, his heavy-lidded gaze traveling down to my cloth-covered breasts and down to my exposed stomach, then dropping lower. I could almost feel the heat of his gaze on my skin, burning me like the sun burned vampires. He raised the knife and started to step forwards. I gritted my teeth and kicked out once again with every ounce of strength in my body, aiming at the hand that held the knife.

He sliced my right side this time. It hurt.

A lot.

I cringed away from him, the inside of my head blazing with a white-hot glare of fury and pain. He stopped right in front of me, grinning as blood slid slowly down my flanks in a thin red line. I glowered at him as he took a cautious step towards me, then another. Waiting. I shifted my weight onto my left leg and narrowed my eyes dangerously, ready to kick him again. He stopped a few feet from me and held up the knife in warning. I saw my own reflection in the blade overlaid with a splash of my own blood, and grew very still.

'There's a good girl,' he murmured.

As he knelt before me and started cleaning his knife on the torn-off remains of my dress, an idea shot into my head. It was so clear, so perfect, I wondered why I hadn't thought of it before. I let my eyes light up as though remembering a secret joke, and pressed my lips together as though trying not to laugh.

Harlem paused in his knife-cleaning, weighting the curved blade in his hand. 'Something funny?' he asked, tilting the knife critically so that light glinted off its newly-cleaned blade.

'Ah, it's nothing.' I spat out blood and narrowed my eyes at him, pretending to think hard. 'Okay, I gotta ask.' I tried to pull myself upright on the leather strap, but I had no strength left. My arms were already numb and useless and my sliced sides blazed with pain. I sagged down, trying to look relaxed and confident as I went on. 'So... I was talking to Cyan before I came down here, and—'

'Cyan?' Harlem paused in his knife-cleaning and his face lit up with a surge of almost pitiable hope. 'She's here? In the club?'

'Yeah. Crazy, huh? Blind drunk somewhere downstairs, the poor thing.' I sucked in my breath, looking down at him in a conspiratorial fashion. 'I heard Harlequin stood her up tonight. *Again*. Can you believe it?'

Harlem narrowed his eyes at me.

'You talked to Miss C and you're still alive?' I jumped as he stabbed the knife experimentally into the toilet wall, an inch from my bound forearms. He pulled the blade out, examined it critically. 'You're full of it, kid. What kinda fool do you think I am?'

'The kind of fool who lets the woman he loves slip through his fingers.' I suddenly kicked the thin wooden wall of the toilet stall hard, making the whole row shake. *Thin wood. Good.* 'Hey! Wake up, dumb-ass. I'm talking to you!'

Harlem raised a scarred eyebrow but I pushed on regardless, before my nerve ran out. 'Do the math, shit-for-brains. She's out there right now, all alone and vulnerable... and you're stuck down here playing footsie with me. What's wrong with that picture?'

Harlem smiled and pushed his face right into mine. He waited until my breathing stopped and I swallowed before he replied. 'So?'

'So, I'm human and you're taking all this time to kill

me. That's kind of lame. You should be up there with her right now. Who knows what kind of guy is picking her up at this very moment?'

'You're lying. She ain't here.' Harlem sat back calmly, sitting back on his heels and pulling his second knife out. This one was a lot bigger, and had a wickedly curved serrated edge. He cleaned the blade on the bottom of my dress, taking his time about it. He laid it on my belly beside the first, as cool and as calm as if he were laying the table for dinner. 'You don't know jackshit about Cyan, and you don't know zip about me. So shut your yap before I cut it off.'

'I know enough to know you're wasting your time with her. You're beneath her and you know it. She wouldn't wipe her royal ass with a guy like you.'

Harlem froze. I saw the knuckles of his knife-hand go white, and I swallowed hard.

'Say that again,' he growled, leaning over me.

'You heard me,' I said, through a big fake yawn. I mimed stretching my arms and arched my spine, as though I was settling down to take a nap, comfortably tied to a toilet pedestal about to get butchered. 'And quit fooling yourself. You know the whole "*Werewolf falls in love with vampire*" thing never works out.'

Harlem stabbed the knife into the wooden wall behind me, an inch from my throat. I heard the tip of it scrape brick as it punched out the other side of the wall, and a bead of sweat ran down my forehead. He leaned over me and grabbed a handful of my hair, breathing in my face.

'And what the fuck do you know about love, bitch?'

I took several careful breaths, willing myself to go on. My legs were shaking with adrenaline. It was now or never. I tried to keep my voice light and look him square in the eye as I delivered my bombshell.

'I know those scars on your face weren't caused by the Televamp, Harlem.' I forced a lazy, knowing smile. 'What do you think your friends would say if they knew that you let yourself get beat up by a woman?'

My head hit the floor on the other side of the restroom an action-packed second later. Harlem moved surprisingly fast for a man of his bulk. Even through the ringing in my ears I marveled at the strength he must have in him to be able to tear a whole toilet out of the wall barehanded and throw it across the room, with me still attached to it.

Water pattered down and I rolled frantically aside as the cistern tank smashed down just a few feet from my face, water spilling over the floor in a cool tide and flowing towards me, soaking into my clothing and pooling around me.

It was gross but I didn't care. All my attention was focused on the empty restroom around me. A single white feather lay on the floor. The tip was stained with blood. The restroom door was wide open to reveal the corridor outside.

*Doll had gone!*

An instant later Harlem's boot slammed down next to my head. He grabbed a fistful of my hair, dragging my face up to meet his.

'My life,' he snarled, 'is none of your business.'

'Oh, but everything's my business,' I wheezed, shock apparently making my mouth run on auto-pilot. I looked down at my hands, noting with a stab of fierce triumph that the rope that had bound me was broken. Most of the skin was also missing from my wrists, sure, but it was a small price to pay for my freedom. 'And you're so cute when you're angry. Give us a kiss, gorgeous.'

I grabbed Harlem's scarred, stubbled face and crushed my lips to his. With the remainder of my strength I rolled my body over on top of his, pulling my feet up off the ground, out of the stagnant cistern water that pooled around us.

Perhaps Harlem thought he'd won at that point, because he'd started to relax when I snapped my hands out on either side of his body and directed every last atom of Dark Arts power inside me at the giant puddle on the floor he was lying in.

Harlem's screaming body shielded me from the worst effects of the bio-electricity. I was flung off him almost instantly as the power poured through him, amplified by the water, making his huge body jump and buck as though possessed. I was already running when I hit the ground on the other side of the room, bouncing off the big rubber trash can and propelling myself through the half-open door out in the hallway.

*I was free!*

I didn't have long before he'd come after me, I knew, as my bruised head pounded with the sudden head-rush of being upright. He was a big guy, and I wasn't exactly running on full power tonight. My suspicions were confirmed when I heard a heart-stopping snarl come from the open doorway behind me.

But there was something wrong here. This growl sounded like it had come from the chest of a mountain lion rather than a human…

Oh, *shit*…!

I craned my neck back just in time to see the monstrous

black *thing* come blowing out of the restroom door, moving so fast that it slammed into the wall opposite, tearing a big chunk out of the brickwork and ripping a six-foot slice of carpet off the floor with its hooked claws as it scrabbled for purchase.

The nightmarish wolf spun upright and came after me.

# CHAPTER THIRTY-SEVEN

I TORE DOWN the corridor, cursing feverishly under my breath as I tried to out-run a killer werewolf the size of a small truck.

As days went, I'd had better ones.

I threw a look over my shoulder as I ran, unable to resist, to see exactly what was about to eat me. Harlem in wolf form was a sight that not many people got to see and live. As a werewolf, he was jet black with sharp dagger-like ears, tall as a grizzly, broad and strong as a black bull. His thick, greasy black mane hung over his eyes and poured down over his massively muscular shoulders in dark oily waves, filling the corridor with a goat-like stench. His sides were carpeted with ragged patches of fur which clung to his huge tattooed wolf-muscles like scrub-grass on a mountainside. Every inch of him was thick with sinews and veins and claws that promised ugly, bleeding, screaming death to anyone who dared to get within a one-mile radius.

Harlem's fur was smoking.

I wasn't even aware that I was screaming as I barreled

along the corridor at top speed, driven purely by the sheer terror of hideous death snapping at my heels.

I sped around the corner, rolling against the wall like a pinball as I slammed into two dividing partitions, kicked open a set of double doors, and ran straight into someone tall and broad who seized me by the shoulders and slammed me into the opposite wall, knocking the breath out of me.

I stared up at the mini Uzi that was pressed against my forehead, and took my first real breath since I'd electrocuted Harlem, about eight seconds ago.

'Hi, Phil,' I squeaked.

Phil stared down at me, his every muscle tense as he jammed the muzzle of the Uzi into my temple, a wild look in his brown eyes. He was wearing a brand new black Hunter uniform that was perhaps half a size too tight, his lean form bristling with strapped-on weaponry.

He did not look friendly.

'Identify yourself,' he snapped, his finger tensing on the trigger.

'Phil! It's me!' I yelled, peering down the corridor after me. Phil had always been a big practical joker, but sometimes he didn't seem to know where to set the limits. He'd crack a joke whilst lined up against the wall before a firing squad, just to get in one final chuckle, but now was no time to be joking around. I heard the heart-stopping scrape of fast-approaching claws and madly batted Phil's gun aside, trying to run. Phil grabbed me and shoved me back against the wall.

'If you're really you,' he barked, 'tell me your name. And what number am I thinking of?'

'I'm Kayla!' I yelled, groaning internally as I tried to

shove him aside to get a clean shot to the doors. 'And I keep *telling* you, Phil, the number thing only works in *Bill and Ted's Bogus Journey!* Now *move!*'

Before he could reply I snatched the gun away from him and dropped into a low fighting crouch. I aimed the mini Uzi down the hallway and shoved my finger into the trigger-guard just as the beating of giant paws and the sound of heavy, echoing panting neared us on the other side of the doors.

*Three.*

*Two.*

*One...*

The double doors exploded.

For an instant I saw, framed against a suspended chaos of shining, spinning glass, the biggest, meanest, ugliest black werewolf I'd ever seen in my life. Glass and tangled wooden struts flew outwards, showering over us and raining across the entire length of the corridor as the giant black shape of Harlem flew through the wreckage, his great hooked claws scrabbling for purchase on the polished flooring.

I ducked down and opened fire with a yell loud enough to match Harlem's howl. I peppered the oncoming monster with nine millimeter rounds, blowing him backwards through the doors until he fell back against a side-wall, his foreleg buckling from a blown knee-joint. He yowled in fury and pain as the bullets cratered his flanks. I held the trigger down till the chamber ran dry, then ejected the cartridge and thrust the empty gun under Phil's nose.

'Reload!' I barked, staring over his shoulder.

'Hey, Kayla. Good to see you too. It's been a while,' Phil said casually, as he whipped off one of his ammo belts and fed it into the chamber. He looked me up and down, seemingly unsurprised by my bloodied, disheveled appearance, my torn and tattered dress. 'How've you been keeping?'

'Just great. You?'

'Never been better. Here.'

'Thanks.'

I grabbed the gun and aimed it directly at Harlem's head, squeezing off several controlled bursts as the nightmarish monster tried to get up. I was close enough that I distinctly saw each bullet blow a bloody crater in his neck and flank. I held my breath, waiting for him to go down. But instead of rolling over and dying, Harlem just gave a massive sneeze and shook his head, as though I was spraying him with a garden hose instead of an automatic weapon firing six hundred rounds a minute. His knee joint had already stopped bleeding and seemed to be halfway healed.

Then the gun was empty again. I swore.

Harlem roared like a lion and lunged to his feet with a powerful, athletic movement, shaking out his black ruff as he turned to square off against us, his eyes fixed firmly on me. I reloaded with trembling fingers as he threw back his head and gave a series of ear-splitting coughing barks, each one jangling my nerves like hammers hitting my spinal column.

I thrust the Uzi back into Phil's hands and spun wildly around to get my bearings. I recognized the corridor that led to the room my friends were being held in. One of the side-walls was spattered with Harlem's blood from where Grey had attacked him.

'Hold him!' I shouted, over the noise of the creepy howling. 'I'll go get backup!'

'No time!' Phil yelled back. 'Harlequin's here!'

'Where?'

'Here! He went that way with that angel girl. Go stop him Kayla, I got this!'

'You sure?' I saw he only had one clip left.

'Hell, yeah!'

Phil fired a short burst of fire at Harlem, driving him back several feet. My Hunter friend backed up, keeping me safely shielded behind him as the Harlem-beast howled and struggled to its feet again.

'Wait!' I clutched at his sleeve. 'You guys went to Washington! To get the other Hunters?'

'We did. *Go, go!*' Phil shot Harlem in the face, making him sneeze.

'And?'

'Don't ask! Just run!'

My face crumpled. *The other Hunters weren't coming.*

'*Move your ass, Kayla!*' yelled Phil, the humor for once gone from his face. He pointed down at his wristwatch. 'It's almost midnight!'

He yelled as I suddenly seized his wrist and tore his watch off. He didn't fight me, he was too busy trying to keep the machine gun in his other hand steady as he pointed at Harlem.

I took off down the corridor in the direction Phil was pointing, buckling on the big wristwatch as I ran. I heard the sound of yelling and gunfire from behind me and concentrated on putting everything I had into running, to escaping the monster snapping and snarling behind me.

Moments later, the gunfire abruptly shut off.

As I started sprinting down the next corridor I

distinctly heard the sound of Phil's Uzi hitting the ground, clattering over and over with an almost obscenely loud sound before it was drowned out by a volley of frenzied snarling and hideous wet tearing noises.

I tried not to think about what might be happening behind me as I fled down the tiled hallway, cut right, dodged left, and finally burst out into an entrance hall which ended in two big glass sliding doors.

Through the doors I saw the round-bellied shape of a grey-green army helicopter sitting on the flat rooftop outside, its propellers whirling in the night air, preparing to lift off. The side-door was wide open, giving me a clean view of the passenger cabin.

Oh, no.

With the stillness and clarity of absolute panic I saw the pale, elegant figure of Doll sitting inside, her long black hair whipping in the downdraft, strapped firmly into the side-seat by the window. Harlequin was standing over her, looking as gorgeous as ever. He clipped Doll in then turned to put a hand on the helmeted pilot's shoulder, barking instructions into his ear.

He looked cool and collected, as though he was heading out for a business meeting rather than preparing to slaughter millions of people.

I didn't even bother stopping to see if the rooftop doors were unlocked. There was no time. If that helicopter took off with Doll inside it, it was all over.

Without breaking stride I snapped up my arms as I ran and unleashed the biggest fire bolt I could muster at the door-lock. It hit the big glass doors with a scream of superheated plasma and imploded, showering the rooftop outside with spinning crystals of safety-glass. I was through the smoking hole before the glass had finished dropping to the ground, yelling Doll's name.

It was windy outside in the darkness. The chopper's downdraft whipped my long hair around my face as I hared across the big graveled rooftop towards the helicopter, waving my hands and shouting. I had to stop that chopper from taking off. Whatever it cost me.

As though in slow motion I saw Harlequin turn and freeze at the sight of me. A look very much like surprise came over his face, mingled with what I fancied was a touch of admiration. He leaned over the unseen pilot and murmured something in his ear in an unhurried fashion, then cracked his knuckles and stepped lightly down from the helicopter.

I breathed deeply, slowing to a winded trot.

*This was it. My big showdown.*

I turned to face off against the master vampire as he strode casually towards me across the wind-whipped rooftop, rallying up the very last of my strength for my biggest firebolt ever, to blast this son of a bitch back to hell, where he belonged. He was right out in the open, unprotected and apparently unarmed. I had a clean shot. I might never get a chance like this again. This was all I had ever wanted, all I had dreamed of.

*Revenge.*

*For what he'd done to me, for what he'd done to Karrel.*

*For the three hundred and fifty-nine Hunters he'd murdered, blown up in their beds.*

As I raised my hands, preparing to strike, Harlequin simply blurred and vanished.

I stared at the empty space, then jumped as a cold

hand clamped down on the back of my neck and squeezed down with an incredible pressure. I distinctly felt the vertebrae in my neck start to separate as though my head were caught in a mechanical crusher, and clutched at his hand in panic, trying to pry his fingers off me.

'I knew you'd come,' Harlequin purred, his lips a bare inch from my ear. 'We've been waiting for you, sweetpea.'

He put two fingers in his mouth and whistled at the helicopter. I stared as the very recognizable punk-rock figure of Niki leaned out of the open side of the aircraft. He gave me a little wave. I replied with a single-finger gesture. He blew me a kiss before shoving the door further open to reveal…

My breathing stopped. My heart seemed to leap into my throat. Of all the nightmares I'd been through today, of all the nasty surprises, this one was by far the worst.

A limp figure was strapped to the seat next to Niki, dazed but still conscious. He was dressed all in black, his spiky brown hair drenched in blood. As I stared at him in shock he lifted his head and gazed back at me in dazed incomprehension.

'Wylie,' I whispered in horror.

Even without looking behind me I knew Harlequin was smiling. The master vampire's grip tightened on the back of my neck as he gestured for me to walk to the helicopter.

'I heard that your Hunter friends are here,' he purred, his tone of voice turning my spine to ice. 'It wouldn't do to be interrupted before I complete the Prophecy. I think it's time for us to take a little ride.'

# CHAPTER THIRTY-EIGHT

THERE WERE SIX seats in the back of the ex-army 206 Bell LongRanger, two sets of three facing each other. The cabin was plush and roomy for a helicopter, and smelled of old cigarettes and citrus cleaning spray. The remains of a Kentucky Fried Chicken takeout was strewn across the back seat, along with a torn copy of the LA Times, open at the Obituaries page. Several were circled in thick red ink.

It was a very ordinary scene, not at all where I had planned to spend the final half hour of my life, which— if I had to choose— would ideally involve Brad Pitt, black silk sheets and a very large jar of chocolate Nutella spread.

I sat down heavily on the cream leather seat next to the window, opposite Doll, unable to tear my eyes off Wylie. Seeing my last 'normal' friend here, in the thick of my own worst nightmare, was a little more than I could handle right now.

Why the hell had they taken Wylie?

Something glinted on the seat next to him. A feeling of

inevitability grew in me as I peered into the open velvet-lined box beside him. An ornate, curved silver knife lay inside. The blade was acid-etched with sculptured tear-drops, and a big bloodstone was embedded in the handle.

'Make it big,' the designer of the knife had obviously been told. 'Make it shiny. Make it very, very obvious this knife has one job, which is turning something alive into something dead. Then go from there.'

If Harlequin had written 'Sacrificial Knife' in big glowing neon letters on the box, he couldn't have made it more obvious what the weapon was for.

So that was it. Harlequin planned to force Wylie to kill Doll on the stroke of midnight, which was—I glanced at my watch—in about twenty-five minutes and counting. Wylie was human, so the Avenging Angels would attack humanity. If I'd thought Phil's sense of humor was perverse, Harlequin had him beat by a long shot.

The cabin door slammed as Harlequin got into the front of the chopper next to the pilot. I heard the crackle of radio tower instructions issue from his headset, and wondered how much money Harlequin had paid the cops to overlook this one short unauthorized flight. Or rather, how many had been killed before they'd surrendered use of air traffic control. The twin snouts of the old-fashioned fifty-caliber heavy machine guns mounted on the front of the chopper gave me a small clue. There was an army base about fifty miles south of here. I didn't have to ask to know where they'd stolen this thing from.

I settled back miserably as the helicopter's engines fired up with a scream, ready for takeoff.

So this was it. I had failed. Not only had Harlequin captured me and Doll, just twenty-five minutes from the Apocalypse at midnight, but he'd got my best friend, too. We were outnumbered and surrounded by enemies, powerless, helpless and weaponless.

So what else in my life was new?

Niki grabbed Wylie's handcuffed arm and half dragged, half carried him across the cabin, dropping him down in the back seat opposite me like a sack of cheap potatoes. Niki clipped my best friend's semi-conscious body into the harness then moved on to me. He avoided eye contact with me as he pulled a set of solid steel police-cuffs out and cuffed my hands together in my lap. I didn't even bother looking up at him as he pulled the cuffs tight, unable to tear my eyes off Wylie.

My best friend was alive, but even a casual glance betrayed the fact that he was hurt, perhaps badly. Blood spilled in a livid red wave across his pale forehead and cheek, and he held himself strangely, as though something inside him was broken.

How the hell had they found him? We had been so careful to take back-roads on the drive to Wylie's house, changing direction a dozen times until I'd soothed my paranoia that we were being followed. Obviously, where master vampires were concerned you couldn't be paranoid enough.

Put that one on a bumper sticker.

Niki sat down next to Wylie, opposite me. He wisely kept his gun trained on Wylie's heart rather than on me. If he moved that gun an inch I'd've been on him in a heartbeat.

Wylie's eyes fluttered open and slowly focused on

mine, his face a mask of fear and confusion. Someone had ripped his eyebrow piercing out and blood ran in a red trickle down the side of his face. I felt a fist of anger close tight in my stomach, let it grow until it formed a white-hot pit of lava in my belly.

Anger was good. I'd need every last drop of it if I was going to stay alive.

'Where are we going, Kayla? Wylie asked quietly, his voice barely audible above the accelerating roar of the engine. His eyes were unfocused. He looked concussed. 'Is this another one of your jokes?'

'Nope,' Niki said cheerfully. He winked at me as he stretched out his jean-clad legs in front of him as though this was a pleasure cruise, eyeing my bloodstained, ragged appearance with great interest. The look on his face mirrored Harlequin's. He had thought he'd never see me alive again, and it showed. He glanced sideways at Wylie, mischief flickering in his blue eyes. 'She never told you what she does for a living, did she?'

'What do you mean?'

'Shut up, jackass.' My gaze was fixed on the back of Harlequin's head. *If I could just free my hands, maybe I could blast the pilot with a fireball before we took off…*

I saw Niki's gaze flicker over my body with languid enjoyment, settle once again on the wolf-bite on my arm. He yawned, ran a hand through his hair, and reached for the remainder of the cold fast-food chicken bucket.

'So when did you get bit?' he asked me in a tough, uncaring voice, through a mouthful of chicken.

'What's it to you?'

'That's a fresh bite, babe. It's full moon tonight. Why are you still human?'

'Why are you still talking?'

Niki's smile remained on his face although his eyes narrowed sharply, a frown stealing over his face. He took another bite of the cold chicken, chewed, swallowed, all the while watching me in a way I didn't much like.

'Just making conversation, my little furry friend.'

'Then don't.'

'Or what?'

I gave him a slow, easy smile, revealing my budding wolf-teeth. I hadn't had a chance to file them down today, and I could feel the alien twin points of my canines creeping down into my mouth like the tips of two tiny knives. I hadn't taken my anti-werewolf serum tonight, and was desperately hoping that the double-shot I'd taken last night would last me through the next few hours. I knew would pass for human on the street but to anyone who knew the signs, right now I was the equivalent of an unexploded bomb.

Niki raised an eyebrow as he saw my teeth, shut up completely. His gaze flicked around the sealed off cabin, back to me. Doing the math. I saw his Adam's apple bob as he swallowed. Newborn werewolves were feral, dangerous, especially in a confined space like, say, the inside of an airborne helicopter.

I let Niki sweat. He deserved it. I still didn't know for sure who had ratted out Cyan to Harlequin, but with Niki's stalker skills being what they were, I had my suspicions.

I turned away with a growl to check on Doll. My heart swelled at the sight of her, despite our bleak situation. She was still alive, thank goodness. Her eyes were bright with fear as she stared across the cabin at me. She was still wearing the thick iron collar that drained her powers, and her wings were folded tightly behind her, bound with the same silver clips they'd used to keep Grey under control.

She started to speak but I shook my head slightly, warning her to keep quiet. She turned her head slightly back to the rooftop outside, then winked at me and went limp. She gave a muffled groan. When Niki turned his head to look at her she pretended to pass out, sagging down in her seat and closing her eyes.

*Doll had a plan!*

Across the cabin from me, Wylie stirred.

'Kayla?'

'Yes, Wylie?' I was still staring at Doll.

'Why does that girl have wings? And what's wrong with your teeth? Wasn't Halloween last night?'

'Don't worry about it, sweetie. Everything will be fine.'

'Are we shooting a movie?' Wylie turned to me, a look of sudden hope on his face. He must have pretty bad concussion. 'I saw the big guns on this thing. They look pretty real.' He smiled glassily, struggling to focus on me. 'I always wanted to be in a movie.'

'I know, Wylie,' I said softly, glaring at Niki. Niki gave a mocking smile and I clenched my bound fists, tensing my whole body to throw myself at him, rip his throat out, somehow gain control of the helicopter and hit the ejector seat, throwing Harlequin to his death, fifteen stories beneath us…

It was a great plan, with the only downside being that I knew I didn't have a hope in hell. Before I was halfway across that cabin, Niki would simply swung the gun a few inches to the right and blow my head off.

I was trapped.

I settled back in my seat, waiting for an opening.

The roar of rotors from overhead got louder and the cabin jolted once. We were airborne. I caught a glimpse of the pilot's face in the mirror, shadowed by his helmet, and my heart froze with fear.

Mitzi the werewolf was flying the helicopter. Wait. Let me rephrase that. Mitzi *the blind werewolf* was flying the chopper. And everyone seemed perfectly okay with this.

What the blazes was going on?

I gave a little cry as the helicopter's runners bumped over the low wall which bordered the rooftop before breaking free and swinging out into space. My nerves were already stretched to breaking point, and Mitzi's questionable flying abilities did not fill me with confidence.

Nor did the sight of his blind, empty black eyes in the rear-view mirror.

Sweating, I turned to look at Harlequin's reflection in the plastic bubble cockpit. He was sitting calmly with his hands folded in his lap, a look of supreme confidence on his face. I noticed that Mitzi oddly mirrored his every movement, copying every turn of his head as Harlequin looked left and right to check on weather conditions. I knew that all vampires had a form of telepathy, the ability to invade the minds of others, most notably through their Thrall. I realized that Harlequin must be somehow telepathically 'showing' what he was seeing to Mitzi.

Great. So we were being taken hostage in a stolen army helicopter piloted by a telepathic blind werewolf. How much worse could things possibly get?

*Don't think it…*

*Shit. Too late.*

I almost jumped out of my skin as a series of pings and plinks raked across the roof of the helicopter. *Gunfire.* I groaned out loud as a hoarse cry filled the air, a primal cry full of hatred and rage, audible even over the thrumming of the chopper's engine.

'*PADRE!!*'

Oh, Christ on a bike. I peered out of the side window in utter horror to see Harlem standing on the very edge of the rooftop, now back in human form again. He must have been still firmly in the grip of Doll's mind-controlling glamour, because he threw back his head and screamed in rage at the sight of Harlequin getting away in the glass-fronted chopper.

It was too dark to make out many details, but by the flickering white light of the chopper's front beams I could see that Harlem was naked and completely covered in blood. A dark mechanical shape clutched in his big hand was all that was left of Phil's mini Uzi.

My insides twisted at the sight of the machine gun. Phil loved that gun. There was no way in hell he'd ever give it up to an enemy unless he was…

I bowed forwards on the seat as a giant cold hand squeezed my heart, gasping, feeling like I was about to throw up.

*Phil was dead.*

*This couldn't be real, it couldn't be…*

The chopper suddenly juddered as a tremendous metallic rattling sound shook the cabin, as though stones were being dropped onto a metal grille from a great height. I hurriedly pulled my legs up to my chest on the seat as the rooftop around Harlem erupted in a blaze of flying debris.

The helicopter was firing on him!

Mitzi's blank face didn't once change expression as he calmly pulled a black mechanical arm from the flightboard. He swung the chopper's mini-cannons around, operating them by remote control, his head once again moving in creepy unison with Harlequin's. His face was expressionless as he raked the gravel around Harlem's legs with machine-gun fire, forcing him to run for cover.

I pressed my face to the plastic window, watching the action. I noticed that Mitzi's bursts were fired an almost deliberate two meters behind Harlem's legs. I frowned. Mitzi had a machine-gun cannon and his control over it seemed faultless. Why didn't he just take Harlem out? I looked up at Mitzi's face reflected in ghostly silver on the bubble-like front windscreen of the chopper and saw his face flicker with pain, just the once, like he was fighting a bad headache.

Harlequin frowned at him and Mitzi's face instantly went blank again. I realized right away what that meant. *Mitzi was fighting back against the master vampire's thrall. Mitzi didn't want to kill his pack-mate.*

Maybe, just maybe, I could use that.

The gunfire shut off. The low lapping of the helicopter's blades increased to an ear-splitting whine as Mitzi banked around the Circus of Sins nightclub, lining himself up with the horizon. It had just started to power forwards away from the building when a terrific *THUMP* shook the chopper, jolting it heavily to one side. The pitch of the rotors shot up alarmingly and Harlequin muttered a string of expletives at Mitzi in what sounded like Japanese, gesturing sharply downwards towards the floor. My heart skipped a beat as I heard the distinct and unmistakable sound of clawed hands scraping and thumping over the undercarriage.

*Harlem was clinging to the outside of the helicopter, trying to get in.*

Niki stood up quickly, craning his head wildly around to follow the sound of heavy knocking sounds, moving steadily across the underbelly of the chopper.

'He didn't,' he muttered.

'He did,' I said with an odd satisfaction.

'What's gotten into the big dumb freak?'

'No idea,' I said, staring hard at Doll again. The pretty young angel looked as though she was still unconscious, passed out in her seat, but I was sure I detected a flicker in her closed eye, a small twitch on one side of her sleep-curved lips.

She was still controlling Harlem, I realized. *Go Doll!*

Unfortunately, that meant that the rest of us were going down, too.

The chopper dipped in mid-air with a stomach-sickening jolt as Mitzi raised the nose of the chopper and pitched us to the side, trying to shake Harlem off. It was hard to hear over the thump of the rotors, but I was sure I heard a faint roar of rage. It looked like Harlem wasn't letting go. Mitzi cursed and tilted the flight stick, turning the chopper around to head back to the safety of the roof of the nightclub.

I glanced at my stolen watch, hardly daring to look. *Eleven forty.*

So this was how Doll was going to die. The chopper was going to crash with us all in it and kill us all. After the other deaths I'd imagined, it seemed almost too easy.

I clung to my seat in terror as the chopper neared

the building, staring frantically out of the window as a series of scraping, bumping crashes came from the undercarriage, like steel nails on a tin blackboard. *Come on, come on!* I had to fight the urge to get up and pace back and forth. If Harlem somehow got into the chopper before it landed, it would all be over. I never thought I'd say this but it was down to Mitzi to save us now.

Another crash rang out from down below, followed by an alarming hissing noise, like fluid or maybe steam being released. *That couldn't be good.* I heard Harlequin shout something to Mitzi in a growling language I didn't recognize. Niki must have understood it because he reached under the seat and pulled out a stubby sawn-off rifle. He aimed it down at the floor, tracking the thumping noises with its muzzle.

I cleared my throat. 'Are you really going to fire that thing in a helicopter?'

Before Niki could reply, the banging sounds from the undercarriage stopped. I frowned, leaning forward, peering down at the floor.

Perhaps Harlem had given up. Maybe he had fallen off...

I leaped back as the small port-hole window next to my head suddenly burst inwards with a loud crunch of breaking plastic. I screamed and jumped back as an enraged, blood-streaked face shoved itself up against the broken pane, snapping and clawing in his mad efforts to get in.

*Harlem.*

THE ENTIRE WINDOW-FRAME gave way with a crunch as Harlem forced his enormous furred head through the hole in the glass, snapping and tearing at the seats next to the window like a dog sticking his head into a rabbit hole. He had half-changed back to wolf form to make the jump, and was now clinging to the side-runner with his prehensile clawed hands.

Harlem punched out the window in a shower of plasti-glass, then forced his fist through, making a grab for Doll. The young angel gave a piercing scream and cowered back in her seat, staring into the furious face of Harlem, who was just a few short feet away from her chained, bound, helpless body.

'Allow me, ladies.'

Niki stepped forwards, our knight in not-so-shining armor. He loaded his rifle with an ominous *KER-CHACK,* swung the barrel around. He fired three times into Harlem's face from point-blank range, grinning like a skull.

Harlem's whole head was blown backwards by the bullets. When it came back down again I flinched. The top of his head was a gory, pitted mess. The bullets had taken out his right eye and turned his cheekbone and ear into a tattered, dangling mess of torn flesh and fur. Blood ran steadily down the broken window.

And still he kept on coming.

As Niki reloaded and stalked closer, lining up a second shot at blank-point range, Harlem's clawed hand whipped out and punched back through the window. He grabbed Niki's rifle and gave a sharp yank on the weapon, jerking it from Niki's hands. Harlem pulled the rifle through the window and hurled it out of the chopper with a triumphant snarl.

'Way to go, clown-ass,' I muttered.

Niki's indignant reply was drowned out by Harlem's

snarl as the big werewolf reared back, clenched his hand into a fist and slammed it into the side of the helicopter beneath the window, at the join where the door met the side of the aircraft. The whole frame shook with the impact and a big piece of plastic popped off the lock and dropped to the floor inside, followed by another. The move would have shattered the fist of any human being, but Harlem wasn't human. Not even remotely so.

Niki reacted immediately. As he reached for the button to disengage the door lock, I aimed a frantic kick at his knee, trying to trip him.

'What the hell are you doing?' I cried. 'You let him in, he'll kill us all!'

'I'm not letting him in,' said Niki, looking insulted. 'Just checking it's locked. This thing was built to withstand gunfire. The doors are armor-plated. I doubt an angry naked dude is going to do much damage.'

'You don't know Harlem,' I replied with a shudder.

Two double bolts slammed into place and Niki stepped back with a grunt of contentment, dusting his hands off. *Like locking the door would make a difference.* I glared at him, wishing I wasn't handcuffed so I could get up and strangle the life out of him. I'd trusted this guy and he'd betrayed me. He'd betrayed his human mother who Harlequin had supposedly killed, and any human siblings he happened to have.

Come to think of it, why was he even here? Didn't he trust his Dad to do the job right? Was Niki really that arrogant?

My scowl faded into a frown of puzzlement as I saw Niki flick his eyes towards Harlequin, then draw his hand swiftly across his throat. Great. So I was supposed to play a game of Charades with him now, while a werewolf was trying to break into our helicopter and kill us?

I made an angry *'What the hell?'* gesture. Niki's schizophrenic behavior had been pissing me off all day, but now I was more than ready to kill him.

As I stared at him I saw something flicker across his face that could've been pain. He pressed his hands to his temples and winced.

'Talk to me,' he said, in a low, soft voice. 'Quickly, please.'

'About what?'

'I don't care. Anything. Just talk.'

He punctuated the last word with another pointed glance back at Harlequin. As the chopper shook with a fresh volley of thumps and scrapes, he lowered his voice so that only I could hear him. 'And do it quick. I can't keep blocking him like this. He hears everything I think if I don't block it…. Ow!'

He broke off with a grimace, clutching his head.

'Right. Fine.' I said. 'You want me to talk about anything? How about we talk about the fact that you're one wave short of a shipwreck, and that's on a good day? That I've known crazy dribbling homeless guys who talk more sense than you do?'

'That's great. Keep going.'

'What the hell are you playing at, Nick? You told me I could trust you, so why do you keep trying to kill me? Which side are you even on, anyway?'

'Kayla, think. I already told you everything,' said Niki, his voice so low and fast I had to strain to hear him. 'Remember when we talked back in my room before… *shit!*'

His legs gave way and he fell to the ground, clutching his head. As he did so I saw Harlequin glance sharply back in his direction, one eyebrow raised as if in curiosity. Niki's blue eyes filled with what looked like a spill of red pigment, which intensified briefly. Niki bit his lip so hard he drew blood, shaking his head. Harlequin nodded briefly, as though satisfied, then turned back around to concentrate on flying.

A memory came back to me. Myself and Niki, lounging on his black-sheeted bed deep underground in the Circus of Sins. The memory was so vivid that I heard Niki's voice in my head as though he had spoken out loud...

*'Telepathy... believe me, it ain't pleasant...Having someone else in your head all the time, seeing your thoughts... it takes a lot of time and will-power to learn to block it. If you don't, then they see everything. He sees everything. It's how he controls us...'*

All of a sudden, I got it. Harlequin could read Niki's mind, and Niki was trying to block him. Niki hadn't lied to me about wanting to overthrow Harlequin, but he'd had to keep up a performance when he was anywhere near him, to block even his own thoughts of his defection in case his father 'overheard' and took him off the project.

Was that what Niki's little performance had been about, back in the jail cell? Did he say all that stuff about hating werewolves because he knew his father would be listening?

I desperately hoped that this was the case.

Before I could speculate on this any further, another crash rippled through the cabin. I watched with horrified disbelief as the lock flew off the door on the inside and a gloved fist shoved its way through the gap, its thick splayed fingers reaching around on the inside for leverage.

The fist tightened on the inside of the door then pulled back, incredibly pulling the side of the door with it, peeling the helicopter side-door outwards at a ninety-degree angle like it was a piece of string cheese. The metal must've been a good half inch thick, but it immediately started to buckle and bend under the insane pressure of the werewolf's strength. The door had been bent outwards a good foot before anyone reacted. Harlem's strength was unbelievable.

There was a horrible grinding sound as the sliding hydraulic hinges that kept the door on finally gave way.

With a grinding tear, Harlem ripped the chopper's door off.

I caught a quick glimpse of it flying over Harlem's head before it spun off into space, dropping like a stone down the side of the buildings below. Cold night air thumped into the cabin and the chopper lurched as the wind buffeted the inside before straightening out again. Wind whistled into the cabin, blowing my hair over my face. I scraped it back with my handcuffed hands, tucking it behind my ears.

When I could see again, I wished I couldn't. A roaring black void was revealed blowing past the side of the chopper. Outside, the lights of the city dipped and whirled alarmingly. The comforting, familiar shape of the Circus of Sins nightclub spun towards us with aching slowness, but it was still almost five hundred feet away from us and a good hundred feet down.

I yelled out, but my voice was instantly snatched away by the roar of rotors as Harlem's snarling, vindictive face popped up in the now-open doorway. His bloodied hands scrabbled for a hold on the slippery metal floor of the hatchway, his one remaining yellow eye revolving in its socket in search of Harlequin.

He locked on me, and he snarled in recognition and rage.

He started climbing into the helicopter.

HARLEQUIN TURNED AROUND in his seat and frowned with displeasure, muttering something to Mitzi. The next thing I knew, Niki was on his feet again, moving strangely, like a puppet with someone else pulling the strings.

'Crap,' he muttered, sweat running down his forehead. 'Kayla. Quick. Take this!'

He stepped briefly between me and Harlequin's range of vision. His hand brushed over mine. I felt something small and metallic drop down into my palm as he strode away, moving towards the door.

I opened my hand and snuck a glance down at it. Niki had given me another key! This one was large and gold-colored.

But what did it open?

I watched in disbelief as Niki moved over to the open doorway, tore a piece of jutting pipe off the side and struck out at the crazed werewolf, trying to knock him off the chopper. Harlem ducked aside as the metal pipe whistled down, then snatched at the pipe with his teeth. *CLINK!* He got a grip on the end and bit down, growling like a dog with a bone, his one working eye blazing a furious cloudy gold. Niki leaned back with all his weight and tried to pull the metal pipe out of Harlem's mouth. I watched in amazement as the inhuman pair had a brief tug-of war over the pipe.

Harlem won. He was too crazed, too out-of-it to give in. Niki fell back as the pressure on the pipe was abruptly released as it slid through his hands. I'd never seen a werewolf that was stronger than a vampire before.

Niki recovered quickly and leaped to his feet with surprising speed. Harlem had gone back to trying to climb aboard the helicopter. Before he'd got more than one foot up, Niki darted forwards. Harlem's head snapped back as Niki kicked him hard in the face with his booted foot. I'd barely drawn breath to yell before Harlem's clawed hand flashed out and he seized Niki's leg.

With a colossal heave, Harlem threw Niki out of the helicopter.

# CHAPTER THIRTY-NINE

THE RUSHING WIND swallowed my scream of pure horror as Niki plummeted away from the chopper, disappearing into the night. I saw both Harlequin and Mitzi turn quickly to look out the back of the stricken helicopter, as though re-assessing the situation. To my disbelief they both turned back around again and leaned together, as though silently conferring. Mitzi hit a button, and a thick glass screen slid smoothly upwards between the cockpit and the cabin, closing them off like the bulletproof window in a limo. *Bastards!*

I felt my palm sting, and looked down stupidly at my hand. Blood was dripping slowly out of the bottom of my fist. I realized I was gripping the gold key Niki had given me so hard it was cutting into my palm.

*Key. Handcuffs. Crazed werewolf trying to get into helicopter. Join the dots.*

I grabbed the key and twisted my wrists up, frantically jamming the key into the lock. My hands were shaking so much that it took several attempts.

It was in. I twisted it.

Nothing happened. The key didn't fit.

As I stared at it in bewilderment, a savage growl rang out. I saw Harlem's head swivel to lock in on me. His face darkened into an expression of hatred. I guessed he was still sore about me electrocuting him back in the restrooms. With a roar he launched himself forwards into the cabin, half his body still dangling out of the door, pulling himself towards me with his gloved hands...

As I scrabbled backwards on the seat, something red smacked down and struck Harlem's hands. Harlem yowled with pain, releasing his grip on the floor just as the chopper tilted sideways. He slid back towards the door, catching himself at the last minute.

I looked up to see Wylie drag himself back up on his seat. He was holding a fire extinguisher between his cuffed hands. His eyes were wide, disbelieving, but he looked almost grimly determined as he rested the fire extinguisher to the floor, shifted his grip on it, and braced himself for another strike.

I didn't want him to. I didn't want him anywhere near this monster. I turned to Doll, waving to her madly.

'Stop it!' I yelled. 'Stop controlling him! He'll kill us all!'

'I have no choice.'

Doll's voice sounded in my head, crystal clear, unaffected by the tumultuous wind which tore through the cockpit. I gaped at her.

'You always have a choice! Just stop!'

Doll shook her head. 'It is a statistical probability that the intruder will kill me if he enters the vehicle. The curse will then fall on the werewolves instead of the humans. My job is to protect the humans. I must obey.'

'No!'

I yipped as the craft lurched sideways. I saw Mitzi glance back at us as he angled the chopper at an even greater sideways angle, trying to tip Harlem off the helicopter. Bits of trash and the remains of Niki's fried chicken bucket tumbled and slid down the forty-five degree angle floor, bouncing off Harlem's head as he slid backwards, trying to get a grip on the slick floor with his gloved fingers.

'Help us!' I yelled.

'Apologies. I cannot. It is my duty to protect mankind. Harlequin plans to use your human friend to kill me at midnight. If we crash now, that will not take place.'

'So delay him!' I yelled. 'Possess Mitzi! Make him land this beast!'

'Not possible. Harlequin has shields up on his mind and in the mind of the blind werewolf. I cannot touch them. I am sorry.' She settled back in her seat as a furious bellow shook the cabin. 'It is the only way.' She opened an eye. 'Unless you wish to kill me yourself? You are a werewolf.'

'I'm not a werewolf yet!' I yelled. 'I can't take the risk that I'm still human.'

'Then it is done.'

I heard a thump. I looked up to see that Harlem had got a good grip on the fuselage, despite Mitzi's efforts to shake him. He was slowly pulling himself up again, his enormous naked muscles bulging in the cabin light, his murderous gaze fixed firmly on me. I yelled as Mitzi dipped and pitched the chopper again, trying to shake Harlem off. My scream was cut off as the craft lurched suddenly sideways, tipping me off the seat and sending me tumbling down towards Harlem's open mouth.

I caught myself on a seat-post, wrapping my arms

around the slippery leather surface in desperation. I snapped a glance into the cockpit as the craft tilted at an angle of forty-five degrees, wondering what the hell Mitzi was doing. Rather than trying to put the aircraft down and land us safely, Harlequin was using Mitzi to simply try and tip Harlem off the side, angling the chopper at an even steeper incline and bouncing it up and down to try and shake him off. I guessed that a thousand year old vampire didn't have the greatest grasp in the world on aeronautics.

Oh, joy.

As Harlem bit and snapped at the now-ragged seat cover, tearing pieces off in frustration, I found myself suddenly thinking of Mutt. I wondered if he had escaped yet, if he and the other wolves had made it. At least he wasn't up here in this flying death-trap, about to get eaten alive by a rampaging werewolf.

I was clinging onto this comforting thought when a massive explosion rocked the building below us. I snapped a glance down through the torn-off door of the chopper just in time to see a hail of flaming glass rain out of the top floor of the Circus of Sins nightclub, followed by a screeching, screaming flock of...

Wylie shot upright, his jaw dropping as he stared down at the Circus of Sins' roof, clearly visible through the open door below us. His finger stabbed downwards.

'What the hell are those?!' he shrieked.

THOSE WERE TELEVAMPS. There must have been at least a couple of hundred of them, all man-sized, winged, snow-white and naked. They boiled out of the flaming hole in the side of the building and took to the sky in a frantic, confused mass, looking for all the world like giant white bats escaping from hell. The mirrored glass high-rise of the nightclub reflected back eerie echoes of their high-pitched telepathic chittering, seeming to amplify it, making it louder by the second.

What the heck had caused that explosion? Had Ninette made it back to us in time, after all?

I could hear the sound of the Televamps screaming even over the noise of the rotors and Harlem's crazed snarling. Police sirens blared down below in response to the explosion, but I figured they wouldn't stick around for too long when they saw whose building had just gone boom.

I swore as a loud screeching came from outside, followed by a series of what sounded like knives being drawn across the roof of the chopper. Outside the window, Harlem turned around briefly to snap at the Televamps, who now seemed to be attacking him, dive-bombing him as he tried to climb into the helicopter through the ripped-off door.

I saw a dozen of them pile on top of him, digging their scythe-like fore-claws into his thick black fur and beating their wings furiously as they tried to pull him off the craft. All breeds of vampires hated werewolves, and judging by the evil look on these creatures' faces, Harlem was about to find this out first-hand.

But now we were in a different kind of trouble. In the front, the engines whined, thrown off by the excessive weight of the Televamps and the broken pipes and wires that hung out into the ripped-off doorway. More and more of the man-sized Televamps were arriving by the second, settling on the runners and tail of the craft, clinging to every available surface. I saw wings fold and tongues flick through the broken end window as my eyes were drawn inescapably to the 'Max Capacity: 8' sign on the far wall.

We were in deep shit.

I heard the muffled squeaking sound of dozens of bare hands slipping and sliding over metal as more and more of the creatures arrived, attracted by the noise of the aircraft and by the smell of Harlem's blood. In the rear-view mirror I saw Harlequin give a beatific smile.

'Ah, my children,' he said. 'They have arrived.'

I looked out of the window. Even in the darkness I could see the pale outlines of dozens of leathery white bodies pressed up against the glass on all sides. I spun around and looked out of the front. Every window was the same. The Televamps were all landing on the helicopter, settling themselves upon it to rest their wings like it was some kind of giant floating sofa.

I turned away quickly as their childlike faces peered through the glass in curiosity, shielding my eyes from their lethal stares. I saw the side of the Circus of Sins building dance drunkenly past about two hundred feet away, and the whole aircraft shook with the strain of the tight turn as Mitzi banked the chopper around in an arc, preparing to land.

As we got closer to the building, a loud growl from the doorway made me look up in fright. Harlem was back, caked in blackish Televamp blood. Whatever fight he'd just been in, he'd obviously won.

He growled in triumph as he pulled himself up into the helicopter, his murderous gaze fixed firmly on me.

In a whirl of fear I spun to look around the cabin. No escape pods. No parachutes. No secret weapon stashes with invitingly large red buttons marked '*PRESS HERE TO KILL EVIL RAMPAGING WEREWOLF.*'

The only way out was through the door, which was currently blocked by Harlem.

We were still a good hundred feet from the roof of the club.

At that moment the aircraft stalled in mid-air, out of control now due to the rapidly shifting weight of the dozens of Televamps clinging to every inch of the craft. I flew forwards, smashing into the side window as the cabin pitched from side to side like a ship on the high seas. I hit my head on the window frame and fell to the ground, which was now on the wall, my ears ringing and a large bruise flaming on my cheek.

Before I could rally my fading wits to get up a furred hand grabbed my bare ankle, squeezing so tight it made me yell in pain. I turned my head to see Harlem's clawed fist was locked around my leg, his muscular upper body wedged inside the aircraft as he used me as a handle to pull himself up.

The aircraft jerked again and Harlem fell back through the open doorway, dragging me half out with him. I yelled as the cold night air rushed over my legs, and seized the metal handhold on the side of the doorframe with both of my cuffed hands. My palms blazed with pain as the sharp metal frame cut into them.

I kicked out as hard as I could and felt my booted foot connect hard with the werewolf's face. Harlem was hanging one-handed from the metal runners, hauling on my foot with his other hand. The craft lurched and he slipped further backwards, dragging me with him.

A cool, slim hand was suddenly gripping my arm, strong as flesh-covered steel. I looked up into the wide lagoon-blue eyes of Doll as the lights of Los Angeles spun around below me like starry constellations. She grabbed my other arm and pulled me back onto the helicopter one-handed, dragging Harlem up with us. I yelled out, feeling like I was being torn in two by his weight.

I lay on the cabin floor, kicking at Harlem's hand, which was still firmly attached to my ankle. Out of the corner of my eye I saw a flash of white as more Televamps flocked into the open hatchway, seizing on Harlem with cries of glee. Harlem snarled as he was seized from behind by a dozen greedy clawed hands. I saw the largest creature slam its foot-long front claw through the back of his neck and Harlem abruptly released his death grip on my ankle.

I shot backwards, landing with a thump next to Doll. I looked muzzily out of the open doorway and saw Harlem's face fill with anger, then surprise, then finally fear as he was dragged unstoppably backwards by dozens of angry Televamps. I looked away before any of them could catch my eye, but out of my peripheral vision I could see that their faces were distorted with rage, their rows of needle-sharp teeth bared. Harlem's face twisted and started to transform back until it was nearly human, his overlong wolf eyeteeth flashing in the floodlights of the club below us.

He reached out towards me, his one remaining yellow eye shining with fear.

'Help me!' he cried.

I didn't even bother to reply.

I pushed myself up off the floor and watched as Harlem was torn off the helicopter and lifted bodily up into the sky, borne upwards hanging from dozens of clawed Televamp hands. The creatures broke into an excited high-pitched chittering as they carried him upwards, their wings thumping as they sought to gain height.

Harlem disappeared into the night with a forlorn howl. Moments later, his howl cut off. Blood and fur spattered down, falling across the side of the helicopter like crimson rain.

I turned away and leaned against the jolting wall inside the helicopter, feeling a great weight lift from my shoulders.

*Harlem was dead.*

*Another one of Karrel's killers had been taken out.*

The helicopter steadied, leveled out as the Televamps took off to chase the creatures who'd got Harlem, as though eager to share in the meal. I jumped back as a white cloud of Televamps exploded past the window, their wings thumping as they leaped for the cover of the night.

I caught Doll watching them go with a look of longing on her face. I raised my eyebrows at her frantically and pointed to the open doorway, mouthing the word 'Go!'

'I can't.' Doll's voice sounded exhausted. Her long-nailed hand crept up and she touched the iron collar bolted around her neck by way of explanation. 'I can't fly with this thing on. It's iron.'

I froze suddenly. All my attention was rooted on the collar, or rather on the small, almost invisible key-hole on one side of it.

The lock was made of gold.

Hardly daring to hope, I looked down at my hand. I was still clutching the golden key Niki had given me. I had almost forgotten about it. I shoved myself out of the seat and almost fell into the seat beside Doll. My hands were shaking so much that I almost dropped the key as I brought it up, positioning it beside the lock on her collar.

The back of my neck burned all of a sudden. My head turned almost of its own accord to see that Harlequin had turned around to face me. He was staring at me with such intensity it almost hurt. I instantly felt my body go numb. The key was an inch from the key-hole.

Mustering all my remaining energy, I concentrated on the key, visualizing with all my might it going into the lock. A levitation spell was far above my abilities, but it was such a tiny object I had to at least try.

I whispered the words of the spell. Nothing happened. I saw Harlequin turn around in the cockpit, reaching for the switch that opened the glass plate between us.

'Come on!'

The glass dividing panel was halfway open when I felt the familiar tingle of power race down my arm and through my fingertips. A small flicker of light appeared in my palm, and the key instantly slipped from my fingers and shot straight up into the lock. I pictured it turning, and watched in delight as it copied my thoughts, spinning with a whir in the lock.

With a quiet jangle, Doll's iron collar fell off.

I saw Harlequin's mouth fall open, and to my amazement the bigger man flinched back, pressing himself against the side-door to the cockpit as though he was afraid of Doll. She stood up to face him, the thick chains that bound her falling apart as though they were made out of candy. She spread her wings in a threatening gesture, and the tips smashed the remaining three unbroken windows in the back of the chopper.

Although she didn't move, she seemed to somehow grow in size.

She threw a look to me.

'Thanks,' she said. Her voice sounded different, as though she was somehow speaking in harmonics with herself. It sent a shiver up my spine.

For a moment I thought that we were saved.

As I turned wearily back to check on Wylie, the helicopter suddenly juddered. I flinched as I heard the distinct *THUNKT* of the main top rotors connecting with something solid and meaty. Blood spattered the window, and I looked up with a cry as bits of white, shredding wings blew past at high speed.

It looked like one of the Televamps had just discovered what the funny whirly bits on the top of the chopper were for.

It was the last straw for the ailing helicopter. We were almost back at the Circus of Sins building now, but it was too late. The whine of the engines turned to a scream and the smell of burning oil filled the cab as the rotor juddered and slowed, starting to stall. The craft dipped further to the side revealing the rooftop of the club fast approaching on our left. We were still a good fifty feet up.

My stomach lurched as we began to lose height rapidly, spinning out of control like a dying moth in a slow death-dive. I clutched frantically onto the seat-post as the entire craft started to flip onto its side.

With a muffled bang, the rotor cut out. Silence descended on the cabin.

I threw a helpless look at Wylie and Doll, who were staring at me in horror as the cabin tilted ninety degrees and began to drop, fast. Wind whistled past the windows as the roof of the club shot towards us at a terrifying speed. I felt sick.

We were going down…

# CHAPTER FORTY

When I regained consciousness, it was snowing.

I groaned and rolled over, licking blood from my lips. I was lying on the rooftop of the Circus of Sins outside the helicopter. I was alive… or so I hoped.

Rooftop? How could I be back on the roof again?

My head hurt. My neck hurt. In fact, everything hurt. My body felt as though it had been run through a blender before being dragged through the streets behind a herd of wild bulls. My head felt weird, as though every molecule in it had somehow been put through a giant taffy-wringer and then rearranged inside-out.

At first, I thought I had dreamed the events of the last twenty four hours. I wound my eyes laboriously around in the direction of the loud crackling sound coming from behind me, and sighed. The blazing remains of the crashed army helicopter lying fifty feet from me on the club rooftop begged to differ.

Something white and fluffy landed on my face, tickling my cheek. I automatically brushed it off, then yelled out loud as a hideous pain stabbed through my arm, centered on my elbow. *Probably a cracked humerus, or at least badly bruised.* I discovered that my hands were still chained, the skin around the hard plastic cuffs rubbed red and raw. Not fun. I held myself still, quivering in pain, and looked down at the white object that had landed on me with a strange detachment.

It was a feather. A fluffy white feather.

When I had convinced my brain that my eyeballs weren't actually going to pop out of my head, I opened my eyes and scanned the rooftop.

I was lying on a mound of strangely warm feathers, about fifty feet from the edge of the big flat roof. The tall mirrored tower of the Circus of Sins loomed over everything like some dark, angry monolith, sending shivers down my spine.

My eyes settled on my watch. *Phil's Hunter watch.* Its glossy face was cracked, but it was still ticking. I could just make out the shape of the hands in the jumping firelight.

It was quarter to midnight.

My breathing sped up. I'd only been out for a couple of minutes. That meant I still had a fifteen minute window in which Bad Things could happen to me. Wonderful.

I rolled over stiffly to see the still, pale figure of Doll lying next to me. She was unconscious but still alive, her pulse beating slowly through the thin skin of her throat like a trapped butterfly. I was lying on one of her outstretched feathered wings. Her other wing was tightly curled, like a cocoon. The edges of her feathers were smoldering and the silver clips that had bound them up had melted. I realized that Doll must have had wrapped her wings around me just before the crash, shielding me from the brunt of the impact. I owed her my life.

There was no sign of Harlequin or Mitzi.

I scanned the rooftop quickly, looking for Niki's body. There was no-one else up here. Could he have possibly survived that drop? I hoped so.

I looked down at Doll and winced. It was clear from the angle she was lying at that one of her legs was broken. That meant I was going to have to try to carry her out of here with a broken leg. *Oh, joy.* She was taller than me and each wing must weigh at least seventy pounds. My gaze moved upwards again and I saw a tuft of brown hair ticking out from Doll's rolled-up wing. *Wylie.*

Thank Christ for that.

I rolled over and pulled myself up into a stiff sitting position. I prayed feverishly under my breath as I hauled Doll's limp wing aside and checked Wylie over for injuries. Amazingly, my best friend didn't have a scratch on him. *It was a miracle.* The sound of his light breathing was like the sweetest music in the world to me, and I almost passed out with relief.

First things first. I had to get Doll and Wylie off this rooftop. I had no idea where Harlequin had got to, but the fatalistic streak in me told me he probably wasn't far away. I looked down at my bound hands in frustration. How was I going to carry either of them with my hands cuffed together? I needed something sharp to pry them apart, maybe break the chain, like a piece of broken metal or a knife or something...

'Would this do?' asked a male voice.

A bolt of terror went through me. I slowly turned my head to see Harlequin standing over me. Whereas I was bruised and battered from the crash, Harlequin didn't have a scratch on him. His charcoal-grey suit wasn't so much as singed. Typical vampire.

Harlequin held the silver sacrificial knife in his hand. He smiled at me.

Fate's a bitch, isn't she?

I LEAPED TO my feet, ready to run. Before I could make a break for it, Harlequin snapped out his hand and caught me by the chain that bound my two handcuffs together. I flinched as I tried to pull away, trembling from the pain of my swollen wrists.

Harlequin looked down at me with bright eyes, a horrible smile growing on his perfect face. 'Fear not, dear child. I have but one final task for you. Do you believe in magic?'

'Which kind?'

'I thought as much. Observe.'

Harlequin closed his fist on the handcuff chain and squeezed tightly. I heard a sound like marbles clacking together. When he opened his fist again, the solid steel had been reduced to silvery powder.

'First rule of physics,' said Harlequin calmly, as he sprinkled the steel filings on the breeze. 'Matter that exists in the universe can never be completely destroyed. It can only change form.'

He dusted his hands off and sighed, and a look of sorrow spread over his face as he gazed down at Doll. 'As it is with all other, more immaterial things. Love being one of them.'

'What would you know about love?' I snapped, rubbing my freed wrists, the snapped handcuffs circling my wrists like big loose bracelets. Why had he just freed me? I really, really didn't want to know.

I breathed deep, shifting my weight forwards carefully as I moved to stand in between him and Doll. I rallied my failing strength for one last fireball.

'I know enough of love,' the master vampire said quietly. He turned to regard the semi-conscious Doll as she shrank back from him, a look of abject misery stealing over his face. 'Love can never be destroyed. It can only change form. To love something completely, you must be willing to give it up completely.'

'You mean destroy it completely.'

'That is inaccurate,' replied Harlequin, his eyes locked on Doll's. 'Love by its very nature invites loss. Nay, it embraces it, for the only way to truly love something is to realize that someday, it might be lost.'

'Let me guess. You got "Quote-of-the-Day" toilet paper?'

Harlequin chuckled as his eyes flared deep blue. He looked up at me and I felt that familiar numbness of the vampire Thrall creep over me. I concentrated hard in an effort to block it, fighting the swimmingly disorientating sensation that I was sinking downwards, falling forwards into the beauty of his eyes. *Damn him.* The spark of the fireball growing in my palm dimmed and went out with a crackle, as though somehow drained away by Harlequin's Thrall…

I was vaguely aware of a rushing noise overhead, then a dull thud shook the rooftop. The thud was followed by another, then another, followed by a sound like a ship's sail flapping in the wind. Out of the corner of my eye I saw the ghostly white shapes of several Televamps land on the roof, hissing and flaring their wings. They cocked their heads at us with interest but kept their distance. I noticed that they were darting nervous-looking glances at Harlequin. They were actually afraid of him. *Huh*. Above us, the rest of the giant flock started to circle in anticipation, like crows drawn to road kill.

I fought with every inch of my consciousness to move. I watched as my left foot slowly reached out a few inches to nudge the sleeping Wylie, who lay beside me on the ground, cradled on Doll's wing. *Wake up, Wylie. Wake up!*

'And now we are all here,' said Harlequin, spreading his arms like a priest. 'Let us proceed with the sacrifice.'

He held out the knife to me like a gift.

To my utter horror, I watched my own arm rise up towards him, *Evil Dead* slow. My white-knuckled fist slowly opened, fingers stretching out to take the knife from him. I gritted my teeth, fighting to close my fist, to pull my arm back. Harlequin's eyes flashed with fire and I cried out as what felt like a red hot poker seared across the inside of my mind. My fingers closed reflexively around the knife and my arm bent of its own accord, bringing it up level with my face.

The knife was curved, a good six inches long and wickedly sharp. I gulped, trying to open my hand, to drop the weapon. I found to my horror that I couldn't so much as twitch my fingers.

I wondered if Harlequin knew I was a werewolf, that my killing Doll would get the wolves in trouble with the angels, rather than the Humans...

I quickly shut the thought off before Harlequin picked up on it. All vampires were telepathic, after all.

'You're completely insane,' I pronounced, struggling

to unlock my arm muscles, which seemed to have developed a life of their own. I watched in numb horror as I lifted the knife and turned towards the semi-conscious Doll, who was trying to get up with a broken leg and not enjoying the experience very much. The young angel's eyes were open wide, her white wings wrapped tightly around herself, as though to ward off her own fate… the very fate she claimed she had chosen when we'd first spoken back at the auditorium.

'Insanity is relative,' Harlequin said, snaking towards me with a sway of hips. 'Surely insanity is being the very cause of what you yourself have taken such pains to try and stop?'

'Huh?'

'You came here to stop Doll's death. Yet here you are, causing it.' The master vampire bent down and stroked Doll's face softly, then turned to me. 'That's called irony. When you've been alive as long as I have, you come to appreciate the finer things in life. Tell me, how does that feel?'

'Feels great. It'll feel even better when I put this knife through your face.'

Harlequin laughed. My arm shook as I tried to break free from Harlequin's power. It was useless. I was no longer in control of my own body. With great ceremony, Harlequin lifted his hand as though holding an invisible knife. My arm raised too, my movements matching his exactly.

'And now… a few words… a few simple ingredients… and it shall be done.'

Harlequin's lips started moving as he began reciting the words of the incantation. A small magical fire sparked to life and began to burn mid-air between me and Doll. He reached down and picked up a small shard of broken glass from the ground, then slashed open Doll's limp arm, drawing out a dark trickle of blood. 'Angel blood.' He dripped some into the fire with a hissing sound, then sliced a thin crescent of skin from the back of his own arm and dropped it into the fire. 'Demon's skin.' Next, he reached out and ripped a small handful of hair from my head, making me wince. 'Human hair.' Finally, he grabbed several Televamp feathers from the rooftop and dropped them in. 'Vampire's wing.'

As Harlequin closed his eyes and began to repeat the words of the Prophecy, I zeroed in on the hands of my watch.

*Ten minutes to midnight!*

I swallowed, beads of sweat breaking out on my forehead. Prophecy or no prophecy, this beautiful monster wasn't about to force me kill an innocent angel in cold blood. The knife in my hand lifted still higher, its razor-sharp tip just a few seconds from plunging down into Doll's heart.

'You know I'm a werewolf, don't you?' I gasped, as I struggled to drop the knife. 'You know this won't work?'

Harlequin opened one eye.

'You have not yet Changed. Technically you are still human. It will be enough to satisfy the conditions of the Prophecy.'

'I already told you that you were crazy, right?' I asked. I focused as hard as I could and felt the palms of both hands start to glow with a spot of heat. It blossomed in seconds, forming a shimmer around each hand. It wasn't enough for a fireball, but maybe I could use it to somehow damage the knife...

As I geared myself up for one last, desperate magical attempt on Harlequin, to kill or be killed, a bloodcurdling war cry came from behind us. I flicked my eyes sideways to see a dark, wraithlike figure burst through the remains of the locked door that opened out onto the rooftop from Doll's trashed room.

The female figure landed lightly on the low wall that bordered the roof, its steel-heeled stiletto boots striking white sparks on the concrete. For one crazy, desperate moment I thought it was Ninette, come to rescue me.

'I tell him he's crazy all the time,' said a familiar voice. 'He never listens.'

It wasn't Ninette. It was the only woman I knew who was scarier than my Team Leader.

*Cyan X.*

IN THE SPACE of a heartbeat the vampiress flicked out her bio-blades and leaped towards us, her blades scything down towards my head…

Harlequin snarled and grabbed me by the arm when he saw who it was, but he wasn't quick enough. I yelped as Cyan hit both of us with bruising force. I dropped the knife and clutched my head as Harlequin's Thrall released my mind like a fist being pulled out of thick tar.

Cyan seized me by the shoulders, spinning me around and dragging me away from Harlequin, who held on grimly. I'd never been fought over by two vampires before. It wasn't fun. Cyan's bio-blades flashed down and I saw a flash of white bone followed by a gush of red blood from Harlequin's hand as he abruptly released me.

I looked down and saw why he'd let go.

Cyan had cut Harlequin's hand off.

Harlequin cried out in fury and pain as Cyan stepped between us and the wounded master vampire, slicing her razor-sharp bone blades through the air, driving him back and away from us. Harlequin retreated, too blinded by the pain of his sliced-off hand to fight back. She drove him back till he was almost level with the flaming helicopter on the other side of the big rooftop. I watched her in amazement. My mortal enemy Cyan had just risked her life to save us.

But why?

'Stay down,' she shouted back to me, her red lips drawn back from her teeth as she stared at Harlequin, an indefinable look on her face. 'Mama's about to get some payback.'

I watched her in bewilderment as she leapt back down and darted over to the blazing helicopter. She leaped boldly into the flames and dealt several sharp roundhouse kicks to the front of the chopper. The metal paneling gave way with a groan of protest and Cyan grabbed something buried beneath the nose of the helicopter. She ripped it free barehanded with a single jerk of her lithe, muscled arms, sending red-hot bolts and screws pinging in all directions.

She stepped out of the flames, and I saw what she was holding.

I threw myself flat across Wylie's unconscious form as Cyan turned to face the wounded Harlequin, opening fire with the twin fifty-cal cannons she'd just torn from the chopper's fuselage. The Televamps scattered in alarm as she sprayed them with armored bullets, blowing them bodily back across the rooftop.

The creatures screeched as the bullets ripped them to shreds, going through their naked white bodies like hot pennies through butter. Blood and feathers flew and flesh tore under the barrage of lead, staining the rooftop crimson.

I saw Harlequin leap onto the low wall that bordered the rooftop. He shot a murderous look back at me, then spread what looked suspiciously like black, membranous wings before diving off the rooftop. *Ladies and gentlemen, give it up for Mr. Harry Houdini.*

I shook my head in disgust. He'd be back.

But for now, we were once again alone.

A sudden wind kicked up, hot and ripe with the small of blood. There was a loud outburst of cawing and hissing above me. A feeling of slow dread filled me as I realized that we were still trapped by these bloodthirsty creatures, hopelessly outnumbered. More Televamps were arriving by the dozen to quickly replace the handful Cyan had slaughtered with the mini-gun, drawn to the scene by the noise and the smell of blood. The flying vamps screeched in delight and started chowing down on their dying companions, their white bat-like faces stained bright crimson with blood.

I looked away, sickened, my mind moving rapidly. I had to wake Wylie up, get him to help me somehow carry Doll off this rooftop while Cyan was distracting the Televamps. It was our last shot at survival, at saving Humanity. While Doll lived, our fate was not set. We could still save her, still change things…

I jumped as a horrible noise rang out, echoing over the concrete plains of the city. I spun round in panic as a feral scream filled the air, making every muscle in my body go rigid. Beside me, the wounded Doll stirred, clutching her bleeding shoulder, her face pale with fright.

'Run, Kayla,' she whispered, rolling her eyes towards the sky.

I followed her gaze. My jaw dropped.

The sky above us was black with silent flying shapes. At first I thought it was a huge flock of strangely large birds... until I looked closer.

*Those weren't birds.*

I swallowed, feeling my blood run cold. I had seen those shapes before, in every dream I'd had for the last year, both before and after Karrel had died.

My premonition was coming true!

I spun around as an eerie, echoing screech rang out from behind me, gawping up into the sky in fear and fascination. The angels were still too high up to see clearly, but lower down the wheeling spotlights on the top of the club illuminated flash-frame glimpses of things I didn't want to see, things I knew I shouldn't be seeing. The Televamps were all in the air around us, screaming like panicked birds, each one visible only by the dull blue glow of its eyes. They shot back and forth over our heads as the angels descended from on high, first by the dozen, then by the hundred, then more, until the night sky overhead was swarming with dark winged shapes.

Doll raised her hands feebly in the air as though trying to ward them off, but she was too late.

*The angels were here.*

I glanced over at Cyan in near-panic as her machine gun finally fell silent. A huge pile of twitching, dying Televamp bodies formed a feathered mound in front of her almost as high as her head, a flesh-and-blood barricade of Harlequin's ugly mutant babies. She kicked the pile over with savage glee, then flicked her long black hair out of her eyes and grinned up at me, her expression the closest thing to happy I'd ever seen.

She was having the time of her life.

*And she was beautiful.*

I saw her head turn as Harlequin hauled himself up onto the roof fifty feet away from where I'd seen him fall. He clutched his sliced-off hand to his chest, coating his flanks with a sheen of blackish blood. He pulled himself up over the edge and collapsed on the rooftop, looking shaken. His chest and face was riddled with bloody, smoking holes from the bullets. His handsome, high-cheekboned face was smeared with his own blood.

Did this monster never die?

Cyan turned to face him then, splatters of blood running down her face. She lowered the massive machine-gun and tilted her head impishly, her violet eyes alight with violence. Ready to kill the man she had once loved. Harlequin shook himself and stood up with a sensuous arch of his back, stretched his neck, dropped his injured arm at his side. He turned and stared at Cyan as though he had never seen her before.

His lips moved rapidly and Cyan cocked her head, skeptical, listening. The roar of flames and the screech of Televamps drowned out most of what he was saying, but his body-language was unmistakable.

He was stunned by her, bowled over by the fierce beauty who had just tried to kill him.

*He'd seen who Cyan really was, and he was hooked.*

Harlequin stepped back and raised his good hand like a peace offering. He held it out to her, his black hair blowing in the hot wind. I watched in disbelief as

Cyan bared her teeth and shook her head, jerking the empty cannon up defensively as Harlequin took a soft step towards her, then another. The Televamps fell back as he advanced on her, step by step.

I started to get up, buzzing with adrenaline. I had to move while Harlequin was still distracted. I got to my feet as Harlequin called out what sounded like a pet name to Cyan. I watched in disbelief as the big tough vampiress paused, clenched her fists and turned, eyeing him doubtfully.

'Cyan,' I muttered. 'You fool. Don't trust him...'

Love made fools of us all, I knew. Trouble was, Cyan had been obsessed with Harlequin for so long that I doubted even she knew who the real fool was any more.

A wash of light from the burning helicopter flooded Cyan's face as she turned to glance over at me, as though trying to make a decision. I threw up my hands in frustration, drawing one hand urgently across my neck. Cyan's face clouded and she frowned, turning away.

I knew right then that she was dead.

I could only watch helplessly as Harlequin held out his hand again, nodding his head and smiling. Cyan bit her lip, then suddenly tossed her head and smiled with fierce pride as she held out her own hand to him...

'Look out!' I cried.

Cyan threw back her head and screamed as the Televamp who'd been creeping up behind her struck, burying both of its foot-long razor-edged talons in her shoulder. She spun around to lock eyes with the creature, growling, then flicked out her bio-blades and lopped off the vamp's head in one casual stroke. It fell back, twitching, but another instantly took its place, attracted by the smell of her blood.

Harlequin backed away from her hurriedly, then shrugged philosophically and glanced down at his wrist as though he were checking the time. He tipped an invisible hat at me, then turned and walked calmly across the rooftop to the decimated penthouse room. The Televamps fell back to let him pass. He reached the penthouse room, which stuck up from the rooftop like the cabin on a submarine. With one mighty leap he jumped on top of the fifteen-foot-high roof out of harm's way, and settled down to watch the action unfold.

*Coward.*

Cyan staggered to her feet as a second Televamp rushed her, spreading its wings in a threatening gesture. Cyan reared back to strike again… then her eyes went wide and she cried out in sudden panic, clutching her head. Her body crumpled beneath her and she pitched forwards onto the ground, bang in the middle of a rapidly-closing circle of hissing Televamps.

'Cyan!' I yelled. I already knew what had happened. She had forgotten the one rule in dealing with Televamps.

'The crow says don't look,' I whispered.

The vampiress didn't get up again. I watched in despair as she rolled over onto her belly, clawing at her back as white, membranous wings started to form beneath her skin, stretching her stolen black dress out into grotesque, moving shapes.

She had looked into the creature's eyes. *Dammit.*

And now she was turning into a Televamp.

# CHAPTER FORTY-ONE

'KAYLA! HELP ME!' cried Cyan.

I started sprinting over towards the stricken vampiress before my brain had entirely caught up with what my body was doing. I already knew it was too late.

I skidded to a halt a dozen feet away and stared down at her, torn. I could see that her polished fingernails were already starting to lengthen, morphing into talons the size and shape of butcher's knives. Her eyes rolled up to me as she flopped onto her back and curled her pink new wings protectively around herself like a newborn butterfly, as white spines shoved themselves out of her sides and back in reptile-like lines.

Her striking purple eyes locked on mine, imploring, begging me for help.

I started towards her, then paused.

A flash-frame vision slammed into my mind. *Cyan giving her wolf-pack the order to kill Karrel, out-numbered five to one in a dark, filthy club basement. Closing the door on them and walking away as the sounds of screaming and tearing flesh filled the Los Angeles night air...*

I hadn't been there to witness it, but in my nightmares I'd seen it a thousand times. This was the vampire who had given the order to the wolf pack to kill the man I loved. I stared down at Cyan, lying helpless on the ground, then turned to look speculatively at the Televamps, who were closing in all around us. I'd wanted Cyan dead for so long it felt like forever. All I had to do was turn and walk away, just as Cyan had done with Karrel, and these creatures would make it happen, avenge the man I loved...

But two wrongs didn't make a right.

Karrel had taught me that much.

I spun to look back at Doll, checking she was safe. She was lying on the rooftop a few dozen yards behind me, Wylie curled up unconscious beside her. It was almost midnight but she seemed to be in no immediate danger. Harlequin was just visible as a crouching figure on the other size of the big flat rooftop. Even the Televamps were ignoring Doll, intent on attacking Cyan.

I summoned the very last of my strength to conjure up an orange plasma ball, blasting the Televamps away from the fallen vampiress. The squawking creatures instantly started to close in again as I jogged to her side and dropped to my knees beside her, panting, wondering what the hell I was doing.

She had already been "bitten." There was nothing I could do.

But even as my enemy, even as one of the people I hated most in the whole world, I couldn't leave her to die like this.

Above us, the angels screamed, circling closer. I glanced down at my watch.

*Two minutes to midnight!*

'Harlequin…' Cyan gasped, clutching at my arm. She was regressing, her small vampire fangs growing out into primitive-looking saber-teeth. I doubted she had long left. 'He did this to me. *Again*.'

'Don't worry,' I promised her. 'I'll get him for you.'

As I turned back wearily to check on Doll, a flicker of movement caught my eye.

'Look out!' I shouted.

Doll rolled aside in panic as a silver knife flashed down, aimed squarely at her back. The sacrificial knife buried itself in the rooftop with a metallic clang. I saw to my horror that Wylie was awake and clutching the dagger I'd dropped. His irises were a strange cloudy orange, his movements unnaturally stiff.

I glared across the rooftop at Harlequin. The master vampire was over a hundred yards away, but when he glanced briefly in our direction, I saw that his eyes were blazing with a bright orange glow like two tiny points of fire in the darkness. The light was flashing in time with the glow in Wylie's eyes.

Harlequin was controlling Wylie!

And if Wylie killed Doll… the human race would be attacked.

Wylie spun around and instantly struck again with an odd, robot-like movement, catching Doll a glancing blow on the shoulder. The flesh-wound sealed itself almost as soon as he pulled the knife out, but it was clear from Doll's face that the iron had hurt her.

I lunged forwards and grabbed my best friend by the shoulders, tried to wrestle him to the ground. Wylie was skinny as hell and weighed less than I did, but it was like trying to topple an iron statue. He pulled away from me almost instantly, bared his teeth and rammed his elbow back into my solar plexus so hard I almost threw up.

I collapsed on the rooftop next to Doll, winded. I clenched my teeth against the pain and forced myself to keep moving, keep fighting. I sat up and threw myself at Wylie's Doc Martens, wrapped the crook of my elbow around his knees and hauled him over backwards. He collapsed across me and hit his head hard on the rooftop as he went down. His knife went flying, clattering out of his reach.

'It's okay!' I panted, wrangling Wylie into a head-lock. 'I got him!'

Even as the words left my mouth I heard an ominous sound. Something on the other side of the rooftop was hissing, with a sound like escaping gas.

'You gotta be kidding me.'

I jerked up my head as an explosion of sparks sprayed out from the front of the crashed helicopter, followed by an intense rush of flame. The fuel tank had caught fire. The explosion and a shower of flaming engine parts blew outwards in an instant. I saw Harlequin yell in fear as the explosion shot towards him, engulfing the suite and blowing the remains of all three glass walls outwards.

The suite collapsed inwards, burying him.

*Twenty seconds till midnight...*

As the flames flew towards me I saw Doll rise to her knees a few feet behind me and snap her wings open wide between me and the approaching wash of fire.

'Get down!' she shouted.

Her hand flashed out almost casually and grabbed Wylie by the belt, dragging him down and pulling him in close to her body.

*Ten seconds...*

I dropped flat on the rooftop and curled up next to Wylie as the fire rushed towards us. My eyes flew open in time to see to see Doll's white feathered wings turn a bright translucent orange above me as the outer edges of the jet-fuel powered fireball blew past us. Her outer feathers instantly caught fire and began to burn. I curled up tighter next to Wylie, yelling in fear as a blast of intense heat washed over my back and side. We were fifty feet from the blast and Doll's wings absorbed most of the heat, but it still felt like I was being toasted inside a jet engine.

*Five seconds...*

As the fire-cloud boiling overhead started to die down I saw Wylie's head turn sideways and his eyes flash bright orange, as though a button had been pressed on a remote somewhere. As Doll bent over us, shielding us with her body, I saw that he was still clutching the knife.

'Doll! Get away from us!' I shouted.

The young angel ignored me, arcing her wings over our heads to shield us from the shower of flaming engine parts that followed in the wake of the blast. In that split second, Wylie twisted sideways on the ground, his eyes locking in on Doll as though she was a target. He raised the knife, ready to plunge it up through her chest into her heart.

'Look out!' I yelled.

Doll started to turn, to look down at Wylie.

*One second...*

I grabbed Wylie's knife hand, wresting with him. He tore free from my grip. As his knife flashed up towards Doll's chest I shoved Doll backwards as hard as I could with my other hand, but I wasn't fast enough. The knife missed her heart and instead buried itself in the side of her neck, embedding itself in her spine.

Doll screamed.

# CHAPTER FORTY-TWO

I STARED, FROZEN, as Doll collapsed on the ground between us, clutching her neck, her burning wings curling tightly around herself like a wounded animal. Wylie cried out in triumph as she fell, then went silent as the orange light in his eyes abruptly snapped off. He blinked at me, confused, then looked down at the bloodied knife in his hand.

He dropped it, then his eyes rolled up and he pitched face-first onto the ground in an insensible heap.

The world swam around me and I sagged forwards, catching myself on one arm as everything went grey and speckled. I closed my eyes.

*Shock. I must be going into shock.*

A wet noise came from above me. I opened my eyes and stared up at Doll, not wanting to look. She rolled over on the rooftop, gasping. The roof around her was stained with a growing pool of blood, which trickled relentlessly from the knife wound in her neck. She fought to get up, her great white wings opening and closing convulsively as she slipped and slid in her own blood. She looked for all the world like a white dove that had just been shot.

Sound came back into my world and I heard a shriek of fear and pain from the other side of the rooftop. The fire from the exploded helicopter had engulfed a pair of the Televamps who had landed on the roof. The flames were still spreading. There was no sign of Harlequin, just a pile of shapeless twisted metal where the crashed helicopter had been, and a mound of glass surrounding the one remaining standing wall of Doll's suite. Burning metal parts littered the rooftop, a thick pall of smoke drifting upwards into the LA night sky.

Cyan had gone.

Above the carnage over a hundred fully grown Televamps circled, dipping and diving on the thermal currents like an aerial joyride, chattering with joy at their newfound freedom. I pressed my hand over my mouth, fighting the urge to throw up.

*The Televamps were free.*

*And Doll had been stabbed at midnight.*

*The Prophecy had come true. She was dying...*

I spun back to Doll, shook her gently. Blood trickled out of her mouth as her eyes cracked open. 'Please. Help us. Tell me how to stop the Televamps, the flying vampires. They're part angel. I need to know how to kill them...'

Doll slowly raised a wing like a spreading hand, watched listlessly as the edges of her feathers darkened and began to shrivel, like dry leaves burning in the fire. Her eyes were wide, frightened.

'Ah, shit...'

I crouched down beside her, putting a gentle hand on her forehead. She wasn't just burning from the explosion, wasn't dying from the blood-loss of the knife-wound. Wylie had mortally wounded her, poisoned her with the iron knife.

When I'd been in school there'd been a kid who everyone picked on because he was allergic to peanuts. Just one tiny bite, just one nibble of one half of a peanut and his body would go crazy, swell shut all his airways, and start to kill him. Angels were immortal in heaven, but once they came down to earth they became as allergic to iron as that kid was to nuts. Just a small amount of it in their bloodstream was enough to kill them stone dead. I'd learned this in my angel research back at the Hunter place. I never thought that someday I'd be crouched beside a real angel who was really dying because of this dumb heavenly screw-up.

'Doll, please...' I whispered, taking her hand. 'Tell me how to help you.'

As I touched her clammy skin her eyes fluttered open, sending a few flakes of ash scattering on the breeze. Her irises were snow-white, with flecks of silver running through them like cracks in pottery. As she opened her eyes her eyelashes caught fire, burning with tiny flickering blue flames. She was burning up from the inside out, as the tiny flakes of iron from her knife-wounds slowly but surely poisoned her.

'You can't help me. It's too late. I'm dying, Kayla.'

As I stared at her in horror, a flash of movement from above caught my eye.

The angels were arriving.

The Prophecy was coming true.

I rose to my feet in fascination as the Santa Ana wind picked up, blowing through my hair in a hot blast. I stood there on the rooftop, no longer afraid. The worst thing that could ever happen to me had already happened, and now I was just curious to watch the end, to find out how I died. I sat down heavily on the low wall that bordered the roof and looked up at the newcomers in wonder as they dipped and dove through the sky around me, cutting intricate patterns through the night. I shook my head in slow disbelief, feeling a grief-stricken smile light up my face.

It was the end of the world.

And it was the most beautiful thing I'd ever seen in my life...

THEY CAME SILENTLY, appearing out of the sky like the lights of the Aurora Borealis, leaving faint tracings of white light in the sky behind them. Some were naked, while others wore an odd mix of pearly white and golden armor, which shone and twinkled in the light of the distant Hollywood spotlights.

I watched as one angel arced directly overhead like a burning meteor, flying so close that I could see more detail. The angel looped around and did a second pass over me, as though checking me out, and I got my first proper look at the invader.

It was a male. He was beautiful— of course he was— but it was an alien kind of beauty. The angel was well over seven feet tall, with multiple sets of fiery red and white wings which seemed to be made out of actual fire and trailing wisps of cloud rather than the feathers I had expected.

I wondered what kind of angel he was. A Militant Angel, perhaps? The name came back to me from my long briefings at the old Hunter base. The name certainly fit him. His body was strong, regal-looking, like the ultimate blueprint for a human, while his face was oddly rounded and childlike, with a blunt snubbed nose and wide-set, colorless eyes.

I wished to hell that I'd brought my camera.

The angel's exquisite face held no recognizable human emotion as he spun in mid-air like a swimmer doing laps and soared back up into the sky, his wings folding back along his body as he headed at top speed towards the chittering cloud of Televamps.

The cloud exploded outwards away from him as he passed through, fleeing from him like a shoal of panicked fish. The angel homed in on one of the slower creatures, separating it from the pack with expert precision. The frightened Televamp performed a series of impressive mid-air maneuvers as it shot down past me, diving down the edge of the building. I peered down over the edge of the wall to see that the Televamp had got itself trapped between the angel and the side of the nightclub. The mirrored walls seemed to confuse it, throwing off its bat-like sonar.

It darted this way and that, yipping in fright with a rapid high-pitched buzzing sound, then spun around to fight as the angel dropped right past me with a rush of air and slammed into it with a sound like a cannonball fired into concrete.

I leaned over the wall to watch as the pair rolled over and over in the air, fighting silently not fifty yards below me in mid-air. The angel didn't make a sound as it grabbed the Televamp by the throat and started tearing apart the creature's membranous, white-feathered wings with its bare hands, as thoughtlessly cruel as a child pulling the wings off a fly.

The Televamp retaliated by raking its claws down the angel's side, but instead of blood flowing out, white light poured from the creature's skin. A split second later, the cuts healed themselves and closed up, leaving not a single mark on the angel.

I could see at once that the Televamp was hopelessly outmatched.

The Televamp shot up past me as though fired from a cannon, the angel in hot pursuit. Ten seconds later it was over. The Televamp dropped out of the sky, its wings torn to shreds. It chittered piteously as it hit the side of Doll's raised penthouse suite before thudding onto the rooftop not twenty feet from me like a giant heavenly road-kill. A beam from the floodlight washed across it and I saw it was fighting to breathe, its lightweight bird-like chest crushed by the impact. It looked down at its ruined body with a remarkably human expression of distress, using its shredded wings and long scythe-like claws as leverage to push itself to its feet.

It collapsed, then threw back its head and screamed.

All around us in the air, the other angels were tackling the other Televamps in a similar fashion. I realized that the 'snow' falling around us was actually the remains of the Televamps' wings which the angels had been remorselessly shredding, hundreds of feet up in the air. Great clouds of feathers filled the air around us on all sides as they dropped gently downwards in a tumbling mass, backlit by the orange glowing urban skyline of LA.

It was incredibly beautiful at the same time as being incredibly horrible.

'They're killing them,' I whispered in wonder, as I

watched another Televamp tumble shrieking out of the sky, its wings torn to bloody shreds. 'They're evil.'

At my feet, Doll stirred. I bent down to helplessly crouch by her, afraid to even touch her as flames flicked up from the cracks in her skin. She slowly started to sit up, a movement which made her abused body crack even further apart.

'Not evil,' she whispered. 'Just doing their job. The abomination must be destroyed.'

'But…' I could hardly get the words out. 'A human killed you—shouldn't the angels be attacking the humans?'

'I'm not dead yet, Kayla,' coughed Doll, a faint note of reproach in her voice. 'They're just killing time till I die. Angels get bored real easy. It's… why I came down here. Great career move, huh?' She gave a little laugh, choked her way into silence. 'Once I am dead, they will come in force. The Seekers will tell them who killed me. Then, and only then, will they strike.'

Her eyes were closing, the light in her body dimming. 'Use your head, little wolf. Save the humans. There's still time.'

'What do you mean there's still time?' I was shaking her now, almost shouting, desperate for more information. I could tell she was about to pass out. Steam hissed up as I touched her and I pulled my singed hands back fast. 'Doll, just tell me how I can save you!'

'You can't save me,' Doll whispered. 'If you leave now I will die from this wound. So don't leave me. You can still save mankind, if you act fast.'

'But—'

'Save the humans, Kayla. Don't let my death be for nothing.'

The light in her eyes flickered and blinked out. She slumped forwards on to the concrete, unconscious. I cursed, loudly and colorfully. I had the feeling she'd been trying to tell me something. Trying to hint at something she wasn't allowed to say.

But what? How could I save the humans?

Above us in the skies, there was a sudden stillness as the winged Televamps stopped fighting back. They seemed to hesitate, then as one they took off in a whirl of wings, darting away from the attacking angels in fear rather than attacking them. The angels pursued them across the rooftops, grabbing and snatching spitefully at their wings as they flew.

I leaped up quickly as several Televamps landed on the rooftop nearby with a series of loud thumps, blocking my escape route back to the penthouse room. The low wall that ringed the rooftop was at my back, followed by a two-hundred-foot drop. *We were cut off.* Their tooth-filled mouths hung open in fright as they lifted their spiny wings and danced back and forth like giant ungainly seagulls, staring up at the predatory angels, their foot-long fore-claws trailing on the gravel.

I took a step back towards where Wylie lay unconscious next to Doll, summoning up a quick fireball to protect them. The gravel crunched beneath my feet and one of them instantly turned its head with a snap and zeroed in on me. I looked away quickly, making sure to avoid its deadly Gorgon-like eyes.

I watched it in my peripheral vision as it lifted its giant, spindly wings, holding them up above its naked white body like a lady hiking up her skirts. It darted towards me with a strange sideways crabbing motion, hissing at me through its bat-like snout...

'Come on!' I shouted, raising my hands.

I stepped around protectively in front of Wylie and the exhausted body of Doll. My fury at the thought that it would even try to hurt my best friend filled me with a limitless feeling of power, blasting away my exhaustion. I drew on that as I formed a spinning ball of orange energy on my upturned right hand.

The Televamp hurtled towards me, mouth gaping, and I pitched the plasma ball at its chest with all my strength. There was a small explosion and it crashed to the ground with a shriek, a smoking hole in its chest leaking black blood. Before the smoke had even cleared the other two Televamps were upon it, ripping it to pieces with gleeful cries before both turning to me in spooky unison, the gleeful sound of their childlike chirps saying it all.

*All the more for us...*

The second Televamp was almost upon me before I had the second fire-spell ready. This time I only had time to throw up a small wall of flame between myself and the attacking creature before it attacked. The few remaining feathers on its wings caught fire instantly and it ran straight past me with an ungodly shriek, diving off the building in a cloud of smoke.

As I turned to face the third Televamp, I heard a terrible sound— several dozen loud thuds on the roof behind me. A horrible feeling of foreboding filled me as I half turned to see that the roof between us and our escape route was packed with squawking, squalling Televamps, flaring their wings at me and chittering in their terrible high-pitched voices.

I was too drained for a third fireball. I needed a moment to recover, to get my strength back up. I backed off, then remembered too late about the third creature behind me. I spun around with a shout, panicking, just as its jaws snapped about half an inch away from my left ear. It folded its horned wings and dropped down onto all fours to sniff at the prone figure of Wylie, wings poking up into the air, its eyes lighting up with interest... then lurched to the side as I kicked it hard in the head.

'Get away from him!' I shouted.

To my amazement it seemed to do what I told it. It backed away, opening its wings in alarm, and emitted a loud, drawn out hiss of fright.

I was just beginning to congratulate myself on being super-scary when I had that feeling again... the one deep in my gut which told me that somehow, some way, the world was about to once again crap on my head and run off giggling.

I turned, but slowly.

A low creaking rumble came from behind me as the pile of wreckage from the chopper shifted and fell aside in a shower of blazing sparks. I was barely aware of more Televamps landing on the roof between me and the chopper, as I stared into the shifting wreckage with a skin-crawling feeling of foreboding.

A tall, powerful figure stood up with a violent lurch, all snapping teeth and bristling spikes. It flexed its sinuous muscles as it spun around and focused its alien-eyed gaze on me, the flickering flames from the explosion reflected on its shiny black carapace. I saw the shredded remains of a charcoal-grey designer suit hanging in tatters around its muscular waist, and gulped.

Harlequin had survived!

And not only had he lived through the helicopter

explosion, he also seemed to have turned into some kind of alien mutant demon-thing.

Wonderful.

# CHAPTER FORTY-THREE

You know what they say about your whole life flashing before your eyes right before you're about to die?

Well, they lied.

I didn't see my own life as I faced Harlequin down on the rooftop, alone and surrounded by dozens of hissing, hungry telepathic vampires. Instead, I saw other people's lives. The many different lives I wish I'd led that would've meant that right now, I'd be cuddled up in bed with my sweetheart after a long day at the office rather than facing the scourge of the vampire race, alone and exhausted on a rooftop, with about as much hope of survival as the last chocolate donut at an all-day LAPD conference.

Something soft and warm touched my foot. I looked down to see that I'd backed all the way over to where Wylie and Doll were lying. Wylie was still passed out. Doll's body was lying on its back, smoking lightly, still glowing with a weird internal orange light.

At first I thought she was dead. But as my foot touched her she opened her eyes weakly and looked up at me before her lids slid closed again.

A fierce hope flared inside me. Doll wasn't dead yet!

Maybe, just maybe I stood a chance of saving the day.

I just had to figure out how.

Adrenaline flowed through me as I readied myself to go out fighting, to protect my best friend. This was it. I shook my hands to limber up as Harlequin drew himself up to his full, impressive height, pieces of flaming helicopter tumbling away from his armor-plated body like so much kindling.

Harlequin was a black vampire, Niki had told me, a demon crossed with a vamp. He hadn't been kidding. An uneasy thought struck me as I backed away from the giant demon towering above me. If Harlequin was Niki's father, that meant Niki was part human, part vampire *and* part demon.

No wonder he was confused.

I stared up at Harlequin in fascination, torn between the urge to run and the weird need to stay and stare. I'd never seen anything that looked remotely like him outside of a late-night Japanese horror movie.

In demon form Harlequin was well over twelve feet tall, winged, scaled and jaw-droppingly spectacular to look at. He was like a living sculpture, a piece of biological artwork. His skin was jet-black from head to toe, so black that his giant form seemed to swallow the light. Muscles rippled across his lean flanks as he turned to face me with a snake-like hiss, black scales flashing across his body like armor plating. His corded arms flexed, his heavy-looking curved claws clacking greedily together. His face and heavy brows flashed and glittered as he moved, and I saw that his skin was inlaid with hundreds of tiny multicolored scales and progressively larger bone-studs, like living gemstones.

Even as a demon, Harlequin was stunning.

He was also about to kill me.

His murderous black eyes locked in on the body of Doll at my feet and he drew up in surprise, his fists clenching convulsively to his chest like a child spotting a dead kitten. There was a beat, and then he relaxed from his attack posture and spun around, yellow alien eyes flicking back and forth, seeming to take in what was happening for the first time. He looked down at the bloodied knife lying beside Wylie, then his great spined head lifted and he regarded the circling, fighting angels above us with what looked very much like approval. I didn't have to know demon body language to know what he was thinking.

The Avenging Angels were here. Even thought they were killing some of his babies, he'd won.

'They have come,' he announced with great satisfaction, his deep basso voice making me jump. I hadn't realized he'd be able to speak in demon form. He turned his great horned head to look at me, and smiled as he saw the Televamps that surrounded us on the rooftop. 'You have failed.'

'I like to think of it more as underachieving on a grand scale,' I muttered. I needed a weapon, fast. My eyes flicked down to the knife, but even as the thought went through my head Harlequin's spiked tail lashed out and he sent the knife flying off the edge of the building. *So much for that.* 'And just so you know, those Seeker guys are way more scary than you could ever be.'

Harlequin laughed at that, his deep, horrible voice

booming out over the concrete canyons of downtown. 'My dear child,' he said, his eyes twinkling. 'Those aren't Seekers.'

'So the world isn't ending?' My heart lifted.

'No. Those are Militant Angels. They come down first and find you.'

'Oh.' I stared into the sky, wondering why I was still alive. 'So what are Seekers?'

'Seekers are Avenging Angels. They come and get you.'

Harlequin pointed a clawed finger over my shoulder. '*Those* are Seekers.'

I unwillingly turned, feeling a terrible sense of déjà vu.

Twin points of lights were just visible in the depths of the smog-cloud above us, growing closer by the minute. A distant, high-pitched screaming filled the air, echoing weirdly off the concrete landscape. At first I thought that two big airplanes were approaching en route to the nearby LAX airport, somehow flying side by side. But then I looked again and the lights resolved themselves into twin fiery comets, hurtling on a collision course down towards LA.

It was a scene straight out of my dream.

And my nightmares.

The Seekers had come.

I TENSED UP, backing off as the hissing Televamps that surrounded us edged closer, poised to attack, but they seemed too scared of Harlequin to get any closer. I realized that I was safe as long as I stayed near the mutant demon rampaging killer.

*Great.*

In fact, I realized, there was a strange kind of balance to the moment. Everything was in perfect equilibrium.

The Televamps were too scared to come near us with Harlequin here.

The Militant Angels wouldn't attack us till Doll died.

The Seekers wouldn't strike down the humans until the Militants reported Doll was dead, poisoned by Wylie's knife-wounds.

And Harlequin wouldn't dare kill me until it became clear one way or another that I had either foiled his plan, or helped it succeed. Only Doll herself knew which race had killed her, and judging by the flames flicking out through her mouth she no longer had anything left to talk with.

It was a fragile balance, and just the tiniest action could tip things one way or another, towards life or death, towards salvation or annihilation for the entire human race. I had to act, and fast.

But what could I, a single human, do?

And suddenly, the answer popped into my head, clear as a bell. I had one shot to fix all this, to save everyone, but I had to move fast. I edged carefully around the prone figure of Wylie and sank quickly to my knees beside Doll.

Harlequin was distracted, staring up at the approaching Seekers and basking in the glow of his impending success.

My fingers were trembling as I brushed through the heaped piles of charred feathers beside Doll, searching frantically through the rubble of helicopter wreckage and Televamp body parts. Within seconds I had found what I was looking for: a piece of broken iron piping from the crashed helicopter. It was an inch wide, thick and deadly with a razor-sharp edge. It wasn't a sacrificial knife but it would do. It was iron. My hand was trembling so much I could barely hold it. Light glinted dramatically off the edge as I raised it. This was my moment, the reason Fate had brought me to this point.

It was perfect.

Ninette had been wrong, I realized. One person could change the world.

I just had to do it quickly, before I lost my nerve.

I put a hand on Doll's shoulder, shook her gently.

'Hey, crazy lady,' I whispered. 'Wake up. You still want to save mankind?'

The angel's eyes fluttered and focused on me, then slid across to the makeshift blade. She stared at it for a long moment, then looked up quickly at me, her eyes wide with sudden comprehension. I lifted her limp hand, curling her fingers around the blade, then turned my head away to gesture up at the screaming, hissing skies.

Doll followed my gaze, then her eyes slid closed in understanding. She nodded once. I squeezed her free hand then turned away quickly, rising to my feet to hurl a piece of wreckage at a Televamp that had gotten too close to us. I offered up a quick prayer to the heavens, watching out of the corner of my eye as Doll slowly lifted the blade into the air and positioned it over her own heart, clutching it in both hands, her thin chest heaving.

I turned quickly away, unable to watch. Doll was dying anyway, but I couldn't just stand there and gawk while she took her own life, choosing to die by her own hand in order to save the humans she loved so much.

My reasoning ran like this. Wylie the human had

mortally wounded her, and the crash of a helicopter chartered by a vampire and piloted by a werewolf had nearly killed her.

But still she lived, although she was dying.

So which race had killed her?

The answer was none of them, as she wasn't dead yet.

At this exact moment, Doll was neither alive nor dead, but halfway in between. If Doll killed herself, the angels would just have to attack themselves, if they were so keen on punishing the race that had killed an angel. I wondered if there was a pre-biblical clause to exclude that, but as far as I could figure it out, Doll's suicide was the only sure-fire way to end this.

I was mentally patting myself on the back for spotting this cosmic loophole when a blinding pain cracked across the backs of my legs. I stumbled, pitching face-down into the feathery ash that blanketed the rooftop. Harlequin had knocked me down with his whip-like, muscular tail. I watched helplessly as his clawed hand flashed out and gripped Doll's wrist. His grip tightened and Doll dropped the makeshift blade with a cry.

I was busted.

I pushed myself up on one elbow and instantly collapsed again, all my strength gone. I tried again, wracking my brain to come up with a plan to get myself and my friends out of danger before the balance tipped. Judging by the shallow way Doll was breathing, I had only a short time left to act.

I swore as Harlequin seized my wrist and dragged me upright, holding me away from Doll. I was powerless, helpless to act, to do anything that would save the day. He lowered his head until it was almost on a level with mine, then smiled and tilted his face to the heavens, as though waiting for me to make my move. Somehow, that scared me more than anything else.

As I lay there, waiting for the end, I heard an inhuman hiss come from behind us. I looked over Harlequin's shoulder and my jaw dropped.

A female Televamp stood behind us. Her snow-white skin was blackened and burned, and she was dressed in the singed remains of what had once been a figure-hugging velvet dress. Before I looked quickly away, I saw that the Televamp had violet eyes.

Cyan was alive!

Before I could react to this, Cyan's clawed hand flashed out. She grabbed the iron bar that Doll had dropped, flipped it in the air like a cheerleader and drove it down through the left hand side of the angel's chest, into her heart.

Doll's body jerked, then sagged, a sigh of what sounded very much like relief escaping from her lips.

Time itself seemed to freeze.

Cyan X slowly turned back to me, her beautiful face distorted by the telemorphic being she had become, but still recognizable. She had horns now, and spines. They kind of suited her. She kept her eyes averted from mine as she stared down at Doll in grim satisfaction.

Cyan had just stabbed Doll through the heart.

Let me rephrase that.

Cyan the *Televamp* had just stabbed Doll through the heart.

But how had she known what to do?

Cyan's mouth twisted into a grin as she tapped the side of her head, and I remembered once again that all vampires were telepathic.

'Great plan,' she said, smiling grimly. 'Thanks for that.'

I STARED AT Cyan, stunned. She grinned back fiercely, still keeping her deadly gaze averted. We both turned to watch as Doll's body started to combust beneath us. She was unconscious now, and I was glad of it. Hairline cracks filled with white fire spread out from her heart where Cyan had stabbed her. Wylie had merely wounded her before. This was a killing blow.

I turned away, sickened, as Doll's body started to break up, white-hot fire belching out of the fissures in her skin. I knew that this was for the best, that this was sparing the lives of millions of humans, but still, I couldn't watch this. The heat coming from Doll's dying body was incredible. I got to my feet and backed off as the fire grew impossibly bright like burning magnesium, whiting out the rooftop, illuminating in horrifying detail the inhuman faces of the angels circling above us.

Their cries echoed Harlequin's scream of rage as he realized what Cyan had done. He bared his teeth and started stalking towards Cyan, his one remaining hand held high to strike her down. But before he could reach her, a new and terrible noise rang out.

*Jesus Christ. What now?*

As one we all spun to look upwards.

The spinning circle of angels above us had got wider, a vertical column of flashing wings like a typhoon twister made of feathers. Above the racket of screeching Televamps and roaring wind I could hear dozens of car alarms going off down below, police sirens sounding, people's voices shouting and screaming in fear at the sight of the approaching angels.

And in the exact center of the enlarging twister, through the calm eye of the storm, the twin black shapes of the two Seekers were hurtling down towards us. They were directly overhead now, getting bigger every second.

They were still too far away to make out many details, but from what I could see of them, I doubted somewhat that they'd look much like the angels you saw on greeting cards. These things were the size of semi-rigs, with beautiful trailing wings the size of ship sails. They looked unstoppable.

But were they?

There was a flash of black scales as Harlequin sprinted away across the rooftop, heading away from Doll's body at high speed. There was no way down from the rooftop and the penthouse suite's door was now partially blocked by flaming rubble, but it was obvious that he didn't want to be anywhere near Doll's body when the Seekers landed.

What did he know that I didn't?

*Time to go.*

I grabbed Wylie by the shoulders and shook him fiercely, shouting his name. He didn't even stir. He was out cold, probably still heavily concussed from the helicopter crash.

Above us, the Seekers screamed closer.

A screech from behind me made me jump and turn. A group of three Televamps were coming at me fast from the side. They had different colored crests. One had what looked like a Beatles haircut made of razor-sharp spines.

*Great.* I was about to get eaten by the vampire version of Larry, Curly and Moe.

I locked my arms under Wylie and heaved with all my strength, arms shaking, trying to do a fireman's lift like I'd seen in the movies. In my panic I over-reached myself. My foot slid on a piece of debris. I fell forwards, landing on top of Wylie on the rooftop, cursing and swearing.

My head snapped up. The three Televamps were nearly upon us...

I raised a hand, tried to summon a fireball to scare them off. I was so exhausted that all that came out was a shower of dull orange sparks.

I gave up and struggled again and again to lift Wylie, as the Televamps screamed in triumph and darted towards us...

'Need a hand, little lady?' called out a deep male voice.

I looked up to see a stocky, grizzled figure striding across the rooftop. 'Magnus,' I cried. A maintenance hatch gaped open in the roof behind the figure, some twenty yards away. The pale, worried face of Motor peered out, gripping the guard rail tightly as he stared up in horror at the approaching Seekers.

'Over here!' I yelled, then yelped and flung a piece of helicopter debris at one of the Televamps who was nearly upon us. The creature squawked and skidded sideways, puffing open a weird-looking frill that reminded me of a cobra's ruff. 'Help me!'

'Nah. I just thought I'd stand and watch.' Magnus grinned and flexed his great fists as though preparing for battle. The three Televamps that had been stalking me drew up short, sniffing the air and screaming at him in outrage. *Vamps hated wolves.*

Magnus paused a short distance away, facing slightly to my left. 'What am I looking at here?' he asked pleasantly.

'A roof-full of nasty bitey things,' I shouted. 'Don't look into their... Oh.'

I looked at Magnus's blind eyes.

Suddenly, I saw possibilities.

Magnus jogged forwards to join me, lifting his nose to the breeze as though homing in on my scent, just as he had back in the circus ring. One of the Televamps hissed sharply as he approached, raising a foot-long claw in warning. Before it had finished hissing Magnus had drawn out a service revolver and shot it twice in the neck. The wounded creature screamed as its two buddies instantly turned on it, drawn to the smell of blood. There was a blur of white skin and slicing claws, and the wounded creature stopped screaming and started dying.

I looked away fast. Curley was now eating Moe. *Gross.*

'Got it,' grinned Magnus, twirling his gun like the Lone Ranger. 'Who's your daddy?'

'There are more!'

'How many more?'

'Hundreds!'

'Jesus, Kayla. You could've warned me.'

'I think he tried to.'

I pointed over his shoulder as Motor stuck his head out of the hatchway, waving his hands and shouting urgently to us.

Magnus gave me a bleak look with his empty eye-sockets, raising his gun. 'Don't listen to a word that old fool says. He always spoils my fun. Here. Aim me. I got six clips in my pocket.'

'No time!'

'Why?'

I looked up. The Seekers were now so close I could feel the downdraft from their fiery descent. 'Don't ask,' I said rapidly. 'Magnus, I got a friend down. He's hurt. Can you get him out of here? Please?'

'No sweat, princess.' Magnus reached out one of his huge hands. I took it and placed it on top of Wylie's unconscious figure. Magnus groped around, then scooped Wylie up with a grunt, lifting him as easily as I'd lift a child. He turned to go, balancing Wylie in the crook of one arm so he could bring his gun to bear. 'You comin', squirt?'

I turned to look at Harlequin, who was cowering over the far side of the roof, surrounded by a protective crowd of his vampire 'children.'

I suddenly felt very cold. *I had to stay up here,* I realized. *I had to see how this ended. And if it didn't end with Harlequin dead, I'd have to figure out how to kill him.*

'I don't think so.' It was hard to get the words out, but I managed it.

Magnus shrugged. 'Your call. Just tell me one thing.' The big werewolf's whole body tensed up. 'Did you get Harlem?'

I nodded. 'The bitey things got him.'

Magnus's face brightened.

'The body...?'

'In bits. You might find an arm if you're lucky.'

Magnus nodded faintly, then took a deep breath and stood up straight, finally seeming to relax. He smiled widely, and for a moment, I saw a spark of the great werewolf leader he'd once been.

'Serves him right,' he said with a grin. 'He was in charge of that breeding program. Thanks, Kayla.'

Motor was shouting to us, whistling and yelling. Brad had poked his head up through the hatch and was waving to me frantically, a look of horror on his face as he stared up at the sky. The Seekers were nearly upon us.

Magnus gave me a curt nod, then turned around, a little stiffly. He started striding back to the open hatchway without a word, using his friend's voice as a guide. I'd half hoped he'd leave me the gun. He didn't. I didn't much blame him. *Much*.

I watched him go, watched Motor shout directions at him as he neared the man-sized hatch. Watched him blow the heads off two other Televamps who got too close. I didn't relax until Wylie was in Motor's arms, handed down safely into the darkness. I breathed a sigh of relief as I saw his dark head of floppy hair vanish down the hatch.

*Wylie was safe.*

I waited for Magnus to climb down after Wylie, lock the hatchway behind him. But instead he paused, one foot on the rung to safety. He seemed frozen in place. The winter wind ruffled through his thick brown hair as it gusted over the rooftop, bringing with it the smell of gunfire and spilled blood. He raised his face to it, breathed it in. He smiled and cocked his head as though hearing the sounds of ancient battles.

And then....

'Oh, no, Magnus. What are you doing?' I murmured. Magnus had climbed out of the hatchway again and was marching off determinedly in the opposite direction. The two dozen or so Televamps left on the rooftop turned to watch him as he passed, gun clutched in one white knuckled fist.

One of them hissed and flared its wings, then another, then another. Within seconds, Magnus had a trail of the white, deformed creatures following him as though he was a werewolf Pied Piper.

More Televamps landed on the roof nearby, drawn by their siblings' vengeful screams. There were so many of them on the rooftop now that that it was getting harder and harder to avoid their malignant stares. Everywhere I looked on the rooftop, ugly freaky winged vampires were jostling each other, dancing back and forth in excitement, scurrying after Magnus. None of them had tried to attack him yet. They were just staring, seemingly puzzled why he hadn't yet become one of them through their telepathic 'bite.'

I thought once again how perfect a weapon these winged nasties were. They could 'convert' anyone who came near them who didn't know their secret.

*They could get anyone apart from a blind man...*

I could only watch in gratitude as Magnus led them away from me, away from the hatch, his back straight as a ruler, gun hanging at his side. When his foot touched the wall on the other side of the roof, he spun around and opened fire.

The Televamps exploded away from him in a white tide.

I threw myself flat on the rooftop. When I looked up, I saw Motor staring at me from the relative safety of the hatchway. The old man shook his head as though in disbelief mingled with a little bit of what I hoped was respect, then vanished back into the service duct, pulling the hatch firmly closed overhead.

As the harsh *boom-boom-boom* of Magnus's service pistol briefly paused, as he reloaded, I heard the distinct sound of bolts sliding back into place with a horrible finality.

'Kayla!' Magnus shouted across the rooftop, his calm façade starting to slip. 'Get out of here!'

There was a sudden burst of squawking and hissing from the other side of the rooftop. I jumped up as I saw a huge crowd of Televamps had gathered around Magnus. Bullets flew with an almost mechanical precision. A dozen Televamps were dead, their bodies being ripped to pieces by the rest. Magnus's gun fell silent again. He had to re-load. Suddenly, as though orchestrated, the flock closed sharply in, obscuring Magnus from view.

When they pulled back, Magnus was gone.

I shouted out to him in panic, but my voice was swallowed as the ring of angels circling above us abruptly opened out. A storm-force wind rushed over the rooftop. The Televamps hissed and screeched like a deck-full of seagulls, craning their scrawny necks to stare up at the approaching Avenging Angels, opening their wings with relish in the streaming wind.

I crouched in the shelter of the low wall and craned my neck backwards, staring up at the sky. The Seekers were maybe twenty seconds away. I could see them more clearly now, and instantly wished that I hadn't. If I'd thought the Militants were scary-looking, the Avenging Angels were a thousand times worse. They'd looked human-shaped from a distance, but close up I could see that I'd been wrong.

*Very wrong.*

The Seekers looked as though they'd been designed by a blind man who had heard the human body described to him, but never seen it in person. The proportions were all wrong. They were twenty feet tall, their bodies long and gangly. Their limbs were multi-jointed and tapered like jellyfish tendrils, and their heads were sleek, smooth domes with no facial features visible. Their bodies were so white they were almost translucent. I could see the fire of their comet-like entry glowing through their limbs. They hurtled down towards us on wings maybe fifty times the size of their truck-sized bodies, each 'feather' in fact being a jet of flame ten feet long. Their incredible wings billowed out behind them like wildfire, hundreds of feet long in flames all colors of the rainbow.

They were heading right for us.

My mouth went dry. I couldn't move. I had never seen anything quite so terrifying or spectacular in my life. A strong smell of burning ozone and oily sulfur filled the air. I was vaguely aware that I was running, stumbling towards the shattered remains of Doll's penthouse suite as their fiery light fell over the Circus of Sins rooftop. I tripped over the dead body of a Televamp and fell hard, clambered to my feet and carried on running, limping as I picked up speed. The Seekers were perhaps five hundred feet straight up, speeding downwards at an impossible rate. The light from their entry lit up the rooftop as bright as day.

*They were four hundred feet away.*

*Then three hundred.*

I snapped a glance back. Cyan was right underneath the Seekers, standing in the exact center of the rooftop, as though daring them to attack. They seemed to be aiming directly for her, as though she was standing on a giant black 'X'.

I saw her bat-like face fill with fear as she stepped back and flicked out her bio-blades as though to defend herself from the fate she'd chosen. She turned her head and stared fixedly at Harlequin, as he cowered on the rooftop with the monsters he'd created.

I felt a sudden, overwhelming urge to save her, even as I reminded myself that this was the woman who'd killed the man I loved.

What should I do?

*Two hundred.*

*One hundred...*

Fuck it.

I started to run towards Cyan, shouting her name. I had barely started running when a giant hand of heat grabbed me and hurled me bodily through the air, bowling me over and over. The breath left my body as the ground beneath me exploded and hit me in the face, whirling me around and around in a maelstrom of shattered concrete and flying debris.

*Impact.*

# CHAPTER FORTY-FOUR

Consciousness returned, slowly.

I lay on the rooftop beneath a large pile of cinderblock rubble, coughing as dust and smoke filled my mouth, my nose, my eyes. The concrete beneath me buckled and rippled with aftershocks and the whole building shook as though a tank had just slammed into it. I could hear nothing but the little plinking and popping sounds of cooling concrete, and the sound of my own racing heart.

I couldn't feel my hands beneath me. Vague shapes flickered through the white dust cloud before vanishing like evil spirits. Giant piles of rubble were heaped all around me. My whole body seemed to have gone numb from the impact. Time seemed to lose all meaning as I lay there in the gritty haze of the massive dust cloud thrown up by the Seekers' landing, gazing up at the sky.

I wondered for the second time this evening if I was in fact dead. I thought they weren't supposed to have pain in the afterlife. If I was dead, I had definitely been lied to.

After what felt like forever, I slowly raised my head from my arms and looked around.

There was almost nothing left of the Circus of Sins' rooftop. A charred, blackened crater almost thirty feet wide in the roof was all that was left of Cyan. Clouds of toxic-smelling smoke spewed from the awesomely huge hole, and the twisted red-hot girders sticking out of the edge were still smoking. It looked like the set of a disaster movie. Half of the crashed helicopter was missing, the impact of the heavenly creatures having sheared it clean off as though it had been cut by a knife.

Of the Seekers themselves, there was no sign.

I pushed a good dozen pounds of crushed rubble off myself, fighting the urge to count all the interesting new bruises I had, and got unsteadily to my feet. Nothing seemed to be broken, although my limbs felt like rubber, and everything that didn't hurt was covered in dried blood and white ash. *Tasty.*

As though in a dream I tottered over towards the edge of the crater. My ears were ringing. I couldn't even feel my feet on the ground. I stared down into the great hole, swaying slightly. I peered down inside then gasped and stepped back quickly, grabbing hold of the twisted shape of a vent shaft for support.

The Seekers had melted a thirty-foot-wide hole down through the exact center of the Circus of Sins, a hole which ran from top to bottom like the core of a carrot. Inside the hole was a blackened, melted mess of bricks and mortar and blackened metal. Here and there I could see whole floors laid bare, truncated pieces of furniture and sparking electrical pipes sticking out into the yawning void. It was surreal.

I wondered how whoever was Up There could justify

such destruction to take out just one person. Then my mind filled with images of hurricanes and earthquakes, and I decided to let it go.

I didn't want to think about the implications of that right now.

I stared down into the yawning void for what felt like an eternity, my mind reeling with vertigo, an uncomfortably tight feeling growing in my chest. Now that the physical shock of the explosion had passed, emotions were coming back fast like the rush of water from a breached dam, fast enough to drown me.

Doll was gone. And Cyan was dead. I couldn't believe it. I knew that what she had done was the right thing, but I couldn't help feeling a pang of regret over her death.

Not sympathy, because I'd heard from the Hunters exactly how many people she'd killed in her long and eventful life.

But regret covered a lot of things that I didn't even have names for right now.

I jumped as a series of small, muted explosions detonated in the sky above me. I looked up, shielding my face against the light. All around me, the Avenging Angels were hurling themselves at the frantically fleeing Televamps, wrapping their arms around them and combusting in small clouds of super-heated flames. *Killing the entire race of the one that had killed the angel.*

There were only a couple of hundred Televamps in existence. As it had turned out, their job wouldn't take that long.

I stood there blinking as the aerial battle raged around me, my nerves jangling as charred feathers and ashy white burned-up Televamp bodies fell downwards, mixing with the rain that fell steadily over the rooftop.

*Rain?* I blinked, wiping the water off my face. A light scattering of rain had sprung up out of nowhere, putting out the numerous fires which blazed around me on the rooftop. It so rarely rained in LA that I was almost as surprised by this as I was by what had just happened.

It was like a miracle.

Almost.

A few minutes later, the last Televamp was dead. I watched in surprise as the remaining angels exploded in small bursts of white light, like fireworks going off in the night. When the light died away, all that remained of the angels was a host of what looked like large white birds. The creatures gathered together into a flock, wheeling overhead with an eerie rush of wings. As I watched they streamed upwards in a rushing torrent and vanished into the grey storm clouds overhead. There were so many of them that their wings carved the cloud-mass in two, sending it drifting apart, slowly breaking up as it went to reveal the bright stars overhead.

Their job was done.

A light breeze sprang up out of nowhere and blew away the scattered fragments of cloud, and within a few moments the night sky overhead was almost completely clear.

I realized I'd been holding my breath, and let it out in a sigh. The Seekers had come. I'd fought Harlequin. And I was still alive.

That meant we'd won.

Didn't it?

Something felt wrong. I turned quickly around to scan the rooftop, searching for danger, but there was nobody there. I stood alone on the darkened rooftop. It took me a moment to figure out why I was feeling so strange.

I wasn't tense any more. The red-hot iron band of urgency which had been constricting my chest for the last God-knows how many days since I'd found out about the Seekers was gone. It was all over.

I took a hesitant breath, then another, delighting in the easy way my chest moved.

No panic, no fear.

The human race was safe.

The world suddenly turned black and pitched sideways, and a shocking pain jolted through my elbow as I caught myself on one arm. What was going on? I stared down at the ash-strewn rooftop just inches from my nose. Why was I lying on the ground?

I gave a sudden giggle, surprising myself. I had a job to do, missing friends to go find, a scarily big cleanup and containment operation to do all by myself, but my body suddenly didn't seem to want to co-operate. A hissing tide of shock descended on me as the events of the last few hours hit me all at once, leaving me gasping as the concrete dam I didn't even know I had built in my chest to deal with all this abruptly burst.

I may have blacked out for a while, for the next thing I knew a black-clad figure was bending over me in concern, shaking me. I looked up through a grey fog to see that it was Niki. Wasn't he supposed to be dead? He'd just jumped out of a helicopter, after all. Niki's lips were moving, his voice seeming to come from a long way away and I couldn't make out what he was saying. It seemed funny to have him here. No matter what I did, I just couldn't get rid of the guy.

I must be going into shock.

More figures appeared behind him out of the cloud of ash, running out of the blown-apart penthouse suite. I saw the familiar faces of my friends as they ran over to where I was lying, staring down at me in concern. Mutt was there, with a pale-faced Mia in tow. Brad and Grids stood behind them looking nervous, their father Motor bringing up the rear. They formed a group around me, but they weren't looking at me. They were facing in the opposite direction, grouped around me in a protective semi-circle, staring at something just outside my line of vision.

Niki reached down and touched my cheek, his own soot-streaked face drawn in concern. I had no idea what to say to him. My gaze flitted almost guiltily around the destroyed rooftop. The place looked like a war zone. How would I even begin to explain all this stuff?

'Kayla?' I could hear Niki's voice now. He sounded shaken.

'I can explain,' I mumbled automatically.

'Save it,' said Niki, hauling me into a sitting position. 'I busted your friends out, but we're not safe. We gotta go. Right now.'

'Why?' I asked. At the same time I felt that weird feeling again in the pit of my stomach. The back of my neck prickled and the dragon charm around my neck briefly flared blue, heating up ready for action. I knew by now what that meant.

Something bad was up on the roof.

*Watching us.*

Right on cue, a low, rumbling growl sounded, scarily

close. I swore, then rolled my eyes slowly to the side.

Oh, Christ.

The wounded Harlequin was lying not more than ten feet from us, his tail whipping from side to side like an angry cat. His left arm was smashed to a pulp. A pile of busted girders from the explosion were lying across him, pinning his legs down. His broken teeth gleamed in the firelight as he opened his mouth unnaturally wide and hissed at us. As Niki pulled me frantically to my feet he rolled onto his side and convulsively lurched upright, the girders dropping to the side with a loud series of clangs.

I groaned and let Niki pull me backwards as the black demon towered over us.

Harlequin's body coiled, ready to attack.

There was a loud crash as a broken AC duct in the roof behind him blasted open so hard that it came right off its hinges, throwing a huge pile of debris and ash up into the air. An unfamiliar werewolf burst out, clawing and twisting to squeeze his huge wolf body through the small man-sized hole. He popped out like a cork from a bottle and landed on the roof in a clatter of claws, revolving to face me.

I backed off quickly, assessing this new threat. At first it looked a little Mutt, but this wolf was far too big. I didn't recognize him from Motor's pack, or from anywhere else for that matter. The wolf was almost as big as Harlem had been, strong and well-muscled with long shaggy chestnut-colored fur falling in thick curly waves along his flanks. His face was blunt with a wicked-looking black mask and ears, and there was blood on his muzzle.

He looked very angry.

I could only stand there, numb with exhaustion, as the new werewolf's amber eyes locked in on me and he uttered a short, urgent bark that sounded like a command. Niki grabbed my hand and pulled me backwards while Mutt and the other wolves moved protectively in front of me, shielding me from the enraged master vampire and the new scary-looking werewolf.

I backed off, shaking my head. It was over. I was done. I could barely stand, let alone fight. If I tried to conjure up a fireball I knew for a fact that I'd pass out.

Niki reached out to take my hand, squeezing it tightly to reassure me.

'It's okay,' he said. 'I got this.'

We both knew that he hadn't. Niki was strong, but he was no match for his father, the master vampire. And he couldn't fight the new werewolf at the same time. Even if he took one of them down, the other one would certainly attack and kill me while he was fighting. Niki bared his teeth and hissed as the new werewolf snarled and shook his lion-like ruff, snorting and scraping his claws on the roof as though preparing to attack.

We all tensed, waiting for the end...

# CHAPTER FORTY-FIVE

TO MY SURPRISE, the new werewolf turned his back on Niki with a snort and spun to face the crouching, bleeding figure of Harlequin. The werewolf let loose a long, loud howl that echoed eerily over the surrounding rooftops.

Then he snarled and sprang at Harlequin.

'Uh, I think that's our cue to leave.'

Niki grabbed my hand and pulled me after him. I threw a glance back over my shoulder just in time to see the new wolf lock his teeth in Harlequin's neck then drop to the ground and roll, using his superior weight to pull the master vampire down in a classic takedown move. I was impressed. I'd never seen an ordinary werewolf tackle a master vampire before. Whoever the wolf was he was either very brave, or extremely stupid.

We'd almost reached the open maintenance hatch when a low roaring sound came from overhead. I tensed, looking wildly upwards. What new hell was this? Attacking swamp dragons from Hades, perhaps?

No. It was another helicopter.

In fact, it was two helicopters. They were both gleaming white and looked distinctly official. I made out some kind of insignia painted on the side of the first one. It seemed to have more spotlights and warning lights on it than a usual police chopper. I wondered who had stolen these ones, and whether they had come to rescue us or shoot us.

As the two choppers raced overhead, a muted thunderclap sounded from above me. I looked up to see the silhouette of a man dressed in black standing on the roof of the penthouse suite. The thunderclap sounded again and I saw a silver harpoon flash past me and thump into Harlequin's side.

The new werewolf hurriedly jumped back out of range and the big vampire hissed, spinning around to fix the shooter with a glare that promised all sorts of pain and death. The figure fired again, and Harlequin jerked to the side as a second harpoon impaled him in the back, right between the shoulder blades.

I saw that the harpoons were connected to long silver steel cables, the other ends of which were still somehow connected to the gun.

The werewolf released Harlequin with a bark and leaped back out of range as the stranger directed the larger of the two choppers to land on the last semi-stable section of the roof. The rooftop trembled alarmingly as its weight settled and a five-foot section of roof collapsed into the smoking crater, cracks radiating dangerously outwards towards where we stood, but the roof held.

For now.

The wolves grouped themselves protectively around me to watch as the great black vampire bucked and kicked, trying to free himself from the huge harpoons. I saw the black-clad man run back to the helicopter and secure the other ends of the cables to a set of steel hooks and reels set into the side of the chopper. The man hit a switch. The winch snapped taut and started to turn, reeling the master vampire in.

Harlequin howled and hissed, but he was powerless to stop his steady slide across the rooftop as the steel cables winched him in. There was no vestige of his previous personality left in his face now, just a lizardlike rage that was frightening to behold. Retractable spines shot out of his body and dug into the rooftop in a vain attempt to protect himself, barely slowing him down as they scraped uselessly over the concrete.

I felt Niki take hold of my hand and squeeze it as the second, smaller helicopter came in to land, carefully skirting around the first, slowly circling the devastation on the rooftop as though its pilot was unable to believe what they were seeing.

A few moments later it began to descend, hovering over a part of the wide rooftop behind the first chopper which was relatively uncluttered. The rotor slowed and lapped to a halt. The door slid open on steel runners.

'Kayla?' shouted a disbelieving voice.

My eyes flew open. I stared.

*'Ninette?'*

Ninette pushed back her black baseball cap and gave me a look of plain surprise. Her long hair was pulled back into a tight, businesslike ponytail beneath her cap, and she was dressed all in black and dark green, the SWAT version of the Hunter uniform. Behind her, a dozen other similarly dressed strangers peered out of the chopper. Their pistols were all trained firmly on me.

I made a big show of looking at my watch. It read half past twelve.

'You're late,' I said, unable to resist a dig.

'We had Bird Strike,' snapped Ninette. 'Bunch of giant flappy things with big teeth hit one of our choppers, almost knocked it down.' She jumped out of the helicopter and looked around her in disbelief. She arched an eyebrow, examining me with disapproval. 'I see you've been keeping busy.'

'Yeah. She kicked Harlequin's ass, and you missed it,' grinned Niki.

There was an instant ripple of clicking sounds as the people in the chopper swung their pistols around to point at Niki.

'Ma'am. Shall we take the vampire into custody?' barked one of the troopers.

Ninette glanced at Niki, then at me. She sighed, shaking her head.

Her incredulous gaze traveled over the demolished rooftop, the crashed chopper and the heaped snowdrifts of vampire ash to me. She looked down at the nearest pile. There was part of a severed Televamp arm sticking out of it. The hand had foot-long talons. They were still twitching.

'Newbie. Did you do all this?' she demanded.

I ran through three or four excuses in my head before deciding on the truth. 'I guess,' I said. I flicked a cautious glance up at her, looked away fast. She looked pissed. 'Sorry,' I added, unable to help myself.

Ninette's eyes narrowed, and I swallowed audibly. In the last twenty-four hours I'd killed one renegade werewolves, helped destroy a parasitic race hell-bent on taking over the world and foiled an evil mastermind's plot to destroy mankind.

But my Hunter Team Leader still scared the crap out of me.

'I'll clean it up,' I started, hanging my head, then leaped back hurriedly as a big furry shape bounded towards me. 'Wolf! Wolf!' I shouted, stabbing a frantic finger over Ninette's shoulder. Everyone turned around as the huge longhaired werewolf who'd attacked Harlequin loped calmly over to us, claws clicking on the ash-strewn cement, tail held high in greeting.

I stared at Ninette, waiting for her to pull out her trusty Rugar and blow the wolf's head off. To my surprise, she simply glanced over her shoulder, then heaved a put-upon sigh.

'What part of "don't tread in the ash" did you not understand?' she sighed, turning around to face the wolf. 'Now you're going to get it all in the chopper, and the rental company'll charge us a cleaning fee. That's coming out of your wages when we get home, mister.'

To my utter shock, the huge werewolf sat down facing her, regarding her steadily with intense golden brown eyes that suddenly seemed just a little too innocent. Ninette put her hands on her hips and glared at the huge creature. The wolf's body language was relaxed and calm, but after a moment I saw its Adam's apple bob as it surreptitiously swallowed. Ninette raised her eyebrows pointedly, eyeballing the creature, and after a few seconds the giant wolf dropped its gaze and looked away, as though unable to face her stare.

'*Men*, I swear,' said Ninette in exasperation, removing her cap to wipe her forehead. 'Can't live with 'em, can't shoot 'em and bury 'em in the backyard 'cause the neighbors'll complain.'

I turned back to the new werewolf and looked him over. I'd never seen this wolf before, but something about him was very familiar. Those calm brown eyes. That expression of long-suffering good humor... where did I recognize him from?

'And I'm hoping to God you remembered to check the cinches on those harpoons,' Ninette went on, folding her arms as she glared at the wolf. 'If he escapes and eats us all, I'm blaming you.'

The wolf rolled its eyes and gave a very passable imitation of a human shrug... just as a huge, echoing crash came from the other side of the rooftop. I heard the sounds of snarling as frantic shouts and gunfire came from behind the other helicopter.

The big wolf froze, then turned to bare its teeth ingratiatingly at Ninette, who sighed.

'Pop quiz,' she said, fixing the big wolf with an accusing look. 'I am about to be very, very upset with someone. Can you guess who that "someone" might be, *Phil?*'

# CHAPTER FORTY-SIX

IT TOOK ANOTHER eight silver-plated harpoons and a dozen sheets of steel netting to bring Harlequin down. I stood behind the relatively safety of the Hunters' helicopter with the surviving five werewolves as the two dozen or so new Hunters fussed around his bound body. They'd just come from the Hunter HQ in Washington, they told me, where apparently the organization was grudgingly getting ready to pay the LA city Mayor a mind-blisteringly large sum of money to cover up this mess.

The Hunters were back in business, although I was told it would be a while before they could afford to rebuild the LA base.

I couldn't wait for them to start.

I watched as they buckled the chains tighter around the furious figure of Harlequin. He snarled and howled at them, his hypnotic eyes covered with a handkerchief and several dozen layers of duct tape.

Nobody seemed to believe we'd finally caught Harlequin.

I was even more relieved when, several minutes later, they dragged Mitzi out of the remains of the smoking building. He was quickly bound to be shipped off with Harlequin to wherever they were taking him, but not before he'd stared at me for several long seconds with his creepy black contacts before slowly baring his teeth. I knew that look by now, even from a supposedly blind guy. That look said quite plainly that he'd be back, and that I should probably be watching my back for a long time after that.

But I wasn't looking at him anymore. Nor was I looking at the maddened master vampire, wrapped tightly in the metal net. They didn't matter to me. I only had eyes for the big brown longhaired wolf who trotted sedately around the whole operation like a trained police dog, helping Ninette tag and bag the howling vampire and occasionally snapping at Harlequin's heels when he broke a chain here and there. No-one paid him that much attention.

*Phil was a werewolf.*

I couldn't believe it. It went against everything I knew, everything I thought that the Hunters stood for. My own team leader was dating one of the very creatures she'd devoted her life to helping put behind bars.

I needed an explanation, and fast.

I finally dared to ask Ninette about it, as we waited for backup to arrive and contain Harlequin. She just shrugged in reply as she handed me back my Hunter ID wristbands. I took them and closed my hand tightly around them as though they were made of gold-dust, which in a way, they were.

*I was back in business.*

'He is who he is,' she said, watching Phil bound over

to greet one of the newly arrived Hunter cleanup crew members from the second helicopter. The recruit darted away with a girly scream when he saw the werewolf, and the whole team laughed like this was some kind of an in-joke.

'We met on a job,' she went on without preamble, motioning me to walk with her. Niki was watching us closely, and Ninette seemed very anxious to get away from him. 'It was one of my first, as a Hunter. I was sent out to track him, got ambushed on the way by a bunch of vampires. There were ten of them, big ugly motherfuckers. Phil saved my life.'

'Why would a werewolf save your life?'

'Because I needed saving,' Ninette said, with a shrug. 'I never told him I was a Hunter, least not to begin with. And he never mentioned he was a wolf, till I asked him flat-out the next day. For just one night, I let him be the brave young man who had saved my life.'

I turned to Niki, staring at him across the rooftop. I could have sworn that he winked at me before turning around, heading back to help the Hunters tie up Harlequin.

As he passed Mutt I saw him flash his teeth in a threat. Mutt growled in reply, and I smiled. I could see that we had some interesting days ahead of us.

'What happened then?' I asked.

Ninette smiled, her eyes lighting up with her memories. Ninette very rarely talked about her mysterious past. I felt like I'd passed some kind of test.

'Took him back to base for questioning. We wound up talking for hours. After that he just kind of… stuck around.'

'And the other Hunters allowed this?'

'Absolutely not. They threw him out, threw me out for "consorting with the enemy." Then the new recruits started dying, and they realized what a piece of fuckin' gold they had in their one and only Dark Arts instructor.'

Ninette flicked her fingers out as though she was lighting a cigarette, and four tiny candle-like flames popped out of each fingernail. She blew them out, shook her fingers with a wicked grin.

'I said I'd come back only if Phil could join the team. They screamed and cried about it for a couple months, then gave in.' Ninette smiled at her memories. 'Werewolves aren't all evil, Phil taught me. Wolves can learn to control their appetites, after the first few changes. Learn not to be such animals, although not all of them are strong enough to make that choice. Phil chose to become a Hunter because he was sick of a few bad wolves ruining the werewolves' rep. He wants people to understand wolves, to not be afraid of them. He taught us a lot. Still took them three years before they'd agree to put him on payroll.'

'Even though he's not a man?'

'Oh, he's a man, alright.' Ninette smiled as she watched Phil leap gracefully over a pile of rubble, and climb up into the helicopter with the other Hunter commandos. Everyone gave him a very wide berth. 'A man is a man, no matter what species he is. I still love my guy, even though he sheds all over the furniture.'

'But I thought you hated werewolves.'

Ninette looked shocked. 'Whatever made you think that?'

'Well, you're a werewolf *Hunter* for starters.' I paused, not wanting to say it, to bring back the memories. 'And... you killed Billy.'

A shadow passed over Ninette's face.

'You thought I killed him because I hated werewolves?' Ninette shook her head rapidly, as though to dislodge the memory. 'No. Not all werewolves are bad, just as not all human suspects are guilty. Billy knows that as well as I do. No. I killed him because he asked me to.'

'He *what?*'

Ninette put an arm around my shoulders and walked me a little away from the big cleanup operation. She paused at the edge of the rooftop, put a foot up on the low wall that bordered the roof. We both stood and looked out at the glittering lights of downtown LA as she went on. Down below, a long line of military-style black trucks were parking in the street outside the Circus of Sins, while cop cars swarmed around them, shouting through megaphones, trying to get them to move on.

It looked like the rest of the Hunter troops were here to begin the cleanup operation.

Ninette gazed out at the city lights, a strange look on her face. It was a long time before she spoke.

'Tell me something,' she said. 'Have you ever had something happen to you that was so bad that you'd rather die than go through it again?'

I thought briefly of my entertaining half hour in the restroom with Harlem. Of the sound the engines on Mitzi's helicopter had made when they had stalled in mid-air, two hundred feet up. Of the way Harlequin's cold, clawed hands had felt as they closed on my throat. I shrugged in what I hoped was a nonchalant way.

'A few,' I said.

'Let me tell you something, newbie. You lost your boyfriend to werewolves. That sucked, right?'

'You could say that,' I replied, closing my eyes briefly. Ninette had never really gotten the hang of tact. I chose to let it go, as I always had.

'Let me tell you something, Kayla. Billy lost his whole family to the wolves. He told me that a newborn werewolf broke into his house late one night. Tore his kids apart and ate them right in front of him. That's why he joined the Hunters. If you think you have nightmares, if you think you hated the wolves after you found out they killed Karrel, just imagine how Billy felt after going through that shit.'

'I'm sorry,' I said, and meant it.

'Don't be. Billy had a two year old daughter. Beautiful little thing, all rosy cheeks and big blue eyes. He showed me a photo of her once. He kept it in his wallet. He told me that she died last in the attack. Be sorry for her.'

Ninette turned away from me, gazed out at the bright lights of the city. The full moon came out from behind a cloud, dramatically lighting up her face in shades of white and silver.

'You have no idea how much that boy hated wolves, Kayla. He told me over and over that should he ever get bitten, that the moment he started to turn, I should "take care of it." He knows wolves can become good, if they choose to, but he knows it takes time. And in that time, innocent people can die. People's little baby girls can die. That's why we sometimes have to kill newborn wolves, if they ever get on the loose around people. Some Hunters even choose to sign a living will, ordering their immediate execution if they ever get bitten and changed into the thing they hate the most.'

Ninette looked away, a shadow stealing over her

face. 'I made Billy swear that he'd do the same for me, if I ever got bitten by a vampire.'

She paused, looking uncomfortable.

'Should I ask?' I said, then frowned, staring off into space. My fingernails were itching. I scratched at them distractedly.

'Don't ask,' said Ninette. 'Just promise me what I promised him. If a vampire ever bites me, makes me into one of them, you'd know what to do…'

She broke off as she suddenly noticed my preoccupied expression.

'Are you alright? You've gone very pale.'

I looked at her, pressed my hand to my mouth. 'I'm not feeling so good,' I managed, with a hiccup. I really wasn't. My stomach was churning, and a hot sweat had broken out on my forehead. I hoped I wasn't about to throw up in front of Ninette. She'd never let me live it down. My team leader examined me closely. Her eyebrows shot up and she reached out towards me.

'When did this happen?' she asked, gingerly touching my neck.

'What?'

'This effing great vamp bite on your shoulder. I never noticed it before. It's huge.' She peeled aside the sticky top of my dress, tilted me into the moonlight so she could see my neck. It was bathed with semi-dried blood. 'Jesus!'

'Oh, that.' I hiccupped again, and pressed my finger to my lips as bile flooded my throat. *Gross.* 'That happened about an hour ago. Harlequin bit me, but it was just a nip. I'll be fine. You have to swap a ton of blood with a vampire to become one, right?'

Ninette nodded, but her face was strangely pale.

'You said you got bitten an hour ago?'

'Uh-huh.'

'Kayla, this is scarred over. This bite looks like it's years old.' Ninette paused ominously. 'We only met you a month ago.'

I twisted my head awkwardly to look down at my own shoulder. A white row of raised torn flesh formed a neat jaw-shaped circle on my shoulder. Without thinking I tilted my wrist to look down at my werewolf bite. *Snap.* The scarring on the two looked the same age. Damn, but I was healing fast these days...

I heard the sound of a safety catch being removed. I sighed deeply, then looked up into the muzzle of Ninette's gun. My Team Leader's aim didn't waiver as she aimed the Colt squarely at my heart.

I knew without asking that there were silver bullets in that gun.

'Phil!' she yelled, not once taking her eyes off me. 'Get over here! We got a problem!'

'Wait! It's cool. I can explain,' I started, then gasped, doubling over. My stomach felt like it was filling up with liquid fire. My eyes widened as I noticed my nails. They were turning to sharp points, and where I gripped my bare knees I saw tiny beads of blood stand out in shocking red.

*My anti-werewolf formula was wearing off!*

And there was no more left...

My body jerked, once, twice. Blood started to trickle from my mouth. My vision went fuzzy and I dropped my Hunter wristbands as my hands turned to claws. I watched them flutter to the ground, spinning downwards to land on top of a pile of charred, bloodied angel feathers.

Ninette's gun didn't waver as I doubled over in pain, clutching at my belly with hands that suddenly felt like they were about to tear themselves apart. A blazing fire had ignited in my heart and was speeding through my system, hotter and harder than I had ever felt it before.

My legs must have given way then for the next thing I knew I was lying on my back, staring up at a ring of concerned faces as shouts rang out all around me. My eyes flew open in fright as I felt my chest contract and squeeze the air out of my lungs, but before I could get truly scared about it, the vertebrae in my spine separated out and twisted inside me, making my ribs pop back into place with a resounding clicking noise, freeing my lungs.

For a moment, I thought it had stopped. I could breathe again.

And then there was only pain, and lots of it.

I cried out as my body folded in on itself, the wolf virus squeezing my human DNA like a child with a lump of Play-Dough. Ninette swore and backed away from my rapidly mutating body as I rolled over on the ground in front of her, twisting and yowling as my body finally gave up its fight to remain human. The werewolf virus that had been chewing at the bars inside me had finally broken free.

I was turning into a werewolf.

A babble of shouting voices broke out over by the chopper. Mutt and his wolf pack had finally noticed what was happening to me. As I rolled over on the ground I saw them all start running in my direction, only to be stopped by a wall of Hunters who aimed guns at them, warning them to stay back. Mutt shouted out to me before dropping down onto all fours, rapidly changing to wolf form in the silver moonlight that streamed down from above, snorting and pawing at the ground. He put his head down and charged at one of the Hunter recruits, who reflexively opened fire before he was knocked down like a ten-pin.

I bit my lip, panting in pain. Through dimming eyes I saw the giant hairy shape of Phil leap out of the stationary helicopter. He sprinted towards the smaller Mutt, barking non-stop. Mutt ignored him and ploughed past the Hunter recruits, heading at full speed towards me. As he passed the helicopter Phil cut sharply sideways and hit him from the side at full speed, T-boning him. The two werewolves went down, rolling over and over on the ash-covered rooftop, while Mia just stood there and screamed.

It was chaos.

I tried to shout to them, to tell them to all stay away from me, but all that emerged was a howl. I saw Mia start to run towards me, changing to wolf form as she ran... but then I rapidly lost all interest in the proceedings as my arms and legs all dislocated at once and flipped direction in their sockets, fur sprouting in a wave down the length of my limbs.

And then everything went blood red, fading not quickly enough to black.

# EPILOGUE

I MUST HAVE been out for a long time, because when I opened my eyes, the wolves and the Hunters were gone. So was the rooftop. I was lying in the back of an open-backed black pick-up truck. It was in motion, flying down a darkened country road at an insane speed, jolting over deep potholes and whipping through stop signs with impunity.

I groaned, lifting my head as the night wind whipped over me. My hair hurt, as though my scalp was stretched too tight on my skull. My face felt numb and my entire body itched. My ribs were killing me, and I still couldn't seem to catch my breath.

I rolled over with a groan, and saw with a dreamlike feeling of unreality that my hands and arms were covered in a light dusting of soft chestnut fur, the exact same color as the hair on my head. The fur seemed to be growing even as I watched. I held up my arm before my eyes in wonder, flexed my clawed hand into a fist. It was huge. I didn't recognize it as being my own.

My hooked claws dragged slowly across the metal

lining of the truck's floor as I tried to haul my feet under me and get up, in the process accidentally snapping the tow-rope which someone had tied around my paws. The rope was an inch thick, but it pulled apart like taffy as I put just a touch of pressure on it. My limbs moved far too slowly, as though my whole body were immersed in thick syrup.

I tried to get up, then collapsed. I whined in frustration. I was as uncoordinated as a newborn pup.

My neck tingled. I shook my head and three large tranquilizer darts clattered to the ground. I sniffed at one of them tentatively, curious, then snorted hard and rubbed my nose… my *snout* on the side of the truck in distress. The chemical smell of the tranquilizer burned my throat like turpentine, and made the hair along the length of my body stand up with a strange prickling feeling.

The truck jolted over a pothole and I staggered sideways, crashing into the low side-panels of the back. I looked up just in time to see the driver's head whip around in the cab at the sound. *It was Mutt! Thank God for that.* He saw me standing up, the snapped ropes dangling from my furry body like Christmas decorations, and his eyes lit up with panic.

He slammed on the brakes, but he wasn't quick enough. Something else had caught my attention in the few short seconds before his truck came to a halt.

*The moon.*

It was a full moon, hanging low and ripe in the sky.

The sight both hypnotized and galvanized me. I heard the familiar *whumph… whumph… whumph* of the moon calling to me, but the sound no longer terrified me. It was like a magnetic heartbeat, soothing and calming, the magnetic rays attracting me as strongly as blood called to a vampire.

The bone-deep tiredness in my cells instantly vanished as the truck came out from beneath the trees onto an open stretch of road. The full-beam moonlight hit me, filling me with an unbelievable feeling of power and strength, draining away the lingering effects of the tranq darts.

Before I knew what I was doing I had leaped out of the still-moving truck, acting on sheer instinct and adrenaline. I sailed effortlessly down towards the road, my adoring gaze fixed on the night sky above me. I hit the ground awkwardly, fell, rolled, popped back to my feet and leaped across the road in a tangle of oversized paws.

The truck screeched to a halt a dozen yards behind me. I heard the sound of Mutt swearing and gears clashing as the truck did a one-eighty and started accelerating back down the road towards me.

I sprang onto the low brick wall that bordered one of the houses which lined the road and paused, craning my neck upwards. The moon called to me with an irresistible force. I shivered as the wind whipped through my long silken fur, and I instantly forgot about Mutt and the truck.

This was new. This was exciting. I'd never felt so alive, so *awake*. My new claws gouged thick slices out of the soft brick wall as I gathered myself and sprang fifteen feet up onto the roof of the little house, effortlessly jumping from wall to garage to roof, propelling myself mindlessly upwards towards the wonderful white light, my strength increasing and my head clearing with every bound. I heard Mutt's frantic shouts echo up from below me, but they no longer meant anything to me.

I was free. They couldn't hurt me anymore. They'd have to catch me first.

I landed on the rooftop of the first house and spun around in a circle of doggy bliss as the moonlight washed over me at full force. Silky fur spilled out of my skin as the moonlight touched it, dropping well past my shoulders in a glossy chestnut wave, forming a thick ruff around my neck. My eyeteeth and lower canines dropped fully down with four little *clunks*, extending a good two inches out of my lips in either direction.

Finally, I was whole.

The transformation was complete.

I turned left, then right, lifting my new pointed nose to sniff at the breeze. I found to my delight that I could hear and smell everything with incredible clarity. The sensory overload was mind-blowing. The trees rustled and creaked overhead, and a million tiny noises filled the night as the woodland animals went about their nightly business.

And then...

Somewhere, nearby, a door opened. I pricked up my ears in interest as I heard a brief snatch of a blaring TV mixed in with the cries of a baby. The door shut again, and I heard soft bare footsteps pad out onto a lawn somewhere close by, bringing with them a new and wonderful smell.

*The smell of food.*

*Warm, fresh, living, meaty food.*

I settled into a crouch on the rooftop, a low growl rising in my throat. I was suddenly aware that I was starving.

Down below me, a soft female voice started singing a lullaby.

I licked my lips and began moving silently downwards towards the mouth-watering smell, as Mutt's mournful howl rang out across the moonlit rooftops behind me...

## ABOUT THE AUTHOR

Natasha Rhodes is the British-born author of a worrying number of books about vampires and werewolves. Her works include the official novelizations of the smash-hit blockbuster movies *'Blade Trinity,'* *'A Nightmare on Elm Street; Perchance to Dream,'* and *'Final Destination: The Movie 1 and 2'*.

This is the third book in her original 'Kayla Steele' series, the first two of which *'Dante's Girl'* and *'The Last Angel'* have been published internationally to occasional critical acclaim.

She lives in Los Angeles, California with a cat called Potato-Head, a fish named Stupid Jerk Fish, and a big drooly boxer dog called Bubba. She is currently considering banning her bassist boyfriend from naming any more of her pets.

Her shiny new website is currently being built, but until then you can write to her at: www.myspace.com/natasharhodes.

# ACKNOWLEDGEMENTS

It would be entirely cheeky of me to continue this series without thanking the many wonderful people who have been there for me in one way or another whilst writing these books.

This series is dedicated to my wonderful parents Kathy and Frank, who were brave enough and supportive enough to let their oldest daughter go galloping off overseas to Hollyweird, California, to live by the beach and write about vampires and werewolves for a living. I love and miss you both!

Thanks also to my gorgeous and sexy boyfriend Chris 'Sixx' Rohner, without whose love, support, unfailing sense of humor, and remarkably tight leather stage-pants this book could not have been written.

Thanks too to my various musical 'families' of *True 2 Crue, Fan Halen, The Drills* and *POWDER* for taking me in and putting up with me whilst I was writing these books. The LA music scene— and my social life— wouldn't be the same without you guys.

To the Crue-heads and clowns of OC, for welcoming me into the Motley family.

To my favorite band *Halo* for their incredible album '*Lunatic Ride,*' which I listened to constantly while I was writing this series. (Great lyrics Graeme!)

To my editors Jonathan Oliver and Jenni Hill, for pulling off last-minute miracles, and to my agent John Jarrold, for just generally being all-round wonderful.

And finally, to everyone who has written to me over the years with love, support, encouragement, and entertainingly-written criticism. This book is for all you guys. Hope you like it! ☺

NATASHA RHODES

# DANTE'S GIRL

A KAYLA STEELE NOVEL

'Natasha Rhodes
brings life to the undead!'
– SFX

www.solarisbooks.com  ISBN: 978-1-84416-666-4

Kayla Steele is a girl with an unusual problem, she's on a mission to learn the Dark Arts so that she can avenge the death of her boyfriend and bring down the cabal of supernatural entities that is stalking the streets of LA. Then, of course, there's the dead boyfriend himself, Karrel Dante. She's really got no idea where that relationship is going at the moment...

NATASHA RHODES

# THE LAST ANGEL

### A KAYLA STEELE NOVEL

www.solarisbooks.com   UK ISBN: 978-1-84416-646-6   US ISBN: 978-1-84416-577-3

An angel is found murdered on the streets of Sunset Boulevard. To the media gossip mongers, it's the biggest story ever. To the Hunters, an underground monster-fighting hit-squad, it's just another case of "whodunnit". To Kayla Steele, their newest member, it means a last chance to bring her murdered fiancé back from the dead, and to others with a far darker purpose it is the means to destroy the human race.

# ◯ SOLARIS DARK FANTASY

"Black Magic Woman is the best manuscript I've ever been asked to read. Keep an eye on Justin Gustainis. You'll be seeing more of him soon."

**Jim Butcher**

# BLACK MAGIC WOMAN

### A MORRIS AND CHASTAIN INVESTIGATION

## JUSTIN GUSTAINIS

www.solarisbooks.com    ISBN: 978-1-84416-541-4

Supernatural investigator Quincey Morris and his partner, white witch Libby Chastain, are called in to help free a desperate family from a deadly curse that appears to date back to the Salem Witch Trials. To release the family from danger they must find the root of the curse, a black witch with a terrible grudge that holds the family in her power.

**SOLARIS** DARK FANTASY

EVIL WAYS

A MORRIS AND CHASTAIN INVESTIGATION

JUSTIN GUSTAINIS

"Justin is a first class writer; he's smart and he's fun. he moves quickly and he takes corners at speed."

Simon R. Green

www.solarisbooks.com UK ISBN: 978-1-84416-653-4 US ISBN: 978-1-84416-593-3

Eccentric billionaire Walter Grobius is attempting to unleash the Black Wind, a devastating evil that has its roots in ancient religion. More than that, he's in a league with a demon that he thinks is an angel of the lord. Our heroes, Morris and Chastain, are drawn into a deadly case as they investigate a series of witch murders.

SOLARIS DARK FANTASY

BRIAN LUMLEY

THE TAINT
AND OTHER NOVELLAS
A Cthulhu Mythos Collection

www.solarisbooks.com   UK ISBN: 978-1-84416-592-6   US ISBN: 978-1-84416-637-7

A collection of thrilling tales inspired by H. P. Lovecraft's Cthulhu Mythos from one of horror's biggest legends. This volume contains the very best of Brian Lumley's Mythos novellas spanning the entire breadth of his illustrious career. From 'Rising With Surtsey' through to the eponymous 'The Taint', these tales plumb the very depths of horror and show Lumley at his twisted best.

**◖ SOLARIS** DARK FANTASY

# BRIAN LUMLEY

*"Since reading Lumley's Necroscope series, I know that vampires do exist!"* – H. R. Giger

The New Necroscope Novel

# NECROSCOPE: THE TOUCH

An insane triad of malevolent aliens called the Shing't, who have left a trail of destruction in their own distant solar system, have found a new target: Earth.

*The Touch* is the long-awaited start of a brand new Necroscope series, which is sure to delight all fans of SF and horror.

# ⊙ SOLARIS DARK FANTASY